Jonni Jordyn

<u>Other books by Jonni Jordyn</u>

<u>The Lost Art of Magic Series</u>
The Lost Art of Magic
The Untold Prophecy
The Old Child
The Orb of Desstiny

<u>The Mother of All Viruses Series</u>
The Mother of All Viruses
The Queen of All Viruses

<u>The Valley of Hope Series</u>
The Calling of the Grull
The Hammer and the Chain

The Beat of a Different Drummer
Something About Nobility

Dedicated to Cathy Stone
My newest and hopefully last muse who has joined me on this journey
as I remake myself in the publishing world and in the real world.

"Is that a gun in your pocket, or are you just glad to see me?"

Mae West

Book Cover by Deena Rae at eBookBuilders

Illustrations by Deena Rae at eBookBuilders

Scene separator graphics by Freepik

Jonni Jordyn

Chapter 1

Prima Donna Francesca Vittoria Agostina La Perla was not a woman to suffer in silence. Her powerful voice resonated throughout the spacecraft's first-class cabin, penetrating the bulkheads and piercing deep into the lower-class passenger sections. "Elizabeth? Why is it we are stopping here? This is not Valdovian Gardens. Ask that woman what is happening!"

Elizabeth Garrett, the overworked personal manager of the great soprano superstar, sat several rows back, still in the first class cabin, but not up front in the more opulent VIP seats. Her cheeks flushed red, as they always did when the Diva made a scene. She timidly raised her hand to flag down the stewardess as she zipped by them. "Excuse me, miss? Hello? Miss?"

The stewardess easily fended off Elizabeth's pleas and rushed down the aisle past her.

"That is not how you are doing it," Francesca scolded her. She sucked in a deep breath and bellowed out in her full stilted Italian accent, "Hey you! She is wanting to know why it is we are stopping here! This is not our stop!"

The stewardess froze and turned reluctantly to face the diva. Tears gathered in her eyes while fear showed on her face as she meekly announced, "Someone will be out shortly to explain. Thank you for your patience."

The Diva wagged her finger and said, "You don't be thanking me for my patience. I am not giving you the patience. You explain it to me now!"

"I'm sorry," the stewardess said, the tears now straining to break their bonds and push over her lower eyelids, "but I don't really know anything. I'm just a stewardess."

"Well miss 'I am just a stewardess', I am the renowned Francesca Vittoria Agostina La Perla, number one soprano for the Vegan Royal Opera, and you will be giving me the explanation."

"I knew it," the man sitting next to Francesca said. "You're one of those Italian singers from Earth!"

Francesca glared at him and said, "I am *the* Italian singer coming from Earth. All of the best singers are being Italian and I am being the best of the best." She wrinkled her nose as if she had just smelled something offensive and continued, "Why is it I am talking to you? You are the nobody." She turned back to the stewardess and said, "You I *am* talking to."

The stewardess cowered slightly and stuttered, "Yes. Ma'am, I know who you are too. It is a pleasure to meet you."

Francesca took full advantage of the roominess of her VIP seating and rose to her full height, which wasn't so great, but seemed more impressive by her commanding posture. She looked down her nose at the young woman and exclaimed, "Ha! It is good you are knowing who I am, but it is being no pleasure. Why is it I am talking to you? Go find someone with the answers."

The stewardess tried nodding her head, but she was shaking too much for it to be noticed, until she felt the comforting hand of her captain on her shoulder. "It's okay Millie, I'll handle this."

The young stewardess bolted from the passenger cabin, the tears now freely streaking down her cheeks.

"This is good that you are here," Francesca said to the captain, "You fix this. I have the schedule to keep."

"I'm sorry Madam La Perla, but you'll have to discuss the particulars of your travel with our reservations personnel. I'm sure it is all just a big misunderstanding that you will be able to straighten out in no time. Unfortunately, however, your tickets to Valdovian gardens have been voided and you and your associates have been reclassified as stowaways. I've been ordered to let you and your associates off at the nearest port. I have no choice in the matter. I know that this is not your intended destination, but you will need to disembark now."

Francesca's eyes widened as she sucked in a belly full of air. "How dare you?" she huffed in a rather deep husky voice. "I am not being the stowaway, I am..."

A large man with a badge on his belt and the butt of a gun poking from under his arm entered the first class cabin and stood behind the captain. He didn't wear a uniform of the space line and Francesca didn't remember seeing him before. Through the cabin window, she saw that their luggage had already been removed and unceremoniously piled onto the runway with the rest of her entourage, except for Elizabeth, already assembled on the tarmac around their belongings. She narrowed her eyes on the man with the weapon and said, "So. I see now how it is you treat your most important passengers." She snapped her head up high, bouncing her dark curly locks to the back of her shoulders, and scowled at the captain. "Out of my way," she barked, "I will be going now to speak with your superiors. You will be regretting this, you can be sure! Come along Elizabeth." She marched out slowly, with each step full of pomp, dignity and mostly arrogance.

The hot dry air assaulted Elizabeth's lungs as soon as she exited the climate controlled ship and began descending the ramp. She left the diva, who preferred to walk in a slow pompous pace, on the ramp as she scurried across the tarmac and over to the solitary pair of kiosks which stood next to a short row of evenly spaced open-sided wooden enclosures where she presumed passengers would wait to be picked up, although this clearly was no ordinary spaceport.

Victor, the diva's stage manager, walked briskly to catch up with Elizabeth leaving Bruno the muscular bodyguard to gather the luggage into a single pile by himself.

As Elizabeth neared the desk, which was oddly festooned with rustic logs and old weathered planks, the two women behind the counter turned out the lights and headed for a small parking lot hidden behind a scrawny-looking hedge.

"No! Wait!" Elizabeth called out breathlessly across the tarmac. "You can't close now! We've just been stranded here!"

"I'm sorry," the younger girl shouted from behind the counter, "but it's late and we've already shut down the computers. We're closed."

"But we have tickets for Valdovian Gardens," Elizabeth panted, still at a full trot, "The captain said you could explain why our tickets were voided. This must be some kind of mistake."

The young girl shrugged her shoulders and said, "Sorry. You must be from the Vegan Empire. It's happening all over. All Vegans have been grounded."

"But we're not Vegans," Elizabeth breathed heavily as her trot slowed to a brisk walk, "We're not from Vega, we're from Earth. We aren't actually part of either empire."

The older, more grizzled looking of the two, turned the light back on and said to her friend, "You go ahead. I'll catch up with you later."

Elizabeth closed the gap between herself and the rustic-looking ticket counter, still gasping for air. "Thank you. Do you think you can help us?"

"Let me see your ticket."

Elizabeth handed over a pack of tickets.

The woman examined them and said, "I'm really sorry that you got tangled up in our politics, but here's your problem. You booked your travel through a Vegan travel agency."

"Can we just re-book it through you?"

The woman nodded and said, "You can, if you have the money."

Elizabeth perked up. She could fix this.

Victor was right behind her and said, "The Diva has lots of money."

The woman squinted out onto the tarmac and asked, "Is that the Italian opera singer we've been hearing so much about?"

Victor smirked. "She's not really Italian. She just likes people to think she is."

Elizabeth hit Victor in the arm and made an exaggerated face at him with her lips pressed tightly shut.

"Well," the woman explained, "she's kind of a big deal around here, but I still can't help you without any Andurian currency. We can't take Vegan money."

"Why not?" Elizabeth asked. "I thought you both used the same currency."

"We did, or maybe if you had cash we could, but if your assets are in a Vegan bank, we've been locked out and can't get to them."

"But," Elizabeth pleaded, "We still have money in our Earth banks. Can't you use that?"

The woman shook her head slowly. "We have always done inter stellar money transfers through Vega. I don't know who could help you."

Elizabeth's recently acquired hopes that she could just book new tickets were dashed as she cried, "What are we going to do?"

"I don't know," the woman sighed while shaking her head, "and it's getting kind of late. You might try the hotel and see if they'll let you work out something to stay one night. Business there has been kind of slow ever since Vega first started cutting access to private citizen's accounts. Now that they have cut access to corporate accounts, they be desperate enough to cut a deal with you to stay."

Elizabeth spun around, but saw only the flat featureless land with no signs of any town.

The woman saw her scanning the horizon and pointed, "It's out there, in that direction. I don't know what else to tell you. Keep watching the news. This whole mess started a while ago, but it got a lot worse today. We're in this too. I don't know how long the resort can keep paying us. Maybe we'll know more in the morning."

Elizabeth thanked her. "Come on Victor, let's go tell the gang."

"So," Francesca asked as Elizabeth and Victor neared them, "what is it you have learned?"

"It's the alliance. The Vegan Empire has apparently broken off relations with the Andurian Empire."

"It's kind of stupid," Victor added. "Most of their banks and the stock market are part of Vega."

"Tut! Tut!" the diva said disgustedly, "I am not caring about their politics. You should have told them we are from Earth."

"I did, but they said our tickets were Vegan, and all of our money was transferred to Vegan banks. I'm sure we can get all this straightened out, but probably not before morning."

"Morning?" Francesca shouted, "I can't stand here in the open with all the bugs till morning!"

"The girl at the counter said there is a hotel. Maybe we can make some arrangements with them to stay the night."

"Si," the diva relented, "and I'm sure they rob us blind for it. Where is hotel?"

Elizabeth started to point towards town when an open air carriage pulled by a single horse joined the group. A tall lanky man with heavy whiskers and a ten-gallon hat sat atop the carriage and gently said, "Whoa!" while he pressed the long brake handle with his boot to stop the carriage. "Excuse me folks," he said, "but I couldn't help overhear your predicament."

Francesca cocked an eyebrow at the strange-looking man. "Who are you? You look like cowboy movie."

"Yes ma'am. Welcome to Emaude Phlott, the highest tootinest, Wild West shootinest, vacation dude ranch in the whole Andurian Empire. Anyway, I thought I'd offer you folks a ride to the hotel. I know you don't got no money, so you can settle up with me when you get yourselves back on your feet."

Francesca's eyes narrowed as she examined the carriage, which was barely more than a wooden wagon with three rows of seats bolted on. She glanced, somewhat wild eyed towards Elizabeth, who stepped forward to help Francesca reluctantly climb aboard and get the first seat behind the driver.

"This is very kind of you," Elizabeth said, "Mr....?" Her voice tailed off, hoping he would fill in the blank.

"Oh, sorry, Ma'am, where are my manners? Matt Starr is my name, and western lore is my game."

Elizabeth climbed in and sat next to Francesca. "Thank you, Mr. Starr. That's a very beautiful horse. We're all from Earth, and your horse looks very much like an Earth horse. Is that where you got him?"

"No Ma'am. It's not a real horse. I got it on Darvian. I showed those boys some movin' pictures of them Earth horses, and they whipped one right up for me. They're very clever, I think."

Francesca's wardrobe manager and stylist both smiled flirtatiously at Mr. Starr as they climbed into the middle seats.

Victor loaded the last of the smaller bags onto the floor of the carriage, around their feet, while Bruno loaded the last of the heavy trunks into the back of the wagon and climbed into the last row with Victor.

"Hang on to your hats, folks, you're about to step back in time."

Emaude Phlott's flat, featureless surface, between the spaceport and the hotel, made it difficult to judge both their speed and the distance covered.

Francesca made an unpleasant face and waved her hands around her nose. "Are you sure your horse is robot? I swear I am smelling it."

"Those Darvians are very detailed craftsmen. I paid extra for that."

"Why?"

Their driver just grinned sheepishly and shrugged.

"It's not a good smell, this smell you paid extra for."

Elizabeth made a face at Francesca and whispered, "Be nice to him. He's giving us a ride."

Francesca nodded her understanding and said, "He is very fast, your horse."

"Thank you, Ma'am."

"And smooth too, don't you think so Elizabeth?"

"Yes," Elizabeth replied, "It's a very smooth ride."

Starr nodded.

The wind whipped in their faces and mussed their hair. Francesca did not know how much longer she could take this. "How much farther is it being? We must be close now."

"Not much farther Ma'am."

Francesca pointed at the horse and asked, "What is that thing your horse is doing now? It's lifting its tail. I don't like that. Make it don't do that. Oh! Did you see that? That's disgusting."

Starr shrugged again and said, "I paid extra for that too."

The carriage slowed as it passed a blacksmith on the edge of town and followed the street between a raft of old buildings, including a sheriff's office and an old bank. It came to a stop in front of the assay office next to the Amber Palace saloon. "Here you go, folks. I'll take care of your bags while you go get checked in."

Elizabeth went straight in to find the registration desk.

Francesca took one look at the saloon and the surrounding buildings and said, "It is cowboy movie." She pushed through the swinging doors and found a prominent spot where she could stand in the lobby, hoping someone might recognize her and offer their help.

Bruno and Victor grabbed Francesca's luggage and followed the others inside.

Once Bruno and Victor had disappeared through the swinging saloon doors, Starr climbed back up in his seat and took off with the other half of their luggage.

"Elizabeth? I don't like this place. Tell me again why is it I am being here? I want to go home." Francesca knew why she was there, but couldn't allow herself to accept that she was marooned on a dirty little moon with no money.

Victor held up some brochures and said, "Look at these. Emaude Phlott, a moon in the Gellian System."

"Mud Flats," Francesca said with disdain, "It even sounds like cowboy movie. This is truly ass end of galaxy." She waved him away. "I don't want to see papers for ass end of galaxy."

Francesca walked to a window and looked out into the evening sky. "Look at those rings."

Victor was still perusing the travel brochures. "It says here that's Gellian Prime."

"Shut up Victor. I don't need to know these things. Those rings make me sad. They make me feel homesick. How can rings make me homesick Victor? I don't live on Saturn. Nobody lives on Saturn. Elizabeth! ELIZABETH! Where is my Elizabeth! You are to be here when I call for you!"

"I'm sure she'll be right back Bella Donna, she's just making..."

"ACK! What was that did you call me?"

Victor bowed down low in an insincere act of groveling and said, "Prima Donna. I said Prima Donna, as I always do, as everyone does."

"You had better."

He kept his head low, but looked up at her through his eyebrows, thinking to himself, *If only I had some belladonna for you.*

"Get up Victor and go find my Elizabeth."

He stood back up and said, "Prima Donna, Elizabeth is busy making the arrangements for your stay here."

"Here? This is not where I am staying. This place must be for you. Elizabeth! Where is it that I am staying? I cannot be staying here. You must take care of my accommodations first! You know this! Elizabeth?"

"I'm here, I'm here." Elizabeth came trotting from the reservation desk with a small handful of keys.

"Elizabeth! Why are you not making *my* arrangements first? I have been standing here calling for you for at least ten minutes."

"Here you go, here you go. You get your keys first."

"What's that? Francesca Vittoria Agostina La Perla does not stay here in the saloon. Have you taken the total leave of your senses? You stupid, silly girl. I don't know why I keep you around sometimes. You are so incompetent. Make this right. Find me somewhere else to stay."

Elizabeth, usually bubbly and energetic, wanted to cry, and would have had her exasperation not taken over and shifted her towards anger. "Do you have any idea how hard it was to get these rooms?"

"Why should it be hard? You tell them I want room; they give you key. It is simple, not hard."

The tears were welling up in Elizabeth's eyes. "It's not that easy. They don't just give their rooms away, they want to be paid for them."

"So pay them! And stop with the silly crying already."

"We have no money to pay them with."

"What do you mean, we have no money? I have much money."

"I told you. Ever since the alliance broke down, your money is trapped in the Vegan Empire and we can't get to it."

"Did you tell them who I am?"

"Yes!" Elizabeth's face brightened immensely. "And they were very impressed. That's why they gave you the Royal Suite!"

"Royal Suite? Here? This I am having to see."

"It's true! And they can't wait to hear you sing. They are quite the opera fans, as it turns out."

"You're making the joke. These people? This place? What can these cowboys possibly know about opera?"

"Never the less," Elizabeth said, "they are most anxious to hear the galaxy's most notable soprano diva in person."

"No! I won't sing for these hilly billys. Take me away from here now. I want to go home where I can have my own money and stay in the proper villa."

"You have to sing! I already booked you; it's the only way they would give us the rooms."

Francesca was on the verge of tears, and cried, "But I don't want to stay here in the Mud Flats."

"They also said they might be able to arrange some transportation to take you to the empire's border. That's halfway back home, and you might even be able to get to your money from the border."

"Well, that's better then. You should tell me this first. I suppose I could stay one night if they can get me home. Show me to my royal suite now."

Two very short, stocky bellboys gathered up her luggage and her old-fashioned steamer trunk and carted them over to the elevator. Elizabeth and Francesca followed, while Victor took the remaining keys and led the rest of the entourage to the two adjoining rooms they would be sharing. The elevator opened on the top floor and the bellboys led them to the Royal Suite. They opened the door, piled the luggage out of the way, and waited for their tip.

Francesca pushed Elizabeth aside and barged into the room. "This? This is what they call the Royal Suite? It is so puny! And everything is dingy." She gave her body a melodramatic shiver, then cast her gaze on the two bellboys. "What are these small creatures doing in my room? SHOO!"

"They're your bellboys, Prima Donna."

"I don't care. They are ugly. Make them go away."

Elizabeth looked apologetically towards the bellboys and quietly said, "I'm sorry, boys. It's been a long trip. We won't have any local currency to tip you with until after the Diva sings tonight."

"What is that you are saying to them? Why are they still here? How long does it take to tell them to go away?"

The two bellboys threw themselves onto the floor at Francesca's feet.

"EEEEEK!" the diva screamed, "They are attacking my feet! Go away! Shoo!"

"We are sorry your Highness," they both said, "You are correct. We are too ugly to bathe in your Majesty's beauty. We only want to serve, so your stay here could be more pleasurable."

Elizabeth started to pick them up, saying, "She's not the queen. You don't need to do that."

"No, it's alright," Francesca said, "they can stay as they are. This way, I don't see their faces."

"Thank you, your Majesty," the bellboys said in unison.

"So, Elizabeth, when is it do they want me to sing?"

Elizabeth looked at her watch and exclaimed, "Oh my god, in an hour!"

"An hour? That's impossible. I haven't eaten yet, and I need to change first."

"About the food..."

"No time to discuss. Boys, go to the kitchen and bring back some caviar, shrimp, lobster, some of those little toasted bread thingies, and your finest champagne."

They looked at each other quizzically, but didn't budge.

"I thought you were making my stay pleasurable?"

The two bellboys nodded their heads this way and that, as if silently trying to decide who would deliver the bad news.

"They can't get the food," Elizabeth blurted out, "the hotel won't feed us until after you sing."

"That's preposterous! How is it they expect me to perform when put under these conditions? Who do they think they are being? Don't they know who it is that I am?"

"There's no use getting all worked up over this, Diva, I tried to reason with them, but they wouldn't budge on this."

Francesca managed to rein in the fury she felt. "Very well, then. You may be going to your room now. Send Tatianna and Gabriella to dress me. You may come for me when it's half an hour."

"Oh, uhmm..." Elizabeth bit her lip while her eyes darted all around the room, looking for an easy way to deliver the rest of the news.

The diva glared at Elizabeth. Her already unpleasant expression frowned even further. "Why is it you are still here?"

Elizabeth took a small step backwards towards the door and said, "About Tatianna and Gabriella..."

"What about them? Why is it you aren't sending for them now?"

"They left."

"What is it that you mean, they left? Go tell them to come back."

"I think they are long gone."

"How can they be this long gone and I am being stuck here?"

Elizabeth tried to smile whimsically, but still took another half step backwards and said, "Well, you know those girls and men. They found a couple merchants willing to give them a ride, for a price."

"They have money?"

"No, diva, they aren't paying with money."

"Who is it that is going to dress me and spritz me if they are being gone?"

One of the bellboys raised his hand and said, "Your Majesty, please, allow me."

"What?" Francesca squealed, "I never! Get out from my presence you filthy little beast! Now! And take your repulsive little friend too!"

The bellboys popped up onto their feet and bowed low at the waist, backing out of the room while saying, "Yes your Highness. Your insults are like songs to our ears." They backed out into the hall and stood by the door in case she needed anything.

"You may be going too, Elizabeth. I'll just be spritzing myself."

Elizabeth closed the door behind her and shared a look of sympathy with the bellboys. She left for the elevator and her room on a lower floor.

Francesca sank into a chair. She didn't want to cry in front of the others, but now that she was alone, she couldn't prevent a single tear from tracing a light trail down her cheek as she thought to herself, *I really hate this Mud Flats.*

Elizabeth allowed herself to rest for twenty minutes before returning to Francesca's room. She knocked on the door and said, "Diva, it's time." She didn't have to wait long.

Francesca's face was pure panic as she flung the door open and said, "I don't have my Gabriella. She always does my hair."

"You look fine," Elizabeth lied. "I have the directions to the venue. The auditorium is part of the resort, just on the other end of the hotel."

"Where's Bruno? Shouldn't he be here with us?"

"I don't know. I haven't seen him since we got our rooms."

Victor met them at the base of the elevator. "Ah, Prima Donna, you look stunning tonight. I have the arias you selected. There are no props on the stage, but I was able to set some proper colors in the lights."

"Thank you, Victor. Have you seen Bruno?"

"Uhmm, why, I..."

Francesca eyed Victor suspiciously and lowered her voice to ask, "What's the matter, Victor? What is it that has happened to my Bruno?"

"Bruno? Why? Do you think something is wrong with Bruno?"

"You are looking like you are hiding something, Victor."

Victor hung his head softly and said, "Well, I didn't want to burden you, but it's about the hall where you will be performing. It's...uhm..."

Francesca bellowed, "Stop with the stuttering and say it, Victor!"

"It's a dining hall."

The diva gasped and registered horror in her eyes. "You mean it is having the dinner tables?"

Victor nodded.

"With the clinking and the cutting and the chewing? I can't do it. I WON'T do it! Elizabeth, tell them I can't be singing here. Tell them I lost my voice."

Elizabeth wrapped her arm around Francesca's shoulder and said, "I know it's distasteful, Diva, but you have to do it. We are desperate. Victor can go fix the monitors so you won't hear any eating. The music will be all you hear."

"Yes," Victor said, "I can do that."

"And you, Francesca, Prima Donna of the Vegan Royal Opera, you only have to sing two arias, then we can eat, and we can spend the night, and they will find us transportation home. We'll even have some of their precious Andurian money to spend."

"Si," she relented tearfully, "I can do that."

When they reached the auditorium, Victor escorted Francesca back stage. She could already smell the food and fought to hold back her tears. He directed her to the center of the stage behind the still closed curtains, then went to the stage sound mixer and prepared to cue the music.

Elizabeth did not follow them backstage, but took the stage entrance to the dining hall and looked around for a table. The hotel manager motioned for Elizabeth to join him at his table for the performance. She said a small prayer that the diva would not throw a tantrum and ditch the event, then she tucked that little fear away and walked to the hotel manager's table.

"Miss Garrett," he said as he stood and bowed slightly, "thank you for joining us. I would like to introduce you to our mayor, the Honorable Roy Bean."

"Roy Bean? As in the famous hanging judge?"

The mayor took Elizabeth's hand in his and held it to his lips. "Yes, Ma'am, the very same. I had my name changed when I took office here. Most everyone in town has adopted a new persona for the tourists."

"And this," the manager continued, "is our esteemed Governor of Emaude Phlott, Kitt Carson."

"How do you do, sir? You know, you might find this funny, since you have selected names from Earth's Wild West days. The Diva took one look at your picturesque setting and thought she heard the name Mud Flats."

None of the Phlotians found it humorous, and an awkward moment followed, but was saved when the lights dimmed half way.

"Ah," the mayor said, "I can't tell you how excited we were to learn who had landed on our fair rock."

"To be honest," Elizabeth said, "I was surprised you even knew who she was all the way out here."

"My dear girl," the governor said, "Opera is our most precious activity. In the old days, even our royalty sang opera. For us, it is like your baseball of your twentieth century."

"Forgive me, your honor, I let your rustic costumes and props mislead me."

"Totally understandable."

The lights dimmed completely, and the curtains parted.

For her first piece, Francesca selected a humorous Italian aria from Rossini's Barber de Seville, which she had transposed for the soprano voice. Leaving all of their difficulties behind her, she stepped forward and gave them a splendid performance.

Elizabeth glanced over towards the two dignitaries, and their faces were pure bliss. Their eyes were closed and she imagined they were picturing a complete setting for the opera. Francesca finished the first song and the crowd around the hall roared with approval. Elizabeth had been concerned that Francesca might not be up to her usual level of excellence, but she put those fears aside, until she saw the mayor and governor whispering together. Something was wrong. Their applause was polite, but their faces showed concern.

For her second piece, Francesca chose a modern aria from the twenty-third century composer Hargrave. It was an English language aria. Her spoken English may have been broken, but her singing English was superlative. Again, Elizabeth noted that the dignitaries were thoroughly entranced by Francesca, but, as with the first piece, when the music ended, their faces were somber and worrisome.

She struggled to hear what they were saying, but could only make out bits and pieces.

When Francesca finished her bows, she joined them at the table.

The governor addressed her first, "That was absolutely angelic. Never before have I heard such sweet tones on this stage. I wish I could stay and lavish more praise upon your deserving ears, but alas, affairs of state are calling for me. Mayor Bean, if you would please accompany me?"

The hotel manager also got up from the table and returned to his work.

Francesca sat down and immediately started perusing the menu.

Victor collected the music recording from the player before joining them at the table. As he left the backstage and took the short stairs to the main floor, he almost ran into the two dignitaries arguing.

"You said she was perfect. I wouldn't have come all the way out here otherwise."

"I know, I know. Jim is usually very reliable."

Victor hadn't planned to eavesdrop, but he loves hearing others complain about Francesca, so he hid himself behind a curtain and listened.

"You mean you didn't check her out personally?"

"There wasn't time. He was very sure, and if she was even half of what he said she was, then I thought we had better move fast."

"Jim just manages hotel operations. You should have checked her out before putting so much faith in his opinion."

"I'm sorry, it won't happen again."

As much as Victor hated Francesca, he didn't have a clue what they were complaining about. Her performance was stellar.

"Sorry doesn't cut it. We're going to lose our shirts if we can't get the tourists to return."

"I know, and Jim knows it too. He's not just the hotel manager, he's a partner with over ten percent ownership. He's as motivated as you or I am to fix this mess."

"But she sings like an angel."

"Better than an angel."

"Exactly! She was magnificent. There's no way Jim could be right on this one, and you should have checked that! It's a lucky thing I didn't contact the rest of the investors, or your thick headed incompetence could have gotten us stranded on the nearest asteroid!"

Francesca had seen enough of this menu and shouted for a waiter, "Hey you? What is this? Do I look like a child to you? Take back this children's menu and bring me a real one."

The waiter was stunned, both by the volume and the command of her voice, and weakly replied, "I'm sorry, Ma'am, but that *is* our regular menu."

"I'm too hungry for you to be making with the jokes."

The poor waiter didn't know how to reply.

"Look at this!" she bellowed, "Beans? Wieners?"

"I'm sorry, Ma'am, but that's what we serve here."

"I am not the tourist! Do you understand that? I am Francesca Vittoria Agostina La Perla, Prima Donna for the Royal Opera, and I do not eat the beans and wieners. Go find me some real food!"

Governor Carson's frustration had his stomach tied up in knots. He wanted to lash out, and Bean was the sorry soul that got to listen to it. "I'm sorry, Roy, but I stand to lose more than you and Jim put together."

"You may have invested a lot in this project, but you didn't invest everything. Jim put every coin that he had into the hotel. Maybe you should talk to him yourself and hear what he has to say."

"You don't think I've invested everything? If the other investors aren't happy with the way things turn out, I'm a dead man! Not you, not Jim, ME!"

"Then that's all the more reason for you to be here in person to judge her yourself. You brought those mobsters here. They're your problem. So, if you really have that much at stake, then you better start being more of the solution and stop delegating, because what they have planned, you can't delegate to me!"

"You really think those thugs will be satisfied with stringing just me up? No, sir. They'll be looking for more blood than just mine, and guess who's next in line?"

Victor joined Elizabeth and Francesca at the table and asked, "What's up with those two?"

"What?" Elizabeth asked.

"Those two that were sitting with you! The tall one was chewing out the other for wasting his time bringing him here."

"You mean they didn't like her? I knew something was wrong, but I don't get it. They seemed to be completely taken by both performances."

"They loved her! That's what doesn't make any sense. He kept saying she is an angel, the most beautiful creature to ever grace their stage. Blah, blah, blah. Then he goes off on a tangent about the other guy's complete lack of judgment. He calls him a bunch of names and starts poking him with his finger. Look for yourself; they are still at it."

"Why are you still being here?" Francesca threw the menu across the table at the waiter. "Maybe I am needing to speak to someone else. Tell me where is your manager. Speak up! Who is being the head waiter?"

"Oh great," Victor said, "She's at it again. She'll get us thrown out on the streets this time, and I haven't eaten yet."

The governor and mayor stopped their argument and returned to see what the commotion was.

"Madam La Perla," the Governor said, "is there a problem?"

"Is there a problem? *IS THERE A PROBLEM*? Francesca Vittoria Agostina La Perla sings two arias for you and you offer her the *HOT DOGS*?"

"Our food, like everything else here, is themed."

"I am not themed. I am not the singing cowboy. I sing the opera for you as no one else sings it, and you offer me beans?"

"Perhaps you would prefer one of our very fine steaks? We have some of the empire's finest steaks, I assure you."

"What I am preferring is lobster and caviar, but if steak is all you have, then I could settle for a steak. It had better be good, though."

The governor smiled broadly and shook the mayor's hand vigorously saying, "She's everything Jim said she would be. I'll be in touch." He pointed his finger at the waiter, who was still frozen. "You! She asked for a steak. Go find the best steak we have and take care of these other people too. Chop, chop!"

The waiter found his feet and bounded off to the kitchen.

The governor was absolutely giddy. "You'll really have to excuse me. I absolutely must go take care of some business."

Elizabeth glanced over at Victor, who could do no more than shrug his shoulders.

Elizabeth went to the registration desk, where the hotel manager had already returned to work.

"Miss Garrett, she was superb. Thank you so much for bringing her to us."

"You're welcome Mr. Diamond. I hope I'm not being an inconvenience to you, but with all of our Vegan money being worthless now, could I possibly trouble you to pay us, in your money of course, for the diva's performance?"

"Of course, Miss Garrett, no trouble at all." He pulled some cash from the register. "Please let me know if there is anything else I can do to make your stay more comfortable."

"Well, you had mentioned that you might be able to get us transportation back to the border. Have you learned anything yet?"

"I've already placed some calls. I hope to hear something by morning."

"Splendid," Elizabeth exhaled in relief.

"Of course, I don't know how long it might take to arrange for the transportation. Would the diva be available to sing for us again should you choose to extend your stay?"

"I'm sure she'd be delighted."

"Marvelous." Jim closed the cash drawer and said, "Did you know that on a clear night, you can see the rings reflected on the garden pond? They say that if you make a wish on the reflected rings, it is sure to come true."

"Really? I could use some true wishes these days."

"It would be my honor to show you."

"That's so sweet of you, but I think I need to get this money to the troops. Thank you anyway."

"Well Victor," Francesca said, "it looks like it is just you and me. Where is our waiter? I need more butter. Victor! Go find our waiter and tell him to bring the butter."

Victor jumped from his seat, perhaps too eagerly, and left the table. He did not try to find their server, but found the bar instead. It was a long, elegant bar with a large mirror behind it, and a beautiful woman standing alone at the end.

He walked the length of the bar to the woman. "She must really take this stuff seriously," he thought to himself. She was clearly role playing, dressed in a fine satin dress with a bustle in the back, a corset in the middle, and a well-defined cleavage up top.

"How do Ma'am?" he said, playing along.

She flashed him a smile and ran her finger around the rim of her glass.

"What's a fine filly like yourself doing in a dump like this?"

She lifted her glass to her lips, flashed him a smile, then shot her head back as she tossed the contents of the glass to the back of her throat. She put the glass back on the bar and locked her eyes on his.

He slid his hand over to hers, toyed with her fingers and asked, "What say you and me take a little walk back to my room for some wild west bronco fun?"

She opened her small purse and pulled out a brochure for him. He accepted the brochure and looked it over. It was full of many of the fun attractions available in this small tourist stop, including horseback riding and steer roping. He was still working his way down the list when she took the brochure and turned it over for him. The backside listed all the more adult oriented fantasies that she could fulfill. At the bottom of the brochure was a company name, "Android Pleasures Incorporated."

"Ah, Victor, there you went to," Francesca said as she entered the bar carrying a small plate of cocktail wieners. "Everybody ran off and that horrid waiter never came back with my butter. What are you doing with that woman there?"

If he'd had the money, he would have accepted the pretty robot's services, just to get away from Francesca. "Nothing yet, we were just talking."

"Barkeep!" she shouted, "Barkeep! Why are you being so slow?"

Victor wondered if robots get annoyed. Maybe she would take him upstairs just to get away from Francesca's voice.

"Hey you!" Francesca pointed to some guy walking by. "Be a good man and go get the rest of my food from my table."

"I don't think he works here, Prima Donna."

"I'll get it for you, your Magnificence," said one of the bellboys that had shown her to her room.

"Victor, you go help the little man."

"Of course, your Malevolence." *Anything to get away*, he thought.

With Tatianna and Gabriella already gone, Bruno, Victor and Elizabeth were the only ones remaining from Francesca's entourage, and nobody had seen Bruno since they arrived. It wasn't like Bruno to skip a meal.

Elizabeth went to their rooms, looking for Bruno, but they were empty. She left a note for him to find her if he ever returns.

When she arrived back at the dining hall, she was surprised to find the table deserted. She slumped into her chair, thankful some of the food was still there, and munched on some fries.

"Your friends have gone to the bar."

Elizabeth looked up from her fries and saw one of the bellboys. "Oh, hello," she said, "I'm sorry, we never did get your name before."

"Aw, shucks Ma'am," he said in a heavy western accent, "Tain't no harm done."

She giggled. "That was pretty good. So, what is your name, so I can tell everyone what a wonderful actor you are?"

"Roy, Ma'am, Roy Rogers."

"Well, Roy, I'd like to thank you for being such a big help to us." She pulled out a few bills and handed them over.

"Thank you!" he said, "Thank you very much!"

"Aw shucks," she said, "Tain't that much."

Roy laughed.

"I mean it, Roy, thank you. The Diva can be really hard to get along with, especially for..." She struggled for the right word.

"Short unattractive people?"

"I was going to say servants, but she was especially rude to you."

"It's okay. We really love opera, and we really love her, in spite of how she treats us. She could be the Queen, as far as we are concerned."

"Well you and your friend have been superb sports. Thank you."

Roy gathered up the Diva's grub and trundled off towards the bar.

Francesca toyed with her food, swirling the cocktail wieners in a bowl of mustard.

A tall man with a bristly face came up to the bar alongside Francesca, and hand signaled the bartender for two beers. "How do Ma'am, I couldn't help noticing you were all alone here."

Francesca threw her shoulders back and said, "I am not alone. Francesca Vittoria Agostina La Perla is never alone." She looked around for Bruno and Victor, but she *was* alone.

The bartender placed two mugs in front of the tall man, and he slid one over to Francesca.

"Get that away from me and take you with it."

"I can't help myself," he said. "You're a powerful figure of a woman, and I just had to meet you."

He placed his hand over hers and she screamed, "BRUNO! BRUNO! HELP! SOMEONE HELP ME! BRUNO?"

Victor never actually followed the bellboy. He just slinked over to a corner of the saloon, where he hoped she wouldn't look for him.

"BRUNO! VICTOR! WHERE IS EVERYONE?"

Victor could not stand to hear her screeching voice, and reluctantly went to her rescue. The man was far too big for Victor to muscle, so he tried to reason with him, "Excuse me sir, but you're disturbing the whole tavern. Do you think you could back off a bit?"

The man backed off and just watched the scene she was making.

"That is better," she said. "You are lucky my Bruno is not being here or he would be teaching you some manners." She pointed at the bartender and yelled, "And what about you? Are you just going to stand there while this brute touch's my person?"

"Diva," Victor said, "I don't think the bartender is real."

"It is a good thing that you are being here, Victor. Where is my Bruno when I am needing him?"

Victor turned swiftly back to the android girl.

"Victor! What is it that you are not telling to me?"

Victor sighed and said, "Bruno quit. He saw a poster for some prize fights and went off to earn his own way home."

"My Bruno is gone?" She was only sad for a moment. "No matter, I am having you. You did good."

Roy returned with her food and asked, "Where would you like this?"

"What happened to you? The steak is looking cold. Besides, I am not being hungry any more. Take me to my room."

Roy sighed, "Yes your majesty. As you wish."

"On second thought," she said, "You can be bringing that with you. I might nibble later."

"As you wish."

"And have your other little friend bring some butter to my room." She didn't wait for a response, but stormed out of the room, bumping into the tall man who was taking notes of the whole encounter. She stopped at the doorway and commanded, "Come Victor, and you too, little man, take me to my room."

Chapter 2

Harvey Kushkin liked to call himself an adventurer, but he really was a confidence man who had been down on his luck until recently when he had won big in a card game. His good fortune didn't last long because he was also a traveler from Vega and found himself stranded on Emaude Phlott when his ship ran out of fuel, but he was a resourceful man and knew how to work a situation to his advantage. His plan was simple. He would present himself as a gem courier who was delivering a briefcase filled with Delruvian Emeralds, but he was stranded here because he only had Vegan credits to spend. Worse yet, his story would claim that thieves were following him and he had to hide the emeralds near the spaceport. He couldn't approach the local buyer for the emeralds, because the thieves knew his face, so he would need someone to go fetch the gems for him, but he couldn't entrust the gems in a strangers keeping without asking for a small deposit to insure the new partner would return with the gems. It was an old, but very successful con.

He took a deep cleansing breath and knocked on the mayor's door.

"Come in."

He opened the door and stepped into Mayor Bean's office. "Excuse me sir, I was wondering if I might have a word with you?"

"Certainly, come in, come in. I've been expecting you."

"You've been expecting me?"

"Yes, of course, but don't worry, we've kept your business here a secret. I must say you certainly got here quickly enough."

"Thank you." Harvey didn't have a clue what the mayor was talking about, but he felt it would be best to hear him out.

"I'm not sure how much the governor told you, but let me assure you she is worth her weight in gold. She has the looks and the character. She is absolutely the answer to all our prayers."

Harvey nodded his head and said, "The governor wasn't very specific. Perhaps you could fill me in."

"It was pure serendipity. She was traveling on Vegan tickets and was dumped here on our doorstep."

Harvey smirked. "I certainly know how that goes."

"Of course, you would. I imagine your office is flooded with people trapped here with foreign papers."

"You were saying she was worth her weight in gold?"

"Oh yes. They arrived yesterday, shortly before the dinner hour, and said they needed a room, but had no money."

"No money? I thought you meant she was rich."

"I'm sure she probably is, but it's apparently all in Vegan banks."

"That's no good to me. Say, you know anything about gems?"

"Gems? No. You know what? I should just take you to meet her. She's going to make us all rich."

Harvey liked rich. "Lead on, let's go meet this woman."

Mickey the Mooch, a.k.a. Benny the Broom and Freddy the Fist, was born Milton Dimplestrom. He arrived quietly on Emaude Phlott, as instructed, to survey the town before approaching the governor. Milton worked for the Stonewright family, one of the largest and most notorious crime syndicates in the Andurian Empire. Emaude Phlott was supposed to be one of their legitimate enterprises where they could launder some of their ill-gotten gains. Unfortunately, they couldn't push much money through a dying business, and business had already been slow, but since the empire split, the resort community was destined to become a ghost town.

Milton's boss still wanted his payments from the resort, but he wasn't too upset by the current imperial crisis. He'd discovered another mostly legitimate source of income. He used the family's Andurian money to buy up properties owned by Vegans whose current financial status had disqualified them for their loans, and the governor was one of them.

This was Milton's first visit, so he didn't know how much traffic it might have had while business was good, but it was in good condition, and with the addition of a casino or two, could be a gold mine.

Despite the smallness of the room, Francesca found the bed to be roomy and comfortable, and she had slipped off to a sound sleep. When morning came, she thought things would surely have been fixed. Things were always fixed while she slept.

"Elizabeth?" she called out loudly, "Elizabeth, where are you?"

She sat up and removed the night mask from her eyes. As the room around her came into focus, she recalled the unpleasant events of the previous day and started to call for Elizabeth again, until she remembered they were on different floors. She rolled over onto her side and picked up the phone and said, "I want my Elizabeth."

"Elizabeth?"

"Yes, you heard me. Hurry."

"Room number?"

"I don't know the number," she said, "it is your idea of Royal Suite."

"Not your number, Elizabeth's."

Francesca heard the operator cover the mouthpiece, followed by muffled talking and laughter. "This is your hotel. Don't you know your own room numbers? If you don't know, you find someone who does and you get my Elizabeth here to my room. I'm done talking to you now."

Francesca needn't have called for Elizabeth, she was already on her way. "Roy?" she asked as she arrived at the diva's door. "What are you doing here? Please tell me you haven't been camping outside her door all night long!"

"No, ma'am. My brother Gene has been trading off with me."

"Roy!" Elizabeth shook her head and all he could do was shrug his shoulders. "Is she up yet?"

"I don't keep my ear pressed to the door, ma'am. She deserves some privacy."

"She's a loud woman, Roy. You wouldn't have to listen very hard."

"I might have heard her yelling at someone, but I swear nobody got by Gene or me all night."

Elizabeth knocked and asked softly through the door, "Diva? It's Elizabeth. Are you up yet?"

"Elizabeth!" Francesca ran to the door and swung it open. "It is good you are being here. I want to go see the gardens I was hearing so much about. I thought we could be seeing them this morning before we go home."

"Go home? Do you know something I don't know?"

"It's a new day. Everything gets fixed for a beautiful day like today. I have the faith."

Elizabeth smiled at her enthusiasm and was grateful that she woke up in a positive mood. "Well, I certainly hope you are correct, but I'm not so sure they are going to iron this thing out so fast."

"You will see, but first, let's go see the Garden with the witching well."

"I think that was a wishing well."

"Whatever. Either way we can be making the wish."

"Diva, do you have your copy of our itinerary? Mine was lost with the luggage."

"I keep those papers in the big trunk."

Elizabeth went to the trunk and started looking.

"Now? You are looking for it now? I already told you I want to be seeing the gardens. You can do that later."

Roy stepped into the room, bowed low at the waist and said, "I'll take you, your majesty. It would be my honor."

"You see that Elizabeth? I think you could be learning the thing or two from the little man."

Roy offered his arm and said, "This way, Majesty."

Francesca stepped into the hallway without accepting his arm, and followed Roy towards the elevators. "You are not being so ugly," she said, "after I am getting more used to you."

The mayor led Harvey across the courtyard and through the garden. "The resemblance is uncanny. Jim was the first to notice, and when he pointed her out to me, I thought the queen herself had come to visit. But when she spoke, the image of the queen was shattered. You'd think she really was a queen, the way she treated people, except that the queen never treated anyone so badly. When we learned who she was, the famous Francesca La Perla, Prima Donna of the royal opera house, we just had to hear her sing."

"I see." Harvey really didn't see yet, but hoped it would become clearer as he went along.

"That's when the governor arrived. She sang like an angel. Who could believe that such sweet song could come from someone as cantankerous as her? Well not the governor. Once he heard her sing, he thought it was all a giant mistake. Who could blame him? It would never work if she was too soft at heart. He even got up to leave, but fortunately, he had not gone too far when she started yelling at her waiter. She was absolutely merciless. The governor was thrilled to see her butcher the poor guy."

"Well, of course he was. So how do you expect this to play out?"

"We don't know what you have planned, and we don't need to know. Once we deliver her to you, we wash our hands of the affair, except of course, we expect things here to return to normal, once you have done what you have to do."

"You think it will be that simple?"

"I don't know, but I sure hope so, for all our sake. Just take her, please, and fix the empire so we can get on with business here."

"So, for you, it's all about the money?" Harvey had been asked that often enough, it felt strange to hear the words from his own mouth.

The mayor didn't even hear the question. He had spotted Milton walking alongside the hotel and writing something in his journal. "Would you excuse me please? I see something that requires my immediate attention." He pointed to the elevator banks just inside the courtyard doors and said, "Take those to the top floor, she's in the Royal Suite."

Harvey shook the mayor's hand and headed off to the elevators.

Harvey exited the elevator on the top floor and could see what he believed to be the royal suite down the hall to his left. It had double doors and a doorbell, but otherwise looked as spartan as the rest of the room's doors. He still wasn't sure what they expected from him, or how he was going to play it. The way the mayor talked about this woman, Harvey almost felt sorry for her. He would probably be doing her a favor if he did take her away from these clowns; at least he just wanted money from her. He could only imagine what they had in store for her.

He stopped in front of the door and tried to think of a quick line that would get him in. He was too puzzled about the mayor's true motives to come up with anything too elaborate, so he chose to go with simple flattery. He brushed his hair back and knocked on the door.

Elizabeth opened the door. "Hello?"

"Madam La Perla, it is such an honor to meet you. I am a huge fan of yours! Huge! When I heard you were staying in this hotel, I simply could not believe my luck! I already called my friends and told them I was walking the same hallways as the great Francesca La Perla! And then it struck me, why should I just walk the halls? I should at least knock on the door and see you in person, and if I may say so, your album pictures do not do you justice."

Elizabeth started laughing while he prattled on through his spiel.

"I'm sorry," he said, "did I say something funny?"

"Well, biggest fan," she said, "I think it's only fair to tell you I'm not her. I think any true fan would know that I wasn't her."

"Perhaps you can tell me where I could find her?"

"Gosh, let me think, would she fire me if I didn't tell her biggest fan, that doesn't know what she looks like, where she was hiding?"

"Ok, you got me. I'm not her biggest fan. I was sent here to get her. I just thought we might avoid a big fuss if she thought I was a big fan."

"Oh, you must be from the embassy. They told me you were coming. You're here to give us a ride to the border?"

"Exactly. I didn't know you were expecting me."

"How soon did you want to leave? I haven't packed yet."

"No hurry. Take your time. My ship's being serviced now anyway."

"I think the Diva is viewing the Gardens. If you want, I can take you to her."

"No hurry there either. Let her enjoy herself a bit. By the way, my name is Harvey."

"Harvey?" she asked. "I thought we were expecting a Philbis."

"I owed him a favor and came in his place."

"I guess he wasn't her biggest fan either."

Harvey tried to laugh, but it looked more like an awkward grimace.

The mayor briskly made his way to the saloon where the governor liked to spend his mornings sipping strong Baldurian coffee. He pushed his way through the swinging gates and didn't wait to cross the floor before blurting out, "Kitt! Kitt!"

The governor had just taken another sip of the bitter fluid. He puckered his cheeks and clenched his lips as the slightly hallucinogenic sauce passed over his tongue. He closed his eyes as he swallowed before smiling and answering, "What's got you all wound up Mr. Mayor?"

"The emissary is here already. I was just taking him to meet Ms. La Perla, when I saw Milton examining the hotel and taking notes."

The governor scowled as the news soured the mellowness from the coffee. He had fallen behind in his payments, as had everybody. Business was bad all over, but Milton's boss wouldn't care. "You say he was taking notes?"

"Yeah. Maybe he was counting occupants or something."

"Or something. I want you to keep your eye on him. Let me know where he visits when he takes his notes. If that son-of-a-bitch thinks he is going to come in here and take us over, I'm gonna..."

"What?" the mayor asked. "Exactly what are you going to do? You're going to fight the mob?"

"No, no, but I'll think of something. In the meantime, you should just keep an eye on him."

"We've already got a plan. Let's just hope this emissary can do his job and get the king to accept her before it's too late."

The governor grunted and nodded his head.

Milton had been observing the resort all morning. He didn't like it here, the style was too rustic for his taste, but that wasn't going to stop him from doing his job. He measured the property, and counted the guests. It was a nice chunk of real estate, but it wasn't exactly the gold mine they said it would be when they took out the loan.

Francesca waited in front of the assay office after sending Roy to fetch a coffee for her, but she didn't know what was taking him so long. She saw Milton inspecting the grounds and called to him, "Yoohoo!"

He either didn't hear her or assumed she wasn't calling for him.

She called again, "You there!"

He looked up from his notebook to see who the loud woman was.

"Yes, you. I see that you are working. This will only take a moment. I need you to show me to this reflection pool I am hearing so much about."

Milton looked to his right and his left to be sure she was actually talking to him.

"Don't worry about your boss sees you. I am special guest in royal suite. Come now, you can show me to this pool and be getting back to your job in no time."

She must have money, he thought, *and he's certainly done worse things for money.* "Yes Ma'am, I'd be glad to show you to the reflecting pond." He didn't tell her it was his first trip and he had no clue where it was.

Mayor Bean remained hidden in the shadows, and behind the hedges. Milton was still inspecting the grounds when the mayor had caught up with him.

He was easy enough for the mayor to follow with most of his attention focused on his notebook and the property he was inspecting, but, when he met up with Francesca, he stopped skulking around and started walking out in the open, looking around, pointing at various things on the grounds.

The mayor had no clue what he was up to now, but whatever it was, it could not be good for them. Milton was going to ruin everything.

Elizabeth opened Francesca's bags on the bed and started transferring clothes from the dressers to the luggage. She'd been packing the Diva's clothing for years now and had a system that started with sorting the clothing, then arranging them into the bags like puzzle pieces.

Harvey leaned against the wall watching. "That's very impressive. You don't mind packing someone else's underwear?"

"Why would I mind?"

"I dunno, you just seem a little more on the ball than a servant girl."

"I'm not a servant girl," she said. "I'm her personal manager."

"Oh, I see, Ms. Personal Manager. I ask again, you don't mind having to pack someone else's underwear?"

"It's not so bad, and it's a hell of a lot easier for me to pack her stuff than it is to replace something that was left behind."

"Uh huh."

She stood tall and looked at him defensively. "We all have to work for someone!"

"So who packs your bags?"

"My bags are not a problem. They were stolen when we arrived."

"Sorry," he said lacking a smidgen of sincerity.

"You're kind of odd for an ambassador."

"Emissary," he replied, "not ambassador, and I was going for mysterious, not odd."

"What does an emissary do?"

"Whatever the ambassador doesn't want to do for himself, I guess."

"Like packing his underwear?"

Harvey just shrugged.

Elizabeth finished packing Francesca's things, closed the bags and stacked them up. "All done here, let's go see if we can find the Diva out in the garden."

Harvey opened the door and said, "After you."

She smiled as she passed him, and he thought he detected a slight twinkle in her eye.

Milton followed the signs. Some of the signs gave the history of various sections of the resort, and Milton made grand gestures to point out each and every one to Francesca, until he finally arrived at the one for the reflecting pond.

The rings of Gellian Prime could be seen rising over the horizon on the far side of the pond. The reflection of the rings on the pond broke into a myriad of hypnotic shapes which undulated with the minor ripples that always bounced across the pond.

Milton gasped at its beauty and said, "Stunning. I had always assumed it would be perfectly flat like glass."

Francesca looked down her nose at Milton and replied, "I thought you would have seen it thousands of times. They must not let the help to look at it."

"Oh no, I don't work here."

"But you look like inspector."

"No Ma'am. I'm examining the property trying to determine its purchase value."

"Ah, you are real estate broker."

"Wrong again. I'm more of a real estate investor. I travel around buying properties like this one."

Francesca changed her posture and said, "Ah, you must be very rich then. I am very rich too."

"Of course you are. You're in the royal suite."

"Si. But my bank is on border, and I need to get to border to get money back."

"Perhaps, if my business permits, I may be able to offer you a ride."

"Si! That would be good. You should speak with my Elizabeth. She will be so happy you can help us."

The governor checked some arrival and departure reports and saw that Milton was here alone, which he took to be a good sign. If his boss had been here, the governor would have had to plan a hasty escape.

He probably should speak with Milton, but he wasn't sure what he would say yet. He left his office and headed in the same general direction that he saw Bean take. He expected to catch up with them somewhere near the heart of the resort, and was surprised when he spotted Bean way out by the reflecting pool. That area had no intrinsic value to Milton or his boss.

Bean was spying on Milton from behind a billboard for the spa, so the governor took a slightly circuitous route to join Bean, hiding behind the same sign.

Judge Bean was spooked at first, when he heard the governor close in on his position, but was relieved when he spun around and saw that it was only Kitt.

Kitt whispered, "What the hell are you doing way out here? Are you still tailing Milton?"

Bean pointed with his thumb and said, "See for yourself."

Kitt pulled alongside and saw what he meant. He couldn't hear what they were saying, but he could see Milton and Francesca chatting and waving their hands around, punctuating what they were saying. He turned back to Bean and asked, "What the hell is he doing with her?"

"Beats me, but they've been pretty chummy and I don't like it. He's going to ruin everything."

Elizabeth and Harvey took a more direct path, having a fair idea where Francesca would be. Elizabeth pointed ahead of them and down the path. "There she is!"

Harvey saw her, but more important, he saw the governor and mayor watching them from behind the billboard. "What is he doing here?" he blurted out unintentionally.

"Oh, do you know him?"

Harvey glanced back in the Diva's direction and said, "Maybe not, I thought he was someone else."

Elizabeth skipped down the slight grade till she was in earshot.

Harvey quietly remained behind, preferring not to be seen by either of the two men spying on the couple below.

Elizabeth yelled, "Diva! I have someone for you to meet."

Francesca spun around to locate Elizabeth and said, "Oh! There's my Elizabeth. Milton, she's the one I was telling you about."

"Diva! I want you to meet the king's emissary. He is here to give us our ride home."

Milton was in no hurry to meet with the king's emissary, so he slipped out the other side and took an alternate path heading back to the center of the resort.

Francesca looked around but only saw Elizabeth. "Who is that you are talking about? No matter, this fine gentleman has offered to take us home."

Elizabeth spun around, but Harvey was nowhere to be seen. She turned back to Francesca and shrugged her shoulders.

"It's okay Elizabeth. You always had the problem holding on to men."

Elizabeth scouted around Francesca and said, "That's odd. Seems neither one of us can hold a man's attention today."

Milton's circuitous exit took him straight to the governor who was now pretending to discuss resort business with the mayor. "Milton? Is that you? Why didn't you tell us you were here?"

The mayor wanted nothing to do with the governor's mob friends, so he shrunk into the brush and re-emerged further up the path. He did not like that he was somehow mixed up with those guys. He was against it from the start, but the governor had engaged their help without asking his partners opinions. He returned to his office and packed an emergency bag in case he had to make an unplanned departure.

Milton just wanted to get back to his job. The governor was a politician, which made him of even less character than Milton and his gangster friends. Milton did not want to hear what was sure to be a well-practiced speech about how they planned to expand the resort.

The governor offered his hand and asked, "Have you been here long?"

"I'm just here to take some measurements for the boss."

"I know we're a little behind, Milton, but we are working on a deal that is going to fix everything. We'll be back at full capacity in no time. I guarantee we will turn this place around."

"The boss likes guarantees. Too bad they don't usually pay off."

The governor made a reassuring face and said, "This will. It's a cinch. We just need a little time to get all the players in place."

"I can't promise you time, but the boss has been pretty busy on some other opportunities. You might get lucky."

With Milton taking the governor out of the way, Harvey rejoined Elizabeth.

"Oh there you are, Harvey, I want you to meet the famous Prima Donna Francesca Vittoria Agostina La Perla. Diva, Harvey is the crown's emissary, and he is here to escort us back to the border."

"Ah, so you are a real man, how nice, and since my Mr. Milton has disappeared, I guess you will have to do."

Harvey was a little underwhelmed by Francesca's greeting, but he wasn't who he said he was anyway, so it didn't much matter to him. "Madam La Perla," he said, "it is a very great pleasure to meet you."

"Yes, of course it is."

An awkward silence followed, broken when Elizabeth said, "Well, Diva, I should probably alert the others. I've already packed your bags, so we can leave whenever Harvey here is ready to take us."

"Yes, Elizabeth, you do that. We wouldn't want to forget about the others. You just go now, take care of the others, I'll be fine, all by myself."

"You will be fine, and you won't be alone. I am leaving you in the emissary's very capable hands."

Harvey offered his arm to Francesca and asked, "Shall we walk?"

She accepted his arm and followed him down a side path past the pool and the reflected rings.

"Milton," the governor asked, "would you like a drink?"

As much as Milton did not care for the governor's company, a drink sounded good to him, so he nodded his head and walked alongside.

As they walked, Kitt pointed to some land west of the resort and said, "Once we get things turned around again, which will be soon, I can assure you, we were thinking of annexing the property over there and putting in a theme park."

"I thought this was a theme park?"

"No, no, I'm talking about rides and games. You know attractions for both the young and the adults."

As they approached the saloon, they could see a man with two escorts in military uniforms standing outside the governor's office.

"I'm sorry Milton, but can I get a rain check on that drink?"

Milton was glad for an opportunity to avoid them and slipped away, returning to his work.

"Gentlemen!" Kitt put on his most gregarious air, "I'm Governor Carson. I'm so glad you could come so quickly."

"I am Philbis Beck, attaché to the emperor's chief advisor's personal valet."

"Welcome Mr. Beck, my office is right over here." He led them to his suite and opened the door. "Please make yourself at home. We have a guest, here at the resort, who you absolutely must meet."

"You brought us here to meet one of your guests? I thought you said it was regarding imperial security."

"And so it is. You will want to meet this woman. The king will want to meet her. Trust me."

Milton's desire to avoid the uniformed men was overcome by the governor's greeting to them. The governor was expecting them. Milton waited outside a window so he could hear.

"Trust you?" the attaché asked, "Why in the world would the king care to meet this woman?"

"You only have to see her, then you will understand what I mean."

The emissary started to leave. "I have no time for this."

"Wait! She sings opera! She sings like an angel."

"The king does not meddle in the opera's affairs."

"But...but...please, you just have to see her."

The emissary signaled his escort to open the door.

"She looks very much like the queen."

The emissary stopped at the door. "And what makes you think the king would be interested in another woman who reminded him of the queen?"

"Well, she...she..."

"Spit it out man."

"She has a rather sharp disposition."

"She what?"

"No, that's not what I meant. She bears a very regal demeanor."

"I heard you the first time. Is she opinionated?"

"Very."

"Rude?"

"Definitely."

"And she looks like the queen?"

"Yes. And she's practically Vegan. She could be the solution to cure the torn empire."

"Practically Vegan?"

"Technically, she's from Earth, but so was the queen."

"No matter, she would have to be royal."

"She sings with the Vegan Royal Opera."

The emissary stopped to consider everything. "Very well, I think I should meet this woman."

Milton left his post outside the window and muttered to himself, "The boss will want to hear this, and he won't like it at all."

Harvey walked Francesca to a lookout point poised over a wide valley. He leaned over the railing and slowly shook his head. "It's beautiful, but it's not home. This whole resort is like a little slice of Earth, but it's still just a strange little moon clear on the other side of the galaxy, and it just makes me miss home all the more."

Francesca wore a fake smile and slightly nodded her head while she backed away a half step from Harvey, his melancholy monologue, and the railing looking over the edge of a cliff.

Harvey turned to her and said, "Ms. La Perla, Diva, I have a confession to make. I am your biggest fan."

Her mood perked up.

"I would have suffered this dingy moon a million times over, for just one chance to meet you. I thought I had landed here by the worst kind of luck. I ran out of fuel and was stranded here, and then, when I learned that my own fortune was inaccessible, I thought it was a tragic turn of events."

Francesca added, "I know, I know. Same thing happened to us. They won't let us have our money."

"It's just not right. Of course, I'm just a lowly trader, I couldn't even imagine the kind of fortune you must have back home."

"True," she said. "My fortune can be much to imagine for someone like you."

"Well, learning that you are here too, is my great fortune."

"But I thought you were emissary sent here to take us home?"

"Yes! Of course!" Harvey had to think fast. "I do some work for the empire, from time to time, and they contacted me to come help you."

"And you are having a ship?"

"Of course I am," Harvey said, "but I'm not sure it's adequate for someone as special as yourself. I still need to find some way to acquire some fuel for the journey."

"You can do that without money?"

"Madam, a clever person can do a great many things with just the promise of money."

Milton found a secluded spot away from the Governor's office before activating his communicator.

A secretary answered, "Hey Milty, he's busy right now."

"I know he's busy, but he's going to want to hear this."

Milton could hear a muffled commotion in the background before she responded, "I'm sorry, but like I said, he's busy...oh, no, wait a minute, he's done now. Here you go."

Vincenzo Stonewright, born Vincent Bartholomew Stonewright, grew up being called Vinny the Wienie until his father hit the lottery, after which, nobody called him wienie, twice. His father made himself into a success by loaning out his fortune out and extorting usury fees in return. His mother changed his name to Vincenzo when she built his father's business into a small empire, after watching too many godfather movies.

Milton heard his boss take the communicator from his secretary. He was short of breath and huffed out, "What is so important, that it couldn't wait for your scheduled report?"

"Boss, these guys think they're going to fix the empire! They even got this guy from the consulate here to meet with them."

Vincenzo motioned for his secretary to return to her desk. She grabbed her clothes and closed the door behind her.

"What are you talking about?" Vincenzo asked. "They can't even run a simple resort, how are they going to fix the empire?"

"They found a broad that they think can replace the queen! She even looks kind of like her!"

"So?" Vincenzo asked, "I'm sure we can find plenty of women that look like her, especially with the right modifications!"

"It's not just her looks, boss, she sounds kind of like her too, except she's real snobby and bossy."

"You mean she sounds like..."

"Yeah," Milton said, "put the king in a dress and you get her."

"Keep tabs on them. I'll get there as soon as I can."

Elizabeth had already searched the hotel for Victor and Bruno, and was just leaving the saloon when the governor came in, swinging the slatted wooden doors wide for some official looking guests.

"Governor?" she said. "Excuse me for interrupting, but have you seen any of the Diva's party roaming around?"

"No, sorry, I haven't. We were just looking for the Diva ourselves."

"I left her down by the reflecting pool, with the emissary."

The governor looked at his guest for a moment then replied, "But, this is the emissary."

Elizabeth shook her head and said, "No he isn't."

Philbis straightened his suit and said, "I assure you, I am. I am Philbis Beck, attaché to the emperor's chief..."

Kitt did not want to wait for his whole title, and interrupted, "Who did you say she was with?"

"I thought he was the emissary."

Philbis signaled his escort with hand gestures and they headed off towards the reflecting pool.

Chapter 3

Harvey and Francesca left the scenic valley behind them and returned to the reflecting pool so Francesca could make her wish. "I never make the wish before," she said. "Do I close my eyes first?"

Harvey was busy scanning the trails for any sign of the governor.

"Mr. Harvey?"

"I'm sorry Diva. I thought I saw something. Your wish? No, I think you probably need to stare into the reflected rings to make your wish."

"Very well then." She stared directly into the reflection. The rings were a variety of colors and shades which danced on the pools many ripples. "I wish I were away from this horrid place, surrounded with luxury and many adoring fans." She turned from the pool to face Harvey, obviously pleased with her wish.

Harvey, on the other hand, thought she should be more careful how she words her wishes. "Well, Ma'am," he said. "If I'm going to help you get off this rock, I'd better be finding us some fuel for my ship. Perhaps you should meet up with your girl Elizabeth. She's really something, the way she handles everything for you."

"Yes," Francesca said dryly. "She is usually being quite reliable. I think she has never failed me before this trip. I hope she will be returning to her old self and we can stop having these problems."

Harvey scratched his head, wondering if he should just let them have her.

Elizabeth bit her lip, waiting for an explanation, but none came. She shifted her focus from the governor to the new emissary. At least she thought he was the emissary, then back to the governor. They seemed to be waiting for her to explain.

"If you're the real emissary," she said, "then who is that other guy?"

"I can assure you that I am the real deal," Philbis proclaimed. "What can you tell us about the imposter?"

Elizabeth stared off into a corner of the room as she recollected their meeting. "He came to the Diva's room looking for her. He said he was the emissary and he was here to take us home."

"He actually said he was the emissary?"

"Of course he did, at least I think he did. Oh no...maybe I said it all for him. I just don't remember." Elizabeth stopped to rewind the morning in her mind. "He said his name was Harvey. Oh God! I left him with her!" Elizabeth started to cry. She didn't want to, but there was no holding back. She held her hands in front of her, not quite sure what to do with them.

The governor turned his back to place a call to Jim at the front desk.

She took a step towards the emissary, but he flinched, apparently repulsed by the thought of offering comfort to her.

"Please don't do that." The emissary pulled a tissue from his pocket and handed it to her. "I'm sure she's in no danger. He was probably just a fan who wanted to meet her."

That really opened the floodgates, and Elizabeth trembled as the tears flowed down her cheeks.

The governor finished his call and asked, "What did you say to her?"

The emissary just shrugged.

Francesca was walking back to the hotel when she saw Milton on the other side of the lawn. "Yoo hoo, Mr. Milton! You disappeared when my Elizabeth was coming."

With the boss coming to handle things, Milton thought he should keep Francesca company until his arrival. "I'm sorry. I had some things to do. Where is she? I can meet her now."

"She went to find the others. We are going home."

"How wonderful for you. As a matter of fact, I just got off the phone with my partners, and they agreed to take you home too."

"That's being very kind of you, but we are having the official escort from the king's own emissary."

Milton could see the two military escorts running down the far path to the reflecting pool. "That's marvelous," he said, "We should celebrate." He took her arm in his and guided her briskly towards the saloon.

Harvey dashed into some bushes to avoid the emissary's guards, but the bushes were on a slope and his footing gave way. He slipped a short way through the shrubbery and landed on a service road that led around the gardens. Things were getting too complicated. He really would have preferred avoiding imperial guards, but fortunately for him, they tended to be more brawn than brains.

Harvey followed the service road around the end of the gardens until it dumped him into an employee area equipped with tables and benches, and best of all, a couple of old friends.

"Hello Roy," he said.

Roy didn't have to turn around to see who was talking.

Gene got up from the table and said, "I need to go finish polishing the brass."

"Easy boys. Sit back down Gene. Let's chat."

Roy shook his head. Harvey wasn't a bad person, but he was almost always bad news. "What do you want, Harvey?"

"From you? Nothing. I was just taking a walk and came across you by accident. I didn't even know you were here."

"Well," Roy replied without looking up. "Gene and I work here. What's your excuse?"

"I got stranded here. Ran out of fuel and my money is no good."

"Sorry about that," Roy said, "but we can't help you. We've gone legitimate. We can barely even pay Gene's bar tabs."

Gene shrugged sheepishly and took his seat again.

Harvey held his hands to his chest, miming an arrow to the heart. "Boys," he said, "That cuts deep. I too have turned over a new leaf and I wouldn't dream of asking you guys for money. You got me all wrong."

Gene stood up again. "In that case, I can go back to polishing that brass."

"There is one thing..." Harvey stroked his chin while he spoke.

Roy finally turned his head to look at his old time colleague. "I knew it. We're not getting involved in another one of your hair brained schemes."

"This is different. I'm wearing a white hat this time, I swear. It's a rescue mission."

Gene managed three steps backwards before Harvey continued, "You know that opera singer?"

Gene shuddered and said, "Yeah we know her. Not too friendly, but she sure does look like the queen."

"Ex-queen," Harvey said.

Roy said, "That's not how we heard it."

Harvey's face blanched. "Wait a minute! Don't tell me you're in on it? I know we've done some low down things in our past, but we never sold anyone into slavery!"

"Slavery?" Roy asked, "They want to make her our queen. You'll be able to buy fuel again. I don't see the problem."

"You don't see the problem? Remember the king? They are going to force this woman on him!"

Roy started laughing.

Harvey didn't get the joke. He glanced back and forth between Roy and Gene, but still didn't get it. "What's so funny? Maybe you can let me in on it?"

Roy stifled his guffaws long enough to say, "I thought you wanted to rescue the woman, but now I see you must be planning to rescue the king from her!"

Harvey tried holding it in, but couldn't help letting a few chuckles slip out. "Come on guys, I'm serious. Let's help the old gal."

"Why should we? She treats us like vermin. Now her girl Friday, on the other hand, is real nice. Have you met her?"

"Yeah," Harvey said, "she's something else, but, let's stay focused on the singer."

"As we see it," Roy said, "if we treat her nice now, we might gain some favor from her when she's queen."

Harvey looked from one brother to the other, expecting one of them to break down laughing, but they were serious. He shook his head and wagged his finger saying, "You can't treat her like that. You said it yourself. You two have gone straight. Helping her is the right thing to do. Besides, she's loaded."

Gene and Roy nodded to each other and shrugged their shoulders. Neither was sure whether they could trust Harvey's good guy approach, but they had to admit he was right. She was loaded, and either way it turns out, if she becomes queen or remains the Diva, she will still be filthy rich.

Governor Carson smelled trouble. He didn't know who or what the imperial guards were going to find, but it wouldn't be good for him. With Elizabeth's sobbing form leaning against the emissary, he saw his chance to slip out and find the mayor. If Milton was passing himself off as the emissary, then the mob was up to something, but that just didn't make any sense. Milton was just a flunky. They had other men they would use for something like this, and Milton had plenty of aliases he could use without telling her his name was Harvey.

He brushed the thought aside and entered the mayor's office. Bean was tossing personal items into a large briefcase. Matching luggage stood waiting by the door. Kitt closed the door and asked, "What are you doing?"

"What's it look like I'm doing? The mob's here to finish us off, I'm going to find a nice quiet planet and disappear for the rest of my life."

"Stop being so dramatic. Besides, the empire sent their emissary here. Milton has more reasons to leave than we do."

"Are you kidding me?" The mayor stopped packing long enough to look Kitt in the eye. "I met the emissary this morning. He doesn't have a clue. He's completely useless to us."

"You couldn't have met him this morning. He just arrived."

"Nope, he came bright and early this morning. I was taking him into meeting with the diva when I spotted Milton roaming the grounds."

The governor rolled his eyes. "He was an imposter, and he's with her now. The real emissary is with the diva's manager in my office while his troops are out there looking for this fake."

Bean slammed a desk drawer shut and ripped open another. "Don't you see how this is getting out of control?" he growled, "It's all going to blow up in our faces."

"No it's not, and stop that packing." Kitt pulled open a drawer and started transferring folders back from the briefcase, but stopped to look Bean calmly in the eye and said, "Put that stuff away. The real emissary is here. He is going to take the diva back with him, and our plan is back in motion. As soon as she marries the King, our business will be thriving again."

Francesca and Milton sat in a high backed booth in the corner of the saloon. He ordered drinks, wine at first, but he smoothly progressed to stronger drinks as they went on. Francesca blindly drank whatever he put in front of her. "I tell you something, Mr. Milton. I don't like this place so much."

The saloon was a bit noisy, which suited Milton perfectly. Francesca was a loud woman, and the more she drank, the louder she got. He appreciated the din that surrounded them. It helped drown out their conversation, which he preferred keeping somewhat private. "Amen to that sister." He ordered more drinks for her, wishing a live band would come in before she got any louder.

Francesca sucked down the shot he put before her and continued, "Ever since we did the landing here, it is like I am stuck in the cowboy movie."

"I know what you mean," he replied, "I just don't understand their fascination with the wild west."

Francesca scrunched up her face as she said, "When we get here, this cowboy man came for us with robot horse, only it smelled bad like real horse."

He lined up two more drinks for her and shook his head saying, "Too much. Too, too much."

"I just want to go home, where I have my money, and royal suite is real royal suite. At home, I am treated like royalty. I am best singer. I think I deserve the royalty treatment."

Milton downed his own drink and thought to himself, *This broad should be more careful what she wishes for.*

Whether or not Harvey went through with rescuing Francesca, he was going to need to get off this rock, and with his money as worthless as hers, the only way he was going to do that was to hustle someone out of some fuel. Since money was scarce, he could try hustling someone out of their ship and transfer the fuel. He wrestled with how he would mix rescuing the diva with taking someone's ship. She might pose a risk to his escape, but he often told people his schemes were for a good cause. This time it might be true. He was venturing into unfamiliar territory and would have to play it by ear.

The spaceport, which was little more than a parking lot with a landing area, was nearly deserted. The economic problems facing the empire were visible in the small number of ships. Harvey wondered how many of these ships had also been stranded here along with his own, the Nova Comet.

The sparsely used rows provided little cover for him as he wandered, careful to avoid surveillance cameras and the infrequent guard patrols. He noted the various models of ships and judged them for their speed and range and also their stealth. His search brought him to his own ship. He had acquired the Nova Comet a long time ago while gambling, at least its former owner gambled it away.

Harvey considered Schatz a game of skill, and he knew how to manipulate the cards when he dealt.

He patted the ship's underbelly. It had been a good ship and had gotten him through many police and military blockades, then turned his back to his ship and tried blocking out the sentimental inclinations that were seeping into his forethought. It took a long time to customize the Nova Comet just the way he wanted it, but it was out of fuel and wasn't taking them anywhere. A paltry dozen or so ships surrounded him, but he only needed to find one of them with fuel, or so he kept telling himself. Even if he can't get the fuel transferred, he could always take the ship and build new secret storage compartments in the cargo hold. He needed a ship that was fueled up and ready to go. Souping up a new engine might be fun, but getting all the specialized electronics he needed wouldn't be easy, or cheap.

Elizabeth was inconsolable. She worked her way back to her room waffling back and forth between uncontrollable sobbing and shorter intermittent bursts where she would regain just enough of her composure to find her way through the hotel to her room.

It was all her fault. History would remember her as the person who delivered the diva into the clutches of an inscrutable kidnapper or worse. She found the elevator and wiped the back of her sleeves across her eyes so she could see the numbers. Everything was blurry. Only her guilt was clear to her. She pressed the number to the diva's floor instead of her own. Her balance wobbled right and left as she ran her fingers along the wall to feel her way to the royal suite. A solitary hallway was the final gap between her and the double doors, which she strained to see through her tears.

The key had sunk to the bottom of her purse, eluding her attempts to locate it. She leaned her back against the wall so she could search her bag with both hands, finally pulling it out and letting herself in. The first thing she saw was the packed bags on the bed, which led to another round of tears.

Bruno would know what to do, and no matter what his personal agenda might be, she was confident that he would not stand by and allow Francesca to be kidnapped. She punched his room number on the phone and listened to it ring and ring, but he didn't answer. Her heart fell again, launching another fit of tears which she tried to stave off by calling Francesca's personal communicator.

Elizabeth heard the familiar tones that were made when the other end was paging its user, then she heard the click it made when someone answered. "Helooooo," Francesca sang into the mouthpiece.

"Diva! Are you okay?"

"I'm fine dear. I'm fine."

Relief washed through Elizabeth's body and she fell limply into a stuffed chair. "Diva," she said. "I have some terrible news. The emissary we met this morning was an imposter! He was planning to kidnap you and hold you for ransom!"

"Oh my," Francesca giggled, "how exciting!"

"Exciting? Are you feeling okay?"

"I'm being just wonderful!" The diva downed another shot and slurred, "I'm simply marvelous, my dear!"

Elizabeth felt another shoe about to drop. "Where are you? I need to find you. The real emissary is here to take us to the border."

"You can be thanking him for me, but that nice Mr. Milton has already offered us the ride to the border."

"You mean he is real? I mean, you found him?"

"Yes dear. While you were off doing whatever the things are that you do, your diva was taking care of the business for all of us. Honestly, sometimes I'm not understanding why it is I hired you."

Their server delivered another round of drinks to the table and Elizabeth heard the clinking sound of glass against glass, followed by the sound made when the other communicator ended the call.

Harvey's spirits were sagging. There were only a few ships in the lot and he'd checked about a third of them, so far, and all of them had been drained. They didn't have enough fuel to taxi out to the departure zone. Forget about trying to escape this rock. He started pulling the hatch to reveal the fuel cells of yet another ship when he heard a new vessel approaching behind him. That ship still had some fuel. He hid behind a large tire and watched it pull up alongside all the other ships. It was a large passenger ship. There was no way he could ever convert that ship to be either fast or stealthy, but he had a feeling that it probably carried huge fuel reserves.

A handful of passengers disembarked. He could see some of them arguing with a tall grey skinned woman in an airline uniform. Harvey could tell she was an officer from the ship. He wasn't familiar with her species, or where she may have been from, but she was an impressive specimen: tall and thin and very confident looking. She moved with an uncommon grace, holding herself upright like a swimmer treading water. He couldn't hear what they said, but he could see her raise her arms up in the air while shrugging her shoulders.

Harvey needed to get closer. He worked his way from ship to ship and wheel to wheel until he was almost next to them, but he was too late. The passengers left in the direction of the two podiums, apparently unsatisfied with the conversation they had with the tall woman in captain's clothes.

She started to head back into her ship when a ground engineer pulled his truck up to the rear of her ship and started opening the fuel bay. She yelled in a tongue Harvey had never heard. She was clearly agitated, and much bigger than the poor engineer. He hooked some large hoses to her ship and started something on his truck. She moved towards the rear of her ship and the engineer. Harvey followed, and the closer he got to them, the taller she looked. The engineer was no small guy, but she towered over him. She looked like she could tear him apart, and approached him like she might just do it.

He ran back in the direction of the mechanics hangar. She immediately followed him. She was slow at first, but her long legs stretched out her stride until she was nearly leaping with each step. He was only half way to the hangar when she began to close the distance to him. "I'm sorry," he pleaded. "It's the new policy. Harry? HARRY? Help me out here! Explain to her that we'll credit her for her fuel and she'll get it all back!"

She was nearly on top of him when they disappeared into the hangar and out of Harvey's sight.

Harvey was tempted to steal the fuel truck and fill his own ship. Nobody was watching it, but it was too impulsive. He didn't like taking uncalculated risks. He'd have to plan a way to get the fuel back from storage to his ship.

While Harvey slipped out of the space port and back to the resort, a quiet ship entered the port low over the horizon and slipped undetected into an empty spot among the parked vehicles. It wasn't an overly large ship, but it most certainly wasn't small. The hatch opened and Vincenzo Stonewright emerged and quietly slipped down to the surface. Vincenzo looked around the port and was satisfied that there was no security alerted by their stealthy arrival.

Two goons followed him out of the ship. The first stepped in front of him looking both dumb and ferocious, obviously undeterred by the lack of interest from security. The second sidled up alongside Vincenzo and asked, "Hey boss, you want that I should go get the cart?"

Vincenzo closed his eyes and shook his head.

"What?" the goon asked, "Didn't I ask it right?"

Vincenzo made all his associates watch and memorize the godfather series so they could walk and talk the parts. "No Tony," Vincenzo said, "You asked correctly, but don't you think that by now you would know that I always want you to go get the cart?"

"Yeah boss, you're right. Be right back."

Tony went to the rear of the ship and pressed a button on a small remote he retrieved from his pocket. A small and silent three seat ground vehicle was lowered from the tail section. The craft was triangular shaped with a single pilot seat in front and two passenger seats in the rear. It had an open top and only a small glass windshield in the front. A narrow ledge in the back was just large enough to accommodate some luggage or golf clubs. Tony took the front seat and glided the cart up alongside of Vincenzo.

Vincenzo entered the rear of the cart and said, "Take us to the hotel."

Tony didn't need to do anything. The cart heard Vinny's instructions and had already plotted a course.

The last goon jumped onto the landing in the back and rode fireman style just as the cart started to leave.

Vincenzo pulled out his communicator and called Milton.

Milton was expecting him and answered, "Boss. How was your flight?"

"Smooth, of course. We'll be there in a few minutes. You got the dame with you?"

He needn't have asked. He could hear Francesca say, "Who is it Milty? Is that our ride?"

Milton replied, "Yeah boss, I'm with her. She's lit up like a Christmas tree and shouldn't pose no trouble for us."

The emissary stood, alone, in the governor's office. He pulled a handkerchief from his breast pocket and wiped his broad lapels where Elizabeth had ground in her tears. He went to a mirror hanging on the governor's wall and checked his appearance. He frowned at his reflection and straightened out a few stray hairs then pulled his communicator from his belt and called the guards he had sent to find Francesca.

"Emissary?"

"Have you located this woman they claim to have found yet?"

"No sir. We've searched the grounds around the reflecting pool, but there's nobody there matching her description."

"Very well. Return to your posts outside my suite."

The emissary went to the governor's desk and wrote on his blotter, "You have until sunrise. If you don't produce the woman, I'm leaving."

Milton raised his hand and motioned for their cocktail waitress. The petite android, decked out in gaudy sequins and a feather boa, promptly attended their table, and asked, "Is there anything else I can get you?" Her eyes were heavily lined in black, and she kept them both wide open and trained seductively on Milton.

"Just the check, please." Milton had already pulled out a charge stick which he held up for her.

She flashed an enticing smile and leaned over the table, displaying her ample synthetic bosom, which nearly spilled out of her corset, and added, "If you are quite sure, happy hour just started. Are you sure there isn't anything I can get for you to make you more happy?"

Francesca watched the woman through her drunken eyes and reached out to play with her feather boa. "I like this," she slurred, "But I think you are far too young and pretty to be working in a place like this."

Milton wanted to explain to Francesca that their waitress was just a robot, but simply shrugged off her behavior instead and waited for their attendant to take his charge stick.

Seeing that she wasn't going to make another sale, she stood back up and in a very well programmed move, adjusted her breasts back in place in the top of her corset. She took his stick and passed it over her portable terminal and returned it to him, then zipped off to the next table.

"Come on doll," he said as he stood up and helped Francesca's wobbly form out of the booth. "It's time to get you home where you belong."

Francesca was more of a handful than Milton anticipated, but he managed to guide her through the swinging doors and out onto the wooden sidewalk.

Harvey was more than a little uncomfortable with his new role as the hero. His life as a con man and smuggler had not prepared him for what must be done, but he was in a unique position to recognize what was going on around him.

He thought the old gal was in trouble when the empire was after her, but he clearly heard the mobster ask if someone had the dame with them. If the mob was after her too, he would have to act fast.

He crept from the parking area to the back of the mechanics hangar where he had seen a parked hover bike. He hated to see perfectly good vehicles, like this, abandoned in the middle of nowhere, so he pulled out one of his favorite gadgets and ran it through a sequence of lock codes until the bike sprang to life.

He swung his leg over the seat and felt the low thrum between his legs. He gripped the handles and goosed the throttle, surging him silently forward, away from the hangar. He was grateful that the bike was well maintained by the mechanics and quickly raced it out of the space port and across a side exit onto a service road.

The main road took a more circuitous route to keep the tourists from seeing the living areas that weren't themed as the park was. Harvey was confident that he could make up considerable time and beat the mobster to the park, but that still didn't put him in time to save Francesca.

It was a fast bike, and he kept the throttle pushed to the max. The service road slipped down into a valley where they kept most of the housing hidden from view. The valley was surprisingly lush. He found himself surrounded with trees as he zipped the bike through the valley along the narrow road. The valley must have looked like a small oasis surrounded by the desert as it was.

He made good time and the housing soon disappeared behind him. The road headed up again and he emerged back onto the desolate flatness of the small moon, with the park and the hotel just ahead. He parked the bike behind the hotel and entered through the employee door. A maintenance smock was conveniently left hanging inside the entrance, so he slipped it on and followed the hallway to the service elevator. He tried to look "maintenancy" as a maid passed by while he waited for the elevator.

So far, so good. He took the lift to Elizabeth's floor and walked nonchalantly to her door. He was about to knock, when the door swung open and there she was.

Elizabeth couldn't hide the surprise on her face. For an instant, Harvey thought she was going to smile, but it never happened.

"You!" she shouted, "What are you doing here? Who are you? I'm calling security. HELP! SOMEONE HELP!"

"Shhh. Shhh." Harvey backed her into the room.

"Get away from me! HELP!"

"Stop that! Listen to me!"

She wouldn't stop screeching for help, and Harvey could not warn her of the danger she was in. He retreated out of the room and ran down the hall to escape the hotel. Now he was really confused. How could he help them if they didn't want to be helped?

Dusk settled on to the small resort of Emaude Phlott. The setting sun cast shadows that stretched across the dusty streets. Gas lamps sprang to life along Main Street and the boardwalk, adding a gentle flicker to the scene. As the sky darkened, the street took on a purple hue cast from the rings of Gellian Prime that shone overhead.

Milton tried guiding Francesca down the boardwalk toward the circular drive outside of the registration desk at the entrance to the park, but she kept tugging the other direction. Holding her upright was hard enough for the small man, but was doubly difficult when she pulled towards her room. The wooden sidewalk offered uneven footing at best, forcing him to double his efforts.

A passing tourist watched the struggling couple suspiciously, and Milton was certain it looked exactly like what it was, so he held his hand to his mouth, miming a drinking action, to which the tourist simply nodded and moved on.

It was a pleasant evening. The emerging stars and the rings provided a romantic backdrop to the quaint little town. He thought maybe he was taking the wrong approach. He didn't have the strength to carry her all the way to meet the boss. Perhaps he should try wooing her into joining him.

"I thought you were anxious to get home," Milton said to Francesca, "but you keep going the wrong direction. They're meeting us over there."

"Yes, but my things," she replied, still leaning towards her suite.

"But you're rich. Can't you just buy new things?"

"Yes," Francesca said. She eased up for a moment, comforted by the reminder that she would be rich again. She started to follow Milton, and he leaned her against a wooden post so he could rest. He reached up and brushed his hand against her cheek, but the lamps cast her face in an unflattering light. His spine shivered and he returned to guiding her towards the main entrance and she resumed her struggle in the opposite direction, slurring, "but my Elizabeth. We must get my Elizabeth."

"Don't worry about her, we'll send for her."

Mayor Bean grudgingly followed the governor to the sheriff's office. Of all the attractions on Main Street, the sheriff's office offered the most authentic decor, from the wanted posters facing the street to the jail bars inside. But it was also the least used place. Customers were never arrested here, and the sheriff seldom spent much time here himself. The dust which had been careful applied just to look like a dirty old west sheriff's office, needed no touch up applications, since the sheriff spent most of his time dealing Faro in the saloon.

The governor just peeked in the window to confirm he wasn't there, then headed directly across the street to the Pink Lady Saloon. They pushed through the swinging gates and found Earp where they expected him to be, dealing cards at the Faro table.

He looked up at his visitors and scowled through his large handlebar mustache, then returned to dealing the cards. He only had one customer, his longtime friend Doc Holiday, and the governor wasn't sure whether they were actually gambling or just playing for show.

The governor tipped his hat and said, "Wyatt."

Earp didn't even bother to glance up at the governor and mumbled, "Kitt."

The governor sat down at one of the empty chairs, but Earp was quick to say, "The seats are for paying customers."

The governor glanced around the mostly empty table then shot a quick look over to Holiday who said, "Now Wyatt, I'm sure we can spare a moment for our good friend Governor Carson."

"Thank you Doc," Carson said, "and this is business. We've got a problem."

Wyatt grunted. He put the cards down and poured himself a shot of whiskey.

Carson said, "Did you hear our new guest sing last night?"

Wyatt nodded his head and said, "She was good."

Doc laughed and said, "For a moment there, I thought she was the Queen."

Wyatt sneered and asked, "What's this got to do with me?"

"Well," the governor continued, "We have a plan. Not only does she sing like an angel and look like the queen, but she has a sturdy enough character to match up with the king. We think she could be the queen; the *new* queen. We'd like to present her to the king so he would end his tirade and the Vegans will be placated. Hopefully then, business will pick up again."

Wyatt tossed the whiskey to the back of his throat and looked thoughtfully into his glass. "Okay," he said, "but I repeat, what does this have to do with me?"

"Well, we have a little problem."

The mayor thought the governor was taking far too long so he spat it out, "The mob's in town and they are going to take her for themselves and ruin everything."

Holiday nodded and patted his sidearm, saying, "So you need us to take care of someone?"

"Oh, settle down John," the governor said, "these guys use real guns. But we do need to secure the woman and keep her from them."

Wyatt shuffled the cards and dealt hands to the three gentlemen. "I still don't see what this has to do with me, and like you said, they use real guns."

Holiday pulled out his six shooter, popped the cylinder to the side and spun it. The well-oiled cylinder spun fast a free, emitting a soft buzz. He cracked the gun open and stared down the inside of the barrel at the governor. "It may be a replica," he said, "but it's a real enough gun with real enough bullets, and I know how to use it."

The governor reached out and gently pointed the empty barrel away, saying, "You're not helping John. I'm sure they don't want to make a scene in public. All we need you to do is escort her to the king's emissary. Nothing more."

Wyatt leaned over and spit into the spittoon at his side. The governor blanched at the sight. "If the emissary is here," Wyatt asked, "then why don't you just go bother him with your problems? Those chicken shits from the empire don't go anywhere without an escort."

"We would," Kitt said, "but he hasn't really come on board yet, but I'm sure that once he sees her, he'll be behind us one hundred percent."

Holiday flipped his gun closed and said, "What the hell, it's been too damned quiet around her anyway." He stood up, tugged his vest down and checked the timepiece in his waist pocket. "Come on Wyatt, we'll be done in time to meet Kate for dinner."

Earp took a deep breath and exhaled loudly and shoved his chair backwards while he stood up. "Where is she?"

Tony switched the cart from automatic mode to manual as they entered the park's circular drive. He pulled the cart alongside the curb at the end of the wooden boardwalk, just before the registration desk.

Vincenzo looked down the street and frowned. He had no love for the west and didn't understand the appeal, but he saw how much others liked it and his mother thought it might be a good place for a casino, so he invested anyway. But now, looking at the dirt streets and aged wooden structures, it didn't look like an investment, it looked more like a sink hole to him.

Looking further down the street, he saw Milton struggling to guide Francesca towards him. From this distance, he couldn't really tell if she was everything Milton said she was, but she had the right build and hair color, and maybe that would be enough.

He turned to the back of the cart and said, "Bruiser, go see if you can help Milton."

The tall goon in the back stepped off the cart and went to assist Milton. His real name was Bruce, and he wasn't nearly as tough as the boss would have liked, but he was big. The wooden boards of the sidewalk creaked under his weight, no matter how gingerly he tried to walk. He didn't like making so much noise when he walked, and would have picked his footing more carefully, if he hadn't been so busy looking up so he could duck to avoid the cobwebs that hung from the awnings and fluttered in the breeze.

"Look," Milton said, pointing down the walk. "There are my friends now."

Francesca leaned heavily on Milton while she waved at Vincenzo.

Bruce was able to offer a considerable amount of support for Francesca, and with her between the two mobsters, she walked a nearly straight line to Vincenzo.

Vincenzo got up out of the cart and graciously bowed and offered her the other rear seat. "My lady," he said. "It is indeed a great honor to meet you. And it is my pleasure to assist you today."

He held up his hand for her, which she accepted. He gently kissed the back of her hand and guided her into the cart, then swiftly followed her and signaled Bruce to jump on back again.

"But," Francesca said, "we must wait for my Elizabeth!"

Vincenzo looked inquisitively at Milton, who answered, "Elizabeth is her assistant."

"Oh," Vincenzo lied, "Elizabeth is already at the space port waiting for us."

Francesca was relieved to hear that and relaxed into her seat.

Milton took the remaining post on the back of the cart next to Bruce, but Vincenzo said, "Milton, why don't you finish your analysis. I'll call you when I need you."

Elizabeth stared breathlessly at the door. The imposter came to her room. He must have come looking for Francesca. Elizabeth would have to warn her about him.

She had heard glasses clinking when Francesca called and unless they were in someone's private room, the saloon would be the best place to start looking. She wished she knew where Bruno was. Everything was getting a bit complicated for her to handle alone.

She peeked through the peep hole and didn't see Harvey. Carefully cracking the door open, she slipped out of the room and made her way to the saloon. A pinch in her head reminded her that she didn't really want to visit the saloon ever again.

When she pushed through the swinging doors, the saloon was too quiet for the diva to be there. The lights dimmed slightly and the crowd that remained had obviously been there a while. Elizabeth ran to the bar tender to ask if he had seen where Francesca went, but he was just a robot serving drinks.

Elizabeth had no time to waste looking for her. If they were going to take her, they would have to take her to the space port. She grabbed some tip money that had been left on an empty table and ran out of the saloon and hailed a cab.

"Take me to the spaceport," she yelled before she had even closed the door behind her.

Harvey saw Milton lead Francesca down the boardwalk towards Vincenzo. He knew where they were taking her, but the hotel where he left the speeder was too far away, so he crossed his fingers and ran behind the saloon where he found an assortment of vehicles. He quickly hot-wired a scooter and took off for the space port.

As he pulled onto Main Street, he saw Milton and one other goon still struggling to get Francesca lifted into the buggy. He sped down the road confident that they would spend their time looking behind them instead of ahead.

The space port was practically deserted, which was becoming a common state for it ever since the empire divided. There was only a single ship being serviced, and the ground crew did not seem to be in much of a hurry. They probably resented working so late when everyone else was home relaxing.

Vincenzo's ship was still being refueled when Tony pulled the cart into the space port. Vincenzo did not like being around the fuel or the fueling stations, so Tony kept the cart a safe distance away. He climbed out of the buggy and helped the inebriated Francesca down to the ground.

A quick check of his watch told Vincenzo that they were falling behind schedule. "Tony? Why don't you go see what's taking them so long. I want to get off this rock."

Tony leaned Francesca up against a stack of crates and ran off to see about the refueling.

Bruce climbed down from the buggy and stood in front of Vincenzo awaiting some kind of orders. Vincenzo hated when they couldn't manage the small stuff and waved him off saying, "Go watch the road. Make sure we weren't followed."

Francesca ran her fingers across the stack of crates, apparently fascinated with the mottled surface of the wood. Still leaning her shoulder against them, she walked around the stack and found writing on the other side which seemed to tickle her plastered brain.

Vincenzo stood on the runway looking off into the horizon. He wasn't really the gangster that people thought he was, or that his mother wanted him to be, but he was the boss and tried his best to always look like the boss, so he never meddled in the mundane affairs of the underlings.

Francesca was still amusing herself with the normally uninteresting crates when Harvey reached out and pulled her between two other stacks of crates. Francesca's face lit up when she saw him and she started to say something, probably in a very loud voice, when Harvey put his hand on her mouth and said, "Shhh!"

Francesca thought he was just being mysterious and romantic with her and fell into his arms so he could hold her. Harvey guided her between the crates to his own ship that still needed to be fueled.

Harvey entered a code into the ships keypad and stairs were lowered from the fuselage. Before he could turn around to get Francesca, he heard a new voice behind him.

"So, you must be the famous emissary I've heard so much about."

It wasn't Milton's voice or Vincenzo's. Harvey put a smile on his face, turned around and without affirming the statement, asked, "And you are?"

Philbis wore a well-practiced smile as he responded, "I am Philbis Beck, attaché to the emperor's chief advisor's personal valet and I've been wondering who was going around impersonating me."

Philbis was flanked by two hefty guards. Harvey would have to talk himself out of this mess. "I never actually said I was the emissary. People around here seemed to be expecting you and just assumed I was you." Harvey shrugged his shoulders and added, "I was stranded here and out of fuel. I thought maybe someone would be generous enough to send me on my way before you came."

Philbis pointed to Francesca and asked, "And was this woman generous enough?"

"Uhh, maybe."

Philbis nodded dramatically and said, "I suppose your type often finds generosity in inebriated women."

Harvey cocked his head sideways and repeated, "Uhh, maybe."

"Well," Philbis said, "as long as I am escorting this lovely young woman off this rock, I see no reason I can't take her companion with us." He turned to one of the guards and said, "Tie him up."

The guard tied Harvey's arms behind him and gripped his arm to escort him to the emissary's ship. The emissary walked in front leaving the other guard to struggle with the tipsy diva.

When the diva stumbled up the gangway, Harvey's guard caught her before she fell and Harvey zipped off the runway into a culvert where he disappeared from their view.

With Francesca aboard, the guard started running after Harvey, but the emissary said, "Leave him. Let's go."

The cab pulled into the spaceport at the entrance near the ticketing podiums. Elizabeth jumped out and gave all the money she stole to the cab driver. She didn't know if it was enough and she didn't care, she was already here.

She doubted that the kidnappers would take a commercial flight, so she ran around the podiums to the back where all the ships were parked.

Crates and boxes were stacked everywhere. She walked blindly up and down the aisles looking for the diva until she ran across Harvey. He was sprawled unconscious on the ground with his arms tied behind him. She kicked him and screamed, "What did you do with her?"

The kick worked. Harvey shook his head to clear the cobwebs. He wobbled and rolled around until he managed to sit up, but his side hurt. He tried rubbing his side, but his hands were still bound behind him. She started to kick him again, but he rolled away, yelling, "Hey! Stop that!"

Elizabeth was out of control. She yelled, "You tell me what you did to her or I'll kick you again!"

Harvey rolled up against the crates and managed to climb back onto his feet and whined, "Do I look like I'm the one who did something to her?"

"So?" she asked. "What happened? Did your accomplices double cross you?"

"No!" he snapped back. "I learned that these gangsters planned to kidnap your girl and I tried to rescue her, which you could have helped me with if you hadn't gone all crazy on me!"

"You really expect me to believe you were trying to rescue her?"

"Yes!" Harvey yelled back. "And I did too! I snuck her away from the bastards, but the king's emissary had his guards tie me up. I barely escaped."

"So?" she asked. "What happened to you next? Why were you unconscious?"

"Does it matter?"

Elizabeth flung her arms around and growled. "Why are you always hiding stuff? Is everything you say a lie?"

"No," he pleaded. "I haven't been lying to you. Not really. Can you please untie me?"

Elizabeth went around him and looked at the ropes, but said, "Not until you tell me why you were unconscious."

Harvey hung his head and grumbled under his breath then said, "Have you ever tried running with your hands tied behind you? I tripped and hit my head."

Something in his voice told her it was the truth. He looked too pathetic to be lying now. She giggled, then said, "Oh, I'm sorry. I didn't mean to laugh."

She untied him and they heard the roar of a ship taking off.

Elizabeth looked up and asked, "Is that the emissary with my diva?"

"No," Harvey said. "That's the mobsters."

Another ship took off heading a different direction and Harvey said, "That's the emissary."

Elizabeth breathed a sigh of relief and said, "Well thank goodness she's safe."

"Are you kidding?" Harvey asked. "Do you have any idea why they wanted her?"

Elizabeth looked at him blankly.

"That emissary plans to use her to replace the Queen. She's practically going to be a slave stuck in a marriage to the worst person in the empire."

Elizabeth's mouth fell open. She paused as it sunk in and shook her head and said, "No. That's just too crazy to even consider."

"Is it?" Harvey asked. "Have you ever seen the queen?"

Elizabeth shook her head no.

"Your girl is the spitting image of the queen. And she can sing opera too? Wave goodbye to her now, because you'll never see her again."

Chapter 4

V incenzo poured himself a cognac and sank into his sumptuous chair as the ship pulled out of the moon's atmosphere. "Boy am I glad to get away from that hunk of rock. Every time we go there I'm afraid we're going to come away with fleas or something."

"Yeah boss," Tony agreed. "I know what you mean. That place gives me the willies, but it's kinda nice to wear my gun in public like they do."

"It looks good on you too. I guess there are some good things about the good old days, but I'm a big city boy. It just don't feel right if we ain't rubbin' shoulders with the crowded sidewalks. And don't forget about the food. I can't imagine life without any of the finer restaurants."

"Yeah," Tony added, "and the ballparks."

"At least they have the fight cards," Bruce added.

"Yep," Vincenzo said, "and I even miss all that snooty upper crust stuff too: the museums, the theatre, and the opera. Speaking of which, I was sure the old gal was going to raise the alarm when you brought her on-board. What did you do to keep her so quiet?"

Tony was confused, which wasn't necessarily so difficult to do. "What do you mean, 'what did I do?' I thought you made her all quiet."

"Not me," Vincenzo admitted. "I guess we got Milton to thank for that. She was sure tanked when we picked her up. She must be sleeping it off."

"Yeah, that's it boss. She must be sleeping it off."

Vincenzo sipped his cognac and said, "Let's remember to keep her good and plastered. Her voice gives me the heebie jeebies. Where'd you put her? Maybe you should make sure she has a refill when she wakes up."

Tony was confused again and asked, "What do you mean, 'Where did I put her? You brought her on-board, boss."

"Why would I bring her on board when I have you to do the heavy lifting?"

Tony just shrugged.

"Oh hell!" Vincenzo said. "Search the ship! Find her!"

Harvey ducked behind a row of cargo containers when he heard the sheriff's siren approaching.

The sheriff jumped out of his remarkably non-themed vehicle and ran to Elizabeth. He heard the roar of a ship engine as he approached and asked, "Who just took off?"

"As near as I can tell," she replied, "one ship was some mobsters and the other was the imperial emissary."

The sheriff strained his neck to see the ships but all he could see was their contrails. "Did they get the singer?"

"We think she's with the emissary."

The sheriff looked at Elizabeth curiously and asked, "We?"

Elizabeth wanted to point to Harvey so he could explain, but he was nowhere in sight. "Me," she replied, "I think she's with the emissary, at least I hope so, maybe. I'm not sure which one is worse."

The governor climbed out of the sheriff's vehicle and said, "Maybe we can see something on the security cameras."

The sheriff grunted and nodded. As he started towards the space port's security truck, he turned and asked Elizabeth, "Maybe you should come with us. You might recognize someone on the surveillance cameras."

Elizabeth nodded and followed along.

Harvey was listening from the next row and knew that if he was on the security recordings, they would show him trying to rescue Francesca. He came out of hiding and said, "I think I'll come along and take a look at those too."

"You!" the governor shouted.

"Why were you hiding?" the sheriff asked.

Harvey shrugged and said, "Ever since I was stranded here people have been mistaking me for one person or another. Either I was one of those gangsters or I was representing the empire."

"The other gangsters," the governor interjected.

"The truth," Harvey continued, "is that I'm just a guy who ran out of fuel and was stranded here and I just went along with whatever anybody said hoping it would lead to a little fuel to help me get home."

The sheriff didn't really buy it, but he signaled for Harvey to come along with them anyway.

Francesca lay back staring up at the ceiling of the emissary's spacecraft. Little black dots mottled on the ceiling captured her attention for the moment. They looked like stars but when she squinted her eyes, they also looked like the many heads of an audience when she was on stage performing. How long has it been since she was on stage? A shiver ran up and down her spine as she quickly discounted that awful theatre with the clinking and the eating. Her true fans must miss her terribly, but she would be reunited with them very soon.

"It's a good thing that you are doing," she said, "You should be rewarded for saving me. In fact, I have just the thing for you!"

She sat up in the chair and looked around her. She wasn't on stage; she was sitting in the back of a small passenger ship, with the imperial guy up in the front. The ship wobbled and spun a bit in her mind, but she forced herself to stand up and look in the back of the ship. "Oh no!" she said, "This is not right. This will not do. We must go back for my things."

The emissary sat in the front of the cabin with his guards. They did their best to ignore her, but she was a loud woman.

"Hey you!" she bellowed. "Are you hearing me? You forgot my things! I have the picture to give you, but we must go back for my things."

The emissary winced as her voice filled the cabin. He looked pleadingly at the guards. He couldn't ask them to knock her out, but he wouldn't hold them responsible if they acted on their own.

Francesca walked a very crooked path up the ships center aisle past the emissary and banged on the door to the cockpit. "Hey you! You driving the ship! You forgot my things! We have to go back!" She banged her fists on the door but nobody answered.

The emissary couldn't ignore it anymore and shouted "We can't go back now. The king himself has ordered us to bring you directly to him. He is your biggest fan and he wants to meet you without delay."

"Well," Francesca said, "it is good that I should be meeting my biggest fan, but not without my things. What will your king say if I am not with the signed autograph? I mean the autographed sign, no that's not it, the pictured photo..."

"I know what you mean, but the king would have my head if I turned around now. Please return to your seat. We have many fine photographers in the empire. I am sure we can replace everything that you have left behind."

"Everything?" she asked meekly.

"Everything you are missing. We will get you new replacements for everything you lost."

"What about my Elizabeth? How are you getting me the new Elizabeth?"

Francesca sat back in her chair and began to cry. She cried softly at first, with soft tears on her cheeks, but her cries morphed into loud sobs that were even worse than her ranting. The emissary put headphones on and played loud music to drown her out. His guards had no such luxury and just grumbled until she finally quieted down and fell asleep.

The spaceport had no actual buildings. It was just a landing strip with stalls for people to await departure, but there was a security team in a truck that parked alongside the fuel dump. The head of security saw the sheriff heading their way on the monitors and met them outside the truck. "Good day Mr. Earp, is there something we can do for you?"

"Yes sir," the sheriff said. "This woman here believes that her boss has been abducted on one of them ships that just left and we'd like a gander at your security logs to see what happened, and maybe catch an identity of them alleged kidnappers."

"Of course," the security officer said. "Help yourselves. I'll go inform Gellian Prime so they can track the ships just in case your allegations prove out."

The security truck was barely any larger than a closet. It was filled with monitors showing every corner of the small spaceport, but was only designed to accommodate two people. Four people squeezed into it was very cramped, and the lack of any windows made it seem even smaller.

The sheriff sat at the controls in one of the two chairs with Elizabeth behind him looking over his shoulders and the other two men squeezed in on either side of her.

"There she is," the sheriff said as he played through one of the video logs.

"That's the emissary," the governor said pointing at the man on the screen with her. "The real one."

"You have to rescue her!" Elizabeth cried.

"From the empire?" the governor asked.

"Do you know what they plan to do with her?" Elizabeth replied.

"I'm sorry," the sheriff said, "but she's off the moon and out of my jurisdiction."

"But they're going to..."

"And what," the sheriff interrupted as he pointed his thumb at Harvey, "do you think this guy was going to do with her?"

"Hey!" Harvey replied. "I was trying to rescue her! Just rewind the logs! You'll see."

"I don't need to rewind the logs," the sheriff said, "I think I know what you were up to."

"Why not?" Elizabeth asked. "I'd think a man in your position would be more interested in the facts before making such accusations. I know that I'd like to see if he is telling the truth."

"Yeah!" Harvey said. "Or are the facts also not in your jurisdiction?"

The sheriff rewound the logs and they saw the mobsters bring Francesca to their ship.

"Those guys," Harvey said, "are all gangsters. They're up to something and you can see they were kidnapping her."

"I don't know," the governor said weakly. "I just see some businessmen offering her a ride. We all know she was trying to find a ride off this moon."

"Look at them!" Harvey shouted. "They're practically carrying her!"

"Sure," the governor agreed, "but she looks kind of tipsy if you ask me. They're just holding her up. Look at how they leaned her against those crates. She looks drunk as a skunk."

"Maybe that's just how they operate," Harvey said. "They get her drunk and then haul her off."

The logs showed Harvey sneaking in and guiding the diva away from the gangsters only to get ambushed by the emissary.

"Nice rescue," the sheriff said snidely. "Next time leave the hero work for the good guys."

"I waited for you to show up," Harvey said, "but I guess you were too busy."

The sheriff frowned at Harvey and returned his attention to the logs. One of the guards took Francesca up the ramp and when the other guard went to assist, Harvey took off. The sheriff switched to another camera and saw Harvey running between two rows of cargo containers, then Harvey hit the stop button on the player and said, "You see? I told you I tried to rescue the old gal, but that guy got the drop on me."

The sheriff looked suspiciously at Harvey and asked, "What happened next?"

Harvey shrugged and asked, "What do you mean?"

"I mean," the sheriff said. "What did you do next, that you don't want us to see?"

The sheriff hit play and the logs continued. Harvey caught his foot in a rope hanging from a container, tripped and slammed his head into the ground. The sheriff erupted into laughter and said, "I'm sorry, I assumed you stole something from one of these crates, but that was priceless."

The log continued and Elizabeth showed up and kicked Harvey as he lay on the ground.

"Ooh!" the sheriff bellowed. "This just keeps getting better and better."

Elizabeth's cheeks turned crimson and she mouthed to Harvey, "I'm sorry."

Tony searched the ship from top to bottom, but Francesca was nowhere to be found. He climbed back up from the lower level and approached Vincenzo with his head drooping on his chest. "Sorry boss, but she ain't here."

"Damn it Tony, why did I ever hire you?"

Tony shrugged and said, "Because you is my uncle?"

Vincenzo scowled and said, "It was a rhetorical question."

Tony looked confused and Vincenzo explained, "That means you don't have to answer it!"

Tony was still confused. "Why would anyone ask a question if they didn't want to hear the answer?"

Vincenzo growled and hit the intercom button to the cockpit. "Turn us around. We're going back."

The sheriff had known that the mobsters were on the premises. The governor had asked him and Holiday to do something about them. He wasn't one of the partners and didn't know that the governor was in bed with them and had no idea that his investigation was the cause of the governor's nervousness.

The logs at the spaceport seemed to confirm Harvey's story, but he couldn't get a good enough picture of the gangsters to make a positive identification. He escorted Harvey and Elizabeth back to the resort and to his office where he hoped to find some better images of them in his own security logs.

Elizabeth sat down at one of the monitors and began pouring through images of guests as they came and went by the front desk. She didn't know what the mobsters looked like, but she knew everyone that was in the diva's entourage and could identify any strangers she found hanging around with the diva.

Harvey, on the other hand, knew exactly what they looked like. He could identify them without hesitation. He fingered the speed control on the logs and fast forwarded through the recordings.

Perspiration gathered on the governor's temples. He knew that somewhere in the logs would be images of him meeting with the mobsters. He tried organizing excuses in his mind portraying them as businessmen who obviously had lied to him about their identities. He stood behind Harvey and Elizabeth trying to think of specific ways that he could deflect suspicion from any suspects that either of them pointed out for the sheriff.

The planetary security council of Gellian Prime was quick to respond to the spaceport's warnings. The current political unrest had put the empire under a great deal of scrutiny and they did not want to allow a kidnapping from their jurisdiction to appear on the news wires.

A swarm of police ships left the surface of the planet and the two space stations that hovered over the planet's north and south poles, clear of the planet's rings. The ships converged between the planet and the moon, then surrounded the moon in a geometrically spaced net to contain any traffic that tried leaving. No ship was leaving Emaude Phlott without being searched first.

Francesca didn't cry for long. She usually got her way just by requesting it. When that didn't work, crying had always taken care of it in the past, but not this time.

She got up from her chair and demanded in her highest and shrillest voice, "You must be stopping this ship right now! I need my Elizabeth and you are to be turning us around to go get her! I need her and she is my friend. I will not go on without her! She knows how to take care of the things so everything is all right. It is obvious to me that you do not know this. You need my Elizabeth as much as I do."

The guards were in agony. They didn't care about Francesca's plight, but her voice cut directly through their heads. She was loud and her voice had a timber that connected directly to their pain centers and erupted in their brains. They looked pleadingly to the emissary.

The emissary squirmed in his seat. His headphones did not do enough to block out her voice and squashing them against his head did not help.

He finally flung the headphones across the ship and stood to face her. "Do you not understand? You have been commanded to come before our King, the Emperor. He wishes a personal audience with you. We cannot simply turn around now because you lost your assistant. The King will assign a new assistant for you when we arrive."

Francesca began to cry in earnest. "This new assistant your king will give me won't be my Elizabeth."

"You want an Elizabeth?" the emissary screamed, "The King will get you an Elizabeth. I'm sure he can find you a dozen Elizabeths. Then, when you get settled in, you can have your new Elizabeth arrange to transport your old Elizabeth to join us. Okay?"

The police blockade expanded and weaved a sensor net around Emaude Phlott. Reports of the emissary's ship had already circulated the police network and a command ship had been ordered to intercept it.

The emissary's speakers crackled to life, "By order of the Chancellor of Gellian Prime, no ships are allowed to leave this moon until further orders."

Philbis picked up the microphone, clicked the send button and said, "This is Philbis Beck…"

Before he could say that he was the personal attaché to the emperor's chief advisor's personal valet, Francesca began screeching, "Help! Help! He won't let me have my Elizabeth!"

Philbis quickly disengaged the mic until she quieted down again. He clicked the mic again and said, "This is an imperial ship…"

Francesca screamed again, "Tell him to go back for my Elizabeth!"

"Unidentified craft," the police commander said, "Your communication is breaking up. By order of the Chancellor, you are instructed to return to Emaude Phlott for inspection, or prepare to be boarded."

"This is outrageous," Beck shouted at his crew. "How dare they stop an official ship on imperial business?"

He turned to Francesca with fury in his eyes. "Madam? How dare you interfere with official business like this?"

She smirked at him and said, "Go back and get my Elizabeth. She would straighten this out for you."

He wanted to strangle her, but forced himself to turn back around and growled, "Take us back."

Vincenzo had always been very lucky. His mother flipped a coin to decide whether she would marry his father or have an abortion. He liked to gamble in the family's card parlors and did well enough that his father put him in charge of running one of the casinos. He had a magical knack when it came to observing their guests and knowing who they should extend credit to. His step brother was first in line to succeed their father, but he was sentenced to twenty years a week before their father was killed. Turning the ship around ahead of the police net was pure luck.

Landing was routine. The ship pulled into the space port and taxied to the same spot where they had boarded. Vincenzo stood at the bottom of the boarding ramp and said, "Now go find the old broad. She probably just passed out where you left her."

"Yes boss," Tony said as he started searching around the stacks of crates that they had leaned her against.

The hotel security had the same basic layout of monitors as the space port, but the room was more spacious and hospitable than the cramped truck.

"There!" Harvey said as he was playing through some recordings. "That's one of them, and that's her with him."

The picture showed Milton escorting Francesca across a grassy area between the hotel and the reflecting pool. They crowded around the monitor and fast forwarded the recording until they saw Francesca boarding into a carriage with Vincenzo.

Harvey pointed and said, "He's the boss."

The governor knew that if they followed Vincenzo around enough, they would find him with the governor somewhere. "You must be mistaken. I recognize him. He's been coming here as a guest for years. I've met with him personally many times. Perhaps he's just being a good Samaritan and helping her out. I understand that he is very wealthy."

"No," Harvey said definitively. "They're mobsters and he's the boss."

Vincenzo climbed on the back of the two seat hover bike with Tony at the controls. It was a quiet vehicle which allowed him to slip back into the resort undetected.

Harvey and the sheriff were still going over the security logs when the Governor saw Vincenzo arrive on one of the live monitors. Everyone else was too glued to the logs to notice.

The governor slipped out and met Vincenzo at the back. "You can't be here."

"I practically own this joint," Vincenzo replied harshly, "I can..."

"No," the governor interrupted, "They've seen you on the security logs. They're already looking for you."

"Oh," Vincenzo said uncomfortably. "I just came back to find the rich broad."

"You're too late. The empire already has her."

"You mean the character that they keep calling the emissary?"

"Yeah," Kitt said nodding his head, "some stranger took her when you left and the emissary took her from him. She's long gone, but you've been positively identified."

"Don't be so sure that she's gone." Vincenzo pulled his communicator from his pocket and said, "Check and see if the planetary police let anyone from the empire through."

Letting the empire have Francesca was the governor's idea and the best chance for saving the resort, but it wasn't the mob's first choice, even though letting the king have her might solve the civil crisis and improve business for the resort, the mob's agenda generally gravitated towards more immediate returns, and the governor had more to fear from the mob than the empire.

If he weren't already in bed with them, he could have just let things go as they were. He wouldn't have worried about it at all if Vincenzo weren't there already, but he was there, and they were partners, and they scared him and the other partners.

He returned to the security room and tapped the sheriff on the shoulder. "I'm putting up a reward for the safe return of the Diva Francesca. Please see to it that my offer reaches all the right people."

Earp looked up at the governor and said, "Yes sir. Will do."

The governor was pleased with his own gesture and glanced around the room with a wide smile on his face. He saw Vincenzo on one of the monitors and added, "In fact, Wyatt, you probably should make sure my offer gets to some of the wrong people too."

"I can go get her," Harvey said, "But I'll need a little money for fuel."

The governor didn't really have the money for a reward and figured he would cross that bridge when he came to it. "If you rescue her, the reward money is yours, but I can't be paying the reward in advance to every guy that comes along and says he wants to rescue her."

Elizabeth couldn't stay and watch the monitors any more. She had to do something. She ran out of the security office and into the hotel lobby. She no longer had e a room there, and with Francesca missing, she had no way to pay for their stay. She needed a white knight to come charging in on a gleaming stallion to offer assistance, but all she saw were hotel employees standing at their posts and a virtually deserted lobby. They glanced at her as she stood in the middle of the lobby, but she was no longer a paying customer, so none of them approached to help her.

Tears collected in her eyes and were near to flowing onto her cheeks when Harvey came up behind her and softly wrapped his hands on her shoulders. She wanted to cry and his grip was comforting, but she needed a knight to save her and all she got was a scoundrel.

She ran from the lobby and burst through the swinging doors and slammed into Bruno's thick chest. Bruno retracted from her and exhaled, "Ooof."

"Sorry," she said before she recognized him. But as she looked into the face of the man she ran into, she scrunched her face and cocked her head to the side. "Bruno? Is that you?"

Bruno's face was beaten and misshaped to the point where it was barely recognizable. He nodded his swollen head, but said nothing.

"What happened to you?"

Victor was at his side and said, "He tried prize fighting to win enough of a stake to get off this rock."

"Oh," Elizabeth said, "I guess it didn't go so well."

Bruno shook his head and said, "I lost three bouts and they wouldn't let me fight anymore."

She hugged him and said, "I'm so sorry about that. We haven't had any luck either. The Diva has been kidnapped and we don't have enough money to go after her."

Bruno grimaced as he shaped his swollen expression into a scowl and looked at Victor angrily.

"Easy," Victor said, "Don't get mad all over again."

"Why is Bruno mad?" Elizabeth asked.

Victor looked away as if he hadn't heard the question, but Bruno growled and Victor said, "Bruno's mad because I bet against him. We have money, but when I went to get passage off this moon, they turned us down saying we could barely pay for the fuel with this money."

"Let me get this straight," said Harvey who had naturally followed Elizabeth out of the hotel, "You have enough money for fuel, but you don't have a ship? I have a ship, but I don't have money for fuel."

Victor's eyes twinkled as he reached for Harvey's hands and said, "A marriage made in heaven."

Elizabeth's spine shivered at the thought of these two hooligans working together, but she saw no other choice and went along.

Roy tugged on Harvey's sleeve to get his attention.

"Hey," Harvey said. "What's wrong now?"

"Nothin's wrong. I heard what you said, that you're going to help the old gal, and we want in."

Harvey looked around but didn't see Gene. "Are you sure Gene wants to do this? It could be dangerous."

"Yeah," Roy said nodding his head, "Gene's in. I'll go get him. You guys want to meet up at the space port?"

Harvey looked blankly at Elizabeth and Bruno and asked, "Do we have enough money to get us to the port?"

Elizabeth shrugged her shoulders, but Roy said, "I got this. I'll meet you guys right here in an hour."

Vincenzo was livid. "How the hell could you lose one loopy dame? Find that emissary and get her back for me!"

Tony bounced his head up and down and said, "Yes boss. Yes boss." He looked at Bruce vacantly and they both shrugged.

Vincenzo closed his eyes and shook his head. "I don't know why I keep yous guys around me. One of yous gotta check with our friend that has juice with the police while the other should go find out what Milton knows about this here emissary."

"Right boss," they both said in unison.

Elizabeth was tending Bruno's face out in front of the Saloon when Roy pulled up with Matt Starr and his wagon.

"You!" Bruno shouted as he jumped up on the wagon and grabbed Starr by the collar.

"You know Matt already?" Roy asked. "Let me guess. He ran off with your luggage?"

Bruno nodded his swollen face as he cocked his arm back to pummel Starr.

"Easy Bruno," Victor said, "Remember you broke a couple bones in that hand."

Bruno winced as he flexed his hand and lowered his arm.

"Well," Roy said, "I guess it's a good thing I didn't tell Matt where he was taking me!"

Matt's eyes darted accusingly over to Roy.

Gene burst out of the swinging doors loaded down with the remainder of the Diva's luggage. "I went upstairs and gathered everything she left behind." He peeked over one of the trunks and when he saw Starr, he added, "And if Matt tries anything with this stuff, I'll feed him to his own robots so they can poop little Matt turds all over this God forsaken moon."

Roy winked at Elizabeth and said, "I told you. Gene was plenty happy for the ride off this rock and a chance to help you out."

Bruno let go of Starr and helped Gene load the luggage onto the coach. Roy climbed up front to make sure Matt didn't try to escape.

Milton couldn't believe he was actually searching for the emissary. He should be hiding from the man. Worse yet, if he finds him, Vincenzo plans to take Francesca from him by force. It wasn't like he had never gone up against the police before, but this was a royal envoy. Going up against the king was treason and carried the most severe punishments if he were ever caught.

He roamed the hall looking for signs of either the emissary, his guards, or Francesca. He remembered how enthralled she was with the reflecting pool and ventured out onto the grounds to hike down there.

Nobody was at the reflecting pool. He looked out over the pool and saw nothing but a pinkish sky.

"Of course nobody is here," he scolded himself, "They only come here when the rings are visible in the water."

He skulked back up the path to the resort, mumbling to himself that it was a fruitless search. If he were the emissary, he'd already be long gone from this rock. He slapped himself in the forehead. He should have checked with the front desk first to see if the emissary had checked in or out.

Chapter 5

Philbis sneered at Francesca. She was the most obnoxious woman he had ever met, which was largely why they wanted her, but he didn't like having to return to this hell hole just because of her tantrum. He should have been able to simply tell the authorities who he was and continue on his way, but there was no way the police would let him go with her screaming and squawking. He had no doubt that his diplomatic immunity would prevent them from incarcerating him, but he didn't imagine they would allow him to kidnap the diva and take her to the emperor under those circumstances.

His crew swiftly guided his ship back to Emaude Phlott and descended to the surface parking in the same spot they had left shortly before.

"I can't believe I'm doing this," he said. "Do you think you can behave yourself if I go get your precious Elizabeth?"

"What does it mean, to behave myself?" she asked. "I am Francesca..."

"I know who you are, but if you say something to make the police suspicious, then this whole deal will be off and you'll never get your money back."

"That is not being the truth," Francesca said. "I will be getting back my money. It is my money. My Elizabeth will do this for me."

"Because you always get your way?" he asked.

Francesca cocked her head and looked at him like he should know the answer.

Philbis shrugged and asked, "What? What is that look supposed to mean?"

"We are here, are we not? You bring me back here to be getting my Elizabeth. No?"

He glared at her and grit his teeth, then spun and growled as he descended the ramp to the tarmac.

Before the emissary had reached the bottom of the ramp, Francesca jumped up and started walking down saying, "I think I should go with you. I will make it smoother to explain to my Elizabeth."

"Oh no you don't," Philbis said as he spun around and marched back up the ramp.

"I think I do," she said flatly.

Philbis put both hands on her shoulders and shoved her back inside.

"You dare to touch me?" she bellowed.

"You're staying here."

"No," she said loudly, "I am going to find my Elizabeth."

"No," he replied, "You are staying here while I go find her."

She started to step towards the exit and he placed his hands on her shoulders again and held her in place.

"Again with the touching?" She opened her mouth and emitted a loud piercing scream that was loaded with all of her operatic training.

Philbis panicked and pulled a tazer from his pocket and shocked her till she fell unconscious. He pointed to his guards and said, "Take her to the panic room to sleep it off." Then, while they were carrying Francesca, he retrieved a syringe from a med kit and gave her something to keep her sleeping for a while.

"That should hold you," he said. He left the ship and descended back down the ramp again wondering why he hadn't used the tranquilizer before.

The Diva's voice was unmistakable. Elizabeth heard it from clear across the tarmac.

Harvey was busy fueling the ship with Bruno and Victor keeping a close eye on where their money was going. They each wore ear protection that they found in a work locker, not because it was particularly noisy, but because they wanted to look like workers who belonged around the fuel lines. Victor paid for the fuel and led the started to show the engineers where they were docked, but Harvey insisted that they could pump their own fuel leaving Victor to suspect that there might be some question of ownership regarding the vessel, but he wasn't going to say anything to jeopardize their escape.

"Did you hear that?" Elizabeth asked, but of course they did not. "I'm going to go find her." Elizabeth paused only a moment for some reaction from them, but decided that the Diva's situation was too dire for her to wait, so she ran off in the direction of the scream that she heard.

She burst out from behind the row of private ships and saw the emissary walking along the deserted tarmac towards a cab. She ducked down behind some crates until he was behind another row of ships, then bolted out in the direction that he had come from. There were only a couple ships in that direction and only one of them had the gangway down.

She tiptoed up the gangway and into an empty hallway. The hall ended in a small room with three doors and a small cylindrical elevator that led up to the passenger compartments and the cockpit. The doors probably opened to storage closets, but she tried them anyway. The first was an empty closet. The second door opened to a small room with two fold down cots for sleeping. She guessed that this was probably the crew's quarters. The third door opened to another closet, but the back wall of the closet was pushed ajar like a door. She pushed it a little more to reveal another small room with a pair of fold down cots and Francesca asleep on the lower cot.

"Diva!" she whispered loudly. "Diva! Wake up!" She sprinted to Francesca and shook her but she was out cold. She patted Francesca's cheeks, afraid to actually slap her.

Francesca half opened her eyelids, but rolled her eyes upwards and went back to sleep.

Elizabeth pulled Francesca upright in the small bed and climbed under one of her arms to lift her, but she was too heavy.

"Come on," she moaned, "You gotta help me here."

Philbis was just about to hail a cab when he heard someone behind him yell, "Planetary Police! We'd like a word with you!"

Philbis turned around and saw two uniformed officers running towards him from the tarmac. "Excuse me," he said, "but I'm rather busy."

"Sir, we need you to return with us to your vehicle for inspection."

"Do you know who I am? I am Philbis Beck and I am the attaché to the emperor's chief advisor's personal valet."

The lead officer held his hand out expecting Philbis to present credentials. Philbis stuck his jaw out and stood tall as if they should recognize from his stature that he was there on official business. The officer just snapped his fingers and held his hand in front of Philbis's face.

"Very well," Philbis said, "but I am here on official business for the emperor and your supervisors will be hearing about this." He produced an I.D. card which the officer scanned. His scanner produced a hologram of Philbis's face and a full description of his office and his full immunity.

The disappointed officer returned Philbis's I.D. card and said, "Thank you for your cooperation."

Philbis snapped the card back into his pocket and turned to hail a cab again, then stopped. The police have already cleared him and the diva is out cold. Why should he worry about this Elizabeth character? He turned and headed back to his ship thinking that he might need to wear earplugs after she woke up.

With his tanks full, Harvey climbed into the ship's cockpit while Victor and Bruno readied themselves in the passenger compartment. Harvey wondered why Elizabeth wasn't pestering him to move faster and chase down the emissary, but he gracefully accepted the peace and quiet as a blessing and started the ships motors. He let them warm a bit then eased the throttle forward and raised the ship just enough to clear any obstacles on the ground. He skimmed along the surface, below the space ports radar until he was out of range, then pulled back on the yoke and aimed the ship up into the sky towards the rings of Gellian Prime.

Elizabeth was unable to lift Francesca by herself. She needed to get Bruno to help her carry the Diva. She laid Francesca back on the bed and snuck down the hallway and was about to descend the ramp to the tarmac when she heard the emissary's footsteps on the bottom of the ramp.

She zipped back out into the hallway and spun around looking at the doors, then ducked into the empty storage locker and crouched down with her ear pressed to the door. She heard the whizz of the motors raising the ramp followed by the cylindrical elevator and Philbis saying, "Nap time is over boys. Get us out of here."

Harvey's ship had a number of high tech upgrades, including an advanced heads up display that used a sophisticated sensor array to track and identify nearby objects. An augmented reality projector highlighted those ships in the cockpit's windows. As soon as Harvey exited the moons atmosphere, he eased up on the throttle and watched his windows light up with the images of a network of police cruisers that surrounded the moon.

He was expecting some kind of a welcoming committee at some point, but was a little surprised that they were already in place and ready for him. He flipped up a protective cover on the control panel and exposed a blue switch. The heads up images identified the threat potential of the police cruisers. Most of them were highlighted blue or green, but a couple of the closest ships were yellow and starting to turn orange. His ship had a stealth skin which made it harder to detect beyond close range. The ships in the heads up display would change to red when they were close enough to detect him regardless of the ships special skin. He flipped the blue switch to engage the ships cloaking devices, but he could only remain cloaked for a few minutes without burning out his engines.

With the cloak engaged, he eased the throttle forward again and headed away from the moon and into the planet's rings. The rings were composed of large chunks of ice that shared a flat orbit around the planet. He was relatively safe from detection while he was floating among the rings' many chunks of ice, so he disengaged the cloak and weaved his way between the ice chunks until he was on the other side of the planet.

From a fair distance, and especially when gazed upon through the reflecting pool, the rings of Gellian Prime were a beautiful thing. The reflecting pool framed them in one of the most relaxing settings imaginable, but here, dodging between chunks of ice as big as the ship, the rings were a daunting obstacle that triggered the nerves that ran from the base of the brain, down the spinal column, and ended in the sphincter muscles.

Victor made the mistake of visiting the cockpit while the ship was weaving between the chunks of ice. His mouth fell open as he watched the ship pass by and around the large floating icebergs. An aura surrounded the ice in the window as the heads up display colored them based on their potential to impact with the ship. The closest ones modulated towards red then back to yellow as the ship corrected its course to slip by them.

Harvey turned the captain's seat slightly and glanced over his shoulder to see who came in. "Hey. Victor, right?"

Victor nodded his head unable to speak.

"Did you need something?" Harvey asked.

"That's okay," Victor replied. "You just concentrate on what you're doing."

"What I'm doing?" Harvey asked. "I'm not doing anything. The ship's navigational computer is plotting our course through these. What do you need?"

Victor acclimated some to the nearness of the large chunks and said, "Nothing important. I thought maybe Elizabeth was with you. Someone should probably prepare a small bag of the diva's clothing."

Harvey leaned the pilot's seat back and put his hands behind his head. "Sorry. I haven't seen her. You might check the crew quarters below.

Victor nodded his head weakly and backed out of the cockpit.

Elizabeth felt the low thrum of the engines through the floor and could tell when they had lifted off. She peeked out of the small storage unit where she was hiding and saw that the elevator was still up on the upper deck and the area was deserted. She tiptoed to the room where the diva was and found her peacefully sleeping.

"Diva? Are you okay?"

Francesca didn't stir, so Elizabeth tried patting her on the cheeks again, but she was out cold. There was no escaping now, so she just sat on the edge of the bed holding the diva's hands and waited for her to wake up.

The glowing police ships on Harvey's imaging system were unmistakable against the inky black of space when he first left the moon. The net they deployed around Emaude Phlott was complete and even though he had kept low to the ground to avoid detection by the space port, he wasn't so fortunate when he pierced the net of police vehicles and entered into an orbit around Gellian Prime by weaving through the ring's icy chunks.

He knew they must have seen him, but that didn't necessarily mean they could follow him through the rings. He doubted that they would physically follow him into the rings. There were very few things in the universe that would warrant a man putting his safety at risk by following a course through the ice field, and that man's superiors wouldn't want him to risk the ship he flew. They would most likely send in drones and try to follow him by sensors.

Harvey wished he could have used the cloaking device all the way around Gellian Prime, but the technology wouldn't support such a long usage. Fortunately, he still had other stealth appliances available to him. The skin of his ship made it look like a small pebble amongst the much larger ice field that surrounded him.

More important than his gadgets was his mind and his experience. He'd spent years avoiding such traps and eluding the authorities. The trick was making it not worth their effort, and he was very good at that.

The emissary sat back and let the crew do the flying. He still had to work out exactly how he planned to introduce the old bat to the king. The king didn't actually send him on this mission. His position gave him early access to the reports about her and it was his duty to verify the accuracy of those reports, or at least, that was his excuse.

Seeing her up close, she was everything he could have hoped for. She had all of the queen's most attractive qualities with a disposition that might be able to match, or at least withstand, the king's abrasive personality. He saw the opportunity presented to him and chose to take action hoping it might result in some upward movement for his career.

"By order of the Chancellor of Gellian Prime, no ships are allowed to leave this moon until further orders."

Philbis sighed and replied back, "This is Philbis Beck attaché to the emperor's chief advisor's personal valet. We are on official business for the king himself." Philbis scanned his identity card, sending his credentials to the police vehicle.

After a short pause, they replied, "You're cleared. Proceed."

The engines hummed and Philbis felt the familiar tingle pass through his body as the ship entered into hyperspace. They'll be back at the palace soon.

Harvey guided the ship through the rings until he was on the opposite side of Gellian Prime and completely hidden from the moon. He had already plotted a course to the capitol of the empire, but he had to exit the rings before he could engage the hyper-drives.

He turned the ship and avoided the last few tumbling mountains of ice and was about to escape when the police deployed a blocker in front of his ship. He couldn't open the hyperspace field around his ship with the blocker field in place.

"Prepare to be boarded," emanated not only from his speakers, but the skin of the ship vibrated and acted as a giant speaker cone. There was nothing for him to do at this point. He shut down the drives and waited. He hadn't given up on saving the diva, but he would have to talk his way out of custody before he could. He ran through an inventory list in his mind. There was nothing currently on the ship that the police could use to detain him. This should be nothing more than a minor delay.

Police troopers entered the ship and went straight to the cockpit and secured Harvey's hands behind his back. It was an ancient practice for detaining prisoners and even though the technology existed to hold detainees by imprisoning their mind and their motor functions, there was something about placing a man in shackles that no doubt gave the police a visceral satisfaction that they were loath to abandon.

Harvey sat alone in the interrogation room. His hands had been released from behind him just so they could be cuffed together through a ring on the table before him. The room could have been cloned from a late 20th century crime movie. The walls were off-white with no decorations on them. The only furniture in the room was the table in the center, and three chairs, the one Harvey sat upon, and two on the opposite side of the table. A single mirror hung on the wall opposite Harvey and he had no doubt it allowed others to view the proceedings through the mirror. A small camera was mounted high in the corner with a view of Harvey's face and the single door that was on the side of the room.

There was no clock in the room, and Harvey wasn't sure how long he had been there, but it felt like a long time to him, and was certainly part of their strategy. He assumed that the others were probably getting the same treatment. Bruno had the look of a trouble maker and Victor talked like a con artist. He hoped that Elizabeth would be the one who did most of the talking. She was level headed and most of all, looked very honest.

Eventually, a burly man entered the room and sat down across the table from Harvey. He was a big man, like Bruno, and had a lot of experience etched across his face in the form of scars. No doubt, his appearance was supposed to be intimidating, but Harvey had no time for games here.

"Let me guess," Harvey said, "You've searched my ship and found nothing suspicious."

"I wouldn't say that," the interrogator said.

Harvey waited for him to continue, but he just sat there staring at Harvey. "So? What did you find that was so suspicious? Let me tell you. You found nothing and now you're just baiting me hoping I would tell you where the secret booty was stashed, so let me tell you: there ain't none. Now if you don't mind, I've got some business in another part of the empire and you're holding me up."

"Not so fast," the interrogator said. "You and your companions are a suspicious lot. Why are you travelling together? What was the purpose of your visit to Emaude Phlott?"

"Our purpose? You guys stranded us there with your petty little civil insurrection. We don't have anything to do with your politics, but you landed us there and left us penniless and without any fuel. My companions and I pooled our resources to buy enough fuel to get off that moon. I don't think we broke any laws there."

"So, why didn't you just come forward and say so?" the interrogator asked. "Why did you break through our embargo and try sneaking through the rings to escape?"

"You had already stranded us there once. We didn't want to give you another opportunity to strand us again."

"Uhuh," the interrogator nodded his head and continued, "I find it curious that you chose to hide your ship in our rings. This seems like a smuggler's way of evading capture."

"Really?" Harvey asked. "I hear those smugglers are pretty good flyers. You really think I fly as good as them?"

"The real question is why you would choose to risk flying through the rings that way."

Harvey grinned and said, "I was just showing off for the lady."

The interrogator scribbled down some notes and asked, "What Lady?"

"You know, Elizabeth. I'm sure you have her locked up in some room just like this one."

"Mr. Kushkin, we have no lady from your ship."

This struck a nerve with Harvey. He had no doubt that the man before him was being completely honest. "Well she was there. I can't imagine how you missed her."

"We didn't miss her, I assure you."

"Then I don't know where she is. We're in this whole mess for her. She needed my help and I was trying to offer it, but I don't know how she wasn't on board."

The interrogator pulled a picture out of his folder and asked, "Is this her?"

Harvey looked at the blurry picture of Francesca and said, "No, that's not her," but he was afraid that his reaction had given himself away.

The interrogator paused a moment before asking, "Do you know who she is?"

"Who? That broad? No, I don't know her."

"You're lying to me. Why would you lie to me?"

"Why wouldn't I?" Harvey moaned. "You seem to think that I'm up to something illegal here. If you must know, we were trying to rescue her. Elizabeth works for her and came to me because that woman had been kidnapped."

The interrogator kept a straight face. He didn't believe a word of this and completely hid his amusement, but wanted to hear the rest of Harvey's story. "Kidnapped? Does she know by whom?"

"Don't ask. You don't want to know."

"But I did ask," the interrogator replied. "I do want to know."

"By the empire," Harvey's voice tailed off as he replied and realized how ridiculous it might sound.

"The empire?"

"That's right," Harvey said trying to sound more sure of himself. "Your empire sent someone over to kidnap her. Elizabeth asked me to help get her back."

The interrogator had heard enough and laughed. "I've heard a lot of crazy stories in my time, but that's got to be the best."

"Ask the governor if you don't believe me. Go to that silly dude ranch and ask the governor. In fact, you can ask the mayor and the sheriff too. They were with Elizabeth and me. They know what I was doing."

"You're serious?" the interrogator asked incredulously.

"Damned right I'm serious. You go ask them."

"Okay, Mr. Kushkin. We'll go ask them."

Elizabeth felt the wave pass through the ship as it came out of hyperspace. There were no portholes or viewfinders for her to get her bearings, but she assumed they were taking the diva to the capitol. She worried about Francesca, but she couldn't ignore the fact that she was a stowaway on this ship and would be in serious trouble if they caught her. She didn't know what would happen next, but there was little chance for her to sneak the diva off the ship in an imperial spaceport.

"Don't worry Diva. I'm not abandoning you, but I have to go back to my hiding place."

She let the diva's hand go and ran from the panic room back to her utility closet and climbed into an empty space on a bottom shelf.

An empty shelf on the bottom metal rack wasn't exactly inviting, but it was a place for her to hide, hoping nobody would have any need to come in for supplies. The trembling in her limbs spread to her whole chest and was matched only by her heart that thundered in her ears. She closed her eyes to hide the unpleasant reality of the room, but could not stop her mind from retracing her situation. There would be no denying that she was a stowaway on an official imperial ship, and they would probably take that pretty seriously, except, that technically, she was already a stowaway stranded on Emaude Phlott. Would being a double stowaway would make matters any worse for her?

A slight change in gravity meant they were close. Sucking in a deep breath, she opened her eyes. There were very few things you could actually feel on a space craft. Inertial dampers shielded the crew and passengers from changes in velocity and course corrections, but they couldn't hide the feeling of the hyperspace field passing through the ship, and they couldn't prevent you from feeling the slight change when the ship touched down on a planet and the artificial gravity turned off.

Governor Carson had been keeping as low a profile as possible. He did his best to avoid Milton who was still surveying the grounds, and especially kept out of Vincenzo's way. Hiding places were at a premium, leaving him in his office with the shades down and the door locked.

Outwardly, he pretended to want what was best for the diva and acted outraged at the empire for abducting her, but to save his own skin, he would gladly turn her over to Vincenzo and his people.

The clock ticked slowly as he drummed his fingers nervously on the desk until he was startled by the ringing phone. The caller's id was blocked. Vincenzo's id was blocked. The phone rang again. He reached out for the handset but hesitated. How would he tell Vincenzo that the empire took her? Maybe it would be just that simple. The empire took her and she's out of my hands now.

The phone rang again. Why oh why didn't he have an assistant to take his calls? His mind plugged in the answer rather than answer the phone: business was down and it was a budget cut. Even the robot assistants were out of his budget. He took a deep breath and picked up the receiver. "This is Governor Carson."

"Governor Carson? This is Captain Follier with the Gellian space police."

Carson swallowed hard and nervously asked, "Captain Follier? What can I do for you?"

"This is probably nothing," Follier said, "but I'm investigating a possible abduction and your name came up during the investigation."

Sweat beaded on Carson's forehead. "My name? An abduction you said?"

Follier continued, "We have a witness here..."

Carson's heart pounded so loud in his ears, that he was sure that Follier could hear it. "You have a witness?"

"Yes sir. The witness claims that you sent him to rescue the woman who was allegedly abducted."

Carson barely heard the captain over the pounding of his heart. "Rescue?"

"Yes sir. I'm sure you have nothing to do with this…"

"What's his name?" The governor asked weakly.

"Kushkin."

"Kushkin?" the governor asked. "I don't recall that name."

"That's what we figured. His story had a lot of holes in it already. At first he tried telling us to ask some Elizabeth what was going on, but there was nobody on his ship named Elizabeth, so I figured he must have thought we wouldn't actually call you to verify his alibi."

"Elizabeth?" the governor asked. "Is Elizabeth missing too? She was with Harvey. Have you seen Harvey?"

"Harvey?" The captain asked. "Do you mean Mr. Kushkin?"

The panic Carson had felt thinking the police were on to him was supplanted by the growing list of missing people. "What happened to Elizabeth? Where's Harvey?"

"If you mean Harvey Kushkin, we have him in custody."

"You what?" the governor bellowed. "How is he going to rescue her if you have him in custody?"

"So," the captain said slowly, "You did send him on this mission?"

"Yes!" the governor said, then thinking about it added, "Wait. I'm not sure how far I trust him. There's just something about him that seems shifty."

"Yes sir," the captain replied, "I would agree with you on that."

"You need to locate Elizabeth and the imperial guy they sent here."

Now it was the captain's turn to swallow hard. They let the emissary go already.

Philbis liked strutting around like a peacock when he dealt with the public. Away from the palace, he represented the empire and he made sure everybody knew it, but here, at the capitol, he was the bottom man on the totem pole. He exited the ship and was met at the bottom of the ramp by his boss, the attaché to the emperor's chief advisor.

The attaché didn't look or sound too happy. "Philbis, you're late."

The smile melted off of Philbis's face as he explained, "She's a spirited woman. Plus, there were some regional complications, but wait till you see here. It was worth…"

His boss waved his hand in the air so Philbis would stop trying to rationalize his tardiness. He looked around Philbis and asked, "Well? Where is she?"

"She's in the crew's quarters sleeping."

The attaché rolled his eyes and snapped his fingers. The guards who had accompanied him scurried up the ramp and into the ship, then, after several quiet moments, emerged from the ship and said, "She's out cold."

"Oh yeah," Philbis said, "She wouldn't shut up so I gave her something to help her sleep."

"Boss," the other guard said, "We can't wake her. I think she's been drugged."

"How much did you give her?" his boss asked.

Philbis shrugged and said, "All of it."

The attaché shook his head and walked off saying, get the medics to revive her and bring her to my office.

"Yes, sir," Philbis replied.

"Not you," the attaché said pointing directly at Philbis, "them." He jerked his thumb to point up the ramp at the guards. "You need to file some reports explaining what took you so long."

Elizabeth heard only bits and pieces of the commotion outside the utility closet. She remained curled up in the bottom shelf where she hid and closed her eyes as if that would make her more hidden. She heard the elevator whir, followed by footsteps descending the ramp. Someone outside had been talking but she couldn't make out what they said.

Heavy feet stomped up the ramp and opened one of the other doors.

"Come on," she heard someone say, "you grab her feet while I lift her by the arms."

"No," another said, "he said to get the medics and then bring her to his office."

"I'm not sure that's what he meant," the first one said, "but she's a handful and it sounds better than lifting her."

Elizabeth couldn't stay hidden so long that she lost Francesca. They've come to take her somewhere. Elizabeth trembled at the thought of being caught, but she couldn't let them have Francesca.

"I'll go make the call," the first voice said. She heard him step out into the round hall and say, "We need a medic on eleven foxtrot tango. Yeah, the ship that just came in. Tell him to bring something to revive a sleeping prisoner."

Elizabeth opened one eye and peeked over at the door. She couldn't fight off one man, let alone two men, and judging from the clomp of their boots, they were large men. She would have to wait for them to take Francesca and follow them.

"So?" Harvey asked. "Did you talk to the governor? Do you believe me now?"

The interrogator took his seat and said, "It would seem that the governor does indeed know who you are."

Harvey shook the manacles that chained him to the table and said, "So I can go now? They have an enormous lead on me and I need to catch up with them if I'm going to save her."

"Not so fast, Mr. Kushkin. There's still something fishy about your story and I'm not convinced that I should let you go."

Harvey had thought he would be in the clear. "But they're getting away!"

"Relax Mr. Kushkin. That's a job for the authorities. I'll have some of my boy's look into the alleged kidnapping."

Harvey fell back in his chair. He had no confidence in the police's plan to follow through.

It wasn't bravery, but Elizabeth decided that they had no interest in her closet, so she left the confines of the rack where she had been hiding, and crept to the door. She pressed her ear to the door, but it was still more muffled than what she could hear through the air vent that was high on the door. She strained to reach the vent on her tip toes and cocked her head over to point her ear at the vent. She heard the rustling of clothing and a strange clicking that she couldn't identify.

The vent was too high. She looked around the room and found a small step stool between the tall racks. It wasn't a light weight folding variety, but a sturdy two step platform. She tried picking it up, but it was too heavy for her to lift without grunting and she didn't think she could quietly place it back on the hard floor.

She pulled it along the floor. It made a horribly loud squeaking sound. She closed her eyes and told herself, "No, it wasn't that loud. You're just scared. Get ahold of yourself." She pulled again. It still squeaked as it scraped along the floor, but if she pulled slowly enough, only she would hear it.

She finally reached the door. "Good job," she told herself. "Now get up there and give it a good listen."

She climbed up, and could not only hear what was going on, but the angle of the vents let her see clearly into the round hall. One of the guards was playing with his weapon. He spun it around and changed hands on it. Occasionally the strap would swing around the weapon and the hooks that fastened the strap to it would clink.

She heard footsteps climbing the ramp. The guard immediately stopped playing with his weapon and went to the entrance. A small man with grey hair appeared at the top of the ramp and the guard said, "This way."

He led the old man to Francesca's room and after a few moments, she heard an older voice say, "Hello! How are you feeling? Do you think you can walk now?"

Francesca groggily replied, "Who is it that you are?"

"I am Dr. Greely. You took too many sleeping pills, but I fixed that."

Francesca's voice grew a little stronger as she asked, "Where is this? Where is my Elizabeth?"

Elizabeth couldn't see what was going on in Francesca's room, but she heard one of the guards say, "We don't know any Elizabeth."

"Shhh," the doctor said to the guard, "Of course you do. Elizabeth is the one who is already inside the palace waiting for us." The doctor returned his attention to Francesca and said, "You're in for a treat, my dear. You've been invited to the Royal Palace."

"The Palace?" Francesca asked.

"That's right," the doctor said. "Elizabeth is waiting for us. Shall we go?"

"Si," Francesca said. "Take me to my Elizabeth."

Elizabeth saw the old man come out of the room with Francesca. Francesca was still a little wobbly, but it wasn't the first time that she had to walk inebriated and she managed to make her way to the ramp and off the ship.

"It's true," Roy told the police. "This guy said he was from the empire and he had all the right credentials, but I heard his plan. He's taking the singer and selling her into slavery."

"You heard all this?" the interrogator asked.

"You'd be surprised how tall people overlook little people like my brother and me."

"And you say they're selling her into slavery?"

"I know it's unbelievable, but she looks just like the queen and these guys figure that if they can sell her to the king, or at least to the right people in the palace, the king can use her to end the feud with Vega."

"Okay," the interrogator said. "I think I heard enough. We'll just let you sleep off whatever you're on in the tank."

A ranking police officer opened the door and poked his head through the doorway to say, "Let him go. We got the smuggler and don't need the saps that were with him."

Chapter 6

The world spun and bounced in Francesca's head as she was walked down the gangway. The doctor's injection went a long way to waking her up and sharpening her senses, but her head throbbed and her eyes still wobbled.

Her escort kept her from falling as they led her away from the ship to a luxurious limo. She nodded her head when she saw the craft hovering on the tarmac and slurred, "Thish is being much better."

The limo crossed the imperial compound from the private space port to the palace's living quarters where it followed the circular drive and pulled up in front of a red carpet. A doorman opened the door and offered her a hand to help lift her out of the vehicle.

The carpet led to a flight of marble steps. Large hedges grew on either side of the steps and except for the uppermost floor, obscured the view of the palace which lay beyond. Francesca's head had cleared dramatically, but her feet still wobbled slightly as she left her escort and climbed the stairs, but too many people were watching for her to stumble for her to make a spectacle now. She took her time and rose up the stairs with a regal bearing befitting the greatest soprano in the known universe.

At the top of the stairs, two rows of servants lined the carpet. She could tell from their uniforms that they were house and kitchen servants. They bowed and curtsied as she approached them. It had been far too long since she had been treated so well, but she refrained from showing her pleasure too easily and simply nodded her head, then held it high as she passed them.

Once she was beyond the hedges, she could finally see the immense size of the palace. It was three stories tall, but each floor was the size of two floors. Gargoyles adorned the roof and watched down over the gardens that surrounded the mansion. A huge fountain shot high columns of water from the garden on her left. The water arced gracefully through the air and crossed other arcs of water before splashing in the pool below.

More staff waited in front of the entrance. The head butler came forward and greeted Francesca, "Your majesty. Welcome to Bristolcutt Manor. Allow me to show you inside."

He offered his arm and she gladly accepted. A young maid ran forward and curtsied deeply while holding out a generous bouquet of roses. Francesca accepted the roses. She could no longer hold back the smile which now beamed freely on her face.

The inside of the palace was even more opulent than the outside. Francesca's head began to spin again from the immense splendor that surrounded her. She was led up the large round marble staircase to the second floor and down a long hallway where two guards stood just outside the double door entrance to a luxurious suite. They opened the doors as she approached.

"This," the butler said as he entered the suite and spread his arms, "is your suite. You'll find a private dining table and a dumb waiter over there and the restroom includes a large tub with therapeutic massage jets. If you need anything at all, just pull the velvet rope and ask for it. This is all yours."

The butler stepped back, pleased with what he had to offer.

Francesca stepped into the room and the smile melted off of her face.

The butler's eyes darted around trying to find what was wrong. Head's would roll if something was not perfect. Seeing nothing wrong, he asked, "Is something not to your liking? We can change the decor if you wish. How may I fix this?"

Francesca's face screwed up as if she had eaten something sour. The butler snapped his fingers and an assistant butler who had been following them ran to his side with a notebook and pen.

The butler looked around again and said, "You don't like the wallpaper? We can change it!"

The assistant butler was furiously writing down what he said.

"No," Francesca finally said, "This room... This room..."

"Yes, your Majesty?"

Francesca spun slowly around looking at the room. The decor was fine. She walked over to the window and looked out over the garden and finally said, "Why is it that I am not being on the top floor? Francesca Vittoria Agostina La Perla stays in the penthouse. This is a nice room for the regular guests, but this is not being the penthouse."

"The penthouse?" the butler mumbled.

Francesca turned to face the butler. Her face and voice dripped with disgust as she said, "This is Palace, no? I am the renowned Francesca Vittoria Agostina La Perla. I am the number one soprano for the Vegan Royal Opera. You may call me Prima Donna, though you have already said the 'your majesty' to me. I am liking the sound of that one, but I do not stay in the servants quarters. I will wait here while you go find out where it is that my real room is so you can show me there."

The assistant was aghast, but the butler was strangely tickled by the reprimand.

"Yes, your majesty," the butler said. "I will go find the proper accommodations for the Prima Donna at once"

Elizabeth waited for the commotion to die down before opening the door a crack to peek out into the round hall. Nobody had remained behind so she tip toed to the door and looked down the ramp. She exhaled a big sigh when she saw there were no guards posted at the bottom of the ramp, but the diva was also nowhere in sight. There could only be one place for them to take her. They weren't holding her for ransom; they were delivering her to the king. She would be in the palace.

She snuck down the ramp and followed the length of the ship where she crossed over to another ship and walked down its length. Her luck didn't hold out. Guards were posted intermittently, some at the base of specific ships, and others at odd intervals along the perimeter of the palace grounds.

Behind the control tower, she saw a small wooded area with trees and bushes that extended up to a long hedge. She dropped down on her belly and slithered under a low lying craft then crossed another aisle until she was able to make a dash to find cover under the trees.

The small wooded area provided even better cover than she had expected. She walked freely beneath the trees all the way to the hedge wall. It was a very well-manicured hedge through which she heard muffled conversations and knew there must be walkways on the other side. She walked the length of the hedge looking for either an entrance or at least a weak spot where she might either sneak through the hedge or climb over.

Bruno stood on the sidewalk looking back at the police station and scratched his head.

"I told them," Roy said, "I told them everything, but they're just too stupid to believe it."

"We all told them," Victor said, "and they didn't believe any of us."

"Well, I guess it is kind of unbelievable," Roy replied.

"Hey guys," Bruno said timidly. "None of this is getting us anywhere. What do we do now?"

"That's easy," Victor replied. "We wait for Elizabeth. She always knows what to do."

"Where is she anyway?" Gene asked.

"She wasn't with us," Bruno said.

"She wasn't with us?" Gene asked. "What do you mean she wasn't with us?"

Bruno shrugged and explained, "The police don't have her, and I don't remember ever seeing her on the ship. She's just not with us."

"Come on guys," Victor said. "If Elizabeth is not with us, we just have to make our own plan. I say we get back in that ship and go back to Vega."

"No!" Roy shouted. "Elizabeth has to be here. We have to go get her!"

"And the queen," Gene added.

"She's not the queen," Victor replied.

"Well she's gonna be if we don't save her!" Gene shot back.

"But," Bruno said. "Where is she?"

"She's with the imperial dude," Victor said. "You know that, big guy."

"Not the diva," Bruno replied. "Where's Elizabeth?"

"She was on the ship," Gene said. "I saw her."

"Yeah," Roy added, "I saw her too."

"When?" Bruno asked.

"Right before take-off," Gene said. "When you guys were messing with the fuel."

"Yeah," Roy said. "I remember watching her and wondering what she was planning, but then something happened that distracted me. I don't know if I remember seeing her after that."

"What happened?" Victor asked.

"I don't remember," Roy replied scratching his head. "Wait a minute. I do remember. I heard someone scream and ran to look out the door."

"I remember that," Gene said. "And it wasn't just anyone, it was her; the diva."

"Brilliant, you two," Victor said sarcastically. "You hear the diva scream and don't notice that Elizabeth is missing? I'm not even giving you three guesses where she is."

Roy and Gene looked at each other and both asked, "You don't mean she snuck onto the other ship?"

Bruno was still looking at the police station, but he nodded his head and said, "Yeah. That sounds like something she would do."

"So," Victor said. "Let's go get her. I guess when we get her, she'll have a plan to get the diva."

"What about Harvey?" Roy asked.

"Who?" Victor asked sounding a little too insincere.

"Harvey!" Gene shouted. "We can't leave him here!"

"Why not?" Victor said. "He's just the pilot."

"Because it's his ship!" Roy complained.

"So?" Victor asked. "He's obviously a thief and a smuggler. He probably loses his ship all the time."

"The little man is right," Bruno said, "We can't leave without Harvey. It's his ship and he's more than just an ordinary pilot. We'll need him."

Victor wanted to argue, but he just pouted instead.

"You're doing the right thing," Roy said while slapping Bruno on the back.

"I don't know about that," Bruno said. "But he flew us threw the rings. He must be a damned good pilot."

"He is," Gene said authoritatively.

Bruno looked down at Gene and Roy who were standing shoulder to shoulder and said, "I just hope he's as good a smuggler as he is a pilot. We may need a smuggler if we ever want to get close to Elizabeth and the diva again."

Roy chuckled and said, "He is."

"Well," Victor said. "I hate to break it to you, but he's not with us and I don't think they plan to let him go."

Bruno nodded his head and said, "I know. So we go get him."

Francesca sat and sulked. The chair she occupied was as comfortable as it was luxurious and like everything else in the room, it was both expensive and gorgeous. She didn't actually hate the room; it couldn't have been decorated any nicer, it just wasn't in the right place.

The furniture was all old and perfect, as she would expect. Almost everything in the room was either made of an old wood, a delicate porcelain, or a precious metal. Even the molding that lined the ceiling was gilded in gold.

The ceiling took her breath away. It was an exquisite painting of cherubs and angels in a beautiful sky with wispy clouds. What was wrong with these people? How could they waste such splendor on the second floor?

Her mood vacillated in waves between feelings of awe when she found some new piece of art to marvel over, to abject disappointment when she remembered how poorly it had all been assembled.

She tired of the emotional roller coaster and went to the window to view the gardens. Everything in view was the exact opposite of that horrid little dusty moon where she had been stranded. Every color imaginable lined the walkways against a backdrop of lush green. Stone walks of many colors crisscrossed the garden which was littered with benches where visitors could sit and view the garden, or even meditate if that were their desire.

It was her desire. She didn't want the room's location to fester and spoil her mood. She would much rather sit and ponder the last few days in the garden.

Francesca went to the armoire to test the butler's assertion that it was stocked with everything she could possibly desire. She swung the doors open and sucked in her breath as she peeked at its contents. The butler spoke the truth and she selected a marvelous satin dress and a delicate shawl.

The dress buttoned in the back, but she didn't have her Elizabeth. It was that easy for her mood to deflate. She struggled with the buttons and tried not to cry.

She managed to get most of them closed, enough that it wouldn't fall off of her. She draped a shawl around her back to hide those buttons that she could not reach.

A tear nearly escaped her eye as she steadied her nerves. It would get better. These people will learn, besides, she won't be here forever. She would be going home soon to her adoring fans.

Francesca went to the door and turned the knob, but it was locked. This must be a mistake. She wiggled the knob and turned it the other way, but it would not open. She thought that maybe only one of the double doors opened, so she tried the other door, but it too was locked.

She spun around and scanned the room for another exit, but there was only the door to the bathroom and the door to the bedroom. She was locked in.

"Wait a minute," Victor pleaded as his companions left him standing on the steps of the police station. "What did you just say?"

It was too late. They were already too far away to hear him. Victor kicked and shuffled his feet while he grumbled about what would most likely happen, but he didn't like being left alone, so he trotted off after them.

"What's the plan?" Roy asked.

Bruno shrugged and admitted, "They don't usually let me make the plans. I just thought I'd walk around the outside and see if we can find an open window."

Roy frowned and said, "I doubt we'll find an open window."

"But," Gene added, "I think I saw someone working on the alarm system in a closet by the interrogation rooms. We might find a door or window with the alarm off."

"That's why I do the thinking," Roy said sarcastically. "We're not going to try a door or window and hope the alarm is off for that particular one. Besides, the ground floor windows all have bars on them."

"Then what do you suggest?" Gene retaliated.

"We use the tools that we have," Roy said.

Everyone stopped walking and except for Roy, they all looked at their empty hands.

Victor finally caught up and saw them examining their hands. He looked at his hands and asked, "Why are we looking at our hands?"

Gene held up his empty palms to show Victor and said, "Because Roy seems to think we're hiding some tools in them."

Roy rolled his eyes to the heavens and said, "What I said, was that we need to use the tools that we have."

Bruno nodded his head because that's what he remembered hearing.

"But we don't have any tools," Gene complained.

"Don't we?" Roy asked. "We have two midgets and one strong man."

"What about me?" Victor asked.

Roy waved his arms towards Victor and said, "And a wimpy skinny dude."

"Thanks," Victor moaned.

"So?" Gene asked. "If we needed to make a circus, I'd say we got a pretty good head start, but how's that going to help us get Harvey out?"

Roy turned to Victor and asked, "What do you do?"

"I'm the stage manager. I make sure the sound and the lights are just right for the diva."

"Great," Gene whined. "Our circus needed a sound and lighting guy."

"Stop it," Roy said. "Do you know anything about electronics?"

"Not really," Victor admitted, "Why?"

"Nothing," Roy said, "It's just that Gene said he saw someone by the interrogation rooms working on a security system."

"I saw him," Victor said, "but he was actually working on their air conditioning unit. Didn't you notice how warm it was in there?"

Roy shrugged and said, "I thought that was just to make us talk."

Bruno returned to walking around the building, saying, "This isn't getting us anywhere."

Roy joined him; still trying to think up a plan, then pointed to a second floor window and said, "Look there!"

Bruno looked and asked, "What am I looking for?"

"That," Roy said, "is going to be the first performance of our new circus."

Everyone looked at Roy like he had completely lost his mind.

"What are you talking about?" Gene asked.

"Our first circus trick. Bruno is going to throw one of us up to that open window."

"Are you nuts?" Gene yelled. "Dwarf tossing? Really? That's your plan? It's beyond humiliating! It's downright insane and, I don't know, dangerous!"

"Not to mention," Victor mentioned, "that it's illegal in most of the civilized universe."

"We're breaking into a police station," Roy said. "Any laws against dwarf tossing are the least of our worries. Besides, those laws are meant to prevent the exploitation of little people."

"Fine!" Gene said. "He can toss you up there."

"Agreed," Roy said. "I'll do whatever it takes. What do you think Bruno? Can you throw me high enough to reach that window?"

Bruno wrapped his arms around Roy and lifted him to test his weight, then he grabbed Roy by the collar with one hand and the britches with the other and swung him back and forth a couple times. "Yeah, I can do it, but I'm not sure if you would be right side up or down when you got there. You might spin a little, and if you don't make it, you could get hurt."

"If I don't make it," Roy said solemnly, "please tell Elizabeth that I tried and that I would do anything for her."

Gene puffed his cheeks and made a face, saying, "I think I'm going to be sick."

"Someone is bound to hear you," Victor said.

Roy frowned. There was movement in the window and Victor was right about that. He looked at Victor and asked, "Do you think you could sneak up to the second floor and make enough of a commotion in the hallway to distract them?"

"I'm sure I could," Victor said tentatively, "but are you going to break me out too?"

"Just act like you're emotionally challenged," Roy said. "Tell them your brother is in jail and you don't know what to do without him."

Bruno smirked and mumbled, "That shouldn't be too hard."

Elizabeth had walked the length of the hedge, as far as the trees provided cover, three times. There was no opening or weakness in the hedge. There was a tree that was big enough and strong enough for her to scale the hedge and drop down on the other side, but she couldn't do it without being seen. She would have to wait until dark.

Francesca banged on the door yelling, "Why is this door being locked? You cannot be locking me in! Do you hear me? The heads will be rolling when someone learns that you have locked in Francesca Vittoria Agostina La Perla!"

Francesca pressed her ear to the door and thought she heard laughter, but definitely heard some muffled talking.

"I know you are hearing me!" She banged on the door again. "Open this door at once!"

The door cracked open and the butler quickly stepped into the small space. "Madame La Perla, this is most unseemly."

"Si, I am agreeing with you." She stepped forward to leave the room, but he filled the space of the partially opened door. "Out of my way!" she bellowed.

"Please, Madame, keep your voice down. This is the palace."

"You tell me to be keeping my voice down?" she asked. "How dare you?"

"Madame," he said in a hushed voice, "I beg of you."

"Beg what you like," she said, "but if you aren't getting out of my way, then I, Francesca Vittoria Agostina La Perla will be showing you the loud voice."

"But you just got here," he said. "Wouldn't you like a chance to rest? Perhaps you'd like to freshen up a bit?"

Her eyes narrowed as she tilted her head back and looked down her nose at him. "Are you saying that I am not being fresh? First you lock me in like I am the prisoner, then you block the door and now you are insulting me. I am done here. I am leaving. Get me the next flight to my home where I am treated properly."

"I can't do that," he said. "There are no transports to Vega, besides you have no money to get there."

"Again with the no money," she said. "You know who I am and you know how important I am and you know that I am with money, but you insist on treating me like I am the charity."

"Even more important," he continued, "the king would never forgive me if I let you go without meeting him."

"That's the first good thing I am hearing. Take me to the king and while I am having the talk with him, maybe you can be looking for the new job."

"Of course, Madame, at once." But as his words still floated through the room, he backed out of the doorway and the door was closed and locked again.

"Aieeeee!" she screamed at a volume not previously heard in the palace. "Maybe you will be losing more than your job!"

Bruno stood below the open window thinking about the trajectory he would need to get Roy in the window. He didn't compute angles and mass like a scientist, he just looked at it like shooting baskets in hoop ball. "Are you ready?"

Roy also stood at the base of the building looking up. It looked a lot higher from here. "Are you sure you can do this?"

"No," Bruno replied, "but I can try."

"What's the worst that can happen?" Roy asked. "I miss the window and sprain my ankle in the fall."

"If Bruno doesn't throw you just right," Victor said, "you could flip over and land on your head."

Gene laughed hysterically and said, "Landing on his head would be the safest way down."

Roy glared at Gene then looked at Victor and said, "Shouldn't you be creating a distraction?"

"Yeah," Bruno added. "Go in there and act like you're the one who landed on your head. You know, just be yourself."

Victor walked around the building and entered through the front. He waited for an elevator door to open and found it surprisingly easy to sneak upstairs and create a scene.

Bruno heard the commotion through the open window and knew it was Victor. "Okay," he said. "I guess this is it."

Roy nodded his head and got in position in front of Bruno. Bruno reached down and grabbed Roy by the collar and the belt.

"Wait!" Gene shouted.

Roy looked at his brother and hissed, "What? You can't talk me out of this. It's too important."

"Wait," Gene repeated. "I'll do it. I'm more coordinated than you are and I'm at least fifteen pounds lighter."

Roy couldn't argue with what Gene said. "Are you sure?"

"Yeah," Gene replied. "I'm sure. Besides, you're the brains of the outfit. I can't have you landing on your head."

Bruno gripped Gene by the collar and belt as he had done with Roy and before either of them could change their mind again, he tossed him up mightily into the air. Flying through the air was quite a rush for Gene, but crashing into the wall below the window was not. He managed to get one hand on the sill and flailed his legs until he had one foothold on a small finger size ledge and pulled himself up and through the window, crashing onto the floor below the sill.

Once he was inside the room, he wondered why they never discussed what he would do next.

Francesca continued assaulting the door. When the heels of her fists became sore, she picked up a small metal statue and banged the base of it against the door. She didn't care if it dented the wood, but it wasn't working. She sucked in a deep breath of air and belted out in perfect high C, "Help meeeeee! I am the hostage!" Then she slid her pitch down and up like a siren, occasionally throwing out words like, "Monsters!"

Francesca forgot about their love and respect for opera. She thought she was raising the alarm, but the palace guests thought it was some new entertainment.

The door cracked open again and Francesca smiled, thinking she had won the battle.

The butler barely entered the open doorway and said, "Madam, our guests are wondering if you would mind assembling in the garden and favoring us with a song?"

She didn't know how he knew that she wanted to go to the garden, but a victory was a victory and she wasn't going to miss this opportunity. She pulled the door open wider and shoved the butler aside as she walked out into the hallway, silently gloating over her victory.

Gene gathered his feet below him and looked out the open window. Roy and Bruno both held their thumbs in the air.

"Great," he thought to himself. "That helps a lot."

He turned and looked around the room, wondering what Roy would do. The office was small and crowded with file cabinets. A large desk dominated the center of the room with file folders littered across the top. In the corner, a coat rack held a rain coat and an umbrella, but Gene's eyes focused on the freshly pressed police uniform that was still on a hanger and wrapped in plastic, and also hung from the coat rack. He grabbed the uniform and held it up, trying to tell if it was Harvey's size, but decided it didn't matter. Harvey would have to make do.

As he was about to exit the office, he spotted a diploma on the wall with a shield. It was framed and obviously meant something to somebody. Gene grabbed the frame and said, "Sorry Mac." He flung the frame against the corner of the desk to break the glass and pulled the shield out.

He could still hear Victor down at the other end of the hall. Victor must have wanted to be an actor before becoming a stage manager; he sure was hamming it up. Gene slipped out the door and found a stairwell away from Victor's commotion. He zipped down the stairs and located Harvey in a small detention room that they sometimes used for interrogation.

Harvey was alone when Gene entered the room, carefully leaving the door slightly ajar so it didn't lock them both in.

Harvey was surprised to see him and asked, "How'd you get in here?"

"You know how tall people rarely even see us."

Harvey had known them long enough to have seen what he meant.

"Here," Gene said as he tossed the uniform to Harvey. "Put this on."

Harvey quickly unwrapped the uniform and pulled it off the hanger. He pulled the top on over his shirt. It was tight in the shoulders, but he could make it work, except when he tried to clasp it, he found that the buttons were on backwards. "You idiot!" he ranted. "It's a woman's uniform."

Gene looked at Harvey and shrugged. "Does it fit?"

Harvey struggled to get the buttons closed.

Gene checked the dry cleaning bag and said, "Lucky for you, she wears pants and not a skirt."

Harvey glared at him and grabbed the pants. The shirt puckered at the chest where the buttons were too tight. He pulled the pants on, but they wouldn't fit over his own pants and he muttered, "That's just great."

Gene shrugged apologetically as Harvey pulled his pants off and tried again.

Harvey got the slacks pulled up, but couldn't button them at the waist and barely got the zipper a little over halfway up.

Gene snickered and said, "Sorry, I didn't think to check her drawer for some unmentionables. Here's a badge to pin over your breast. Don't worry, you look cute."

Harvey lunged for Gene, but he was already slipping out the door.

Gene headed directly for the backdoor that he had planned to break in before Roy had this brilliant plan.

Harvey tried to look matter of fact as he walked briskly behind Gene. He couldn't slip under people's view like Gene did and hoped the uniform would make him invisible enough to get out.

Gene closed his eyes and held his breath as he pushed open the backdoor. No alarms went off and he zipped outside wishing they had just gone in that way instead of tossing him up to the second floor.

The butler caught up with Francesca and offered her his arm, asking, "Madame? If you will?"

Francesca smiled sweetly as if to accept his offer then scowled and turned her nose up. She brushed by him and marched down the hallway.

The guards had to swallow their chuckles as the butler rolled his eyes and followed her.

She didn't know her way around the palace or out onto the grounds, but she walked with a purpose as if she did. She knew she would have to descend the grand staircase and assumed that if she exited the atrium on the opposite side from where she had originally entered, she might find a rear door to the gardens.

The palace was full of people. Dignitaries scurried about trying to look more important than they were, while servants circled in the shadows trying to look busier than they were. Some of the consuls collected in small groups in the corners and whispered while others stood in conspicuous places, hoping to be noticed. Francesca could feel their eyes follow her as she marched down the hallway. Servants stopped and either bowed their heads or performed a mini curtsey as she passed.

She heard a smattering of excitement coming from the atrium, but as she descended the marble stairs, the atrium grew silent as a church. The servants again bowed and genuflected when she passed. She liked the servants more than the other patrons who only stared and whispered amongst themselves.

At the bottom of the stairs, she saw light at the end of a dark corridor in the back of the atrium. It looked like an exit with light coming from the outside. She turned and walked briskly to the back. The butler and a small entourage followed behind. She stopped in front of the back door and waited for someone to open it, but when nobody did, she scowled and pushed it open herself.

Now she was in a real foul mood and didn't know if even the gardens could help. The sun was comforting upon her face and the sound of a nearby fountain was soothing to her ears. The room they had given her was on the far end, so she turned and followed a path which ran parallel to that wing.

The scent of flowers was powerful, but her mood was still too sour to enjoy them. She turned and looked over her shoulder. Those people were still following her. She picked up her pace, but she was a singer, not an athlete.

The gardens here were as beautiful as the ones she had seen from her window, but she continued walking. Her legs burned from walking too fast, but she wanted to lose the butler and his minions. Just before she reached the end with the room where they had placed her, she came upon tall hedges that lined the walk. She could see that the hedges extended far off to the walls where the gardens ended. Sixteen more paces brought her to a break in the hedges. It was a maze. This would be the perfect place to lose those meddlesome stalkers.

She slipped into the hedge maze and tried to lose herself, not thinking that they lived here and probably knew the maze very well.

Bruno snickered when he saw Harvey. He pointed at the uniform and asked, "Isn't that…"

Harvey didn't look amused and immediately said, "I don't want to talk about it. Let's get out of here before they catch me and accuse me of impersonating a…."

"A girl?" Bruno finished for him.

Harvey grit his teeth and said, "I was going to say a police officer. We can't stay here."

"Sure," Roy said, "but we can't leave Victor behind either. He helped get you out of there."

Harvey counted heads and saw that Victor wasn't among them. "Yeah? Well we don't have to stand next to this building to discuss it."

"I'll go get him," Gene volunteered. "I'll just tell them that I'm the brother he was looking for."

"You do that," Harvey said while taking off the police woman's blouse. "I have to find some real clothes."

"Why?" Bruno asked. "Since you kept your own clothes on underneath, just ditch the pants."

"I can't do that," Harvey said.

Bruno started laughing.

Harvey hit Bruno with the rolled up shirt and asked, "What's so funny?"

Bruno took a moment to stop laughing and wiped the tears from his eyes. "Nothing, except I didn't realize that they came with matching panties."

Harvey didn't care how big Bruno was or that he was a professional prize fighter. He was going to take a swing at him anyway.

"Hey guys," Gene said. "I got him. But I had to drag him away. He got into the role and was really hamming it up."

"Let's go then," Harvey commanded. "I have another pair of slacks on my ship."

Harvey wasn't concerned about getting his ship out of impound. Acquiring vessels was a specialty of his.

As they approached the fence that surrounded the lot, Roy asked, "How long do you think it will take for you to get us to the imperial palace?"

"The imperial palace?" Harvey asked. "That would take an eternity."

Roy scrunched up his face and asked, "An eternity?"

"As in I'm not going there. This was about all the imperial fun I intend to have."

Everyone's face fell on that announcement and Bruno asked, "But what about the diva?"

"What about her?"

Bruno poked his large and hardened finger into Harvey's chest and asked, "Why do you think we broke you out of there?"

"The big guys right," Roy said. "We could have left you there."

"Well I sure don't think you broke me out for my sake. You guys need a ship, and I have one. That's all you wanted."

"We needed you," Bruno said. "We already had your ship. We could have taken it. But we need your skills. We need you and the diva needs you."

"And," Roy added, "Elizabeth needs you."

Harvey pictured Elizabeth in his mind. A scowl crossed his face as he jumped the fence and realized this was something he had to do. His mind was clouded with all the feelings that had entered into his life lately that had nothing to do with him. Victor and Bruno practically crawled between the rows of impounded ships, but Harvey barely even bothered to duck his head as he made his way to his ship and entered the override code to lower the ramp.

Gene nudged Roy in the side and jerked his head towards Harvey. They crept up the gangplank and took their seats, but Harvey was like a robot as he climbed aboard and prepped the ship for launch. With the exception of Harvey's machine like lack of emotion, a palpable excitement filled the air. Everyone was even more excited to leave Gellian Prime than they were to leave Emaude Phlott.

"Did you remember to relieve yourself?" Bruno asked Victor. "It's a long trip and I don't want you having any accidents on the way."

Victor tossed the nearest loose object he could find, a book, and hit Bruno in the head.

Bruno smiled and shrugged, saying, "Sorry, but your acting job was so good, I believed it."

Victor was already buckled into his seat, but he spread his arms and bent at the waist in a dramatic bow. "Thank you, sir. I accept this award and want to thank all the little people who helped me get here."

Gene pointed his thumb at Victor and said, "You hear that Roy? He's thanking us for helping him act crazy."

"I don't think he was acting," Roy replied. "That was the real Victor. Now is the acting when he pretends to be sane."

Victor looked around his seat for something else to throw, but there was nothing.

Mirth and relief filled the passenger cabin, but not the cockpit. Harvey completed his computations and engaged the button to start their ascent. He plotted a course that returned them into the rings and let the computer take him there. Once he was in the rings, he manually guided them around the planet until he had a window to take him to the capitol of the Andurian empire.

He double checked his computations and glanced at a few more diagnostics, then pushed the throttle forward to leave the rings. He never even bothered to check his sensors to see if they were being followed. He left the planet until he was at a safe enough distance to engage the hyper-drive and put the ship back into auto pilot.

Harvey pressed the final button instructing the computer to follow the plotted flight plan and they were off. His mind was still replaying the last few days and his encounters with Elizabeth and Francesca. In spite of his first instinct to wash his hands of the whole affair, he understood his desire to save Elizabeth, but he found himself also compelled to help Francesca, no matter how caustically she treated people. The diva was especially mean to Elizabeth and he should have wanted to abandon her there, but he found himself wanting to save her too. The old Harvey was losing the internal struggle to the new Harvey, and that only required him to remember Elizabeth.

He closed his eyes and leaned his chair back to take a nap. Normally, he would have jokingly announced going into hyper-drive to his passengers, but this new more serious Harvey might as well have been making the trip solo. Bruno and Victor didn't know him well enough to notice the change, but Gene and Roy sure did, and they found it a bit creepy.

Francesca thought she had lost the butler and his assistants as she navigated through the hedge maze. She found her way to a large center area and when she tried crossing it to another opening in the hedge, people started pouring in, blocking her way. She turned to find more openings in the hedge, but they too had people streaming into the courtyard at the center of the hedge maze.

The people formed a thick ring around Francesca. They didn't get too close and left a generous space for her to maneuver, but there was no gap in the ring of people for her to exit. The butler came forward and gestured towards the people as he said, "Madame, they have come to hear you sing."

Francesca was thrilled that they wanted to hear her sing, but she despised the butler and his people. "I already told you that you are to be calling me Diva or Prima Donna. I am not being your Madam."

The butler bent low at the waist and said, "My apologies, Prima Donna."

A stranger took two steps forward from the ring of people and also bowed at the waist saying, "Please, your majesty, honor us with a song."

Francesca was touched. She remembered the ugly little man on that horrid little moon who also called her "your majesty." She liked that little man, in spite of his unfortunate appearance, and she liked this stranger.

"Very well," she said. "For you I will sing, but not for him." She pointed at the butler. "I want him to leave."

In unison the crowd turned their eyes to the butler. Anger projected from their eyes and he remained bent low at the waist as he said, "As the Prima Donna wishes." He backed away from Francesca into a gap that opened in the crowd to allow him to back all the way out.

"And take your little friends with you," Francesca shouted, "or there will be none of the singing."

Five people made their way through the crowd and joined the butler. He stopped when he reached the outer layer of the ring, but the throng of people continued giving him the evil eye until he left through the nearest opening in the hedge.

With the butler and his people gone, the people turned their attention back to the diva with only love and honor in their eyes.

A smile crossed Francesca's face. Ripples travelled up and down her spine as she felt all those little hairs on her body stand at attention. She loved a truly adoring crowd.

She launched immediately into an a capella aria. Her performance was stunning and the people were mesmerized. Somewhere in the recesses of her mind, she remembered wondering why her agent had booked her to play in this part of the empire, but seeing them swoon here, as they had done on Emaude Phlott, was all the answer she needed. These people truly loved her.

There had been no question in Elizabeth's mind that she had heard more and more people gathering on the other side of the hedge. It would be impossible for her to cross the hedge on the big tree without being seen by that large of a crowd, but when she heard Francesca sing, and there was no mistaking her voice, the throng of people on the other side of the hedge had grown so large that Elizabeth considered the possibility that she could quickly scale the fence and lose herself in the crowd.

To her own surprise, even while she considered the rash action, Elizabeth had already begun moving and quickly climbed the tree. The tree was tall enough for her to see over the hedge. The crowd pressed into a central court and all eyes were on Francesca. She scanned the hedge maze and tried to memorize the way in, but it wouldn't have mattered to her. She slithered out on the sturdy branch and dropped down, hanging from her hands. It was a lot farther down than she had thought. She closed her eyes, held her breath, and let go. The fall was only about five feet, but in her mind, with her eyes shut, it could have been twenty.

To her own amazement, she landed safely and quickly wound her way through the maze. She hadn't memorized the path as well as she should have, but eventually found her way to the court and slipped into the crowd of rapt people just as Francesca was starting a second number.

Chapter 7

Francesca's performance was perfection as always. The throng of people swooned around her and rocked in time to her voice.

Elizabeth had seen many appreciative audiences in the time she had worked for the diva, but this level of rapture was unprecedented. The courtyard was packed with listeners standing shoulder to shoulder. They rocked back and forth like waves of water rippling in a bowl.

Francesca spread her arms and held the last note.

The crowd held their position leaning towards their left, not breathing, but they hung on the last note.

As Francesca let the note die away, the people relaxed into a more balanced position. They were like jelly as ripples of appreciation flowed through the crowd.

Francesca smiled and looked over the crowd. She saw the rapture in their faces and waited for them to return to reality. They opened their eyes and put their hands together for her. A roar of approval rose from the throng and they pushed into an even tighter formation.

Elizabeth tried reaching Francesca, but the crowd was impenetrable. She waved her hands in the air and yelled, "Yoohoo! Diva! It's me!" but her voice was lost in the applause.

The butler returned to the throng. His guards parted the masses to let him in.

Their anger for him had long ago been forgotten and they allowed him into the center where he bowed before Francesca and escorted her out of the garden.

As Harvey approached the Andurian capitol, he plotted a large arc to take the ship into the shadow of the Andurian moon. He stayed in the moon's shadow until he was close enough to engage the ship's cloaks and slip into a little known blind spot in the Palace's sensor array. The blind spot extended to the far end of the palace's space port where he was able to park the ship amongst the other private ships. He turned off the cloaks to preserve the coils and engaged the camouflage circuits which drew very little power.

With the ship disguised, he led the small troop to a hiding area in the woods outside the palace grounds.

The butler led Francesca back to the palace, but this time he avoided the grand staircase and took her to an elevator near the rear entrance. The lift only had buttons for two floors on it, but he waved a badge in front of the buttons and the doors closed

"Here," he said to her. "This key card will grant you access to the penthouse suites."

Francesca accepted the card and said, "It is good that you are being more reasonable now."

He grit his teeth and faked a smile for her. The elevator door opened into a hallway with three doors. "This way," he said pointing to the left. She followed him through the door on the left and found herself in the same room he had put her in before.

The satisfaction she had felt for winning the penthouse suite faded from her face. "What is being the meaning of this? Are you tricking me?"

"No Madame. I can see that you are confused. If you follow me to the window, you will see that you are indeed on the top floor now. Since you liked the decor of the other room, we transferred everything up here for you."

Francesca went to the window and looked down. "It is good that you are not tricking me. This is much better than the other room."

The butler smiled thinly and said, "Yes diva. A dinner will be prepared in your honor. It won't be a formal banquet yet, though that is most certainly coming. I do hope you will honor us with your presence and let me assure you that the staff at the palace prepares the most marvelous meals."

"Si," she replied. "We certainly don't want to disappoint our fans."

"Very well," he said. "You will find an assortment of gowns in the armoire, but if they are not satisfactory, you need only pull the velvet rope or pick up the phone and more will be presented for you." In his heart, he expected that she would probably make the call regardless of how much she liked the gowns. "I'll come for you around five."

She waited for more from him, but hearing nothing, said, "Thank you. You're excused." She waited again, this time for him to close the door, then looked in the large mirror over the fireplace. She had only worn this gown for a couple hours, and already it looked tired and drab. She hated selecting gowns. That was something that Elizabeth did for her.

Francesca returned to the window and looked out over the hedge maze. A ship landed in the space port and parked just beyond the woods that bordered the hedge maze. "Oh, Elizabeth," she sighed, "Why are you not being here to help me?"

Elizabeth saw Francesca being escorted away. She hadn't been able to attract the diva's attention and she couldn't push through the crowd fast enough to catch her, but she was able to circle around the throng of people and follow the diva up to the palace.

Guests and staff crossed the atrium in a continuous stream of traffic. Elizabeth slipped in behind a maid and walked to the elevator that Francesca had taken. She pressed the up button, but a voice behind her said, "Excuse me, can I help you?"

She froze momentarily then spun around with a big smile on her face and said, "Hi! Aren't you sweet? My name is Elizabeth Garrett and I'm the diva's personal assistant. I just saw her take this elevator and I still need to go over her appointments for the week."

"Yeah, sure you are," the guard said, "like I haven't heard that one before."

"But it's true. You can ask her yourself."

The guard grabbed her by the arm end twisted it slightly behind her. "Out you go."

"You're making a big mistake."

The guard took her through the front entrance and pushed her down the lane that led off the palace grounds.

She walked down the lane until she thought he wouldn't still be watching her, then slipped to the right past the hedge into the wooded area where she had climbed the tree into the hedge maze.

As soon as her feet hit the ground on the other side of the hedge, she heard, "Well, that wasn't your finest hour," and felt arms wrapped around her waist. She looked down and saw Roy hugging her.

"We were really worried about you," Roy said.

Francesca remained in the window for quite some time, looking down over the gardens. The view was only slightly different from the previous room, yet the satisfaction she felt was priceless.

She eventually left the window and perused the amenities of the room. It had everything she could possibly want; everything, except her Elizabeth.

The armoire was filled with several beautiful gowns in a rainbow of colors. Elizabeth would know which one to wear. She tried thinking which one her assistant would select and chose the blue one. Again she had trouble buttoning the back by herself.

She returned to the window and wondered where Elizabeth could be. She was probably still stranded on that horrid little moon with that phony bad smelling robot horse. Another ship landed in the space port and she prayed that Elizabeth might be on that ship, but she knew that it was just a silly prayer.

A knock on the door drew her attention away from the scene outside. She waited for them to knock again before saying, "Entrare."

The door opened only a few inches and the butler said, "Madame Diva, dinner is ready."

Francesca sighed and said only, "Si." Her shoulders slouched as she shuffled slowly to the door, but when she arrived at the door, she straightened her shoulders and wore a regal bearing. Nobody would see her sadness.

The dining hall was on the second floor. It was a modest hall dominated by a table that could seat no more than two dozen people. The table was laid with fine porcelain plates and bowls surrounded with gold forks and spoons. Highly polished silver bowls and platters were held by an army of servers waiting for the guests to be seated. Even the chairs were fine antiques which, to Francesca, meant expensive. One chair, at the end of the table, was grander than the others with the royal crest emblazoned on the back cushion.

Francesca was led to the large chair. The seat of honor, she thought to herself, but as she began to take her seat in it, she was quickly ushered to the seat next to it.

The butler saw the change in her posture and quickly explained, "That is the king's own chair."

Francesca looked harshly at him and said, "So I am to be sitting in the same chairs as everybody else?"

"No, Madame," the butler hemmed and hawed, "I mean yes Madame, that is. Normally you shall have your own chair at the opposite end of the table, but tonight, the king wanted you near him so he could speak privately with you."

"The king is being here?" she asked. "And he wants to be speaking with me in the private?"

"Yes Madame, if he comes, that is. I meant to say, if he attends, he wanted you near him."

This festered on Francesca's irritation nerve. "*If* he comes?" her voice rose, but was not bellowing yet. "You bring me here to be meeting with the king and maybe he does not come?"

"Yes Madame, I mean no Madame. He might come."

Other guests were admitted to the room and seated around the table. Francesca took a moment to collect her feelings and smiled to the other guests.

There was a small amount of quiet tittering among them, but there were also a number of bows and nods towards her.

Harvey held field glasses to his eyes and monitored the palace.

"These hedges are part of a maze," Elizabeth said.

"Yeah, I know."

Elizabeth ignored the annoying know it all tone of Harvey's reply and continued, "Francesca was taken inside to an elevator. That was the last time that I saw of her."

Harvey zoomed the glasses to the upper windows of the palace. "She was probably taken to one of the queen's suites then. I don't understand why these people let them parade her around like that. The Andurians are good people, mostly. I would have thought that they would have kept her hidden from the public."

Elizabeth was confused and asked, "Why?"

"Mostly because she looks like their queen," Harvey said. "I would think that dragging their queen around in handcuffs would create too much scandal."

"Oh," Elizabeth laughed. "She wasn't in handcuffs."

"No?"

"No," she said flatly. "And they weren't dragging her around. She was on her own. She came out here to the courtyard in the center of the maze and sang for them. Then, when she was done, she returned to the palace."

Harvey removed the glasses and looked at Elizabeth. His puzzled expression amused her. He looked around to see if anyone else was as confused as he was and asked, "Was she drugged?"

"I doubt it. She sang too well to be drugged."

Harvey laughed and said, "I've known plenty of musicians that performed on drugs."

"Ha ha," Elizabeth retorted. "Well, not the diva."

Harvey turned to Roy and Gene. "Why don't you guys go in there and see what's up."

"How are they going to get in?" Elizabeth asked. "Didn't you see what they did to me?"

Harvey looked at Roy to explain, but Roy let him squirm. "They have special talents. They've done this before. Trust me."

Roy laughed and said, "It's because we're little and people don't like to stare at us."

The doors to the dining hall were closed after the guests were seated. Very little was said at the table, and what was said was in private whispers between only two people at a time. Francesca waited for her meal in near silence.

Soup tureens were eventually carried around the table by the staff and ladled into their bowls. It smelled as fine as any she had ever sampled. She smiled across the table and said, "Well, it certainly smells wonderful."

Guests around the table whispered to each other, but towards Francesca, they were very careful about what they said and chose mostly to say nothing.

Francesca carefully ladled a spoonful of soup off the back of the bowl and slurped it from the spoon. She smiled appreciatively and said, "The soup is quite good, no?"

Nobody else in the room had picked up their spoons yet and many gasped at Francesca's remark. Expressions from the other guests ranged from being caught unprepared to answer to absolute terror at being asked.

Francesca raised her spoon and yelled towards the kitchen, "You must give to my Elizabeth the recipe. This soup is absolutely divine."

A wave of whispers rippled down the table to the other end, and still none of them had tried the soup.

"Elizabeth is my personal assistant," she said to the guests. "I hope she is arriving here soon. I find myself being swamped with those mundane little things that she is usually taking care of for me."

The guests nearest her looked back at her blankly, unsure if they were supposed to respond, while further away from her, the guests conveniently looked the other way as if they hadn't heard anything.

"You know what I am meaning," she said directly to the woman sitting across from her. "There are just some things that a person of my station should not be having to deal with."

The woman across from her turned to her husband and whispered, "Am I supposed to say something? Do something! Help me out here!"

The woman's husband shrugged and whispered back, "How do we address her?"

"How would I know?" the woman whispered angrily. "You're supposed to know these things."

The husband bowed his head to Francesca and simply said, "I couldn't agree with you more."

The doors were flung open and a thin man at the door announced, "Presenting His Royal Majesty, King of Anduria, and emperor to all of Greater Anduria and the Vega colonies, Marcel Dogian Pernupt."

The guests at the table immediately stood and bowed their heads, but Francesca was in the middle of slurping another spoonful of soup. The table was dead silent, and her slurp was unmistakable.

"Mmmm," she said as she slowly rose from her seat. "You must try the soup. It is exquisite."

The king stared at Francesca. The resemblance was intoxicating. He approached his chair, but before taking his seat, asked, "Has it always been your habit to sample the soup before your king arrives?"

Francesca narrowed her eyes and said, "Only when he is coming late to supper, but I forgive you this one time. Do not be making it the habit." Francesca sat back down and picked up her spoon again, then added, "Besides, you are not being my king. I'm not from here."

The king was struck by her directness and didn't know how to respond. He slowly took his seat and as he recovered his composure, he said, "Even if you are from the Vega Colonies, I'm still your king and your emperor."

"No you're not," she sang with a lyrical quality to her voice as she dipped some bread in the soup and consumed the soggy end.

"I beg your..."

"You needn't beg," she said, "It is, how you say, unbecoming of a king. I am not being from Vega either. Do you not know who I am? I am finding this rather insulting."

The king smiled to his guests and said, "Of course I know who you are. I make it my business to know everything going on in my empire. You're that singer from Gellian Prime that I've heard so much about."

"That singer?" Francesca asked, unable to hide the displeasure in her voice. "That singer is what you call me? I am the renowned Francesca Vittoria Agostina La Perla, number one soprano for the Vegan Royal Opera."

"So you are from Vega!" The king looked proud of himself for catching her in a deception.

"No," she said curtly as she sampled the wine. "I am being from Earth. I only sing for Vega."

The king looked perplexed and an aid whispered in his ear, "Earth is from a neighboring galaxy still outside the empire."

"Too much talking," Francesca said. "Your soup is cold by now, and I am being ready for the next course."

"Of course," the king said weakly. He nodded to the waiters and the next course was brought out. Guests around the table quickly sampled the soup and set their bowls aside.

Harvey watched Roy and Gene approach the servants' entrance of the palace with his binoculars. The sun was falling low on the horizon, but his glasses compensated for the lowering light.

Elizabeth pulled alongside and said, "So, even if they get in, what is your plan?"

"First thing we have to do is assess her situation. Roy will find out how much freedom she has and whether we can use that to our advantage."

"So, you think that if she's free enough, she can just walk right out of there?"

Harvey put the glasses down. Roy and Gene were inside and out of sight already anyway. "I think that if she is free enough, she may not want to leave, and before we can mount a rescue, we need to know that she wants to be rescued."

"Of course she wants to be rescued!!" Elizabeth objected.

"She's not like you and me," Harvey reminded her. "She likes her luxury a lot and she likes being the Prima Donna. Don't you think the palace just might be like heaven for her?"

Elizabeth opened her mouth to object, but said nothing. He might be right.

"If she doesn't want to stay, we'll get her out. If she's free to roam about, then we'll just walk her out of here to the gardens and sneak her to the ship. If she's not that free, then Roy will have to find a way to sneak her out. Don't worry. He's good at this."

Elizabeth sighed as she watched the Palace lights come on. The grounds were as beautiful at night as they were during the day. Francesca might want to stay, for a while at least.

"I think we got off on the wrong foot," the king said. "Let us start over. Are you enjoying your stay in my home?"

"To be telling the truth," Francesca said, "it has been quite horrid. I don't have my Elizabeth with me and it's just been so primitive without her."

"But your room is acceptable?" the king asked.

"It is being okay now," she replied. "Now that I have it straightened out, but I had to do the straightening myself, and my Elizabeth would have had it right on the first try."

"I'm told you sang for the court today," the king said trying to change the subject away from Elizabeth. "They tell me it was quite exquisite."

"Si. I sing, but my Elizabeth would have made sure that Victor had everything ready for me."

The king motioned for his sergeant of the guards and asked, "Who is this Elizabeth and where is she? Did you not mention an Elizabeth in your reports?"

"Sire," the sergeant said, "one of the palace guards reported that a woman claiming the name of Elizabeth tried taking the elevator to the private suites. He said that she claimed to be the diva's personal assistant."

"Well?" the king said, "Bring her here. The diva obviously wishes to be reunited with her servant. Bring her at once!"

The sergeant grimaced and admitted, "We cannot. She was ejected from the grounds."

The king slid his chair back from the table and said sternly to the guards, "Then find her! Search the grounds and the spaceport, but find her! And put that ninny that ejected her on report. I regret the day when my ancestors removed the stockades from the palace grounds."

The sergeant left immediately and the king turned to Francesca and said, "I will find your Elizabeth. It is possible that she is here on the grounds and was mistaken for, let us say, one of your more aggressive fans."

Francesca reached for the king's hands and held them warmly, asking, "My Elizabeth is here?"

Inside the servants' quadrant of the palace, Roy found the laundry room. The laundry had three sections: a table where incoming laundry was sorted; the machines that washed and dried the articles; and the tables where everything was pressed, folded and stacked.

Roy and Gene searched through the piles of laundry for something to wear. Most of the clothing was too large, but they knew from experience that they might find a woman's or child's top that could fit, and they weren't disappointed.

Disguised as waiters, they were even more invisible than they were before. Now they could slip through the hallways unquestioned.

The main course consisted of braised chicken on the bone served over a layer of diced fruit that had been soaked in brandy and syrup. The fruit's light colored flesh offered a pleasing contrast to the chicken's crispy dark skin. The fruit's syrupy sauce added a light sweetness to the chicken pieces, but also made the chicken, which was held in the fingers, a bit sticky.

Water bowls had been placed by the guest's dishes alongside the main course and the guests would frequently dip their fingers in the bowls to wash off the syrup.

The king was especially fond of the brandy soaked fruit. He liked to roll his chicken pieces around to layer it with the sticky fruit before taking a bite.

Francesca didn't like eating food with her fingers, but tried dipping her chicken in the fruit like the king did, although without his level of gusto. She carefully lifted the sticky concoction to her mouth and took a dainty bite. "Mmmm," she said with a practiced smile. She didn't like the syrup that had dripped onto her fingers and immediately dipped her fingers in the water bowl.

The king took another fruit covered bite and returned Francesca's smile, saying, "It's good like this, isn't it?"

Francesca pointed a finger to the corner of her mouth and pretended to wipe a crumb.

The king cocked his head, not understanding her gesture.

She leaned over and whispered, "You have a thing, right there, on your mouth."

"Oh!" he said and deftly wiped the fruit morsel into his mouth with his finger. He motioned for one of the servers and was presented with three more chicken legs on his plate. He promptly rolled them around in the fruit and took an enormous bite leaving several bits of fruit stuck on his lips.

Francesca took a dainty bite from her chicken, then wiped the corners of her mouth with her napkin and said, "You see how I do it? Perhaps you should try taking the smaller bite."

The woman across from Francesca gasped, but the king simply replied, "As you will soon see, the emperor does nothing small." The king continued to tear through his meal until the fruit was devoured, then he dipped both hands into the water bowl and sloshed water near Francesca's plate.

She looked coldly at him and was about to say something cross when he said, "I am sorry I didn't get to hear you sing this afternoon. I do hope you'll favor us again so I might hear you sing."

Gene was the first to spot Francesca while she was still at dinner. He nudged Roy and nodded his head while they carried away trays of dirty dishes that the servers had collected from the dining table.

"How do you know that's her?" Roy whispered. "Are you sure that's not the queen?"

Gene shrugged. They were difficult to tell apart.

"I think I'll have a grand ball," the king said. "I'll invite all the planetary dignitaries and introduce them to the court's new favorite performer."

Francesca's voice dropped low and dry as she replied, "You say that like I am being your new pony to be showing off?"

"We do not view you as a mere pony," the king said while stuffing an oversized bite of sweet bread into his mouth. "You are more like a prize filly. The grandest equine ever bred."

Francesca slammed her napkin on her plate and pushed her chair away from the table. She stood and bellowed as few others could, "I am Francesca Vittoria Agostina La Perla. I am number one soprano for the Vegan Royal Opera. I am renowned throughout the known universe and I will not be called the filly by the backside of a fat pompous horse."

The room was quieter than a chapel and Roy whispered, "Yup. That's her."

The king's face flushed red. He jumped to his feet and matched Francesca's volume as he yelled back, "Well I never..."

Francesca quickly ratcheted it up a notch to cut him off and sang in a clear soprano,

> *"What have you never?*
> *Have you never had the manners?"*

"How dare you Madame?"
The king's guards moved towards Francesca, but the king flicked his wrist and waived them off. His voice rose into the tenor range and he sang,

> *"Did you just call me a horse's ass?"*

Francesca sang in a low mezzo soprano voice,

> *"I used the poor description just now..."*

She raised her voice one note on the chromatic scale and continued,

> *"When you eat,*
> *you are more like a..."*

Francesca pulled all the stops and jumped to a high A and finished,

> *"a big fat cow!"*

Throughout the room, guests wanted to sneak out and not be witness to this, and yet they were mesmerized by the impromptu opera that presented itself before them.
The king wanted to continue the argument, but Francesca stormed out of the room.

She wanted to leave the palace and go home, but without Elizabeth, she didn't know how, so she returned to her penthouse room where she could sulk.

Gene and Roy dumped the dirty dishes in the kitchen, then quickly ran out of the palace to Harvey's location without even bothering to lose the disguises.

"She's in there alright," Gene said while still gasping for air.

"Yeah," Roy added. "That was most definitely her."

"That was never the question," Harvey replied. "We knew she was in there. Are they holding her hostage, or is she free to come and go."

Gene and Roy looked at each other and shrugged. "I guess," Roy ventured, "that she's free to come and go. She sure got up and left the table on her own."

Harvey turned to Elizabeth and said, "Sorry. I'm not going to kidnap her just because you thought they kidnapped her first."

"No!" Roy said. "I don't think she wants to stay."

"Yeah," Gene added. "You shoulda heard how she shot the king down."

"She shot the king down?" Harvey repeated.

"Yeah," Roy replied. "She called him a horse's ass."

"Great," Harvey moaned. "Now we'll have to break her out of jail."

"No!" Gene said. "The king waived off the guards and let her go."

"He let her go after that?"

Roy laughed and said, "He even let her go after she said he ate like a big fat cow. Those were her exact words, 'a big fat cow.'"

Gene added, "I'm a little surprised they didn't slap her in irons and drag her to the dungeon."

Roy bopped Gene on the head and said, "They don't do that anymore. I doubt that they even have a dungeon these days, but I can't say she didn't deserve it."

Elizabeth was on the verge of crying. She'd watched and listened to the conversation and her face contorted worse and worse as they kept piling up the insults Francesca had flung at the king.

Pacing the room and sulking were not enough for Francesca. A rage boiled within her which continued to manifest itself as an aria,

> *"That man!*
> *How dare he speak to me like that?"*

She pulled a bottle from the wine rack and poured herself a glass. "And he's the king? He's the one. He blocks me from my money!"

She quickly downed the glass of wine and poured another. She stared into the glass of wine and sang,

> *"The world must have the sense of humor,*
> *for such an ill-mannered chimp*
> *to be emperor!"*

She swallowed the second full glass and went to the door. She bellowed out, "He shall have a piece of my mind!"

She turned the knob, but it was locked. "Ahhh!" she screamed, then dropped her pitch into the mid alto range and sadly sang,

> *"Like a prisoner,*
> *I'm locked in my room,*
> *Without my Elizabeth,*
> *this room is my tomb."*

The king knocked on her door and sang,

"*Madame!*"

He started in the high tenor range and dropped his voice into a baritone as he sang,

> "*You insult me!*
> *You do me grievous harm*
> *when you leave my table!*"

She sang back,

> "*You are a thief!*
> *You steal my money*
> *and strand me in hell!*"

The king jumped up to the tenor range as he asked,

> "*A thief?*"

Then returned to a baritone to sing,

> "*I am the emperor!*"

Francesca laughed and sang,

> "*You?*
> *An emperor?*
> *No! You are a kidnapper!*"

He belted back,

"You go too far!"

Francesca pounded on the door and sang,

"Then let me go!
If what I claim is not so…"

The king took a deep breath and belted out in his deepest bass,

"I cannot!"

Francesca took a step back from the door and sang softly,

"So you admit it,
You are what I say"

Francesca heard the door unlock and the king sang softly,

"There.
You are free to go,
but you cannot leave me…"

She was near tears as she sang back,

"How am I being free to go
if I cannot leave you?"

The king repeated himself, soft and low,

"You cannot leave me…"

"You said that," Francesca replied blandly.

The king dropped back to a deep bass and sang,

"Or I will die..."

"What was that?" she asked, "Did you say that you will lie?"

Francesca opened the door, but the king was gone. "What a strange man," she said, "but his voice is not so bad. Very good range for him being the novice."

Francesca realized that she was talking to herself and closed the door.

Tears still collected in Elizabeth's eyes as Harvey held her in his arms to console her. "Don't worry. We'll find out what is going on in there."

Roy and Gene returned to the servants entrance. The kitchen was filled with talk of the argument between Francesca and the king. The women thought there was something romantic about the two of them confronting each other with opera, but the men thought the king showed weakness by allowing her to say what she did.

This wasn't news to either of the brothers. They worked their way through the kitchen, as invisible to the staff as they were to the residents. They were about to leave the kitchen when they heard someone say, "And that's when she stormed out and returned to her room."

"Yes," another said, "and the king went after her."

"He didn't!"

"Truly, he did."

"Keep your voices down," a maid said, "and I'll tell you what happened next. I was checking the towels in the penthouse suites and the king was there outside her door. They were singing through the door."

The servants hushed and waited for her to continue.

"And then the king says he'll die if she leaves him."

"What?" a waiter asked. "That old cow?"

"She's not that old."

"And boy can she sing."

The conversation deteriorated into idle gossip and Roy nudged Gene. "Let's go."

Gene nodded and followed Roy to the elevator. The guard at the bottom of the lift actually noticed them, but did nothing to stop them. They looked official enough. They used a servants card to take the elevator to the top floor and regrouped in a small alcove while they tried to determine which door would be hers.

Francesca tried forgetting the whole incident, but she couldn't. Why would the king say he would lie? Did he plan to keep her here forever and lie to the world about her? Or did she misunderstand him? Maybe he said he would cry. That makes more sense, except kings don't cry, or do they? She had never heard of a king who sang opera before either. Maybe what he really said was that he would sigh. She's made men do that before. It makes more sense than if he said he would fly, although he does have his own spaceport.

"Arrrgghhh!" Francesca growled. Why couldn't she get that horrid man out of her mind? She searched the bar for something to eat. She wasn't really hungry, but she had to change her train of thought before she went mad. If she had her money, she could go shopping. It always made her feel better to buy things.

"That's it!" she shouted. "He said he wanted to buy!"

She ran to the door, but stopped when her hand reached the doorknob. "What did he say next? What did he want to buy her? She turned back towards the center of the room. It's best to leave these things for a surprise, but she couldn't.

She spun around and raced for the door. She flung the door open and ran to the elevator.

Gene and Roy tried catching her, but the lift doors had already closed before she even saw them.

Harvey took Elizabeth back to his ship. "You had us real worried when you disappeared."

"Really?" she asked. "Somehow I didn't think you would even notice that I was gone."

"Well we did," he lied. "We searched all over for you."

"But you came here anyway? I guess you didn't search very long."

"You were gone," he replied. "You were long gone and as far as we knew, you might have been kidnapped too. Where did you go? And how the hell did you end up here ahead of us?"

Elizabeth scowled as she remembered Francesca calling for help. "Someone had to save her, and since you weren't man enough to help her, I did."

"Not man enough?" he growled. "What do you think I'm doing here? I'm here to rescue her. I came a long way to help the old broad, and not because she's such a nice person either."

"You wouldn't have had to go such a long way if you had saved her in the first place."

Harvey wagged his finger at Elizabeth and yelled, "How did you expect me to save her before she was even taken? Am I supposed to be psychic?"

"You should have acted when you heard her!"

"Heard her?" he yelled, his voice rising with each sentence. "What the hell are you talking about?"

Elizabeth wasn't letting him intimidate her. She pointed her finger and stabbed him in the chest. "She yelled for help, but you were too busy with your damned ship!"

Harvey shrugged his shoulders and held his arms out at arm's length. "When did she yell? I never heard her!"

Elizabeth couldn't believe that he would lie to her like this. She involuntarily sucked in her breath to yell some more, but she had already run out of steam.

"That's right," he said, adopting a smug posture. "I never heard her."

She swung her arm like she was swinging a hammer and pounded her fist into his chest, but she wasn't satisfied, so she hit him with her other fist, then began a barrage of punches pummeling his chest. "How could you not hear her? She's a very loud woman. Probably the loudest woman you'll ever meet."

Harvey had had enough of her punches and reached up, grabbing her by the wrists. "I can't really argue with that. She *is* very loud,"

Elizabeth's anger began to fade into despair. She cried, "The loudest you'll ever know."

"Maybe," he said, "and maybe not. Seems to me that you're giving her a good old fashioned run for the money."

Elizabeth's rage was gone and she fell into a full cry. Harvey pulled her against his chest to comfort her, but she pushed herself away and cried, "No!" He gently pulled her back to him again and she didn't resist, but laid her head on his shoulder and let it all out.

"I'm sorry," he said, "that I didn't hear her, but I really didn't. She must have yelled for help while I was fueling the ship. The fuel pumps are really loud when you're working so close to them, and we were all wearing protection over our ears."

Elizabeth blubbered, "They drugged her and stowed her like luggage. Even here, I was so close to her, but she couldn't see me and they wouldn't let me see her."

"You will. We'll get her and offer her a ride home."

Francesca stormed out of the elevator. She had no idea where she should go, so she stomped off towards the dining hall which was almost the only place she knew, but before she reached the dining room door, she saw the king at the end of the corridor. "Oh, there you are being," she said, but he turned a corner and never heard her.

She set her jaw and hustled down the hall after him. The hall was bare of ornaments and there were very few people milling about. She wondered why he couldn't hear her, or if he really did and was avoiding her.

Francesca reached the end of the hall and saw a door close on the left. Nobody was in the hall, so she headed directly to the door she saw close. She burst into the room and found two men looking over the king's shoulders as he sat at his desk reviewing some reports.

"You!" she bellowed.

> *"What is it that you said to me?*
> *Something about wanting to buy me?"*

"Buy you?" the king asked incredulously. "I never said I wanted to buy you."

"Don't be the hard headed," she said, then slipped into a low monotone alto voice,

> *"You said that if I left you,*
> *You would buy...*

but you never finished what it was you were saying."

The king waived his guests out of his office and replied in a low baritone,

> *"No, Madame.*
> *If you leave me I will buy you nothing."*

Francesca raised her pitch one note and sang,

> *"So you think I will stay*
> *If you buy me something?"*

The king sang,

"No Madame,
I would not try to buy your affection."

She pitched up another note,

"But what is the something?"

He shook his head and sang,

"I know not of what you speak."

Francesca jumped to full soprano and belted out,

"You tease!
You lie!
You said that you would,
now you say that you won't.
I'm not the young girl
So impressed with your gold
That you buy her affection
But inside you're cold."

Francesca let the note die away before adding,

"and don't be so secret
when you buy me the gift."

The king opened his mouth to say something, but he was too perplexed to reply. Francesca was glowing. She looked so much like the queen, but she stood with more pomp than the queen had ever displayed. She looked down upon him with the kind of authority and entitlement that should have been his. He had never known anyone with her regal command.

Seeing that he would not reveal what she thought he would buy for her, she stormed out of the room with all the anger and flair with which she had entered.

The king was practically speechless. He managed only a low soft baritone,

> *"I know not what you thought I would buy*
> *If you ever leave me,*
> *I said I would die."*

Elizabeth tossed in her bed for most of the night. She hardly slept and was convinced that even if she had, she just would have had nightmares anyway. The room Harvey gave her was considerably nicer than the crew's quarters which Francesca had when they brought her to the palace. She wondered what kind of quarters they may have given her now. Francesca was probably lodged in a servant's room and trotted out just to sing for the dignitaries. She may even be forced to share a room.

Elizabeth curled up on the thin mattress and hugged her pillow, but even that made her feel guilty knowing that Francesca was probably being kept in squalor.

Harvey knocked on the door and said, "Sun's up. We have work to do."

Harvey had left some dresses in the closet. When she asked him why he had so many nice dresses, and he just said they were payment for a shipment he had delivered.

Harvey entered the palace through the front gate with Elizabeth on his arm. She never even noticed when he bumped into the three men smoking cigars in front of the steps. He led her up the steps where he showed an invitation to the front guard and they were allowed through.

"We have an invitation to brunch?" Elizabeth asked when safely inside. "Where'd you get that?"

Harvey glanced sideways at her and asked, "Why? You don't think I get invited to nice places?"

Harvey walked Elizabeth calmly through the atrium. "The brunch is in..."

A ruckus brewed behind them and she clearly heard a man yelling, "But I had my invitation..."

Elizabeth spun her head around to see, but Harvey continued to usher her forward and said, "Don't look."

She didn't have to look. She could hear the authoritative guard and the whining dignitary. "I'm sorry sir," the guard said, "but you'll need an invitation to enter."

"Do you know who I am?" the guest whined. "I'm Ferdinand Lupino. The king invited me personally!"

"I'm sorry sir..."

"Check your list!" Ferdinand demanded.

Harvey was almost to the back door when he heard, "Hey you! Stop that man!"

"That's our cue," he said as he pulled Elizabeth into a side hallway. They ducked down a servants' hall then turned to the right and ran directly to a servants' stairwell.

The servants' hall whizzed past Elizabeth and they practically flew down the stairs as Harvey led her through the engineering level.

"How do you know your way?" she asked breathlessly.

They crossed the engineering level, running past boilers and generators.

"Did you hear me?" she asked again. "How do you know your way around here?"

"I used to work here," he replied.

He led her through a door at the end of engineering and then up a stairwell to a rarely used guest wing. They burst through the door into the hallway and saw Francesca turn the corner at the end of the corridor. They started to follow, but a guard popped into the hallway and Harvey ducked through the nearest doorway to hide.

As Francesca was leaving the king's office, a maid bowed low and smiled sweetly. "Is there anything I can get you milady?"

"NO!" Francesca bellowed. "You are not my Elizabeth! I need my Elizabeth! Only my Elizabeth can help me!"

The poor maid was shocked to tears. Francesca didn't mean to make her cry and sang,

> *"I'm sorry.*
> *Do not cry.*
> *I'm sure you can do many things.*
> *That Elizabeth does without asking."*

The maid's lips trembled. She had only wanted to be of service for Francesca, but she was so harshly shot down that she nearly cried. She shouldn't have been so shocked, it wasn't the first time an aristocrat had yelled at her, and it wouldn't be the last, but Francesca apologized, and that was a first. The maid loved to sing around her house, but she had never before sung in public. She blotted the tears from her eyes and timidly sang,

> *"I know not your Elizabeth.*
> *I know not where she is or what she does for you.*
> *But if you'll give me half a chance,*
> *you'll learn what I can do."*

Francesca was speechless. She hugged the maid and together, they found their way to Francesca's room.

On the other side of the door, the king called his steward and sang in a deep clear baritone,

> *"You must find this Elizabeth,*
> *for only she will do.*
> *And if you can't find her today,*
> *then bring the guard that sent her away."*

Roy and Gene were down the hall when they saw Francesca leave he king's office. She walked down the hall past a guard and into the elevator that led to the penthouse suites.

"Did you see that?" Gene asked.

"Yeah," Roy said. "She's in the penthouse suites."

Gene shook his head and said, "She doesn't look like a kidnap victim to me."

"I know," Roy replied. "We gotta talk to her."

Gene pointed at the guard and said, "I know that one. He won't let us pass."

Roy headed the other direction and said, "I guess it's time for room service."

Chapter 8

The king hadn't been himself since the queen had left him, but since the arrival of Francesca, he had changed again. He knew it and was afraid that others saw the change in him too. He wasn't supposed to care about their opinions, but he did. He didn't want to appear weak in front of his subjects, and Francesca made him feel weak. For years he thought that being the emperor meant being invincible, but he was learning how wrong that belief was.

He'd only been married six years, and it created quite a scandal when he wedded the outsider. She was so far outside, not even from within the empire, that many considered her to be less than a commoner, but she was anything but common.

She wasn't pompous, but she had a regal bearing. She walked like a royal and talked like a royal. The king believed that she must have been royal in her own land, though she denied it. She looked every bit like a queen, and pictures from the wedding proved nothing to the contrary.

But, she changed. Her appearance was the same, as was her speech, but her actions betrayed her. She ventured out into the public and didn't maintain her regal aloofness. She connected directly with the people and they loved her for it. The more they loved her, the less they loved the king, their emperor.

The king wasn't without sympathies, and did nothing to dissuade his wife from her philanthropic adventures, but when her public kindness began to drift from his official policy, a rift grew between them. She sought to treat the Vegans as equals to the Andurians, but he saw them as money grubbing misers. Their whole society was built around money transfers and the accumulation of wealth, but she insisted that there was much more to Vega. She crossed the border countless times and drew attention to the cultural and artistic beauty in Vega, but the king only saw them for their banks and stock exchanges. When the economy was bad, he pointed to them as the cause, but when the economy was good, he saw it as Andurian supremacy in spite of Vega.

The more she tried to sway him, the further he set his resolve. She was very vocal with her opinions and he found himself spending more time spinning her comments and actions so they wouldn't affect the people's confidence in his leadership, but it did. As their politics grew apart, so did they, but he still refused to use his authority to squash her activities, until she lowered the boom and demanded a divorce. He was the emperor, yet this woman, someone below the commoner caste, had utterly destroyed his life. She wanted more than he was willing to surrender and he wasn't going to stand for it.

He confined her to her suite, but the people loved her and spirited her away. He knew where they had taken her, and as long as they kept her in the palace, he allowed them to believe she was hidden from him. He set his spies to keep track of her, but he suspected that his spies also loved her and might not be loyal to him. The whole empire seemed against him in this. Someone had to pay, and he saw to it that it would be the Vegans. It was the Vegans that created the divide between them, so it was the Vegans who would find themselves divided.

Things were bad in the empire, but he believed that things would be even worse in Vega, yet it did nothing to improve his mood. Then this singer came to the palace. She had all of the queen's beauty and bearing, but none of her flaws. She treated servants not as friends and confidants, but as servants, as they should be treated. He was the emperor and not prone to silly whims of the heart, yet Francesca looked so much like the queen, that it was as if he had been in love with her for six years already. She was the queen, or at least, she should have been the queen.

She didn't just talk like a royal, she spoke her mind like a royal and she looked down her nose at all those mealy mouthed nobles that constantly swarmed around him hoping to garner some favor. They were like beggars on the streets, only in better clothes.

Francesca had spunk. She pulled the king from his funk and brought excitement to his life. She was perfect.

The king sat at his desk, thrilled over Francesca's lambasting of him, yet more than a bit annoyed that she could walk away like she had won the argument. He must do something. He can't let her believe she won.

There would be another opportunity, and he must be better prepared.

Having given the king a piece of her mind, Francesca felt that she had somehow earned the amenities that her penthouse suite had to offer. She tired of looking out the window at the gardens and rang the bell for a room service attendant.

A small rap on the door preceded a maid pushing the door open a crack and asking, "Did you need something ma'am?"

"Yes, I'm feeling a bit peaked…"

"Would you like the doctor, ma'am?"

Francesca scowled and said, "No, I do not want the doctor, and why is it that you are interrupting me?"

The maid bowed her head and said, "Sorry ma'am."

"I think I would like some tea."

The maid bowed her head again and said, "At once ma'am."

The servant disappeared and started to close the door when Francesca said, "Wait! Where is it you are going? I am not dismissing you yet."

The servant entered the doorway again and apologized, "Of course ma'am. Sorry ma'am."

"With my tea, I am wanting the crackers."

The maid trembled slightly as she bowed her head yet again and said, "Yes ma'am."

"No, toast."

The poor girl struggled to keep her voice from wavering. "As you wish."

"With the jams and jellies I think."

"Yes, ma'am."

Francesca waited a couple heartbeats before barking, "Well? Why is it that you are still here? Aren't you knowing how to do your job? Go to get my tea and toast."

Harvey led Elizabeth back into the hallway after hearing the guard pass by. This area of the guest wing was barely any better than the staff's quarters. The doorway they had seen Francesca enter led to another hallway. Harvey knew this hallway. It contained bedrooms that were usually reserved for guests in hiding, or sometimes guests having secret rendezvous.

They crept down the hall and listened at the doorways, certain in their belief that Francesca would not remain quiet, but they heard nothing. They reached the last bedroom and Harvey shrugged his shoulders and said, "We can go back again if you want."

"What about that door?" Elizabeth asked pointing to the next and last door in the hall.

"That's the stairwell," Harvey said.

"How do you know?" Elizabeth asked.

"It doesn't matter. It leads to the barracks and the king's offices. I doubt that she went upstairs to get there."

"I doubt that she would take the stairs," Elizabeth added.

The stairwell door opened and Harvey impulsively pulled Elizabeth into the last bedroom, which was thankfully empty. He heard two guards pass by and cracked open the door to peek out.

They banged on a door that was just down the hall and across from them. The door opened.

Harvey couldn't hear what was said, but he clearly saw Francesca come out, looking very concerned as the guards took her by the arms and led her away.

Francesca waited in her room for her tea. She sat in the oldest most elegant chair in the room and counted the moments as they passed by until she heard a soft knock on the door.

"Well it is about time," she said. "Come in and try being quick."

The door opened and Roy and Gene came in the room and fell to their knees.

"Your majesty," Roy said. "We have come to rescue you."

"You!" she shouted. "What is it that you are doing here?"

"We're here to rescue you," Gene repeated.

"We thought they were holding you prisoner," Roy said.

"Ah, yes. I am seeing that. I thought so too at first, but it is being better now."

The king's guards took Francesca's doppelganger, the actual Queen, directly to his office. She stood in the center of the room with her head hung low as he waved the guards away. She didn't know when he had found her, but she always knew that this would be a possibility. She tried desperately to get a ride off the planet, but the people most inclined to help her were the Vegans, but they had cash flow problems on this side of the border making fuel nearly impossible for them to get. She didn't know anyone who would help her if she were to be tossed into jail, but she wasn't in shackles, so maybe he had something else in mind. She couldn't tell what he wanted from his expression, but whatever was rattling around in his head, there was absolutely zero chance of a reconciliation. She can't let him think that he can keep her in this marriage by force. She waited for the guards to leave, and when the door closed behind them, she lifted her head defiantly and said, "So, you found me. This doesn't change anything."

"My dear," he replied. "I never lost you. I've always known where you've been hiding, and I've decided that you may remain hiding. In fact, I insist that you remain hiding."

"So, you're granting my divorce?"

The king laughed. "The queen does not divorce the king. I will consider your petition and decide whether or not I will divorce you, but later. For now, your king has other matters that require his attention. You may stay in your quarters while I deal with the mess you have made of the empire."

"The mess that I..."

"That is all," he said interrupting her. He pressed a button on his desk and said, "We are through here, you may escort the queen back to her new quarters."

The door opened and the guards led her away.

"She may look like the queen," the servant said as she prepared the tea in the kitchen, "but she is not the same. She is a horrid woman!" The servant stared at the tea pot and contemplated whether she should spit in it.

The butler took the tea pot and placed it on a silver tray with the tea cups and a bowl of sugar cubes. "Be careful what you say, she may be our next queen."

"Why?" the maid asked. "Why would our king want such an awful, egotistical woman?"

"Think about it," the butler said. "Who does she remind you of?"

"Who does she remind me of?" the maid repeated, "I already said she looks just like the queen, but that don't mean she reminds me of her."

"Forget what she looks and sounds like," the butler said. "Consider what she says and how she treats you. Now, who does she remind you of?"

Recognition dawned in the maid's eyes. "She's just like the king!"

The butler nodded. Several other staff had collected around them. Some had not yet met Francesca.

"I saw her in the dining room," a waiter said, "and if you ask me, she's worse."

"One pompous royal ass is enough," someone in the back of the growing crowd said.

"Now stop that at once!" the butler said. "We cannot have talk like that."

"You mean in public," the voice said, "where someone can hear us, but it's what we're all thinking!"

The butler couldn't argue with that.

The maid said, "Then we have to get rid of her."

"You want to kill her?" the waiter asked.

"No," the maid said, "but we can make her hate it here."

"Before you are rescuing me," Francesca said to Roy, "I am needing to know where you are taking me. I am not going back to the cowboy movie."

Roy and Gene shared a blank look. They hadn't planned that far ahead.

"So!" Francesca exclaimed. "You were thinking we would go back to that, what you call it, Mud Flats?"

Roy was quick to reply, "No! No, your majesty. We were focused on getting you away from here. Do you know what they have planned for you?"

"They ask me to sing for them."

Roy nodded and said, "That's part of it, but that's mostly to make you feel wanted. Do you not know how much you look like the queen?"

"Why would I be knowing that?"

Roy pointed to the mirror and said, "Look there! That's what the queen looks like. This whole civil war..."

"It's not a war," Gene said, "it's just a...a..."

"Yeah," Roy continued, "It's hard to explain, but the reason you can't get back to Vega, and the reason you can't get your money, is because the queen left the king."

"I am not blaming her," Francesca said. "He is a horrid man. He's rude and arrogant. He is not a nice man. She should leave him."

Roy closed his eyes and exhaled loudly. "You explain it to her, Gene."

"Majesty," Gene said, "The king cutoff all travel and ties to Vega when the queen said she was leaving him."

Francesca nodded and said, "I left off from what I said that he is being very controlling."

Roy said, "Rude, arrogant, controlling. Does that sound like anyone we know?"

Francesca thought about it a moment then shook her head and said, "No. I am not keeping people like that around me."

Gene continued, "The economy crashed when the king split the empire and cut off Vega."

"He's a bad king too," she said.

"Don't you see?" Roy asked. "He did all this to keep her here."

"So?" she asked. "I'm not seeing what this is having to do with me."

Gene spoke slowly as if that would make it clear, "They think..."

Roy interrupted Gene and blurted out, "They think that they can replace the queen with you and the king will put the empire back together."

Francesca looked puzzled, then she looked disturbed.

"You see?" Roy said. "They want you to be the new queen."

The anger melted from Francesca's face. She actually started to look happy. "You mean they are wanting ME to be queen? That's not sounding so bad."

"What?" Roy exclaimed. "You WANT to marry the king?"

The joy left her face and she said, "Oh. That must be the other shoe that is dropping. I am not wanting to marry him. Even the cowboy movie is not sounding as bad as that. Take me home."

Harvey led Elizabeth to the gardens to wait for Roy and Gene.

"This is where she sang for them," Elizabeth said. "Right here, in the center of the hedge maze."

Harvey checked his watch. "They should be here by now. I hope nothing has happened to them."

Elizabeth's eyes glassed over as she reminisced, "You should have seen the people. They adored her."

Harvey checked the gaps in the hedge to see if they were approaching.

"That's what's so confusing," Elizabeth said. "She didn't look like she was under any kind of duress. She looked real happy."

"No sign of them," Harvey said.

"Are you even listening to me?"

"Sure, you said she looked happy. I bet she always looks happy when she has an audience."

"True," Elizabeth agreed.

"But she didn't look so happy in the hallway when they took her away."

Roy and Gene came in and said, "Hey guys, we're here."

"You're late," Harvey said.

"Sorry," Roy said. "But we had a longer talk with her than we planned."

Harvey was surprised and asked, "They let you talk to her?"

"Who?" Gene asked. "We just went to her room and knocked on the door. She was alone when she let us in."

"She let you in?" Harvey asked. "By herself?"

"She's a big girl," Roy said. "She knows how to use a door."

Harvey shared a look with Elizabeth and said, "But we saw her hiding in the lower quarters!"

"Yeah!" Elizabeth added. "Then two big guards took her away!"

"No way!" Roy said. "There were no guards on her. She's in the penthouse suite living it up like the queen herself, but we explained the situation to her and she's ready to go."

"She sounded kind of pissed," Gene said, "when we told her what the king had planned for her."

Bruno had been quietly watching them discuss their findings. He'd stayed behind watching the guards patrol routes while they had gone to find Francesca. "I don't know why you have such different stories, but it don't make much difference to me and Victor which of you is right. We'll still need to get her past the guards if we want to sneak her out."

"He may be right," Roy admitted. "Even if she is living it up in the penthouse, it doesn't mean they'll let her walk out of here."

The king needed to plan his attack before he confronted Francesca again, and in order to do that, he would need to learn more about her. He had already sent requests to his personal liaison at the imperial intelligence agency and to the performing arts czar. He should have answers back from them soon.

Impatient for his replies, he checked his mailbox for a response. The performing arts czar was painfully inept and may not reply very quickly, but his intelligence group was the model of efficiency and should get back to him with a report quickly. To this day, he still shudders when he remembers the pomp and ballyhoo that accompanied the empire wide inauguration of the tragically named department of Words, Obscuration and Cryptology. Within moments of the announcement they were flooded with messages suggesting they read it backwards. Others volunteered equally inappropriate alternatives like the Galactic Information Program or The Bureau of Messages and Ultimate Decryption.

Embarrassed at first, his intelligence wing decided to pretend it was intentional by keeping the name and adopting a new slogan, "Don't have a COW, we'll know if you do."

The king could wait no longer. He waved his hand over his desk and the beautiful wood grain finish was replaced with a black glass top displaying a screen and some icons. He pressed a button on the glass to open the communicator and said, "Mr. Nell's public line."

A woman on the other end answered, "W.O.C."

"Mr. Nell, please."

Nell answered, "Nell here."

The king was annoyed and asked, "How long must I continue calling you through the public lines?"

Nell was equally annoyed. It wasn't the first time the king had asked him that. "Only until you have no enemies who might want to intercept your communications."

"But you said our communicators were encrypted."

"Take it from me," Nell said, "The encryption is worthless."

The king was annoyed with his tone and said, "I don't think I like the way you are talking to me, I'm your..."

"Sir," Nell interrupted, "You're anonymous. Maybe you'd like to keep it that way?"

The king growled and asked, "What have you learned about the singer?"

"Her name is Francesca Vittoria Agostina La Perla..."

"I know that," the king snapped. "It's something she is quite fond of reminding people."

"She's a singer..."

The king just sighed, hoping the report would reveal something new.

"She's from Earth, a relatively new planet in our circle of extended trading partners. She joined the Vegan Royal Opera three years ago. She's supposed to be quite extraordinary. We don't have any information about her childhood or her family on Earth. In fact, if I thought she might be a criminal, I'd be suspicious that she just suddenly showed up out of nowhere in her late teens. She has money, well, she has money on Earth which she converted to Vegan money when she came here. This is her first visit to the Andurian Empire. She was on her way to sing at the Valdovian Gardens, a very exclusive private resort. The resort was rather upset when she didn't arrive and I hear they were more than a little peeved when they heard that you snagged her. Someone in the embassy received an anonymous tip about her when she was marooned on Emaude Phlott, an offbeat resort moon circling Gellian Prime. Since she's been here, she's managed to absolutely delight the public with her performances, but she's also completely alienated most of your staff. Apparently, she can be a bit brusque with the help, and possibly some of the guards as well."

Most of Nell's report was irrelevant to the king. He needed to know something he could use against her in an argument. "I really don't care what the help thinks of her, I need some real dirt on her. Something I can fling at her when she gets uppity. What about this Elizabeth she keeps asking for?"

"Her personal manager's name is Elizabeth Garrett. They were travelling together when they were dumped on Emaude Phlott. Also with her was her stage manager Victor Fink, a personal body guard Bruno Bulgazzi and her personal stylists Gabriella and Tatianna."

"Have you located this Elizabeth yet?"

"No your mmm...sir. She's still at large."

"Okay, Nell. Send me a written report of what you have. You said her history started when she was in her teens. Find out why. Does she come from a crime family? Was she a witness to a crime? Is she a clone? Could she be the queen's clone? See if the problems she has with the staff might relate to some bigger problem from her past. Maybe you can find out for me exactly what ticks her off."

The king waved his hand over the desk again and it was once more a beautiful wood grain.

"How dare he?" Francesca fumed. She paced back and forth in her room as her rage grew. "He thinks he can kidnap the great Francesca Vittoria Agostina La Perla and force her into the marriage? I am not being the horse to be traded for and put on the display."

She poured herself a drink and looked into the mirror. "Well, I have a surprise for Mr. *'I'm the emperor.'* I won't be waiting here for him when he is coming for me."

She sucked down her drink and rummaged through the bar for something stronger. "No, not being here is not good enough. I should be getting the donkey here to wait for him. That would make a fine wife for him."

Her feet wobbled unsteadily below her as the bottles piled up on the table. She stopped pacing and plopped down in the soft cushioned chair. "He won't be getting it. If I leave the ass here for him, he won't know why unless I am telling him first."

She downed another glass and said, "That's it! I can't be leaving without giving him a peace of my mind before I go!"

She stood to march for the door but the room rocked around her and she fell back into the chair and passed out.

Bruno and Victor dressed as groundskeepers and positioned themselves just inside the palace atrium. They pretended to inspect plant leaves while the others went to Francesca's room.

Vincenzo entered the palace grounds with forged documents. He dressed as a dignitary and had no trouble getting past the guards. He recognized Victor and Bruno from the surveillance recordings that he had obtained from the space port. He watched them from across the atrium. They were up to something, and that probably meant that the broad was here.

He approached Bruno from behind and asked, "Where's the dame?"

Bruno spun around and asked, "Huh?"

"Don't play dumb with me," Vincenzo said, "I know how you'se been working with that two bit low life Harvey Kushkin, and I ain't letting da bunch of you mess up my plans."

Bruno looked blankly at Victor for help.

Victor just shrugged and said, "You should probably ask Harvey."

Vincenzo looked around, but didn't spot him anywhere nearby. "Where is he?"

Victor shrugged and said, "Maybe he's on his ship?"

Vincenzo nodded to his beefy associate and said, "Take me to him."

Victor shrugged again and said, "I can take you to his ship, but I don't know if he's there."

Vincenzo scowled and motioned for Victor to lead the way.

Nell knew that when the king had asked him for a written report on Francesca, he wanted it right away, like yesterday. It may not have been as complete as it could have been if it weren't rushed, but it was delivered to the king's inbox with the greatest haste and the king wasted no time opening it and reviewing it. He pressed the icon on his desk for the butler and said, "Johnny? Bring that singer to me. I'm ready to see her now."

"Right away."

The butler left his drab office and rode the elevator to the top floor. He knocked gently on her door, but she didn't answer. He rapped more forcefully and Francesca sang out sweetly, "Who is it?" then darkly lowered her tone to say, "If you are being that bully of a king, then nobody is home."

The butler scowled. He came here thinking he would simply tell her the king wanted to see her, but she didn't sound like she would go with him to see the king. He knocked again and said, "It's me. I'm here to take you to your next appointment."

Francesca held her latest bottle upside down. It was completely drained. She scowled at the empty bottle and said, "What is this next apartment being? I don't have the next apostment."

"Oh don't you remember?" he lied. "Didn't you get your itinerary? No matter. Are you decent? I'm opening the door now."

"No!" she shouted. "I'm not doing the intinnerarer...itintery...I don't have the apponstment."

She didn't sound right. He opened the door and saw the empty bottles that surrounded her. "Oh my, you don't look so good."

"What is being wrong with my looking?"

"You're wasted. I'll get help." He called the infirmary on his communicator and said, "Code White in the penthouse suite."

She waved him away saying, "Why are you being here? I'm not going anywhere with you."

"But your appointment..."

Francesca got up and stumbled forwards into his arms. "I told you I'm not going with you. I want to see the king! I am wanting to give him a piece of my mind!"

The butler sighed and said, "If you insist..."

"I do," she said.

He helped her out the door and was met in the hall by one of the nurses. "Here," he said, handing her the glass the nurse brought. "Drink this."

Roy led the way through the servant's quarters. Harvey had to see Francesca for himself before he would believe Roy's claims that she was free to come and go, especially after Harvey and Elizabeth had both seen her dragged away in custody.

The guards had grown accustomed to the two brothers passing through, but they looked suspiciously at Harvey and Elizabeth. Roy simply shrugged and pointed at them with his thumb saying, "Personal hairdresser."

The guard's expression softened some as he looked appreciatively upon Elizabeth, then asked, "So who's the dude?"

Gene snickered and said, "She's his assistant."

The guard looked surprised at first then looked over Harvey again and winked at Gene saying, "Ohhh."

They entered the elevator and after the lift doors closed, Gene laughed hysterically and Harvey smacked him hard on the back of the head. "You know I don't joke around about people's gender identities."

"Except," Elizabeth asked, "when it pertains to you?"

"That's not it," Harvey said. "I'll tell explain, I swear, but this isn't the time."

Gene was still rubbing his head, but couldn't stop laughing long enough to reply.

"You deserved that," Roy said.

The elevator doors finally opened and they went to Francesca's door. Roy knocked and said, "It's me. Let me in."

Several seconds passed by and Roy tried again, "Majesty? I have Elizabeth."

Still no answer and Elizabeth said, "Diva? Are you in there?"

Harvey wasn't waiting any more. He got down on one knee and inserted some needles that looked like dental tools and picked the lock.

Harvey went in first, but when Elizabeth entered the room, she whistled while she scanned the room. "Maybe she doesn't want to leave. I'm not sure I would want to give this up."

"Maybe so," Roy said. "But she hates the king and doesn't want to be his next wife either."

Gene was going through the empty bottles and said, "Looks like she might have had a party and not invited us."

"Oh no," Elizabeth said.

Harvey mimed drinking and asked, "Is she a...?"

"No," she replied, "not really. But when she gets really upset, she has been known to binge."

Gene found a bottle that wasn't completely empty and drained it. "The gal has real nice taste when she binges. A hell of a lot better than the fermented rocket fuel we usually get."

Harvey stood at the window looking pensively out over the garden. "I was really hoping you guys were right, but I know what I saw. How are we going to get her out of detention?"

"Wait a sec," Roy said, "Just because she's not here right now doesn't mean she's been taken into custody. I'm telling you she's free to leave on her own. Maybe she just went for a walk."

Harvey took a melodramatic look at the empties that littered two tables and asked, "How far do you think she could get in her state?"

"I don't know," Roy said, "but I'm not going into the imperial jail to search for her."

"I though you guys worshiped her!" Harvey exclaimed.

Roy and Gene looked at each other and shrugged.

Gene wagged his finger at Roy and said, "I knew we should have run the other way when he first showed up!"

Vincenzo and his thugs followed Victor and Bruno to Harvey's ship. Vincenzo's muscle men kept Bruno especially close while Victor was allowed to lead the pack.

"What is this?" Vincenzo asked when they searched the empty ship. "Where's the broad?"

"The diva?" Victor asked. "She was never with us, but Harvey was right here the last time I saw him."

Bruno nodded his head but added nothing more.

"Bah," Vincenzo growled. "If you're running a flim-flam on me, I'll float you in space. Do you read me?"

Victor nodded quietly.

"Let's get out of here," Harvey said.

He pulled the door open and found the doorway filled with two large guards. A woman's voice behind them said, "See? I told you I heard strange voices."

One of the guards pressed a button on his lapel pin and said, "Can we get a couple more guards up to the singer's apartment? Looks like we'll be escorting some guests to detention."

The guard looked at the four of them, then pointed to Harvey and said, "I'm guessing that you're the ring leader. "What's your name and what were you all doing here?"

Elizabeth stepped forward and said, "Excuse me, but I think you've got the wrong idea here. We're all friends of the diva's. You can ask her if you want, but I don't think the king would like it very much if his prize singer's friends were thrown in jail."

The guard didn't like being interrupted and squinted at her like he had a headache. "What's your name then?"

"My name is Elizabeth Garrett. I'm the diva's personal manager."

"Yeah, sure, and I'm the king's long lost brother."

The other guard stepped forward and whispered in his ear, "Wasn't there a memo that his majesty wanted us to be on the lookout for someone named Elizabeth being on the grounds?"

The first guard scowled. He didn't want to be involved in anything complicated. "Okay," he said to her. "You come with me. The rest can wait in detention."

"No!" Elizabeth said. "We're together. We're all with the diva."

The guard looked confused, so Elizabeth explained, "The singer! You understand? We're all with the singer!"

The guard still looked unimpressed, so Elizabeth continued, "You said the king was looking for me? Well they're with me, and you don't get me without them."

The guard sneered at her and said, "Follow me, and don't try nothing funny."

As they filed out of the room, Harvey asked Elizabeth, "Why would the king be looking for you? How does he even know your name?"

Elizabeth shrugged, but Roy suggested, "Remember who we're here for. I'm willing to bet that she's been whining to anybody who would listen that she needs Elizabeth for one thing or another."

Outside the elevator, the guard said, "Ya know? This don't work for me." He turned to the other guard and said, "Take them to holding. She can try convincing the king to send for them."

"Welcome," the king said as Francesca was brought in, "Come in, please have a seat."

Francesca's gait had steadied tremendously since imbibing the butler's curative cocktail.

"Francesca," the king continued, "May I call you Francesca?"

She squinted at him sideways and asked, "What is it that I am calling you?"

"Let's keep it informal," he said. "No 'Your Highness' or 'Your Majesty' here, how about simply 'King' or 'Sire'?"

"Well then, King," she replied, "You are to be calling me 'Diva' or 'Prima Donna'"

He had practiced using her name and had to retrace his arguments in his mind now. He should have used his given name, but it was too late for that now. "Diva," he said, feeling the weight of the word on his lips, "can I get you anything to drink?"

Her expression turned chilly. She wasn't going to sit here and be ridiculed by this horrid little man because she, in a moment of weakness, had drunk too much. "You know?" she said. "I am thinking that we don't have anything to be talking about. I should be going."

"No, wait!" he shouted. "Let's talk."

"Talk?" she asked. "We already talked. First you say I am the prize horse, but that wasn't worst. I found out what you really plan. I'm not the girl who just fell off the hay wagon. I am Francesca Vittoria Agostina La Perla. You cannot be locking me up and kidnapping me! I am not belonging to you!"

"I know," he admitted, "I know. My people were wrong to bring you here by force, but their intentions were good and they weren't wrong to recognize the kind of impact you would have on me."

"Bah," she replied. "They...."

A loud knock on the door interrupted her and the king barked out, "Not now."

Francesca frowned at the interruption, but turned her attention back to the king and continued, "As I was saying..."

She was interrupted again by another knock on the door. The king stormed to the door and swung it open. "Which part of 'NOT NOW' did you not understand?"

The guard bowed apologetically and said, "Your highness, Elizabeth."

The king pointed at the woman who the guard had escorted and raised his eyebrows. The guard smiled smugly and nodded his head.

"What was that?" Francesca asked.

"Diva!" Elizabeth shouted as she pushed the guard out of the way and brushed past the king to hug Francesca.

Imperial officers scurried around the detention center while Harvey sat with his hands still bound in an uncomfortable chair. It was an altogether too familiar scene for Harvey. Time seemed to be the law's number one tool. In Harvey's opinion, the only thing they did fast was to draw the wrong conclusion. When it came to actually working an investigation, it seemed like they believed time was on their side, and when booking or interrogating a suspect, they relished any opportunity to make them sweat.

Roy and Gene were left at the same desk like they were children that couldn't be separated. Roy scanned the room for a familiar face, and when he spotted one, he tried nodding to get the guards attention.

Gene laughed and asked, "Are you hoping one of them asks you out on a date?"

"No, Dufus. I'm hoping they'll recognize us as part of the staff and let us go."

One of the guards finally did recognize Roy and asked the sergeant of the guards, "Why are the bus boys in custody?"

"Who?" the sergeant replied.

"Them," the first guard said pointing to the brothers, "the midgets."

"They were in the penthouse suite with the tall guy."

"Well, they work here. I've seen them around."

The sergeant approached Roy and asked, "What were you doing in the penthouse suite?"

"We were collecting the empty bottles. They must have had one hell of a party up there."

"What about the tall guy?" the sergeant asked.

Roy shrugged and said, "We saw him with the singer earlier, but she wasn't there this time."

The sergeant took a scanner from a drawer and pointed it at Harvey. The screen displayed, "Harvey Kushkin, a.k.a. Malcolm Broadland, a.k.a. Horatio Groves. No warrants. Wanted for questioning regarding suspicion of smuggling, suspicion of dealing arms, and illicit gambling. Known associates include the Klausten fence ring; the Stonewright mob; and the Parvloovian Rebels."

The sergeant tsked and said, "Well, Mr. Kushkin. It looks like you've been a bad boy."

"Don't you mean," Harvey replied, "that it looks like I have a suspicious past? I had a troubled youth and fell in with the wrong crowd. I was in the wrong place at the wrong time. That's the old me. I'm a good guy now."

"Is that why you're here?" the sergeant asked. "Are you being a good guy?"

"Sure am," he said. "That girl I was with; Elizabeth is her name. She asked me to track down her employer who had gone missing. Her trail led us here. We were just waiting for the old gal to return to her room so we could all have a big laugh about the whole adventure when your men arrived."

"That's a very interesting story, Mr. Kushkin, but I think we'll just hold you here while we see what you've been up to lately."

"What about us?" Roy asked.

"Don't you have some work to do?" the sergeant asked. "Get out of here."

Roy overheard one of the guards confirm that Elizabeth had been taken to the king, so he and Gene went directly to the king's office. He grabbed a tray and a bowl of ice while Gene grabbed some clean towels to drape over their arms.

They knocked lightly on the door and let themselves in. They planned to remain invisible as they placed the ice bowl near the drinks, but Elizabeth shouted, "Roy!"

All attention turned to them and they joined her before the king. Roy bent low and said, "Your majesty."

"Who are these?" the king demanded.

"These creatures are mine," Francesca said dryly.

"Where's Harvey?" Elizabeth asked.

Roy shook his head and said, "Harvey's..."

"Oh God!" Elizabeth screamed. "They killed him?"

"No, no," Roy said. "They locked him up."

The king looked to the butler and asked, "Who is this Harvey person?"

The sergeant of the guards entered the room in time to hear only Harvey's name and asked, "Does the king know Mr. Kushkin?"

"No," the butler said, "The king wants to know who this Harvey is."

"He's a scoundrel," the sergeant reported. "He's wanted in several sectors for numerous crimes."

"He's wanted?" Elizabeth asked.

"He's wanted for questioning," Roy explained. "Tell the truth sergeant. He has no warrants."

The sergeant shrugged and said, "We've found no warrants yet, though his past suggests that we're bound to find one if we keep looking."

"He came here on a rescue mission," Gene said. "Why are you so intent on finding some reason to detain him?"

"Let him go!" Elizabeth demanded.

The sergeant ignored Elizabeth and she got in his face and screamed, "Let him go!!!"

He grabbed her by the arms and Francesca bellowed, "Take your hands off her!"

The sheer force of Francesca's voice shocked the poor man and he released her.

Elizabeth turned to the king and pleaded, "You must let him go. He came here on my behalf. We were worried about the diva's safety."

"Why were you so worried?" the king asked.

"Because she was abducted by imperial troops!" Elizabeth blurted out.

The king was shocked and could only ask, "She what?"

"That's right!" Elizabeth continued. "We were stranded on a resort moon until your emissary came in with troops and spirited her away. She was taken by force and drugged. Why wouldn't we worry for her safety?"

"You thought I did this?" the king asked.

Elizabeth meekly nodded her head yes. "We thought you were holding her prisoner here."

The king turned to Francesca and asked, "Is all this true?"

"It's all confused in my head," Francesca said. "The first emissary was very nice to my Elizabeth, but he wasn't being the real emissary who wasn't so nice to me, but I don't care so much so long as he gets me home to my money."

The king was confused.

"At first," Elizabeth explained, "I thought Harvey was the emissary, but I was mistaken."

"Then I met a nice man," Francesca added, "who was giving us a ride to get my money."

"But he was a gangster," Elizabeth said, "and they tricked Francesca into going with them, so I got Harvey to rescue her from the gangsters. That's when the real emissary abducted Francesca and took her on his ship. He drugged her and brought her here."

The king found this all as intriguing as it was confusing, but it wasn't what he wanted to talk to Francesca about. It wasn't what he was prepared to argue about with her.

He pointed to the sergeant and said, "Please escort all these people to the throne's antechamber and wait with them there, except the Prima Donna. Leave her here. I wish to have a private word with her."

The king watched them file out of his office then went to the sergeant and said, "Release her friend, but have someone follow him to see what he's up to."

Vincenzo returned to the palace with Bruno and Victor in time for Victor to spot Roy and Gene being led away from the king's office. Victor nudged Bruno to see if he had spotted them too.

Vincenzo saw the small gesture and asked, "Do you know those guys?"

Victor shrugged, but Vincenzo saw through his subterfuge.

"Come on," Vincenzo said. "We're following them."

Francesca had barely been reunited with Elizabeth and didn't want to be separated again so soon, but the king jerked his head to signal the butler to lead her out.

Francesca turned to the king with anger on her face.

Good, the king thought, *I have her emotionally distracted.*

Francesca sneered at him and said, "I don't know why it is that you are having to send them away."

"Nothing sinister, I assure you. I just wanted to have a private chat with you."

"Bah," she said, "You and I don't be having anything to be talking about privately."

"Oh but we do," he said. This is what he had been preparing for. He'll start off soft, and then turn hard on her. He smiled at her as he took a deep breath and sang in a sweet tenor,

"The people love you..."

Francesca tried to look disinterested in anything he had to say, but she always liked flattery and a sly smile started to curl on her lips.

The king noticed the slight curl of her lips and continued,

"...and I love you..."

The smile that almost appeared on her face morphed into a frown. She looked as if she had just eaten something bitter.

The king continued singing, punctuating each word in a descending staccato,

"But,
my
staff
seems
to
hate
your
guts."

Francesca forced a fake smile for him and replied in a soft alto,

> *"My staff loves me.*
> *Your staff means nothing."*

The king replied,

> *"Your staff is criminal."*

Fire burned in Francesca's eyes as she belted out,

> *"I think you're bluffing.*
> *My staff would do anything,*
> *If I just asked them."*

The king replied in a lilting tenor,

> *"Tell me truly*
> *Why you protect them...*
> *They're low life misfits*
> *Who do nothing for you."*

Francesca dropped the alto and screeched, "You can ask my Elizabeth, oh, but you sent her away."

She belted out in a strong soprano,

"Let my people go!"

The king wanted to talk about Francesca's issues with his staff, not hers. He lowered his voice to a clear baritone and sang,

"What did you say to make them hate you?
What did you do to make them flee?
What can I do to make them love you?
Love you as much as they love me?"

Francesca looked at the delusional man and wagged her finger while she bellowed, "Bring me back my Elizabeth! And you heard her, bring her friend Harvey too."

The king maintained a poker face and refused to tell her that he had already ordered Harvey's release.

Roy, Gene and Elizabeth were led to a large room that connected to the main atrium. It stood between an even larger auditorium that was used for public presentations and a throne room that was rarely used at all. The atrium served as a lavish display of horticulture prowess with a variety of flora collected from all corners of the empire. Water fell like raindrops from the dizzyingly high ceiling and splashed on the broad leafed jungle plants before collecting in crystal blue pools. Finding cover here was child's play and Vincenzo easily located a small alcove where he could hide with Bruno and Victor. They had a perfect view of the room where the three were taken, but a guard stationed himself outside the door.

Vincenzo pointed to the room and asked, "Is Harvey in there with them?"

Bruno and Victor both shrugged.

"Honestly," Victor said, "we just don't know where he is."

Vincenzo looked around the atrium for some way to distract the guard. "I gotta ask those pint size thieves then. They seem to always know where he is."

Victor also wanted to talk to Roy. He had no doubt that Bruno could take Vincenzo, but Vincenzo's thug would put up a fight, and win or lose, it would not go well for Bruno's already battered face. He thought that if they combined forces with Roy and Gene, Vincenzo might leave them alone, but that required getting past the guard.

"I scouted out this place earlier," Victor said, "and I know a back entrance to that room."

Vincenzo waited for Victor to lead on, but seeing no such initiative, prodded him on, "Must I invite you to lead the way?"

Victor led them to the back of the atrium and down a service stairwell. The stairwell exited to a busy hallway with waiters, maids and guards using the network of halls to cross under the palace atrium. Victor pushed out into the hallway, but Vincenzo grabbed him by the collar and pulled him back.

"Would you look at that?" Vincenzo asked.

Victor followed the line where Vincenzo pointed and saw two guards leading Francesca down the hall away from them and further away from the room with Roy, Gene and Elizabeth.

"We're following them," Vincenzo said.

The guards took Francesca to a room at the end of a hallway and pushed her through a doorway, then locked the door and left.

Vincenzo rapped his knuckles on Bruno's chest and said, "Did you see that? It'll be like taking candy from a baby."

The king walked in a dramatic circle around Francesca like an animal preparing to pounce on its prey. She tilted her head down and sneered at him through her eyebrows as she turned slowly to remain facing him.

He drew in his breath and sang,

> *"I can give you everything,*
> *You will want for nothing,*
> *But you must accept that...*
> *My*
> *Staff*
> *Is*
> *The*
> *Best."*

"Hah!" she spat back at him.

> *"My Elizabeth knows my thoughts before I do.*
> *She tends my needs when I give no clue.*
> *She fixes things when your people mess them up.*
> *As servants go, she earns the galactic cup!"*

The king nodded and sang,

> *"One girl, okay, a compromise,*
> *My staff can teach her how things work.*
> *If her background checks out, I'll let her stay."*

Francesca's irritation showed in both her face and her song. She stomped her foot and sang,

> *"You'll let her stay? You pompous jerk!*
> *Bruno is my personal guard.*
> *He protects me from men like you, you retard!*
> *And Victor is my...Victor!*
> *You control too much. You're a....a..."*

The king shrugged his shoulders and finished her line,

"A boa constrictor?"

"Arghh!" she screamed, "Now you are mocking me. Let my staff free."

"And what about this Harvey? He seems to be quite the scoundrel."

"Well," she said, "He's MY scoundrel and I am wanting him released!"

Francesca ran out of his office and slammed the door, then, unsatisfied with her first attempt, she opened it and slammed it again, then returned to the penthouse.

"Well now what?" Gene asked.

Elizabeth circled the room examining the artwork on the windowless walls. "What an odd place for them to detain us," she said. "It's certainly no jail. Just look how comfortable the furniture is."

"Yeah," Gene said as he plopped into an overstuffed chair. "It's nice and cozy. We know what they want from Francesca. They're just keeping us comfy so they don't alienate her."

"Not all of us," Roy said. "Harvey is still locked up in a real jail."

The room was suddenly quiet and felt colder.

Elizabeth hung her head as she toyed with a vase of flowers, spinning them around, but not paying particular attention to them. She sniffled slightly and blotted the moisture from her eye before it formed a tear. "If only there were some way for us to see him."

"We can," Gene said. "There's a back door that can get us down to the detention level, but what would you say to him?"

Roy perked up and said, "We're not going to say nothing. We're gonna break him out of there."

"Again?" Gene asked. "These aren't the local bumpkins this time. These are imperial troopers."

"So? What makes you think these guys are any smarter than them others?"

Gene opened his mouth but had no reply.

Elizabeth's eyes had followed the conversation back and forth, but finally settled on Roy. "Even if they aren't any smarter, they can get just as lucky, and the penalties would be much more severe here."

"True," Roy said, "but I noticed you didn't say we couldn't do it."

"We can't do it," Gene said authoritatively. "There. I said it. How are we supposed to pull something like this off without Bruno and Victor?"

Roy mulled that over a bit and said, "We're going to miss Bruno's strength. That's for sure. And Victor..."

Gene finished Roy's sentence, "We have nobody to sacrifice without Victor."

"If we're going to do this," Roy said, "I'm going to need another look at the detention center."

"I don't suppose there's any point in arguing with you." Gene said as he jumped out of his chair. "Let's go."

Elizabeth followed Roy and Gene into the hallway at the bottom of the stairs. "Are you sure one of us shouldn't have stayed behind? What if they come back for us? What if the diva talks them into letting us join them?"

"What about Harvey?" Roy asked. "Harvey put himself on the line for you, and it's up to us to spring him. I need you to focus."

Elizabeth didn't feel very focused, but she nodded her head and said, "Okay. Focus." The hallway itself was pretty bland. The floor was probably the dirtiest she had seen in the palace, but how could it be otherwise? The traffic in here was intense. The guard traffic alone was constant, and then there were the maids pushing their little carts with fresh towels and dirty laundry. The waiters whizzed back and forth, filling the hall with a confusing array of scents.

"Elizabeth?" Roy said gently, but when she didn't respond he said sharply, but not loudly, "Elizabeth!"

She snapped her attention back to him.

"Where did you go?" he asked.

"I was focusing, like you said."

"You were..."

Gene prodded him in the arm and said, "Hey Roy, look over there."

Roy looked first at his brother, then followed his arm and finger down the hallway. He squinted his eyes and asked, "Is that Victor?"

Roy put his hands to his mouth to shout something, but Gene tugged on his arm and said, "Shhh! Wait till you see who he's with."

Victor stood in front of a door looking around nervously, then Bruno came out and Roy said, "It's Bruno."

Roy tried shouting again, but Gene stopped him once more and said, "Wait for it..."

Roy didn't know what Gene was getting at until Vincenzo came out behind Bruno.

"Why, that snake," Roy hissed. "What's he doing with them?"

Somewhere behind them, Harvey called out, "Hey guys!"

Roy and Gene spun around and saw Harvey approaching with the butler just as Francesca followed Vincenzo out the door.

"Look!" Elizabeth shouted, but when they turned back, Francesca was gone and nobody else had seen her.

Roy turned back to Harvey and asked, "What are you doing down here?"

Elizabeth stared down the hallway searching for Francesca and blankly asked, "What's she doing down here?"

"They let me go," Harvey said.

Chapter 9

Elizabeth wasn't interested in exchanging pleasantries with Harvey or hearing about his exploits in their jail. She saw Francesca with the same mobster that they had seen at the resort. She immediately took off down the hallway, intent on catching the diva and rescuing her from Vincenzo. They had a significant head start on her, but they were dragging the diva behind them and Elizabeth felt confident that she should be able to catch them. She didn't know what Bruno and Victor were doing with the gangster, but she was confident that they would help her.

"Where the hell is she going?" Harvey asked as he pointed down the hall.

Roy turned to see where he was pointing, but she had already ducked around a corner and was out of sight. He looked for Elizabeth to ask if she had seen anything, but she wasn't with them anymore.

Harvey took off after her.

Roy and Gene shared a look and shrugged, then started down the hall behind Harvey.

The servants that filled the hall were strangely quiet as Elizabeth passed by them. Some stood in small groups whispering amongst themselves, while others were getting up off the floor as if they had been knocked down. Elizabeth stepped up her pace. If those monsters were willing to knock over strangers, there's no telling what they would do to Francesca.

The hall opened up into the atrium. She scanned the room looking for the diva. The tall tropical trees that filled the space obscured her view, but that was not enough to make them impossible to follow. She only had to follow the trail of servants climbing back to their feet to know which way they had gone. The trail led across the glass domed room towards the main entrance. She thought it was odd they would go through the most heavily guarded point of entry.

The king stood in his office with his mouth slightly ajar, stunned by Francesca's exit. He won that round, at least, he thought he had. He flustered her and out sang her and even finished her line when she faltered, yet she ran out of the office and slammed the door leaving him feeling like he had lost. He planned the whole match so carefully, yet she stole his victory from him.

A scowl crossed his face as he left his office and headed to the antechamber where he had his guards stash her friends.

"Follow me," he said to a couple guards on the way, "and when we get there, I want you to arrest all of them and throw them in the dungeon!"

"But sire, we don't have a dungeon."

"Stop telling me we don't have a dungeon," he bellowed. "Find the deepest, darkest corner of the prison and BUILD ME A DUNGEON! And get that pirate friend of theirs back in custody!"

Vincenzo led Francesca halfway through the atrium, then through a side exit that dumped them into some more back hallways and out of the palace. As they ran through the atrium and the halls, the maids and waiters fell to their knees, but the guards sprang to their communicators. Bruno and Victor didn't want to follow Vincenzo, but Francesca was their meal ticket and Elizabeth would kill them if they let him have her.

Vincenzo exited through the servant's entrance and ordinary people in the gardens fell to their knees and cried out, "Your Majesty!"

Francesca stopped to say something to them, but Vincenzo grabbed her arm and pulled her forward. He didn't know what was going on with the people, but he had to reach his ship before things got any stranger.

"Stop that!" someone in the crowd yelled.

"He's hurting her!" another yelled.

The people loitering in the garden quickly turned into an angry mob.

"Oh shit," Vincenzo muttered. "Pick up those feet, sister. We gotta get you out of here."

The king burst angrily into the antechamber followed by the two guards that had trailed him from his office plus the one standing guard in front. None of the guards knew what was going on in the king's head, but it wouldn't be the first time that he had lost his temper. They didn't need to know why he was upset; they only needed to follow his orders.

The king spun around expecting to find Francesca's friends cowering in a corner somewhere. "You can't hide from me!" he growled. "Come out and show yourselves!"

There weren't many places to hide here. The auditorium had rows and rows of seats to hide between and the throne room had pillars and alcoves to hide in, but this room was plain and simple by comparison. He turned to the guards and spit out, "Find them!"

The guards weren't entirely sure who they were searching for, but figured if they found anyone hiding, it would be 'them'.

The search didn't last long. They quickly followed the contours of the walls and checked between the seats and under the tables. "There's nobody here, sire."

Before the king could even ask, the guard that had stood in front volunteered, "Nobody came in or out of the front door. They must have used the servants' entrance in the back."

Harvey had nearly caught Elizabeth when she ducked out of the atrium and a pack of guards descended upon him. Roy and Gene tried ducking behind a large palm tree, but two more guards followed them there.

The butler was slower to follow them and only rejoined them after they were already in custody. "What is going on here? The king has already ordered their release. I was just taking Mr. Kushkin to join the king."

The guard holding Harvey said, "The king ordered them back into custody."

One of the other guards said, "I think his exact words were for us to build a dungeon and throw them in."

The butler shook his head and said, "I'll go speak with him."

Two of Vincenzo's goons had been guarding the ship at the base of the gangway and saw him running towards them. One of them yelled up into the ship, "Hey, the boss is coming, and he looks like he's being chased. Maybe you should warm up the engines and get ready to take us out of here."

Vincenzo was indeed being chased, but not by the king or even the king's guards. At the head of the group was Elizabeth followed by a mob that had fallen in behind her just because they didn't like the way Vincenzo had handled Francesca. Others joined the mob just because they saw them chasing some guy who was running with Francesca.

The two goons separated from each other, allowing entrance to the gangway.

Vincenzo pushed Francesca onto the ramp, but grabbed Bruno's and Victor's shirts and held them back. "This is the end of the line for you boys."

"I'm going with the diva," Bruno said. "I'm her personal body guard."

Vincenzo sneered at him and replied, "Well, you may consider yourself a failure in that regard."

The two goons, who were Bruno's equal in size and strength, stepped between him and Vincenzo, then backed up the ramp as it was being raised.

The king looked at the guard who had been left to watch the antechamber and yelled, "You knew there was a back door, and you didn't have someone guarding it?"

The guard quaked under the king's anger and said, "Sire, I don't give orders, I just follow them."

"Your orders were just to guard them?"

The poor guard nodded his head.

The king poked him in the chest and asked, "Then why didn't you guard them from the INSIDE?"

The other guards tried to quietly step back away from the scorching their brother was receiving, but the king turned to them and growled, "Tell your sergeant to distribute pictures of that woman Elizabeth. I want everyone on high alert. Find her! Tell him to cancel all leaves. Search the grounds and search the spaceport. I don't want them getting away!"

"Yes sire," the guard said meekly as he reached for his communicator.

The guard from the door whispered to his friends, "Sheesh. My exact orders were to guard the door."

"You should have done something," Victor said as he watched Vincenzo's ship lift up and disappear out of sight.

"What?" Bruno asked. "Look at me. I'm still beat up from my prize fighting. Those guys were both as big as me and there were two of them. Were you going to take one of them on while I fought the other one?"

Victor hung his head and said, "No. I know you're right, but the physical stuff is your job. I just thought you would go all commando on them."

"Me too," Bruno admitted. "I wish it were more like the movies where I could run through a hail of bullets and never get hit."

"Except," Victor added, "for a flesh wound to make it even more dramatic when you kick their ass single handed."

Silence fell between the two of them.

"What now?" Bruno asked.

Victor shrugged and said, "I guess we can wait in Harvey's ship."

Bruno spotted the mob of people spilling out onto the tarmac and said, "I don't know what that is all about, but I think we better hurry."

The king left the antechamber and was immediately surrounded by an excited crowd of palace staff workers yelling, "The Queen! The Queen!" The crowd pointed in the general direction of the spaceport. The king watched his guards cut through the crowd ignoring the people. He closed his eyes and shook his head wondering what had become of the empire's proud military.

The butler swooped in and directed a few guards to make a space for the king. "I just released Mr. Kushkin from detention, per your instructions, and before I could get him to you, he was taken into custody again. They said you wanted to throw him in a dungeon."

"I changed my mind," the king said. "I can do that you know. I can do it as often as I want."

The butler raised an eyebrow and said, "I suppose, but can you tell me why?"

"I don't need a reason," the king barked. "I just felt like it!"

"Is it the woman?"

The king just set his jaw and refused to respond.

"Okay," the butler said. "It's the woman, but I thought things were going along so well between you two."

"What?" the king barked. "With that viper? She's the most unreasonable woman in the empire. I don't know what you were thinking when you brought her to me."

The crowd grew thicker and the guards had to muscle a path through the chanting throng.

"What is wrong with these people?" the king growled. "Get them out of the way!"

"We're trying," the butler replied.

"What is going on?" the king asked. "Why do they keep chanting 'The Queen'?"

"Sire," the butler said, "this has been brewing for quite some time."

The king looked at the butler like he had lost his mind. "You think the people have been shouting for the Queen and pointing to the space port before?"

"No, sire, but the people miss their queen and they miss their Vegan friends. The economy has been in a shambles and they all want you to fix it."

The king's expression turned dour. He marched back in the direction of his office, forcing the guards to change direction and plow a new path for him. He scowled as he said, "Oh. The Vegans again. I suppose you blame me for that?"

"No," the butler said, "I know what happened and I know she forced your hand, but your people only know that it has become harder to put food on their tables. Jobs have been lost and some can't feed their children regularly. In places where things are the worst, black markets have swooped in and taken advantage of the peoples plight putting them even further in debt and at risk."

"What would you have your king do? The Vegans declared themselves apart from the empire, not I, yet you tell me that the people blame me for this?"

"The Vegans only protested against you for imprisoning her."

The king's pace quickened as his temper worsened. "She wanted to divorce me! I'm the king of all Anduria! I'm the emperor for God's sake and she said she was leaving me! I would have closed the borders even if the Vegans had not declared their independence."

"Free her then! Allow things to drift back to normal."

The king stopped and looked his butler in the eye. "I cannot do that. You know me better than anyone and you are perfectly aware of what happened to me when she left."

"Yes," the butler replied. "I know exactly what you were like during those dark days. I know just how depressed you were and I even feared for your safety. It was almost like the time when we were children and you romanticized about going off to war, but your father forbade it."

"And you want me to return to that state? How will that be good for the empire?"

The king started walking again, but the butler stepped squarely in front of him and said, "Think back. Why are you no longer like that? What has changed in your life?"

The king nearly crashed into his old friend. "You know I could have you imprisoned for blocking me like this."

"I know. I've seen you do it before, but never to someone who was like a brother to you."

The king's stern face softened. "You are like a brother, and your point is a good one. Everything changed the moment she got here, did it not?"

The butler smiled broadly and clapped the king on the shoulder. "It most certainly did."

"Very well, then. Release the queen. Set things in motion to make this right and make certain the Vegans know that it was my doing."

Elizabeth started out following the trail of servants through the atrium and out the side exit into the servants' hallway. The faster she went, the more the staff did not look like they had been knocked down; they looked more like they had been kneeling and bowing.

She had no explanation for the strange behavior and turned to ask Harvey, but he wasn't behind her. She had no time to stand around and ponder it, so she continued her chase and raced to catch the diva and her captors. The trail had led through the garden courtyard and out to the space port. It grew harder to follow them as the number of people dwindled. By the time she ran out onto the tarmac and spotted Bruno and Victor running through the parked ships, she was leading the crazed mob, except she didn't know they were there.

The crowd no longer saw the queen and eventually scattered across the tarmac. Many of them pointed to the ship that lifted off, correctly assuming that she was on it.

Elizabeth tried catching Bruno and Victor, but she was already out of breath and they were too fast for her. She tried yelling, but her yell was barely more than a heavy breath. They never heard her, but they too were running out of breath and slowing down. She followed them and finally caught them when they were bent over and breathing heavily at the foot of Harvey's ship.

"Where's the diva?" she gasped between breaths.

Victor was hopelessly winded, but Bruno was able to respond, "He took her."

"Who?" she asked. "The mobster?"

Victor nodded his head up and down.

Elizabeth ran up the gangplank while yelling, "You know how to fly this, don't you Victor?"

Victor followed her up the ramp saying, "Me? No. I mean maybe, but..."

"What about the sensors?" she asked interrupting him.

"Not a chance," he said. "I seen how he tracked the ice chunks in those rings, but I don't have a clue how it all worked."

Elizabeth looked pleadingly at Bruno, but he just put up his hands and said, "Don't look at me!"

"Arrrgh!" she screamed as she ran back down the ramp. "Now we have to get Harvey back, and quick, before they get too far away."

Bruno and Victor just shrugged their shoulders and followed.

The butler worked his way through the servants' halls to the queen's room and knocked on the door. When nobody answered, he knocked again and said, "Your Majesty?"

"She's not there," a maid volunteered.

"What do you mean? Where did she go?"

The maid pointed down the hall and said, "They went that way, but I don't know where they went after that."

A pair of maids joined them and said, "I heard that they went through the atrium and back into the servants' bay."

The butler's first reaction was to run down the hall, but he stopped himself to ask, "They? Who was she with?"

The first maid shrugged and said, "She was with some man."

"Three of them," the other maid said, "two big guys and a little one."

"Two big and one small?" the butler asked. "Are you sure it wasn't two little guys and one big one?"

"No," the first maid said, "She got it right. Two big guys and a little one."

"Well now that you mention it," the second maid said, "it might have been two little and one big."

The butler bounced his eyes back and forth between the two maids not sure what he was looking for anymore. He clicked his communicator and called the detention center.

A pleasant woman's voice answered, "Detention dispatch."

"Do we have that Harvey character back in custody yet?"

"No sir."

The butler frowned and asked, "How about the two midgets that worked here?"

"No again," she said, "and about those two, we can't find any records that they were actually employed here."

The butler grimaced and muttered, "Just great..."

He went back to the queen's room and tried the door. It was unlocked, so he pushed it open and searched. She wasn't there, but he wasn't going to take any chances, especially in light of the contradictory witness accounts.

The king went up to the penthouse suites and knocked on Francesca's door. He sang in a sweet tenor,

"Francesca darling..."

She was almost done fuming in her room until she heard his voice and screeched back, "Don't you be darlinging me. I am not being your darling."
At least she was listening to him. He tried again,

"Francesca darling..."

She didn't rebuff him this time so he continued,

"Please let me in
so
I
may
explain."

"Bah," she said, "How will you explain that it is your fault I can't get my money? You go fix things so I can have my money back."
He smiled. She was really talking to him now.

"I will do as you ask."

"And get me my Elizabeth back!"

"As you wish."

"And my Victor and my Bruno and those funny little guys that treat me good."

"As you wish.
But there's a catch..."

"What is this catch being? There's no catch. You fix what you broke. No catches."

The king dropped down into a baritone and sang,

> *"I can do*
> *As you request*
> *If at dinner*
> *You'll be my guest."*

"What?" she yelled. "You do this to me and now you want me to be going to the dinner with you?"

He pulled a deep breath then started in the same baritone but swooped down into a deep bass,

> *"That's the...*
> *catch."*

Francesca was surprised by her feelings. This man was manipulating the situation and she should be absolutely furious, but he was willing to negotiate with her to fix everything that he broke if she went to dinner with him. She was flattered beyond the fury she felt and sang,

> *"If you do as I request,*
> *I'll be your dinner guest."*

The king sprinted to his office and called for his secretary. "I wish to make an announcement. Share this with all the media. Effective immediately, the embargo on Vega is lifted. All traffic and all shipments and any other means of transportation to or from Vega are to be resumed at once. All fines and late fees resulting from the embargo are suspended as of this very minute."

His secretary stood slack jawed, just inside the door to his office.

"Well?" the king barked. "Which part of immediately did you not understand?"

"At once sire."

Elizabeth didn't know why Harvey hadn't followed her. They could have been in the air already if he had. She ran directly through the front entrance of the atrium hoping that maybe he would still be where she left him outside the room where she saw the gangster holding Francesca.

She ran through the atrium and into the hallway, but skidded to a stop when she saw one of the king's guards stationed outside the door. She ducked behind a potted hedge that was trimmed into a tall cylinder, only to have Bruno and Victor crash into her.

"Hey there!" a guard shouted. "Watch it!"

"Sorry," Elizabeth said, managing to look at least somewhat innocent. Victor, on the other hand, looked guilty of anything and everything.

"Wait a second," the guard said, giving them a second look. "You aren't the girl the king wants apprehended are you?"

"Of course not," she replied, but Victor looked even more guilty.

"Oh yeah?" the guard asked. "Maybe you should come with me."

Bruno bowed his head to Elizabeth and said, "Sorry for bumping into you, ma'am."

"All of you," the guard said pointing to Bruno and Victor.

Bruno shrugged his shoulders and said, "It was worth a shot."

Vincenzo believed that he had gotten away cleanly; he grabbed the singer before she could upset his plans and ruin his fortune, and nobody was on his tail as his ship sailed out of the reach of the imperial guard. He couldn't relax yet, though, he had to know for sure, so he turned on the view-screen and tuned to a news channel.

"...is over. In a stunning move, the emperor has released the queen and declared the conflict with Vega to be resolved. Vegans all over Anduria are already contacting their embassies to submit petitions to regain title over their lost properties..."

Vincenzo stood up and numbly dropped his drink on the floor. "NOOOOOOOO!"

"...Andurian authorities have already issued statements that they will rescind all late charges and forgive all debts resulting from the embargo. Unconfirmed reports have suggested that many Vegan owned properties have been swooped up by the Stonewright mob. No word has been issued regarding the status of these transactions, but the bureau of major crimes is actively investigating all such claims..."

Vincenzo fell back into his chair. He put the family's entire fortune into this adventure. Every purchase he made was through legitimate channels and he convinced himself that he was turning the family holdings into an honest enterprise. He never considered the coercion that he used to force purchases through as illegal.

Elizabeth was taken to the detention center along with Bruno and Victor.

"Welcome to the party," Harvey said as Elizabeth was guided into the cell next to his.

"Hey Liz," Roy said sadly.

Elizabeth screwed her face into a scowl and yelled, "Why didn't you follow me?"

Harvey looked around, but there was nobody else that she could be yelling at. He looked around again and said, "What difference would it have made, Sweetheart? We all ended up in here anyway!"

"We wouldn't be here," she yelled back, "if you had followed me! We'd be up there chasing Francesca in your ship!"

Harvey looked for support from the others, but even Roy and Gene sided with Elizabeth. "Listen sister, I did follow you, but the guards jumped me as soon as I entered that stupid hot house."

"He means the atrium," Roy explained.

"Whatever," Harvey barked. "And I'll tell you another thing, we might not be in this mess if you hadn't run off on your own without even consulting us. We could have made a plan instead of you taking off like some kind of lone cowboy."

Gene saw his point and nodded his head.

"They had the diva!" she cried back. "They were dragging her away! I had to follow them!"

"Who had the old bat?" Harvey asked. "I never saw her. I only saw these two goons come out of that room with the Gangster. By the way, how did the two of you get away from him?"

Victor opened his mouth to answer, but Elizabeth interrupted, "Just because you didn't see Francesca, doesn't mean she wasn't there!"

"Well it does in MY book," Harvey yelled back. "You might have hallucinated the whole damned thing!"

Victor tried speaking again, but Elizabeth yelled, "I what? ARRGGGHHH! You're the most horrid man I have ever known!"

"Hmmmph," Harvey replied. "Somehow I doubt you've met very many horrid men."

Roy flashed a strange look at Harvey, and Harvey meekly said, "Well, it sounded different in my head."

Elizabeth turned to run away, but the cell was only eight feet by eight feet and she had nowhere to go.

Victor finally got to say, "It's true. Vincenzo has Francesca. We tried staying with him so we could keep an eye on her..."

"But," Bruno added, "he cut us loose when he took her on his ship. Elizabeth wanted us to follow him in your ship..."

"But," Victor said, "we didn't have a pilot."

Harvey looked at Elizabeth to apologize, but she kept her back to him and he was pretty certain she wouldn't listen to him anyway.

The butler entered the detention center and saw everyone gathered in the jail cells. "Does nobody in here keep informed anymore? Release those prisoners and bring them with me. The king wants to see them."

The cells were opened and the butler counted six heads and said, "Please follow me." He pointed to two guards and said, "You two follow in the back and make sure we don't lose anyone."

He led them through the hallways and up the lift to the king's office. Elizabeth made a point of walking as far away from Harvey as she could.

The butler opened the door to the king's office and said, "Enter, please."

Elizabeth stepped into the doorway and froze. Her mouth fell open. She couldn't move.

"What is this?" Francesca asked. "Why is it you are looking so funny at me?"

"This is impossible!" Elizabeth cried. "We saw him take you away!"

"Uhuh," Harvey said. "It's just like I said before, hallucinations."

Victor recognized Francesca's voice and pushed past Elizabeth and said, "No, Elizabeth is right. I saw her too. This is impossible."

More than the Stonewright fortune was on the line. If this gamble failed, Vincenzo's life would be forfeit, even to his own family. He sent a note to the imperial palace. He addressed it to the king and kept it short and sweet:

> *"I have your precious singer. If you want to see her alive again, you will deposit ten billion Andurian credits into an Ulvarian bank account. Gather the credits. I'll contact you again with the account number."*

Vincenzo looked smugly at the communicator, then turned to the hold, but didn't see what the fuss was about. She certainly was no raving beauty. From all accounts, she was a very difficult woman to deal with. The empire had weathered enough difficult tantrums between the king and queen. Why would the king want more from this woman?

Asleep, as she was now, he saw no threat in her and wondered what she was really like. She made no effort to escape as he led her to the ship. He'd heard that she was a real ball buster, but she was more of a sheep in his custody.

He returned to the cockpit and checked the screen for a response, but there was none. Too soon, he reminded himself, but the stakes were too high for him to relax.

How do regular people survive? He thought that turning the family fortune into a legitimate enterprise would make life better for everyone, but it wasn't working out so well right now, especially for him. How do straight people make a fortune without skirting the law? Or are all rich people really crooks that haven't been caught?

Vincenzo poured himself a bourbon and stared out through the viewfinder at the stars, but still with one eye on the communicator waiting for a returned message.

A messenger entered the king's office and whispered in the butler's ear. The butler snapped his fingers and a slip of paper was placed in his hand. He read the note, then glanced over at Francesca and re-read the note.

"What's that?" the king asked.

"It's a ransom demand," the butler replied.

"Ransom?" the king asked. "Ransom for what?"

The butler glanced at Francesca, then back to the king and said, "For her."

"But she's not missing," the king said, stating the obvious.

The butler and the messenger went next door to the communications center with everyone else following behind him. He sat down at a message console and typed a response,

> *"Your demand has been received. We obviously need some sort of proof that you have what you say you have before we can treat this as a credible threat."*

Vincenzo was quick to respond,

> *"She's missing, ain't she? How much proof do you need? Here's a picture of her sleeping. Whether she ever wakes up or not is up to you."*

An attached picture showed the back of his hostage's head, sleeping on a cot.

Francesca burst out laughing. "That poor woman must be looking like me. He thinks he is having me for his hostage, but no. I am being here."

"But we saw him," Elizabeth said. "We saw him take you, er, her away. It was you. I was sure of it. No wonder he mistook her for you."

"Well," Francesca said, "it wasn't me. You should be knowing me well enough to know that it wasn't me."

"When did you see this?" the butler asked.

Elizabeth shrugged, but Harvey said, "It was when you captured us again."

The butler looked to the operator at the next console and said, "Find the security recordings of the atrium from a couple hours ago. She must be on them."

"Why bother?" Francesca asked. "She's not me. I'm fine. Just tell him he is having the wrong person."

"We can't do that," the butler said, unable to hide the concern in his voice.

"Why not?" Francesca continued. "She is nobody. He'll let her go."

"You don't know that," the butler replied.

"Let's go," Elizabeth said. "Let's go to the penthouse and let them deal with this poor woman."

"Got it!" the operator exclaimed.

Everyone crowded around the monitor and the king opened his mouth to say her name, but it was Francesca who exclaimed, "Valentina!"

"Valentina?" Elizabeth asked.

"Valentina," the king growled.

Harvey's mouth fell open while Victor slowly shook his head in disbelief and said, "She looks just like you, Diva."

The king placed a hand on the butler's shoulder and said, "Tell him he has the wrong person and there will be no ransom."

The butler looked up to his friend and said, "But, she's..."

"She's the wrong person," the king repeated. "Francesca is here with us."

"Who is Valentina?" Elizabeth asked.

"She's my sister," Francesca replied, "my twin sister."

"She's a woman who used to live here," the king said, "but she wanted to leave, and now she has left."

Francesca put a finger squarely in the center of the king's chest and said, "Get her back."

Elizabeth's eyes opened wide as she exclaimed, "Francesca's sister is the queen?"

Roy nodded his head and said, "Yes, and she's the most wonderful person in the entire empire."

"So?" the king asked. "People liked her, but she didn't want to be here anymore. I gave her the good life, but she wanted to leave all this for something else."

"You mean," Roy corrected him, "that you wanted to keep her here against her will, but she wanted to leave you."

"Who is this small person?" the king asked, "and why isn't he in my dungeon?"

Francesca stepped in front of Roy and said, "You don't be touching my little man. You pay the mob person and get my Valentina back!"

Everyone looked to the king for a response, but he just growled and returned to his office.

"What is that meaning?" Francesca asked. "Why does he walk out of here like that?"

"I don't think it means that he is helping you," Roy volunteered.

"Can you blame him?" the butler asked. "First she broke his heart, then his whole empire fell apart, and finally, you showed up."

"What does that mean?" Elizabeth asked. "What does the diva being here have to do with her sister being kidnapped?"

Roy didn't want to answer and looked down at his toes while he said, "Some people here think that Francesca is going to replace her sister and then the king would fix the rift with Vega."

"What?" Elizabeth exclaimed. "That's preposterous! Francesca hates him. Tell him, Diva."

The butler wasn't concerned with their personal squabbling. His priorities were with the king. He didn't wait for Francesca's answer and didn't even bother to excuse himself. He just stormed out of the room after his friend.

"I tell you something," Francesca said. "That man; their king, and I am meaning *their* king because he is being no king of mine, is an impossible man. He's rude and he thinks only of himself. I tell him what it is I am needing and he only hears what it is meaning to him. First he sticks me in a room on the second floor and it's like he is not knowing the insult that was on me! I can't be with a man like that. Sure, he's rich and not so bad to be looking at, and he sings pretty okay, but I am needing more from a man. My man has to have the backbone. I need him to be strong. When I tell him that I am needing him to go save my sister, it is because I need him to go do it and to not be thinking only of himself. Were you seeing the look he was making on his face when he sees the video of my sister being kidnapped? He makes the little smile. That's what he did. He smiled because she was gone. One day that could be me that is on the video. Do you think I am wanting a man who smiles when I am being kidnapped? No sir. Not Francesca Vittoria Agostina La Perla. I need the man who is doing the doting on me and knows when is the time to go the extra distance. I need..."

The conversation around the room stopped as Francesca went on and on about a man she said she didn't like.

"Okay, Diva," Elizabeth interrupted. "I think you made your point. You said you don't like him."

Francesca furled her eyebrows and said, "Yes. That is what I was saying. He just makes me so angry, I could..."

"Well," Elizabeth interrupted her again, "that just leaves us to figure out what we do next."

A burley soldier entered the room with two guards in tow. Harvey recognized him from the great twisted nose on his face and the cauliflower right ear. He walked up to Harvey swinging a pair of hand cuffs around his finger and shrugged his shoulders.

"What?" Harvey asked. "Again?"

"'Fraid so," the soldier replied. He placed Harvey's hands behind his back and shackled them together.

Roy and Gene tried to quietly back out of the room, but the other two guards were quick to take them by the arm and say, "You too. Come with us."

The three were led back to the detention center.

Harvey tried to laugh it off. "I hope you still have some of those cinnamon croissants. I liked those, and I want plenty of that sugar cream to dip them in."

"I like them too," the guard said, "but I'm afraid that one of your miniscule waifs here absconded with the last of them when we released you last time.

Gene forged to the front of the group and quickly changed the subject. "I bet you guys are getting real tired of the paperwork every time you have to book us in then let us go."

"Tell me about it," the guard said. "Just be glad we don't have a dungeon. That's what the king keeps requesting for you, but you'll have to settle for the hospitality of our little old detention cells."

"Maybe," Roy suggested, "you should hold off on the paperwork until you know we'll at least stay with you long enough for the ink to dry."

Harvey watched Gene a little closer, wondering if he still had one of those croissants in his pockets.

Elizabeth shuddered as she watched the guards take Harvey away. If the king actually refused to pay the ransom, Harvey would have been her first choice to rescue the queen.

Francesca still stared at the monitor watching the replay of her sister's abduction.

Elizabeth wrapped her arms around Francesca and said, "The king won't really abandon your sister. He must be planning a rescue."

Francesca glanced over at the operator who was watching the monitors and asked, "Is that true? Will the king really help my sister?"

The operator looked away from the two women, unable to tell them what they wanted to hear.

Elizabeth frowned and asked, "Now what?"

Francesca started to cry and Bruno said, "Don't cry Diva, you still have us."

Elizabeth wiped Francesca's tears and said, "We have each other, but none of us can fly Harvey's ship."

Victor shrugged and said, "Then we have to go get him."

"Be serious," Elizabeth said. "He's in the imperial detention center. Are we supposed to just waltz in there and escort him out?"

"They're probably getting used to it by now," Victor replied with half a smile.

"How can you make jokes?" she cried back. "They'll probably put all of us in the cell next to him!"

The operator turned his head and quietly said, "They don't know that the queen has been kidnapped yet."

"What was that?" Francesca asked.

The operator raised his voice slightly and said, "The king, the butler, and your three friends are the only people outside of this room that know the queen has been taken."

Elizabeth released Francesca and sat down next to the operator. He was young for a guard, but he had an honest face and a friendly expression. "Would they be sympathetic if we told them we were going to rescue the queen?"

"That's not what I'm saying," he replied.

"What are you suggesting?" Elizabeth asked.

"I'm not suggesting anything. That would be treason, but if the queen went down to the detention center and demanded that they release your friends, she might be successful."

"How is that supposed to help us?" Victor growled. "The queen is missing you moron."

The operator looked coldly at Victor. He didn't like being called names and he didn't like being forced to betray his king. He glanced over to Francesca then back at Victor, but Victor still didn't understand. He stared deeply into Elizabeth's eyes, then glanced at Francesca again, then back to Elizabeth.

Elizabeth sucked in her breath and said, "Do you think they would mistake Francesca for the queen?"

The operator looked back at his monitors and shook his head saying, "You didn't hear it from me."

"Why?" Francesca asked. "Why would you help us?"

The operator shrugged and said, "I don't know what you are talking about. I didn't do anything, but I do love the queen and would do almost anything for her, if she were here."

Chapter 10

T he butler entered the king's office and found him pacing back and forth between the windows and his desk. The king glanced over at his friend, but chose to continue pacing and ignore him.

The butler walked around the desk and sat on the edge, content to let his friend walk off a few more laps before asking, "Do you really plan to let them kill the queen?"

He continued pacing while he replied, "They wouldn't dare."

"They might dare if they believe she's the singer and not the Queen. Are you really going to take that chance?"

"Why not? She embarrassed me in front of the whole empire. I am the laughing stock on hundreds of planets. I hate her."

The butler shook his head and softly said, "You loved her once."

The king finally stopped pacing and barked, "I wet my bed once upon a time too, but I have no plans to take that up again!"

"Nobody said you have to take her back. Just rescue her. The people love her and they'll love you for saving her."

"What do I care if they love me?" The king resumed his pacing and added, "Besides, they'll never love me. It's far too late for that."

The butler sighed and asked, "But are you ready for them to hate you?"

"They already do. So what?"

"The Vegans have practically seceded from the empire already, and you've done nothing to prevent it."

The king stopped pacing and growled, "I don't think I like your tone."

"You don't like my tone?" the butler growled back. "What do you think would happen to your reign if the queen is killed and your subjects, who already hate you, learn that you did nothing to save her?"

The king balled up his fists and spat, "You're excused. Get out of here."

The butler left the room with his fists balled up as tightly as the king's, but before he closed the door behind him, he asked, "Have you considered that your affection for her sister might somehow stem from your love for the queen? Speaking of Francesca, are you prepared to have her hate you if you let her sister die?"

The king glared at the butler until he left and closed the door behind him.

Vincenzo barely breathed as he waited anxiously for a new message. One of his henchmen brought him a brandy, which he accepted, but never took his eyes off the communication monitor. He took a sip then grit his teeth and threw the glass and the remainders of the brandy at the lift.

"Sorry boss," the henchman said, "but you looked agitated. You want me to get you something stronger?"

"Why haven't they responded?" he asked.

The henchmen didn't know what to say. He was there to lift heavy things and break unwanted things. He never offered advice and was never asked for any.

Vincenzo patted his man on the shoulder and said, "Sorry. I just don't know how to convince them I'm serious."

"You want me to send them one of her fingers? That works sometimes."

Vincenzo's mother always said he was soft. The repulsion he felt from his man's offer proved that she was right. He fought to prevent his gut reaction from showing on his face and said, "Not yet, let's give them some more time before we do that."

"Okay boss. You're the boss." On his way out, he stopped to pick up the pieces of the broken glass and added, "You think maybe they don't want her back?"

"After all the effort they went through to get her?"

The henchmen pressed the button for the elevator, still holding a pile of broken glass in his palm and said, "My mama always told me, 'Be careful what you wish for, you may get it.'"

Vincenzo waited for more wisdom from his man's mother, but getting none, he prodded the man, "What does that mean?"

"I dunno, it's just what my mama used to say in times like this. If they don't want her back, maybe there's a reason."

Vincenzo pointed to the monitor on the wall with the live image of the queen sleeping. "Look at her. Do you see anything wrong with her?"

"I don't see nothing," he replied, "and I wish I didn't say nothing too. I'm just gonna keep my mouth shut from now on."

"Bullshit!" Vincenzo barked. "I've heard you guys talking before. You guys got plenty to say amongst yourselves, but you don't think you can share it with me?"

"I gots to get rid of this glass."

"Tell me!" Vincenzo shouted. "What do you guys talk about when I'm not in the room? What do you say about her? What do *THEY* say about her?"

The henchmen paused the lift and said, "They say she's a royal bitch. Ain't none of them that likes her. That's what they say. Can I go now?"

"Yeah, go on. Get outa here."

"This is the craziest thing you ever dreamed up," Francesca said.

Bruno's eyes glanced thoughtfully up and to the left as he furrowed his eyebrows and replied, "Not really; it's just that you aren't usually asked to participate in Victor's crazy schemes."

"My schemes?" Victor objected.

Bruno shrugged and said, "You're the brains, ain't ya?"

Elizabeth led them down a hallway towards the lift to Francesca's room and stopped a maid to ask, "Can you tell me where the queen's room is?"

The maid looked suspiciously at Elizabeth and asked, "Why don't you just ask her?"

"Oh," Elizabeth replied, "she's not...I mean, the queen is not feeling herself and I'm just trying to get her back to her room for some rest."

The maid didn't look convinced, but she agreed. "Follow me."

She didn't lead them to the penthouse, but instead took them through some halls to the servant's quarters and into a rather pedestrian room.

It was Elizabeth's turn, now, to look at the maid suspiciously. "Is this it? The queen doesn't live on the top floor?"

"No ma'am," the maid replied. She stared directly at Francesca and slowly shook her head in near disbelief. "It's uncanny. I heard about this one, but this be the first time I ever laid eyes on her. The queen didn't like the penthouse; she lived on the 2nd floor so she could be closer to the people."

Francesca rolled her eyes and said, "That is sounding like my sister. She was always wanting to be loved by everybody."

"I loved her," the maid said. She opened the door and examined Francesca again, asking, "Sister? Really? You sure do look like her, but you don't sound nothing like her, and from what I hears, you couldn't be more different."

"My sister hated my being famous," Francesca said. "The more well-known I was becoming, the more harder she tried being more like normal people. She really hated it when she was being confused for me."

"Is that why you never talk about her?" Elizabeth asked. "Because you two don't get along?"

"No," Francesca replied. "I love my sister, but I made her the promise to be keeping her a secret to protect her privacy. That's why all of this is being such a surprise. Being the queen is hardly being the normal life."

A lull in the conversation gave everybody a chance to digest what was said. Elizabeth walked to the center of the small room and said, "Well, if she wanted to be normal, this room was a success. Where's the closet? Let's find something for Francesca to wear."

"Begging your pardon," the maid said, "But don't she have a closet full of dresses?"

"Yes," Francesca said dryly, "but these schemers are thinking that I should be dressing more like my sister."

"Why would you want to do that?" the maid asked. "From what I hears, you got way better gowns than the queen."

Elizabeth glanced at Victor who only returned a blank expression and shrugged, then she said, "The queen has been kidnapped and we intend to rescue her, but we need to fool the guards into letting a friend of ours go."

"Kidnapped?" the maid asked. "Won't the king rescue her?" The maid paused only briefly before saying, "No, I guess he wouldn't."

"And," Francesca finished Elizabeth's statement, "they are thinking that if I looked like the queen, I could simply march right into the detention center and do the asking to release him."

"Aye," the maid replied. "That would work, but you won't find none o' that in this closet. Let me take you to the 2nd floor."

Vincenzo opened the door to the queen's cabin. Her body rocked slightly as she breathed, but she still faced the wall, hiding her face from him. He wanted to ask her why they didn't seem too excited to get her back, but he didn't want to disturb her sleep.

His henchmen came up behind him and asked, "Boss?"

"Shhh," he whispered. "She's sleeping."

His man pointed to the lift and whispered, "I'll just go finish mopping up the mess."

Vincenzo waved him on while he continued to watch her sleep.

"I'm not actually sleeping," she said without turning over.

"May I come in and speak with you?"

"Of course you may," she replied while she rolled over and sat up on the bed. "How could I ever refuse my rescuer?"

His mouth fell slightly open for a moment, but he quickly shut it to hide his confusion. She just called him her rescuer. "Well, sister, I don't know if I'd call myself your rescuer, exactly."

"Nonsense. I've been trying to get out of the Palace for some time now, but you're the first one that actually freed me. I wish I could offer you some reward, but I'm afraid my personal money is locked up in Vegan banks and I'm as broke as everyone else."

Vincenzo scratched his head. She wants to pay the ransom that the king does not.

"Are you okay Mr. ...? What do I call my rescuer?"

"I'm sorry," he said bowing low. "Where are my manners? My name is Vin-cenzo."

She offered her hand for him to kiss and said, "So pleased to meet you Vincenzo. You may call me Valentina."

"Valentina?" he asked genuinely surprised.

"Oh gracious," she said, "You look absolutely exhausted. Please sit down before you faint to the floor."

"Valentina?" he repeated. "You're...you're..."

"I know," she said. "I'm the queen, or at least I was. I gave up that office when I told the king I was leaving, except he didn't let me leave. Oh I hope you aren't in any danger from him."

"No," he said as he pulled up a chair, "I honestly don't think I'm in any danger from him."

"Hmmm," she said, "and why don't you think that?"

"Forgive me for saying this, your highness..."

"What did I tell you?" she scolded him. "My name is Valentina."

"My apologies Valentina, but I think the king let you go. In fact, the top news story is that he has kissed and made up with Vega too."

"That's wonderful," she said. "Now I can reward my rescuer!"

"Yeah," he said, making no attempt to hide his disappointment. "Ain't that something?"

"Was there more?" she asked.

"No," he said shaking his head. "Just something about him saving them that lost their homes in all this."

"That doesn't sound very much like the man I knew," she said.

"No," he admitted. "It certainly don't. Listen sister, I got some things to go clear up before I can get you to your bank. You go ahead and rest up, if you want, or enjoy the hospitality of my ship. Mi casa es su casa."

"This was the queen's apartment," the maid said as she led everyone into the 2nd floor luxury suite, "at least, it was until the whole Vegan controversy began."

Francesca entered and said, "It's not at all like the one the king had arranged for me."

Victor toured the room turning over things to check their manufacturers and asked, "You mean the penthouse suite?"

"No," Francesca replied. "I am meaning the 2nd story suite he was giving me first. This is much more like my sister."

The maid went to the closet and opened the double doors, saying, "Well, if you want to pass as the queen, you'll have to dress like her, and her wardrobe is one area where the king insisted she accepted her royal responsibility."

Elizabeth walked into the huge closet and ran her hands along the rows of beautiful gowns.

"Selecting and wearing the right gown is not enough," the maid said. "You must look regal in it."

Francesca clucked her tongue and said, "I can do that."

"But," the maid continued, "you must look like you're embarrassed for being so fortunate."

Victor, Bruno and Elizabeth each shared a look of fear. Bruno muttered, "We're sunk."

"No we're not," Victor said. "She only has to fool the guards."

"Aren't they trained to observe tiny details?" Elizabeth asked.

"Sure, but they also tend to rely on what they already know. We'll be in their home with their queen. They won't even question her."

"Okay," Elizabeth said, "as long as you are so sure."

He wasn't.

Elizabeth pulled some gowns down and carried them to the bed.

"That one," the maid said pointing to the gown on the left. "The queen liked wearing turquoise for casual functions. I'll find the matching shoes while you try it on."

Elizabeth nudged Victor and Bruno into a corner facing the wall while Francesca carried the gown back to the closet to put it on.

The maid put a pair of black and copper pumps on the floor in front of Francesca and said, "See if you can slip into these while I button up the back."

Francesca tried squeezing her feet into the shoes, but gave up saying, "They are too tight."

"Not to fear," the maid said as she returned to the back of the closet. "Here's a pair of copper sandals. We can loosen the straps to make them fit."

Francesca slipped into the shoes and the maid adjusted the straps. Francesca looked in the full size mirror and said, "Look at my hair. Where's my Tatianna to do my hair? I can't go out looking like this!"

"Nonsense," the maid said, "Your sister preferred a simple brushing. In fact, she hated having her hair done up and only relented for really special occasions."

"Hey boss!" Vincenzo's henchman ran breathlessly down the ship's corridor.

Vincenzo was walking blindly through the ship, with his head hung low, staring at his shoes. His mind alternated between replaying the news that all property sales would be reversed, and his conversation with the queen. He barely nodded his head to acknowledge his man, but he paused and waited to hear what more could happen to him now.

"Boss?"

Vincenzo grunted.

"It's your mother. She wants to talk to you."

Vincenzo knew it would be bad news. She was always bad news. Even her good news came with calamities attached. He groaned and turned in the direction of the lavatory.

"She's on an open channel...now...waiting for you..."

Vincenzo tilted his head as if that might block the sound from reaching his ears and tried looking like he didn't hear his subordinate.

The henchman watched Vincenzo walk away and asked, "You okay boss? Didn't you hear me?"

Vincenzo still ignored him, until his man said, "Your mama said that it's real urgent that she talks to her little man."

Vincenzo cringed and the henchman snickered.

"What was that?" Vincenzo growled. "Did I hear you laugh?"

"No boss," the henchman lied. "I sniffled. I wish my sainted mother, God rest her soul, could be here today to call me her little man."

"Well, you better not be laughing, or you can just giggle yourself right out the air lock."

"You wants me to tell your mama that her little man will be right there?"

There was no levity in Vincenzo's face. "Why don't you go find something to polish. I'll handle my mother."

Vincenzo didn't hurry. Little man was a name she only used when she was really upset about something, but planned to pretend she wasn't really angry. This was not good at all. He took the lift to the control level and entered the comm room, shutting the door behind him.

The room was empty and she wasn't on the projector, but he didn't need a holo-image of her to picture her tapping her foot impatiently. "What do you want Ma? I'm really kinda busy here."

"Is that really how you want to talk to your motha? No 'Hi Ma' or 'I loves you Ma', just 'What do you want?' Twenty-one hours is how long it took me to get you into the world. Twenty-one excruciating hours, and you think you're too busy to talk to me now?"

"Ma! The last time you told the story, it was only nineteen hours. Do you think you can reverse this time-warp and get to the point?"

"Shame on you Vincenzo Bartholomew Stonewright! Your mother ain't gonna live forever..."

"From your mouth to God's ears," he thought to himself.

"And," she continued, "you just might regret some of the awful things you is sayin' to me."

"I regret them already Ma, now what can I do for you?"

"Vinny, sweetheart; far be it for me to tell you how to run your business, but it is the family business. Your father, God bless his soul, built it up from nothing. Now, there was a good man..."

"Ma?"

"He built it with his own hands..."

"Ma?"

"He was such a good looking man too. I miss him so much."

"I miss him too, Ma. Where's that point you were getting to?"

"Have you seen the news, Vinny?"

"Yeah Ma, I seen it."

"What's going to happen to us when the empire reverses all the purchases you been makin'?"

"For cryin' out loud," Vincenzo barked. "Is that what you're worried about? If that happens, then we get our money back."

"Will we Vinny? Do you really think the empire is going to gleefully hand us back our money?"

"They were all legitimate transactions. Of course we get our money back."

"Were they Vinny? Are you telling me that you didn't lean on nobody to make them sell?"

"No Ma. Nobody. Well, almost nobody. So what if a few of them cry foul. We'll be fine Ma."

"Are you sure?" she asked. "Remember when they trumped up your pop on racketeering charges and said they could confiscate everything, including what we got legally?"

Silence fell between them. She was right. The imperials liked making up new laws and new rules to screw with them. "Don't worry Ma. I'll figure something out."

When the butler had first returned to the security room and found everyone missing, he started to track them down, but then decided he really didn't care. If his boyhood friend wanted to exercise his rank and treat him like any other staff member, then he could clean up his own mess.

He went to the private lounge and ordered half a dozen doubles that he hoped would erase the sting he was feeling from the king's last words. The waitress knew better than to let him have that many drinks on a bar stool, and instead delivered them to a corner booth where they were lined up in single file. He started with the glass on the right and was onto his third when the king found him.

"Johnny?"

His head turned and glanced up before he could stop it. He quickly jerked his head back so he could examine the nearly empty bottom of his glass. He swirled around what little amber liquid remained as if there was something very intriguing to be found there.

The king motioned to the opposite end of the curved bench and asked, "May I?"

The butler waved his hand and said, "You're the God damned emperor, you don't need my permission."

The king frowned, but said, "I guess I deserved that." He sat down across from his friend and reached for one of the filled glasses, asking, "Do you mind?"

The butler just sneered. He thought he had already answered that question.

The king took a sip while his friend took the next glass and drained half of it. "Johnny, I want you to handle this discretely. Find out who has her. Get her back. Pay them what they want if you think that's best, but do it quietly. I don't need to look like any more of a fool than I already do."

"Nobody ever said that you looked like a fool."

"They wouldn't dare, but I could see it on their faces."

The butler put the half-finished drink down and said, "Okay, I'll do this for you, but if she doesn't want to return here, I'm taking her wherever she wants to go. If you want to talk with her or send her belongings to her, that's up to you."

The king sighed, nodded his head, and downed the remainder of his drink.

The guards led Harvey back to his cell, again, where the shackles were removed. He sat back and watched the guards remove the cuffs from both Roy and Gene. There was no malice in the guards' actions, and he may have even detected some sympathy for their situation. "Do you guys know what is going on out there?"

"With what?" one of the guards asked. "You mean with Vega?"

"No," Harvey replied. "I'm talking about the queen."

"Yeah," the guard said softly. "We know how unhappy she's been and how the king has kept her locked up. Sometimes we have to escort her to and from her room. If she ever wants anything, I see that she gets it."

"So you like her?"

"Of course we do. We all like her."

Another guard chimed in and said, "We love her, but we are sworn to serve the king."

Harvey saw all the guards nodding their heads and said, "Then you don't know she's been kidnapped?"

"What?" the guard barked.

"Yeah," Harvey explained. "A gangster is holding her for ransom, and it doesn't look like the king is going to help her any. We were going to go rescue her when you took us back into custody."

"You?" the guard asked. "Why would you care?"

"Don't listen to him," another guard said. "He's just trying to charm his way out of here."

"It's true," Harvey insisted. "We know the queen's sister, and in fact, we came here to rescue her sister who had also been kidnapped by an imperial man."

"I told you," the other guard repeated. "Don't listen to him. His story just keeps getting wilder and wilder."

Vincenzo's mother had a knack for making him depressed. It was even worse when she was right. He left the comm room and returned to the helm where he found the queen looking out the view screens at the cosmos. She was absolutely radiant as she viewed the heavens from their off-world position, until she saw his expression.

"What's wrong?" she asked. "Bad news?"

"Some investments I've made might go wrong for the family. My mother is worried that we might lose everything."

"Is there anything I can do to help my rescuer? I may not have any more official influence, but I suspect I can rally support from the people."

He exhaled loudly and slouched his shoulders, saying, "I can't keep doing this. You really shouldn't be so trusting."

"I don't understand."

"Listen sister. I ain't here to rescue you."

She was thoroughly confused now.

"I kidnapped you for a ransom," he explained.

"My," she laughed, "aren't you the bold one."

"Why are you laughing? I'm being serious."

"Let me guess," she said. "He won't pay."

Vincenzo shook his head sadly.

"So now what?" she asked.

"What do you think?"

Alarm registered on her face and he said, "I'm not really going to kill you, you're too nice."

"Well, that's a relief."

"Don't feel so relieved," he said. "My family may kill us both."

"Your own family?"

"It's your own fault. You created this huge real estate opportunity when you left the king, and I invested the family fortune buying up everything dirt cheap, but the king said he's going to reverse all them deals."

Valentina laughed lightly and said, "I'm sure the board of commerce will return your money."

"Well, my mother ain't so sure. Ain't you never heard of the Stonewright family?"

"Oh," she said, finally understanding.

Francesca stood outside the door to the detention center, sucked in her breath and formed a commanding regal scowl on her face. She set her jaw and started to enter the doorway, but the maid grabbed her by the bustle and pulled her back. "You can't go in there looking like that. The queen held her head high, but she always smiled. She would sometimes go in just to say good morning and deliver scones from the kitchen."

Francesca stretched her lips, but her smile looked more like she had gas.

"That won't do," the maid said. "Try smiling like you are visiting friends."

Victor laughed and said, "She doesn't have any friends."

Francesca shot him a dirty look and he corrected himself, saying, "Try smiling like you just completed an aria and everybody is applauding."

"Yeah," Elizabeth said. "Remember last year after you sang in Antares?"

A beautiful smile formed on Francesca's face and the maid said, "Now you look like the queen. Go in there."

Francesca strolled into the room and said, "Good morning all of you, my friends. I am wondering why it is that my friends, who I am friends with, have my other friends being locked in here where they cannot be my friends with me."

Elizabeth slapped her palm to her forehead. They never even considered her accent when they cooked up this plan. She whispered to the maid, "Please tell me that the queen talked like that."

"She used to," the maid explained, "when she first come here, but even then, she made more sense than that."

One of the guards shot a look at Harvey and said, "So, the queen's been kidnapped has she?"

Harvey's jaw dropped and his shoulders shrugged. For one of the very few times in his life, he didn't know what to say.

The sergeant of the guards wasn't convinced that Francesca was the queen, but she did look like the queen, and considering Harvey's outlandish story about the queen's sister and both of them being abducted, he was willing to go along and see how this played out. He bowed politely and said, "Your majesty, how may we serve you?"

Francesca held her smile, but still looked down her nose at the sergeant. "Release my friends."

"But the king ordered them here."

"The king has gone mad. I am needing this man...and his little friends."

"Well," the sergeant said, "I don't know about the king going mad, but this gentleman has been spinning the most outlandish tales about the queen's sister being abducted and the queen herself being kidnapped, but here you are, so surely this man is quite insane."

"You are knowing about my sister? I mean, the queen is requiring your help."

The sergeant went to close the door and saw Elizabeth and the rest of their party listening from outside. He nodded his head for them to enter. The maid looked like she was about to faint, but Bruno put his arms around her and walked her inside. Elizabeth and Victor followed and the sergeant closed the door behind them.

"So," the sergeant said, "let me see if I understand correctly. The queen has come to me because she needs this scoundrel to rescue her sister."

"Not exactly," Elizabeth said. "You see, this is actually the queen's..."

"Shhh!" the sergeant said. "I know my queen when I see her, and I am sure the king won't begrudge us for helping the queen rescue her sister."

"But you don't understand," Victor said.

Elizabeth put her finger to her lips and said, "Shhh. I think he does."

"You know," the sergeant said, "that this man is a scoundrel and for whatever reason, the king loathes him, but I am unaware of any actual crimes that he has committed, so I'm inclined to acquiesce to my queen's wishes."

Elizabeth leapt onto the man and wrapped her arms around his neck. "Thank you."

"That's quite all right ma'am. Is there anything else you need?"

Elizabeth climbed down from the large man and asked, "Can you help get us to his ship?"

The sergeant nodded and said, "I can do that." He ordered a detail to escort them to the spaceport.

The king had asked the butler to discreetly locate the queen, and he knew no better place to do this than in the center of the intelligence corps' department of operations. They tracked and recorded all ship movements and deep space communications. The only problem he foresaw, wasn't getting them to cooperate, but sifting through the mountains of recordings that they were likely to provide, given his limited search criteria.

"Perhaps, if you could tell us what you are looking for, we might be able to assist you?"

The butler smiled a half smile, but shook his head. "It's not that I don't want your help. Lord knows I could certainly use it, but the king asked me to handle this matter personally."

"But..."

"Quietly," the butler stressed.

"Oh," the intelligence officer said. "I understand. If you have any questions, of a more general nature, I am at your disposal."

"Thank you," the butler said.

He waited for the man to leave, but instead of going he fished through his pockets and pulled out a piece of paper. He jotted down a few notes and handed them to the butler, saying, "If you use this command before your query, then when you are done, your request will be erased instead of recorded."

The butler held up the scrap of paper and said, "Thank you; not from me, but from the king."

The man backed away to a safe distance and said, "I'll be over here. Just call me if you have questions."

The butler stared at the blank screen and drummed his fingers, then typed a command to pull up the security recordings of the gangster leading the queen away. From across the room, the intelligence officer said, "We have voice recognition. You can just ask your commands."

The butler looked annoyingly at the man and asked, "Can you hear me?"

"Perfectly. Just ask if you need help."

The butler remained staring at the clueless man.

"Oh," the officer finally said. "I'll just wait outside. Shout if you need me."

The butler turned to the screen and said, "Security protocol seventy-seven, no logs."

The screen replied, "Confirmed."

"Display departures within one hour of the selected security footage."

The display showed over a dozen lines radiating from the imperial spaceport out to a variety of destinations.

"Display incoming communications within four hours of the selected security footage."

The screen lit up with thousands of bright points of light, obscuring everything else on the screen.

"Overlay the last two screens and show only those communications that came from an endpoint for any of those departures."

Only three of them remained illuminated.

"Show me only the communications that were sent to the palace."

Now there was only a single point of light on the screen.

"Play the communications for me."

The computer's voice read the message, "*I have your precious singer. If you want to see her alive again...*"

"Stop," he commanded. Then, he stuck a memory card in the port and said, "Record everything about the ship and all communications to or from the ship since its departure. Record navigation instructions to reach the location of the ship. Secure the information on my memory card, then delete the logs and end this query session."

The display replied, "Confirmed."

The butler took his card and left, thanking the clueless officer on his way out.

The guards formed a protective detail around Francesca, and with Harvey and the others in tow, escorted her through the back of the palace to a private garage where they boarded a fancy, expensive vehicle.

The interior was considerably more posh than Harvey's ship which Victor and Gene were quick to appreciate. Victor squirmed in the softness of the luxurious seat while Gene went straight to the wet-bar and pulled out a frosty bottle of Andurian lager. Victor nudged Gene in the shoulder and a second bottle of lager found its way out of the cooler.

Harvey kept his face glued to the window. Even though they had treated him well enough in detention, he had no desire to return. The cars glided smoothly out of the garage and down the road to the spaceport. Harvey examined every corner of every building, wondering where this plan would fall apart. Francesca did not fool these guys into believing she was the queen, yet they seemed sincere in helping, but he still remained skeptical that this trip out of the pokey would last.

When they pulled up to his ship, Harvey sprang out of the car and ran to the gangplank, but froze at the bottom of the ramp.

"What's wrong?" Victor asked.

Harvey shrugged and meekly said, "What if it's a trap?"

The sergeant of the guards joined him at the ramp and said, "It's no trap."

"How can you be sure?" Harvey asked. "You didn't even know the queen was missing."

"Fair enough," the sergeant said. "I'll go first and check it out for you."

Bruno followed the guard up the ramp. Harvey entered a code on the keypad at the bottom of the ramp to open the portal to the ship.

The sergeant crinkled his nose as he entered the dark musty interior. "It smells like an old gym sock in here."

Bruno took a deep whiff and shrugged his shoulders saying, "I don't smell nothing."

Bruno smacked his hand against the motion detector and the lights came on revealing the lower quarters and storage. The sergeant opened a couple cabin doors and peered in, then moved on to the single person lift and rode up to the cockpit. Bruno poked his head out the portal and said, "Ain't nobody here."

Victor went back to the car to pocket as many lagers as he could while Harvey climbed up to his ship. "Where's...?"

Bruno pointed to the lift with his thumb and said, "He went up to check the cockpit."

Harvey did not want to hear that. He sprinted to the lift and rose to the upper levels. He arrived in the cockpit to find the sergeant turning on some of his more customized pieces of equipment.

"This is your ship?" the sergeant asked.

"I didn't steal it, if that's what you mean."

"Oh no," the sergeant replied, "but these instruments aren't what you usually find on a private ship."

"I wouldn't know," Harvey said. "I haven't actually owned it that long."

"Oh? How long?"

Harvey tried his best to look nonchalant as he leaned against the door jam and pretended he was uninterested in what the sergeant was looking at. "Let me see, ummm, I think it was just a couple days before the whole Vega incident. Yeah. I remember because I barely used up one tank of fuel before coming here."

"Ah, I see. It must have set you back a few credits. How much? If you don't mind me asking."

"Well, you see, I won it in a card game."

The sergeant whistled. "A card game? That's a pretty high stake game, to win this. You must really be some kind of high roller."

"Me? No. Not really, just this once, it was a really good hand."

"Do you remember who you won it from?"

Harvey tried looking thoughtful and said, "Not really. Why?"

The sergeant finally stopped playing with the gadgets and said, "Nothing. It's just that you must have won it from a smuggler. This would make one cherry smuggling rig."

"Oh, I doubt that," Harvey tried to laugh it off. "The guy I won this from was some old dude. He was wrinkled like a prune and had snow white hair. He played like he was nervous that his wife was going to catch him losing."

"Huh," the sergeant said. "Well I guess I should get going and let you go about your business."

The sergeant rode the lift down and left the ship. Francesca and Elizabeth remained at the foot of the ramp. "It's safe now. Good luck."

"We're not going," Elizabeth said.

The sergeant raised an eyebrow and Elizabeth explained, "They don't need us for this. We might even be in their way, but here in the palace, we can monitor the king's mood. If both the queen and Francesca are missing, we don't know what the king would do."

The sergeant just grunted and said, "Okay, let's head back."

The king was alone in his office reading the latest polls about his popularity. Everybody had an opinion about something, and when the opinion was about him, they printed it. Just because it was a monarchy, didn't mean he didn't allow them their rights, although he wished they weren't so quick to exercise them.

The butler came in and asked, "Why are you reading that trash again?"

"I don't know. It's not like I really care what they say about me."

The butler slid the tabloid out of the king's hands and said, "Yeah you do. You're just too stubborn to let it affect your policies. Why don't you just shut them down?"

"I can't do that. I swore to uphold the charter my ancestors wrote centuries ago. It's the law."

"Then write a new law."

The king groaned and made no effort to conceal how annoyed he was. "Did you want something? Or did you just come in here to pester me?"

"We found him, I mean her."

"Who?"

The butler swung his leg over one of the chairs in front of the king's desk and slid down to the seat. "The queen, of course. Who else did you ask me to look for?"

"So soon?" the king asked. "I figured you'd have to crack codes and chase down a billion forwarding addresses before you could triangulate a position."

"Yeah, that's right. I did it fast. You should give me a raise."

The king raised an eyebrow and pointed to it with his index finger. "There's your raise."

"He's an amateur. Whoever took the queen, I mean. He used no sophisticated, or even unsophisticated, tricks to hide his whereabouts."

The king turned to look out the window while he thought about it. "Send in a team. Go get her."

"Yes sir."

The butler rose from his chair and opened the door when the king added, "Quietly."

The butler paused a second, then nodded his head and turned towards the door when the king interrupted again, "Make sure they can't be linked back to me."

The butler waited for more, but after a quiet pause elapsed, turned again for the door when the king said, "Never mind. I'll handle this."

"You will? Personally?"

"Don't be silly. I'll get our intrepid friend out of detention and offer him his freedom if he does this one little job for me."

The sergeant led Francesca back into the palace the same way they had left. She followed him through the hallway to the detention center and was about to say goodbye when an angry king exited through the door.

The king froze when he saw Francesca and the anger on his face morphed into bewilderment. "What are you doing here? I mean, I thought you were..."

"You thought I was what?" Francesca asked dryly.

"Oh," the king said, the anger returning to his face. "What are you doing in those clothes?"

Francesca scowled and said, "You thought I was being my sister?"

The king's face turned a dark red as he barked, "Never mind. Where are my prisoners?"

The sergeant fumbled for an answer, but nothing came to him.

"You thought I was my sister?" Francesca repeated. "You mistook me for the queen? Well so did everybody else. Your queen ordered their release."

"You what?" the king yelled. "You haven't the authority!"

Francesca put her hands together and held them in front of her chest. She took a calming breath and formed an angelic expression on her face, then took a deep breath and sang in a deep alto,

> *"In the name of the king,*
> *I did this thing*
> *For these men that I know*
> *I let them go."*

The sergeant's jaw fell open as he witnessed Francesca's beautiful voice, but his head spun when the king belted out a tenor response,

> *"These men were mine,*
> *They weren't for you.*
> *I had a job for them*
> *Now what shall I do?"*

Francesca responded,

> *"Your concern is poorly placed*
> *Your actions are disgraced*
> *It's my sister you should save.*
> *If you fail...*
> *If you fail..."*

The king finished her last line in a deep baritone dropping down to a low bass,

> *"I'll,*
> *carry*
> *the,*

shame,

to my,

grave."

Harvey wasted no time sealing the ship and lifting off.

Victor fastened himself into one of the seats behind Harvey. He was no pilot, but he thought he knew a thing or two about how things worked and asked, "Don't you need to file some kind of a flight plan? Won't they chase us if you try slipping out of here like this?"

Harvey just chuckled at Victor's question, but Roy replied, "It's not the first time he has ever left a planet without filing a proper flight plan."

"Or the second time," Gene added.

Roy and Gene settled into the seats across the aisle from Victor.

Harvey mumbled under his breath, "Or even the twelfth." His only hope to find Vincenzo was to wait for another ransom demand, but when he turned on the homing radio, it was already locked onto a far beacon.

"What the hell?" he asked out loud.

"What's wrong?" Gene asked.

"Nothing," Harvey said, "but we seem to be locked onto some ship's transponder, and I don't remember doing it."

Roy left his chair to join Harvey and look at the screen and the array of controls beneath Harvey's gaze. "Could you have left it locked onto that emissary's ship?"

"I might have," Harvey replied, "but I never locked onto his transponder. I used the advanced radar sensors to follow him."

Victor said, "Maybe we have a guardian angel that snuck in and set it while we were gone."

"Maybe," Harvey said, "but maybe not while we were gone."

Gene got up for a closer look at the screen. "Do you really think it could be him?"

Harvey shrugged and said, "I can't be sure unless he broadcasts another ransom demand, but it's in a location that I might choose to hide."

Roy shook his head and said, "That's too simple. He's got to know that we'd find him if he broadcasts."

"No he doesn't," Harvey said. "He's a boss man, not a worker bee."

Victor was still more focused on why they were getting the signal than whose ship it was. "Who could have locked your equipment onto that ship? And why?"

Harvey returned to the pilot's seat and said, "Let's go check it out for ourselves."

Victor asked, "You're not even curious about who did it?"

Harvey replied, "There's only one person I can think of who had showed any interest in my gear. He even turned on some of this stuff."

Chapter 11

Vincenzo granted the queen the freedom to roam the ship, but instead of wandering around blindly herself, she chose to follow him as he moped aimlessly along the hallway.

"Why do you do it?" she asked as they walked slowly through the hall.

"Do what?" he replied, "Kidnap you? I thought I already told you. I'll be ruined if the king does not return my family's money."

"No, why do you break the law? Doesn't your family have enough money?"

He looked at her coldly and she added, "I mean before the real estate thing."

Vincenzo shrugged and said, "It was the family business. I took over from my father who built it up from nothing. I couldn't turn it down."

"Would you have?"

"I always wanted to be a chef. I wanted to create new foods with rare ingredients that people would travel all the way across the empire to try."

"Really?" she asked. "I think everyone should try to be what's in their heart, even if only as a hobby."

"I tried it when I was a kid. My mother threw a fit and forbid me to ever go into the kitchen with the help."

"But you're a grown man now. You can't let your mother control your life."

He chuckled and said, "You don't know my mother."

Vincenzo turned into the observation lounge and opened the shields for a view of the cosmos. "This is one of my favorite places on the ship."

"It's beautiful," she said, "but I hope you're not trying to change the subject. If you're the one who took over the family business, why do you let your mother control you like that?"

"Ahah!" he blurted out. "You think it's so simple, but you just don't understand the women in my family. The men are in charge. They make all the decisions, but they always make sure the decisions they make are what the women want. The only way my mother could lose control of me is if I marry."

"So why don't you?"

He opened his mouth to answer, then shook his head and said, "Nah. We ain't goin' there. Besides, it's too late now. I gotta think how I'm gonna get the money back."

"It's not true, you know. You could take control if you wanted to. I think you're chef idea is a good one. People would come to see the mobster chef. Your motto could be, 'You're gonna like it, or else'."

Vincenzo laughed and said, "That would be swell, but my mamma wouldn't like it."

"You already said the real estate thing was legitimate. Imagine if you converted the family business into a legitimate one? You could teach them that crime isn't the only business that pays."

"Well I can guarantee you this, sister. If I lose my shirt on this real estate, they ain't gonna learn nothin' good about goin' legit."

"That's sad," she said. "I'll try to do what I can to help."

"How you gonna do that?" he asked. "The king don't even care enough to pay a ransom for you."

"The king and I may have our differences, but I still have some influence with the people, and there are a lot of people in the empire."

Harvey assumed that Vincenzo would be watching for someone to approach, so he plotted an arc that put the ship in a slingshot around a moon, flinging his ship in a trajectory that aimed beyond Vincenzo's current location. He kept his eyes glued to the monitor ready to start entering course corrections the moment their quarry moved out of position, but he never did. Even after Harvey had looped around the moon and slowed to an approach speed, Vincenzo didn't budge.

Harvey flipped some switches on another console and brought up the other sensors. This began to smell like a trap to him, and if Vincenzo's ship was just bait, he wanted to see the ambush before it reached him. He kept his finger poised over the cloaking button, ready to disappear at the first sign of hostile ships, but the sensors remained quiet.

Vincenzo sat in the observation lounge with the queen, watching Harvey's ship approach. "Well, what do you know? Do you see that? The king cares after all. He sent someone to come rescue you."

The queen went to the window and watched Harvey's ship approach. "That's not an imperial ship."

Vincenzo went to the window for a better look. "You mean the king didn't send it?"

"He might have if he was more afraid of a scandal."

Vincenzo just shook his head in disgust.

The queen backed away and asked, "What if they're pirates?"

"This close to the capitol? They'd have to be the stupidest pirates in the empire."

"So?" she asked. "Aren't you going to do something?"

Vincenzo shrugged.

"What if they throw you in jail?"

"I thought you said they wasn't imperial."

"What if they are out of work pirates and the king really did send them and they throw you in jail?"

"Now you're getting silly."

"Still," she said. "You don't look like you're planning to put up a fight."

"Nope. They can have you. Wait a second. That came out wrong. Look sister. I'm not going to hurt you. If they hadn't come for you, I'd probably have taken you back myself."

The queen asked, "But what if I don't want to go back?"

"Where would you want to go?" he asked.

She shrugged while Vincenzo settled back in a comfy chair with his feet up, calmly watching Harvey approach.

She looked thoughtful and said, "I may not be able to protect your family money, or keep you out of jail, but I can at least guarantee your safe passage... unless they're really pirates."

"Thanks, sister."

"You know, I really don't like being called sister. My name is Valentina."

"Yes ma'am," he said, getting up out of his chair and bowing low, "Valentina."

Harvey became more suspicious with each passing moment. The closer he got to Vincenzo's ship, the more he feared what might happen next. His eyes were glued to the long range sensors, but there was no movement anywhere around them.

He nearly jumped out of his skin when his speaker sputtered, "Approaching ship, this is the *IONE ALL*, please state your business."

Harvey looked around the room and shrugged, "How should I answer?"

Roy muttered, "Oh brother," as he walked up to the console and took the microphone. "IONE ALL, IONE ALL, do you require assistance?"

Harvey's ship continued to inch closer to Vincenzo's. Vincenzo replied, "Unidentified ship, please state your business."

Roy looked up at Harvey and asked, "What's the name of your ship?"

"NOVA COMET."

"IONE ALL, IONE ALL, this is the NOVA COMET. We're supposed to meet a friend, but we lost the coordinates and thought you looked like you were waiting to meet someone."

"NOVA COMET, sorry to disappoint you, but we're just enjoying the view before we head into the capitol."

"Affirmative, IONE ALL. It is a breathtaking view from here. Can we interest you in a bottle of distilled Curoberry?"

"NOVA COMET, thank you, but no. We are well stocked."

The queen gasped, "Should you have said that? What if they are pirates?"

Vincenzo clicked off the mic and said, "Shhh! The mic was open when you said that."

"Did you hear that?" Gene asked.

"That's her," Victor said. "Except for her accent, she sounded too much like Francesca to be anyone else."

Harvey pulled alongside the ship and launched magnetic grappling hooks to secure it. He extended the air-locked gangway from the NOVA COMET to the IONE ALL. The airlock sealed the ships together and he said, "Let's go."

Bruno was right behind him, but Victor said, "Let's go? He's a gangster. Shouldn't we have weapons or something?"

Harvey said, "The armory is by the airlock."

"Do you think they heard me?" the queen asked.

"Yes, sister, I mean Valentina, I think they heard you loud and clear, and I think they probably are pirates, but I also wouldn't be surprised if they were sent here to rescue you."

"So, do we trust them or not?"

"Not yet."

Harvey distributed weapons to the others and crossed the gangway to Vincenzo's ship. As soon as he opened the door to Vincenzo's ship, they were sucked inward into the depressurized man-trap that Vincenzo had built to welcome pirates. The door slammed shut and locked behind them, then the room filled with air for them.

Vincenzo offered Valentina his arm and said, "Let's go greet our guests."

The butler returned to the king's office and said, "It's done."

The king looked up from his desk and asked, "You know where the queen is?"

"Not yet, but I put some people on it. We should get a report from them soon."

The king nodded and got up from his desk to look out the window and down to the courtyard. "Excellent. The singer will be very happy."

The butler joined the king at the window and said, "You do know that her name is Francesca, don't you? You don't have to call her 'the singer' all the time."

"Of course I know her name, but I'm afraid that if I start to get too personal, I might slip and call her Valentina. They're very much alike you know."

"Not really," the butler replied, "They only look alike."

"Perhaps," the king admitted. "She's very spirited. Francesca, I mean. You should have heard her rip me a new one about rescuing her sister."

The butler laughed. "I heard."

"She also wanted me to end this blasted civil dispute with Vega."

"I'm sure the queen would want that too."

The king turned to his friend and sighed. "I never should have let it go this far, but if I end it now, how will I keep her here?"

"Who?" the butler asked. "The queen?"

"Really? After all this? You don't know me any better than that?"

The butler gripped the king's shoulders and emphatically said, "I know exactly what you meant, but I need to know that you truly understand what is in your heart. You need to know it and you need to say it."

"I know what I want. I want Francesca to stay with me. Everyone else treats me like I'm the most important and most powerful person they know, but Francesca practically treats me with disdain. She looks at me like I need to prove myself to share her space. I like that. I need that! Is that what you wanted to hear? Does that make me some kind of pervert?"

The butler snickered while he replied, "I'm not qualified to say you're not a pervert."

"What?"

"Never mind, it was just a joke. If you want to keep her here, you may want to plan a strategy to woo her, because if you keep her prisoner, you'll lose her, just like the queen."

"Yes," the king said. "It seems to me that there is a distinct lack of loyalty in this palace and I want you to find out who let the queen escape."

"Why? Do you intend to punish those who failed to recognize that the queen was being abducted for not being loyal to you?"

"You make it sound crazy."

"That's because it is crazy. You need to focus on getting her back if you want to woo Francesca."

"I've already done that," the king replied.

"No you haven't," the butler said. "You've asked me to discreetly ascertain her location."

"Fine. When we know where she is, I'll send in troops to get her."

"That's a start," the butler said.

"No, wait. I can't do that. I'll have to send someone in covertly."

"Just as long as you rescue the queen, I think Francesca will be duly impressed."

"Then it's settled. I'll woo Francesca by saving her sister."

"Do you think that would be enough? She's not eye candy. Francesca is a very opinionated woman. You can't treat her like she's Valentina version two-point-zero. If you want to woo her, you may need to listen to her views on policy and consider whether or not you can make some concessions."

The king scowled and asked, "Vega?"

The butler nodded.

"Okay then. Where's that fool Philbis? Send him to Vega to invite them here for talks. I'll throw a banquet for them."

Vincenzo crossed the ship to the inner side of the man-trap. Heavily armored walls and doors stood between him and his guests. In the center of the wall was an armored window, but it was currently blocked with plate armor. On the far right was a locked door, and between them a simple control panel was placed at shoulder height.

"Valentina, my dear, would you mind waiting here in the back of the room while I chat with our new passengers?"

Valentina shrugged and nodded, then found a spot with her back against the opposite wall while Vincenzo approached the control panel and turned a knob to dim the back of the room where she stood. He then pressed a button and the armor in the window slid down revealing his new guests in the next room.

"Did I not make myself clear?" Vincenzo asked. "I am perfectly well stocked and not in need of assistance."

Harvey growled back, "That's sure one hell of a way to welcome guests."

"Guests?" Vincenzo asked. "Maybe it would be, if you were guests, but I think it's appropriate for pirates. Pirates are never welcome here."

"Pirates?" Harvey asked. "What makes you think we are pirates?"

"For one thing," Vincenzo said, "you boarded without my permission and against my wishes, and then there's the sidearms you and your crew are packing. Speaking of which, maybe you can stow them in the chest behind you?"

Victor shook his head no, but Harvey said in a low voice, "Perhaps you'd rather let him open the outer air lock and send us all into space?"

"Won't that just eject us back to your pressurized gangway?"

"Look again. He has two air doors leading out of here."

Victor turned to see the side-by-side doors and dropped his weapon in the chest.

Harvey turned back to Vincenzo while the others were stowing their weapons and said, "Just so you understand, we aren't pirates. We're here on a humanitarian mission."

"Funny," Vincenzo said, "You don't look like do-gooders."

"I guess it's like they say, you can't judge a book by its cover."

"I'm curious," Vincenzo said, "how can you afford to pay such a large crew if you are doing humanitarian work?"

"Well," Harvey said, "mostly I don't pay them much."

"Yeah," Gene agreed.

"But sometimes we pick up odd jobs for people who can pay, and sometimes a job can generate more goodwill than any amount of money is worth."

"And which is this?" Vincenzo asked, "Were you hired to come here, or is it for good will?"

"A little of both, actually."

"And what did you expect to find on my ship?"

Harvey was through playing cat and mouse and decided to throw his cards on the table. "Frankly," he said, "we expected to find the notorious Vincenzo Stonewright holding the imperial queen for ransom."

Harvey's frankness was refreshing and potentially time saving. Vincenzo smiled and asked, "So you're working for the empire? I didn't think you guys ever worked for them. Does that mean you have the ransom on you? Can I see it?"

"No," Harvey replied. "We aren't working for the empire exactly..."

"Who then? We're dying to know who else would have sent you all the way out here looking for a kidnapped queen?"

"We?" Harvey asked. "So you're not alone then. Is she okay?"

"I'm askin' the questions here, bub. Who sent you?" Vincenzo held his hand up to the control panel and added, "Tell me now or I'll blow you out the airlock."

Harvey didn't question Vincenzo's sincerity and quickly replied, "Her sister sent us. The queen's sister Fran..."

The queen stepped into the light and asked, "Francesca? She's here?"

Harvey's jaw dropped as he laid eyes on Francesca's twin. Roy and Gene fell to the ground chanting in unison, "Your Majesty."

The king returned to his desk thinking he had made the great decision that would set in motion a chain of events to heal the empire. He arranged papers on his desk into neat little stacks. Nothing mattered except healing the rift with Vega so Francesca would stay.

He looked up and saw that the butler had not left yet.

"Was there something more?" the king asked. "Did I not ask you to have Philbis extend an olive branch to Vega? What more do you expect of me?"

"It's not what I expect of you, it's what can you do to impress her."

"Well?" the king demanded. "Tell me."

The butler leaned against the door jamb and crossed his arms. "What do you suppose has happened since all this trouble began? Do you even know?"

"Of course I know," the king growled. "It's my job to know. Revenues are down. Businesses are hurting, especially the hospitality sector. I haven't seen one single damned credit in taxes from Vega. Those criminals have nearly bankrupted the empire, but I'm going to be nice to them because she wants it."

The butler shook his head slowly and asked, "What about the people? Do you know what has happened to your people?"

"I just told you. Business is down. Everyone suffers."

"Where are the biggest banks held?"

"What do the banks have to do with anything?"

The butler returned to his seat in front of the king's desk and asked, "And where are the biggest stock markets located?"

"Yes, yes, yes! I see what you are getting at, but we can build our own banks and our own stock exchanges. We'll be stronger than ever."

"Who will?" the butler growled back. "Your subjects have invested their life savings in Vegan banks. Their investments and retirements are tied up in Vegan exchanges. They can't get their money!"

"So?" the king asked. "Things are a little tight, but we can all get through it if we just stick together."

"Are you really that blind? They are selling their belongings, even their homes! They're selling them for a handful of credits just so they can eat! Your people are losing their homes and you think they just need to tighten their belts?"

The king didn't respond. He shuffled some papers on his desk, then turned to look out the window. Nothing outside his window looked as bleak as his childhood friend had just described. "You are sure about this?"

"I am. You can ask your precious Francesca why she can't get her money."

The king sighed heavily and said, "Very well then. Have my secretary draft a moratorium on all real estate transactions. Freeze all assets held in escrow. I will sign an order that invalidates all sales since Vegan banks were cutoff."

"Why so surprised?" Vincenzo asked. "I thought you already figured out that I had her."

Harvey just shook his head, still in shock, and Victor answered, "We had heard that they looked alike, but we didn't expect them to be exactly the same."

"We're not the same," Valentina said. "We were twins at birth, but separated as children. I reached out for her once, but I didn't like what fame had done to her and she decided that she wanted nothing to do with me."

"That's not true," Harvey said, "She sent us to rescue you."

"Yeah," Victor added, "She even pretended to be you when she ordered the guards to take us to the space port."

"Francesca did that?"

Vincenzo pressed a different button on the control panel to open the door. "Why don't you gentlemen come in? If you don't mind, I'd still rather you leave your weapons in the airlock."

Harvey entered the room and slipped right past Vincenzo's extended hand which Victor grabbed and shook enthusiastically. Harvey went straight to Valentina and said, "Your sister is quite forceful. She has been very vocal with the king and..."

"With the king?" Valentina asked. "How is it that my sister even knows my husband?"

"That's a long story, but he's quite taken with her. She, on the other hand, has not been quite so enamored with him. They fight publicly and loudly."

"They fight?" Valentina growled. "Did that lout hit her? She's a spirited one. I hope she hit him back."

"No," Harvey replied. "There was no hitting. Sometimes they yell, and she is quite loud..."

"Yes," Valentina snickered. "I remember."

"But mostly," Victor said, "they sing opera."

"Opera?" she asked. "Did you say 'they' as in both of them sing opera?"

"Yup," Harvey nodded his head.

Valentina's head swirled as her mind struggled to absorb this new fact about her husband. "I knew he loved opera and he would sing in the shower, but are you telling me he sang with her in public?"

"Not with each other," Roy said. "It was more like they sang at each other, and she sure had a lot to say, and not always kind."

"That's right," Gene added. "We even heard her sing that the king ate like a cow."

"A big fat cow," Roy corrected him.

"In front of him?" Valentina asked.

"In front of the whole dining room filled with guests," Roy replied.

"You'd be proud of her," Harvey said. "She insisted that he patch up relations with Vega and she insisted he rescue you."

"I see," Valentina said nodding her head slowly. "You are here to rescue me, so I guess the great lout wouldn't listen to her. Take me back. I want to see my sister, and that good for nothing husband."

She turned to Vincenzo and said, "I promise that I will do everything I can to help you recover your investments."

Vincenzo held her hands and said, "You're a lovely lady and I apologize for putting you through this." Then, he bowed at the waist and kissed her hand.

Harvey was last to enter the airlock and Vincenzo grabbed his arm, saying, "When the time comes, if she needs to reach me, I'll be on vacation somewhere where I can ride horses. I'm sure you know what I mean."

The financial devastation that resulted from the rift between Anduria and Vega was far wider spread than the king knew. Had he known how many people in Anduria were cut off from their fortunes, it could have been construed as an act of war. Throughout the palace, staff members had been separated from their savings and retirement funds. Consequently, news of the king's new plan to freeze and reverse all transfers of assets had spread quickly and widely throughout the palace.

Francesca and Elizabeth were in the penthouse suite when they heard the whispering through the doorway.

Elizabeth heard it first and pressed her ear against the door.

Francesca twisted her mouth when she saw her manager eaves dropping and asked, "Why is it you are doing that?"

"Shhh!" Elizabeth replied.

"Shhh?" Francesca shot back, "You don't be shushing me."

"Shhh, I'm trying to listen."

"Well if it is listening you want to do..." Francesca pushed Elizabeth aside and swung the door open.

The maids in the hall stopped talking and stared at Francesca.

"What is it you are saying here?"

The maids looked at each other a moment, then bowed and one of them said, "We beg your pardon Madam. We didn't mean to disturb you."

They started walking off, but Elizabeth said, "No! Wait! What were you saying about the king?"

The maids looked frightened, but the younger of the two managed to admit, "Please, it's not our place. We don't want any trouble."

Francesca put on her stern face and said, "If you are not wanting the trouble, then you will be telling us what was being said."

The maids looked up and down the hall, afraid someone was listening.

"Come inside then," Elizabeth offered. "Tell us in private."

The maids entered the private suite and the older one took a deep breath, then revealed, "We heard that the king is drafting a new ruling to patch things up with Vega."

"Yeah," the younger one said. "He's going to stop people from selling their homes just to survive."

"Reverse all the sales," the older one said. "That's what they said. He was going to freeze all the assets and put things back the way they was before."

"Thank you," Elizabeth said. "You may return to your duties."

The maids scurried out of the suite and quietly closed the door behind them.

"I did this," Francesca mumbled.

"What did you do Diva?"

"I made him fix things."

"You did what? Why did you...no wait a second, why are you smiling?"

Francesca shrugged and said, "I don't know. It just is feeling good. I did something that is helping the millions of people, and it is making me feel all warm on the inside."

Elizabeth backed up a step and looked at Francesca like she might be cracking up. "You mean, we can get your money back and finally go home?"

"Sure," Francesca said, "that must be what it is I am meaning. I have to go find him...to be thanking him."

Once aboard his own ship, Harvey retracted the gangway and set course for the palace.

Roy led the queen to the master cabin. It was Harvey's room, but he didn't expect any argument for such a short trip.

Gene followed close behind and said, "Majesty, is there anything I can get for you?"

"I got this," Roy said.

Gene elbowed him in the rib and said, "I asked first."

"No," she said, "I'm fine."

"Oh," Gene said, unable to hide the dejection from his face.

"On second thought," she said, "I wouldn't mind a nice iced tea."

Gene's face brightened as he replied, "On the double!"

"While he gets your tea," Roy said, "may I offer you a massage? A foot rub perhaps?"

"Oh my," she said. "That's just too much!"

"Nonsense," he replied while motioning her to the reclining chair. "Nothing is too much for our queen."

"But, I don't intend to be your queen any longer. I left the king which means I abdicated that position."

"You're still queen to me," Roy said.

"As is you sister," Gene said while handing over her drink.

"She can have him," Valentina said. "No wait, I don't want to wish him on her. I have to warn her."

"You might be surprised," Roy said, "at how she handles the king."

"Yeah," Gene added as he returned with her drink. "You'd think she was royal and he was just her man toy."

"I'd like to see that," she said. "I'd like to see my sister. I hope she wants to see me too. Did she really send you to rescue me?"

"She insisted," Roy said. "And when she learns we were successful and the king did nothing, I'll wager that she chews on the kings ear for more than just a quick moment!"

Francesca stepped into the king's office and let the door close behind her. He wasn't really doing anything, but his head was hung low staring at his desk. He didn't hear her come in and she was content, for the moment, to just stand there watching him.

The phone rang and he was quick to snap it up. "Johnny? Oh, it's you. No, that's fine. No. No. Can we discuss this some other time? I'm waiting for another call." He clicked the receiver with his fingers, then pressed a button to call his friend, the butler. "Johnny? Have you located the…" The king looked up and saw Francesca staring at him. "…the missing report yet? I'll get back to you, someone is here. Come see me when you can."

He hung up the phone and said, "Francesca. As always, it is a pleasure to see you. Is there something I can do for you?"

She smiled and feigned sudden interest in a picture hanging on the wall. "This painting is very nice. Very realistic looking."

"Thank you," he replied. "It's a photo, actually."

"So," she asked, "how is your day being? Are you doing anything important today?"

"I think everything I do might be important to someone somewhere."

"Ah, yes," she replied. "I think I am seeing this. How goes things with Vega?"

"Vega? Improving I think."

She stomped her feet and said, "Stop with the toying around. I am hearing what you did."

"What I did? I haven't really done anything."

"No?" she asked, then sucking in a deep breath, she sang,

> *"They say you fix the banks today.*
> *That's what I hear,*
> *That's what they say."*

A shiver ran down the king's spine. Each time they sang together was a greater thrill for him than the time before, but it came with risks. He had to focus on not saying the wrong thing to her. He stood from behind his desk and sang,

> *"I made a plan,*
> *To right a wrong.*
> *It's not done yet,*
> *but it won't be long."*

She curtsied and sang,

> *"Only a good king*
> *Would do what I heard.*
> *A king who's heart*
> *is as good as his word."*

He replied,

> *"I'm grateful, of course*
> *that you think I'm so good*
> *Perhaps we can talk*
> *Over dinner, if you would?"*

Francesca couldn't help smiling and nodded her head exuberantly before running out of the room. She practically giggled all the way back to her suite, wondering how this man could make her behave like a teenager.

Valentina followed Harvey to the cockpit and watched him as he settled into the pilot's seat, sliding it forward to the console and slowly eased the ship away from Vincenzo's and towards the palace.

"It's a very impressive ship," Valentina said. "I don't believe I've ever seen some of these instruments."

"Do you frequent many pilot consoles?" he asked.

"A few," she replied. "I have a class three license, or at least, I had one before coming here."

He engaged the autopilot and programmed it to plot a course to the previous destination. "I do like return trips," he said. "They are so much easier to plot." He flicked a few more switches and engaged the sensor avoidance mode.

"What is that display for?" she asked.

"That's part of the guidance system. It's plotting our course back to the space port."

"Hmmm," she replied thoughtfully, "that's certainly not the usual approach pattern."

"No," he said, "given the unusual circumstances of your departure, and the king's unpredictable nature, I thought it might be best if we slipped in through the back, undetected."

"So," she said, "Vincenzo was right. You are a pirate."

"Ouch," he replied. "I don't like that label. I came here to rescue your sister. Now I'm rescuing you on her behalf. Doesn't anyone appreciate the free enterprise system anymore?"

"Call it what you like then," she scolded him. "but the king will probably call you a pirate too, only not as sweetly."

"Well, that's just one more good reason to sneak in through the back."

"I'm just saying that if this is how you ply your trade, and you're proud of what you do, then you should just own up to it. Are you a proud pirate? Or are you just one of those guys who thinks there is something romantic about plundering ships and stealing other peoples fortunes?"

"I'm not a pirate!" he demanded. "I don't steal or plunder."

"So how is it that you are piloting a pirate's ship?"

"I won it in a card game, and for your information, this instrumentation comes in mighty handy for some trade skills other than pirating!"

She waited for an example, but when no explanation came, she asked, "What exactly is your trade skill?"

"I'm an exporter. Sometimes I need these extra instruments to avoid thieves and pirates who wish to plunder the goods I transport."

"Ah," she said, "a smuggler."

Harvey shrugged and mumbled, "I've been called that, but I'm not a thief and I've never killed anyone."

Valentina tired of the conversation and left to tour the ship. She hoped Harvey was also not a liar and he told the truth that he wasn't a murderer. She wouldn't want to stumble into a room full of secret artifacts that would put her life in jeopardy. The command deck and crew quarters were smaller than she expected. The ship wasn't overly large, but she thought it looked bigger when it was approaching, than the living space. Maybe the engines took up that much space, or maybe she just hadn't discovered the large secret storage compartments where he stored the cargo.

There wasn't much to see and she ended up in the observation lounge where she settled into a chair and watched Anduria against the great backdrop of stars as the ship weaved its way through the security net that surrounded the capitol. It was a soothing sight, and she was nearly asleep when Roy found her.

"Your Majesty," Roy said. "We'll be landing soon. The captain wants us to assemble in the crew quarters so he can lead us back into the palace as quickly and quietly as possible."

She smiled slightly to hear Harvey referred to as the captain and glanced one more time at the sea of stars that created a velvety curtain behind the center of the empire. "Very well," she said, "lead the way."

Roy led her to the central lift and rode with her down to the crew deck. Victor still hadn't grown accustomed to the striking resemblance between the two sisters and nudged Bruno in the side when she entered the hallway from the lift.

Touchdown on the planet was barely perceptible, masked by the inertial dampeners, but the ripple that ran through the ship when the dampeners were shut down was almost pleasurable. Harvey rode down the lift as the door opened and the gangway was extended to the ground.

"Okay," Harvey said, "Let's go. Keep close and keep quiet. No unnecessary chatter. We don't want to attract any undue attention."

Harvey took Valentina's hand and led her down the ramp. He walked briskly across the tarmac, tugging her only slightly as she managed to nearly keep up with him. Harvey jumped the fence into the garden maze. Bruno lifted Valentina and placed her atop the wall where she was able to slide off into Harvey's arms. There was only one exit to this corner of the maze. Harvey went to the opening and scanned right and left while Bruno lifted Roy and Gene over the wall.

Valentina stayed behind and helped them down from the wall until it was Bruno's and Victor's turns. She joined Harvey at the opening, but he still hadn't decided which way to go.

"Oh, for heaven's sake," she said. "Follow me." She plunged through the opening and turned right. "I assume you want us to enter through the servants' entrance?"

"Yes," Harvey replied weakly, "then to the servants' elevator."

She hustled off and Harvey glanced behind to see if everyone was with them.

"Don't worry about us," Roy said. "We'll be fine. We'll meet you in Francesca's penthouse suite."

"That's easy for you to say," Victor complained. "Bruno and I will probably be locked up again before we get there."

Harvey sprinted to catch up with Valentina. Heads turned and servants bowed as they hustled through the hallways to the service lift. Valentina started to press the button for the second floor, but Harvey gently gripped her wrist before she contacted the button and said, "Top floor, please."

Valentina glanced at him sideways, then pressed the button to select the top floor. The hallways were empty, which was a relief to Harvey, until they arrived at the locked door. Harvey looked up and down the hallway for a maid who could let them in, but the corridors were deserted.

Harvey frowned and went down on one knee. He pulled a leather pouch from his belt and inserted the old school lock picks into the antique door locks.

Valentina slowly shook her head and said, "Not a thief you say?"

"I'm not a thief," Harvey repeated, "but sometimes I need to escape from some awkward places."

Harvey turned the tumblers and opened the door. He led Valentina in just as Roy and the others arrived.

Valentina looked around at the room's opulent decorations and said, "Don't tell me. This is my sister's room?"

Elizabeth came out of the bedroom and said, "Oh, Diva, there you are."

Roy stepped forward and said, "Your majesty, allow me to introduce Elizabeth Garret. She's your sister's personal manager."

Elizabeth curtsied and said, "I'm sorry, but you look so much like her."

"That's quite all right," Valentina said. "This is her room and I'm in the company of her friends. What else would you think?"

"They're not so much alike," Victor said, "after you talk to them. Are they?"

The butler paced back and forth in the king's office reading the official pronouncement drafted by the king's secretary. The king's eyes followed his friend's movements until he could stand it no more and said, "Johnny, would you please sit down? I feel like I'm watching a tennis match."

Johnny plopped himself in a chair and finished reading the statement. "It's good. The Vegans may not like it. It undermines the position of power that they hold right now, but your people will probably appreciate it."

The king waved his hands back and forth and said, "Who cares about them? Will *SHE* like it?"

"Who cares about *THEM*?" the butler repeated. "I would hope you do! They're your people. You are supposed to look out for them."

"Yes, yes," the king spat back. "Of course I care about them, but right now, I'm more concerned about whether it would impress her."

"You don't think she'll be able to tell if your concern for them is insincere? If you want to woo her, you're going to have to take a real stand and hope that she approves what you really care about, and not just your words."

"Why must this be so complicated?"

The butler snickered and said, "If you want her, I think you'll need to get accustomed to complicated."

The king sneered and said, "Fine. Send it out and make sure everybody hears about it."

"Just like that?" the butler asked. "You just want to send this out onto the news wires?"

"Why? Should I sign it first?"

"No, you should read it."

"I have read it, and now you've read it too. I thought you said it was okay? What's wrong with it now?"

The butler reached across the desk and dropped the document in front of the king. "Nothing is wrong with it. I just think you should read it...*ALOUD*...to your people."

"Aloud?"

"You want to ease the people's concerns?"

The king nodded.

"You want them to know for sure that this comes from their king?"

Again, the king nodded.

"You want to really impress a certain singer?"

"Very well," the king relented. "I'll read it. Have my secretary schedule a press conference."

Francesca ran down the hallway and pirouetted in front of the elevator. She looked at her reflection in the polished gold doors and sang,

> *"Who is this girl I see?*
> *What does she have to say?*
> *Why is she dancing now?*
> *Francesca Vittoria Agostina La Perla doesn't dance ballet."*

Francesca set her jaw and turned away from the mirrored doors, but couldn't help turning back for another peek and softly sang,

> *"But she looks a lot like I do,*
> *Perhaps younger than I feel.*
> *No that's not true, I feel young*
> *Is it true? Is that me? Is this real?"*

The king settled back in his chair and spun around to face the windows.

> *"What is this weight upon my heart*
> *That tugs me out the door?*
> *Is she the one, like her sister was,*
> *Or is she just one more?"*

The elevator doors opened and Francesca entered the lift singing,

> *"What fool am I to feel this way*
> *About my sister's love?*

I wonder, when he looks at me
Which sister he's thinking of?"

The king rose from his chair and pressed his forehead against the window, singing softly,

"You cad, you scoundrel, bite your tongue,
For, married you are still.
You cad, you cur, you can't expect
Her sister's shoes she'd fill."

The elevator stopped on the top floor and Francesca shuffled sadly out of it singing,

"I cannot take my sister's man
Though she did leave him behind
No matter how I feel inside
He never will be mine!"

Francesca opened the door to her suite and stopped cold when she saw Valentina standing there. They stared at each other for a moment, neither of them seemed overjoyed to see the other at the moment.

"Well sister," Valentina said. "I guess I have you to thank for my rescue, so, thank you."

"I couldn't be letting you rot away as some criminal's prisoner."

Valentina adopted a royal posture and elegantly seated herself in a chair. "It wasn't so bad, in fact, it was a lot more pleasant than being locked up here in the palace by that horrid man."

"Locked up?" Francesca asked. "Here? You are the queen. You are having everything you could possibly want."

"Except my freedom," Valentina replied. "I couldn't stand one more moment with that arrogant jerk."

Francesca was puzzled. "Who is being so arrogant?"

"My husband," she snapped. "Who else? That man is the devil incarnate. Oh, he looks kind enough and smiles when the cameras are around, but deep down, he's a rotten plotter of schemes whose hobby is to steal lives away from unsuspecting women."

"Your husband?" Francesca asked. "The king? You are being mistaken. He's nothing like that."

"He's heartless!" Valentina exclaimed.

"No," Francesca retorted. "His heart is having the shield built up by his many responsibilities and you just have to do the hard work to reach it."

"So it's true!" Valentina said accusingly. "You and my husband!"

"It is not being my fault," Francesca said. "I was kidnapped here before it was you that was the one kidnapped."

"Don't change the subject," Valentina screamed. "You have been with my husband!"

"Maybe not like you are thinking," Francesca explained. "I was brought to him because I am looking like you. But we only sing together."

"Oh yeah?" Valentina asked. "Well I was kidnapped because I was mistaken for you! Wait, did you say you sing?"

Francesca nodded her head and said, "He is your husband. If you want him, then you take him. I am not standing in the way. We only do the singing together."

Valentina rose from her chair and went to her sister, then wrapped Francesca with her arms. "So you do like him?"

"Not if you are telling me that I cannot."

Valentina stepped out of the hug and held Francesca's hands saying, "He can be very charming at times."

"Hmmm," Francesca said, "You think he is charming? Maybe I am not seeing so many of those times."

Valentina laughed and led Francesca to the couch so they could talk.

Harvey headed for the door and said, "We'll just go find someplace for a drink. Don't be too long, you two. We'd like you to come find us before the constable locks us up again."

Elizabeth stood awkwardly alone with the two sisters and said, "Well, Diva. I have things to do, but before I go, you've had several requests asking when you might grace the garden with another recital."

Francesca waved her off and said, "Of course I will do the singing for them. You handle it."

"Very well," Elizabeth replied. She went to the door and exited saying, "Diva, Your Maj...." she stopped short of finishing the word *Majesty* when she saw Francesca's eyebrow twitch. She closed the door behind her and scurried down the hallway. She had nothing else to do and set about tracking down the boys. This called for a drink.

Chapter 12

P hilbis Beck sat quietly and patiently in the waiting room at the Vegan consulate. They'd left him sitting there since he first arrived. He'd been there long enough to see plenty of delegates who could have taken the time to see him arrive and ignore him. They made no attempt to hide the fact that they were there and he was quite sure that they would have paraded through a second time had he not acknowledged their arrivals with morning pleasantries. He didn't blame them. He would have done the same if the roles were reversed. He didn't fully understand their reaction to the king's marital problems. He might have understood if she were Vegan, but there was no doubt that the queen's split from the king had precipitated their civil action. Philbis knew it was because of the queen before anybody else, which was why he had ventured out to bring Francesca to the palace. Hopefully, things can turn back to normal now that the king has a suitable replacement.

The lunch hour had come and gone. This may have been their plan. They may be waiting for him to go to lunch so they can come out and wonder where he went, thus blowing the whole meeting. His stomach growled, but he vowed to wait for them. Other guests had come and been invited in ahead of him. He reasoned at first that they probably had appointments, until one very agitated and slightly surly gentlemen hovered over the receptionist demanding to be seen. They let him in. Perhaps Philbis should be noisier and more threatening.

The waiting room grew increasingly warmer after lunch. The weather outside was sunny, but Philbis doubted it was an act of nature. They must have raised the temperature on the environmental controls. The warmth is probably localized to just this area.

The receptionist unbuttoned the top two buttons of her blouse and ran a cool damp cloth from her neck down the center to her newly exposed cleavage. Philbis almost sneered. If they thought they could distract him with that, they were sadly mistaken. But they did distract him, not with her bosoms, but with the puzzle of how her visible cleavage would make him leave. Did she plan to seduce him and lure him off to a secret rendezvous?

Philbis's mind was lost in his thoughts when she said, "It sure is hot in here today." She walked to where he was sitting, and leaned over at the waist, displaying the depths of her ample cleavage when she asked, "Would you like some water? It's cold."

"No, thank you," he replied.

The glass and icy pitcher were in her hands already, so she poured him a glass anyway. She flashed him a quick smile and offered a last opportunity for him to appreciate her body, then returned to her desk. He chuckled quietly at their immature assumption that he would find her body intriguing.

The minutes ticked away. The ice shifted as it melted in the glass she had poured for him. It was hot, and he was thirsty. He started to reach for the glass, but stopped himself. They were very clever. First he would drink the water, then more hours would tick off the clock until finally he must go relieve himself in the lavatory. He retracted his hand and suffered in silence, but he couldn't tear his eyes away from the glass. He watched the ice melt and re-balance itself until there were only shavings floating atop the water.

"Mr. Beck," the receptionist said, "you can go in now."

He stood. His knees were stiff and he wobbled a bit as he stood. He snatched up the water and downed it in a single motion. His gait was stiff as he walked past the receptionist. She winked as he passed by and he involuntarily returned the wink, telling himself that his wink was merely to celebrate his victory over their waiting game, but he had no idea why she would wink to him after his victory.

The ambassador was a rotund man with a smile seemingly as wide as his girth. "Mr. Beck, I'm so sorry for keeping you waiting, but I think I have a good idea why you are here, and I've been trying all day to get parliament to grant me the authority to negotiate with you. They had to put it to a vote, of course. We're just lucky that they didn't make me wait for a press conference first."

"We could have saved us all a lot of trouble," Beck said, "if you had just greeted me first. Like you, I can't negotiate without being granted the authority first. I'm sorry, Mr. Ambassador, but I'm not here to negotiate anything."

"You're not here to negotiate?" the ambassador asked. "Does that mean you are here to make demands and throw out inflexible terms?"

"Not at all," Philbis said. "I'm here to personally invite you and your delegates to a ball at the palace, after which you can negotiate directly with the king and his advisors."

"What kind of nonsense is this? Has the king gone completely mad? You can't celebrate before we negotiate. We intend to be heard. We're not rolling over for him. Tell him no. If he cares to partake in real negotiations, then call on us again."

"Sir," Philbis said, "I don't think you quite understand. The king has a new view of life. He wants to celebrate his new vision with you. He may even invite you to meet the new singer at court. She's quite incredible. Then, he wants to patch up things with Vega. I believe him. I believe he is sincere. May I tell him he can expect you?"

The ambassador scratched his head a moment, then said, "Fine. Tell him we'll be there, but he better have some of that Grubian Port for us."

Philbis bowed his head and shook the ambassador's hand. "Thank you sir. Till then." He walked out past the secretary and out of the corner of his eye, he caught a bit of a frown on her face as he passed by without a word. He still didn't know what she was thinking.

Elizabeth didn't catch up with the boys in the elevator, but there were only so many places they could go within the palace. She rode the elevator down and headed directly to the visitor's lounge. The lounge had a retro motif and looked like something from a 1940's Earth movie. It even produced a non-toxic haze to give it that old fashioned smoky appearance that was only seen in those old movies. She peered through the smoke and saw the five of them in the corner.

Harvey already had shots lined up in a circle around the table of the corner booth.

Gene raised a shot and said, "Here's to another successful adventure."

Bruno lifted his glass and said, "I'll drink to that."

Victor smirked and said, "You'll drink to anything."

Elizabeth approached the table and said, "Hello boys. You got room for one more?"

Harvey didn't hesitate. He slid to his left and shoved Gene into Roy who blocked one end of the circular bench. Had he given it more thought, he would have shoved both of them clean off the bench so she could sit next to him, but as it was Bruno slid over next to Harvey and Victor slid in making room for her.

Elizabeth grabbed a shot and said, "So, to the mission!"

They all replied, "To the mission!" and downed their drinks.

Elizabeth gave it a moment while the liquid assailed her throat, then said, "I never got a chance to thank you for what you did. I know the diva really appreciates it."

Harvey blushed and said, "We just did what anybody would've done."

"Except the king," Gene added, which brought laughs from everyone's lips.

Harvey motioned for the waitress to bring more. With six of them, the drinks weren't going to last very long.

Valentina smiled as she looked into her sister's eyes. "So, Franny, tell me how you got here."

"It's is being such a long story," Francesca said. "I was going to the Valdovian Gardens to perform, but they say we are the stowaways and dumped us into this awful cowboy movie. Then they tell me I have no money, but I tell them I have much money, and they say my money is in Vega, so it is no good. I have to sing for the cowboy's just to have the food and a miserable room. They even call the dump a royal suite. Then everybody wants to give me a ride. I was getting ride from my Elizabeth's friend when the man from the embassy took me away. I was thinking he was a nice man at first, but he was not. He force me to go with him and he gives me the drugs when he brings me here."

Valentina was more interested in what happened when she was here than how she got here. "What happened next?"

Francesca smiled weakly and said, "I guess it was not so long a story after all."

"But what did they do with you? Did they throw you in a jail cell?"

"Almost," Francesca replied. "The king gives me this awful little room on the second floor."

"You mean my room?"

"Your room?," Francesca asked. "No. We went to your room when I was needing a gown to look like you. He gave me another room that was just like this one, but it was on the second floor. I explain to the king that Francesca Vittoria Agostina La Perla only gets the penthouse and he fixed it for me."

"So you only just met him and he already accommodated you?" Valentina asked with surprise.

Francesca shrugged and suggested, "Maybe when he is looking at me, he only sees you."

Valentina laughed and said, "Nope. After I told him I was leaving him, he relocated me to the servants quarters."

"Ah, yes," Francesca said. "That is where I was to get your dress at first, but the maid tells us your real dresses are on second floor."

"That was when you needed to look like me?"

"Si. I was needing to look like you when I order the guards to free my friends."

Valentina's eyebrows rose high on her face as she asked, "You did that for your friends?"

"I did that for you. I think the guards knew that I wasn't being you, but they let the trick work anyway because I was freeing them to rescue you."

Valentina shook her head slowly. "You've changed sister."

"Was it just me," Harvey said with a slight slur, "but did the two sisters not seem so overjoyed to see each other?"

"Oh no!" Elizabeth said a little to loudly. "Well maybe, but they haven't talked to each other in years."

"It's true," Victor slurred. "Francesca hates her sister."

Bruno nodded his head but was too drunk to say anything intelligible.

"No she doesn't," Elizabeth said. "She loves her sister."

Victor wagged his finger and said, "That's not how she talks. She says some mean shit about her."

Bruno came out of his stupor long enough to add a, "Yeah."

Elizabeth yelled out to the bar, "Where's that next round?" then turned to the table and said, "She talks tough, but that's just because they had a big fight the last time they spoke, and they've been fighting ever since. The diva might say shit, but deep down, she still loves her sister."

"Well," Victor replied, "it must be way, way, deep down there."

Bruno's eyes had been rolled up into the back of his head, but they rolled forward long enough for him to add another, "Yeah."

The table grew quiet and they could hear the news on the screen over the bar. "Citizens, Andurians and Vegans, your king..."

"Shhh, shhh, shhh," Elizabeth said, even though the table was dead silent. "I want to hear this."

"I'm not here," the king said, "to point fingers or lay blame. I had hoped that our financial system would have righted itself and stayed afloat on its own, but that is not the case. All of our biggest banks are located in the Vega system. Our stock exchanges are in the Vega system. Our businesses have been unable to pay their employees and our citizens have been forced to sell property and other precious belongings just to put food on the table. We have guests, who are neither Vegan nor Andurian, that have been marooned on the nearest inhabitable planet simply because their travel tickets were Vegan.

"I say enough! Effective immediately, all real estate transactions, and any other high value sale, which has occurred since the Vegan civil action are hence forth negated. All assets involved in real estate transactions are hereby frozen. A palace hot-line will be established to handle what I expect to be flood of calls. All sellers are urged to contact the palace with the details of their sale. We have a lot of work ahead of us, but we will see this through. We will not allow our people to suffer from a political difference. I stand united with you.

"Thank you."

"Did you hear that?" Elizabeth asked. "She made him do that."

Bruno missed it. He had already passed out with his head on the table. Gene was also asleep, leaning against Harvey's shoulder.

"I did," Roy said. "I wonder if she heard it too? Maybe we should go tell her about it."

"How was that?" the king asked as he returned to his office and dropped the speech on his desk.

"I was worried," the butler said, "that even though you said you weren't going to point fingers, that you were about to accuse Vega of using the banks to wage war upon us."

"And if I had? Is that not what they are doing?"

"Perhaps, but they would probably not be willing to come to the bargaining tables if you had."

The king returned to his window and looked outside. The empire didn't look any different, but his thoughts were on Francesca. "Do you think she saw it?"

The butler shrugged. "Even if she didn't, she's sure to hear about it."

The bartender had long ago declared that Harvey's table had had enough and stopped delivering drinks to them. Bruno and Gene were the first to pass out. Victor and Roy hung on by a thread. Their heads nodded forward and sprang back to attention repeatedly. Roy finally took a deep breath and laid his head upon the table so sleep would find him.

Victor grabbed his last shot glass and tilted his head back to drain the last drip from the shot, but as the blood rushed to the back of his brain, his eyes rolled backwards and he fell back against the booth's cushions and slept.

Harvey chuckled and said, "Looks like it's just the two of us, kiddo."

Elizabeth blushed slightly. "I wonder where the sisters are."

Harvey shrugged and said, "They have their own bar in her suite."

Elizabeth laughed and said, "Yeah. That makes sense."

"So," Harvey said, "What's a nice girl like you doing in a place like this?"

"Shhh!" she said abruptly as she returned her attention to the news.

"This just in. Communication lines at the palace are already jammed with people requesting an audience to get their homes back. Officials at the palace say to keep trying. More operators are being brought on staff to handle the extra volume."

Harvey nudged Gene who was still sleeping against his shoulder. "Come on Gene, time to wake up and go home."

Elizabeth laughed. "You want him to wake up so he can go home and sleep it off?"

Harvey replied, "I want everyone to wake up and go to their own beds. I'm the captain. I'll carry them if I have to."

"Even Bruno?"

Harvey looked at Bruno and swallowed hard. "I might need some help with him."

Roy woke up when he heard Harvey wake Gene. "I'm okay. I'll take my brother. You two concentrate on Victor and Bruno."

Elizabeth shook Victor and asked, "Do you think you can get back to your room?"

"What room?" Victor asked.

"On my ship," Harvey replied.

"Yeah, sure," he said.

Elizabeth climbed out of the booth and Victor followed.

Harvey tried waking Bruno with no luck. "You'd think a guy his size could hold his liquor better."

Elizabeth grabbed one of Bruno's arms and pulled while Harvey pushed. Bruno finally rolled open his eyes and climbed out of the booth, leaning heavily on Elizabeth until Harvey was able to get under his other arm.

"All right big boy," Elizabeth said gently as she guided him away from the table. "Let's get you back to the ship."

"Oh my," Francesca said, "are you looking at the time? We are supposed to be back with the others."

"The fault is mine," Valentina said. "It's just been so long and we have so much to catch up on."

"And you are having so much to be warning me about."

"Oh, don't listen to me. He can be a wonderful man and I'm the sister who couldn't make it work with him."

Francesca shook her head and smiled. "I am not knowing why you are not being more jealous."

Valentina pointed at her sister and said, "You're the jealous one, not me."

Francesca turned her head to the back of the suite and yelled, "Elizabeth? It is time that we should be going to find the others."

"Besides," Valentina added, "if I were to be brutally honest, I'd admit that if you want him, it just means I'll be free from here."

Francesca did not understand what her sister had against this marvelous place. She turned again to the back of the suite and furrowed her brow as she yelled, "Elizabeth? Why are you not being here when I call you?"

"I think she left with your friends."

"Did she?" Francesca asked. "That girl is being so unreliable lately. I don't know why I keep her sometimes."

Vincenzo saw the king's pronouncement and thought that if he were really going to be a legitimate businessman, he would have to pursue getting his money back in return for the properties. His mother wouldn't approve. Nor would most of the family, but this had been his dream since he had been a child. He played the role of the gangster boss to keep the underlings in line, and he sometimes had trouble seeing the wrong in the way he was raised, but his true ambition was to make a good honest living.

The king said he would reverse all transactions and there was no doubt in Vincenzo's mind that the properties he had purchased would no longer be his. If he doesn't recover the money, then his family would probably come to him for vengeance. If it came to that, his own mother would probably sign off on a hit.

He had watched the route Harvey's ship took with his long range scanners. Harvey met with no interference from the space patrol. It could mean that

Harvey was working for them and they allowed him back, but Vincenzo suspected that Harvey knew a secret way in to avoid the detection. Pirates and smugglers are good at that sort of thing. Vincenzo plotted a course to exactly follow Harvey's route.

As he was about to enter the planet's outer atmosphere, three patrol cars de-cloaked and had him surrounded.

Elizabeth's head pounded and throbbed like a fire alarm. She pulled the sheets over her head but the pounding continued. She opened one bloodshot eye to peek out from under the covers and saw an alarm buzzing next to the bed. It wasn't her clock. She reached over to stop the alarm and the sheet fell around her waist revealing her bare breasts. She didn't want to look, but she had to. This wasn't her room. She looked next to her in the bed, but she was thankfully alone.

"Hello?" she asked weakly, but nobody answered.

She closed her eyes and started to cry. This was why she did not like to drink so much, but she didn't know how much time she had to escape and didn't want to waste it feeling sorry for herself.

Her head still pounded as she gathered the sheet around her and crept out of the bed looking for her clothes. The starkly bare room with its unadorned white walls gave no clue to her location. Neither did the purely functional bed with no headboard or footboard. The sunken light fixtures and lack of decorative lamps sealed her impression that this was not one of the finer hotel rooms. Tears collected along her lower lids as she considered what she must have done last night. She wished that she hadn't noted how functional the bed was.

She needed to find her clothes and sneak out quickly. A night stand with the alarm clock stood on one side of the bed and a dresser with a view screen was on the opposite wall with a sliding closet door next to it.

The floor was carpeted, but her clothes weren't scattered across the rug, nor were they tossed into the closet. The room had a desk and chair along one wall next to the dresser and a small round table with two chairs stood in the corner, but her clothes weren't piled on the desk or dresser. Nor were they in any of the chairs. Panic gripped her as she realized her clothes were missing. It was a small cabin and she had searched every inch. The only clothes she had found were men's clothes in the closet and dresser drawers.

If she hadn't shed her clothes here, then where were they? Her memory of last night ended at the table drinking rounds and watching Victor pass out. She may never recall what happened, and if her missing clothes were any indication of how the night went, she may not want to remember.

She dreaded the thought of shamefully creeping down the hall wrapped in only a bed sheet and glanced over at the dresser drawer, but before she resorted to wearing a strange man's clothes, she started a second desperate search of the cabin.

If this is a ship and not a hotel, and she doesn't find her own clothes, she'll have to walk all the way back to the palace; to Francesca's suite, where her other clothes were. "Oh God!" she exclaimed to the empty room. "I hope we're still in the space port!"

The guards led Vincenzo into the palace's detention center. "I'm a legitimate businessman. Why are you detaining me?"

"You're a known mobster trying to sneak into the imperial palace."

"I'm a suspected mobster," Vincenzo corrected them. "Twelve arrests and no convictions. I can't help my association with my family, but that's all that you people ever see. The queen is the only one who ever looked at me and saw me for who I really am."

"The queen?" the guard asked. "You really expect us to believe that you know the queen?"

"I do," Vincenzo said. "That is, I do know her, not that I expect you to believe me. You can ask her yourself. She's a lovely woman and she'll vouch for me."

"Nice try, buddy, but she's missing. She's missing, and you're here. Coincidence?"

"No," Vincenzo said, "she was missing, and now she's back."

"It may be true," another guard said, "I just heard someone say they saw her in the hallway, but he may have been drunk. He said there were two of her."

"That would be her twin sister," Vincenzo explained. "I'd really appreciate it if you'd find her for me. I'm here on legitimate business, despite what you think of me or my family."

A second search of the small cabin revealed nothing new for Elizabeth. She had no choice but to resort to borrowing clothes from the dresser. She slid open the top drawer and found a jumbled mess of men's undershorts. Her face blanched as she gingerly fingered through the disgusting pile. She had no idea whose shorts these were or how disgusting he was. She briefly considered sniffing the shorts to see if they were at least clean, but heaved a bit of bile in her throat at the thought.

She set aside the most masculine garments and tried to find something that at least may be a bit softer, but as she sorted through them she heard someone unlocking the door. She slammed the drawer shut and leapt onto the bed, but the sheet was caught in the drawer and she landed naked on the sheetless bed. The door started to open and she darted into the miniscule clothes closet which barely had room for her as she parted the hanging clothes and slipped inside. She slid the door shut just as she heard someone enter the room.

Harvey held a package under one arm and a tray of boxed food in the other. He closed the door behind him and looked curiously at the empty bed. "Elizabeth?"

She felt her face warm as her cheeks turned a dark crimson. She was glad to be hidden in the unlit closet.

Harvey saw the sheet hanging from the dresser drawer, which was even odder than the empty bed, and asked again, "Elizabeth? Where are you?"

Why did it have to be him? Of course it had to be him. What other scoundrel would have taken advantage of her? Hiding was pointless, but she wasn't going to expose herself to him, at least not while she was sober, so she cracked open the closet door and stuck her arm out and waved.

"Ah there you are," he said. "You hungry?"

She could smell the food and the coffee. She was starving, but she wasn't leaving the closet. "No, thanks. I'm fine."

He set the food on the table and sat down to enjoy it. "Suit yourself."

The sound of him eating infuriated her. She had no doubt that a guy like him thought nothing of a brief encounter with a woman, and he probably had thousands of them, but for him to sit down and eat while she was stuck in the closet had to be the coldest thing a man had ever done to her.

"You should really try some of this," he said. "It's very good. And I got some pain killers too. I'm guessing your head probably hurts a bit."

"You son of a bitch," she spat at him. "You know god damned well that my head hurts." Her head pounded from yelling at him, but she only half regretted it.

"Wow," he said. "I try to be a gentleman and take real good care of you, and I get called names. I even brought you one of those fancy coffees with a double shot."

"Oooh!" she growled. "You really are an asshole!"

"Does your mother know you talk to men that way? I find your whole tone to be a bit offensive."

"I'm offensive?" she screamed. "How dare you?"

"How dare I what?" he asked. "I protected you from God knows what kind of harm you would have gotten yourself into."

"But who was there to protect me from you?" she asked.

Harvey got up from his breakfast and walked to just outside the closet. "You don't remember last night do you?"

She didn't, but she wouldn't let him know that or he would deny everything. "Of course I remember, it's just that you weren't all that memorable."

"That's what I thought," he said. "You don't remember anything. It's nothing to be ashamed of. You were pretty lit up."

But, she was ashamed. She was ashamed that she couldn't remember and she was ashamed of whatever she had done even though she couldn't remember it.

"Do you remember us walking Bruno home from the lounge?"

"Of course I do," she said truthfully.

"And do you remember Bruno stumbling into the fountain in the atrium?"

"Yes," she lied. "Is there a point to this?"

"How about falling in after him?" Harvey asked. "Do you remember that?"
She didn't.

"And do you remember shivering because your clothes were soaking wet?"
She didn't remember that either.

"Here," he said as he shoved the package he brought into the closet.

She opened the package and found her clothes dried and neatly folded inside. "But how did you get my clothes off of me...oh never mind. I don't need to know."

Harvey went back to his breakfast mumbling, "And I bet you don't remember me sleeping on the floor, either." She didn't hear him and wouldn't have remembered that either.

Valentina and Francesca arrived at the lounge long after the others had left.

"You see what you did?" Francesca said. "You talk too much. Now they are gone."

Valentina ignored her sister's caustic remarks and asked the bartender, "Did you see some strangers come in here last night?"

Francesca joined her and added, "One of them was being very big and two of them were little tiny guys."

The bartender looked back and forth between the two sisters, not sure who he was addressing, then finally said, "Yes, I saw them, your majesties. They drank too much and headed off towards the atrium. If I had to guess, I'd say they left the palace."

"Thank you," Valentina said as she tugged her sister's arm and headed for the atrium.

"Were you hearing that?" Francesca asked. "He called us both majesties."

Valentina laughed and said, "Two of us is just one too many."

They entered the atrium, but before they crossed it, Francesca pointed to the far side and said, "Look! That's one of the men who tried to rescue me from that awful cowboy place."

Valentina pointed and asked, "Him? He's the one who tried rescuing me from here!"

Valentina turned and followed them to the detention center with Francesca right behind her. They hadn't even gotten Vincenzo into a cell yet, when Valentina bellowed, "What are you doing with him?"

The guard's complexion paled a shade as he asked, "Your majesty? This man was trying to sneak onto the palace grounds."

"This man is my guest," she said in her most commanding voice. "I invited him here and you will release him at once!"

"But your majesty, the king wants us to hold him."

"Is that right?" Francesca bellowed. "Maybe you didn't notice, but there are TWO of us and we want him released!"

The guards had always favored the queen, but there were limits to how far they would bend the king's commands and were relieved when he entered the room and demanded, "What's all the shouting about? I can hear you all the way down the corridor."

"This man is our friend," the queen proclaimed.

"And we demand that he is released at once!" Francesca finished.

"This man?" the king asked. "You mean the notorious Stonewright mobster? You want him released?"

The king laughed, but the sisters stood their ground. "Yes!" the queen bellowed. "He is trying to turn over a new leaf and go against his family's illicit ways."

"I'm sorry, my dear, but I can't let him go just because my estranged wife wants me too."

Francesca drew in a deep breath and sang,

> *"You little man,*
> *You small hearted lout,*
> *If you ever want me,*
> *YOU'LL LET HIM OUT!"*

The king sang back,

> *"I'll free him now,*
> *But not to leave,*
> *Let the courts decide,*
> *Who they believe."*

"Really?" Francesca asked. "You are rhyming leave with the believe? That's practically the same word, and you call yourself a singer?"

Valentina stood in stunned silence as she watched the two of them sing and bicker. "I think we should take him and go, before my husband changes his mind. We can help him prepare his defense, I think."

"You go," Francesca said. "I will be speaking with the king."

It wasn't a trial and there were no witnesses. The judge had hundreds of transactions electronically recorded, and was prepared to summarily reverse every one of them, but this time, one of the parties stood before him to plead at least his own case. The judge pointed to Vincenzo and asked, "Why is this man here?"

Vincenzo stood and said, "I'm here to help the court reverse these sales. I did what I could to help the people and made a great many purchases over the last several weeks, but when I heard the king's speech, I knew I should come and help unravel this mess."

The judge took another look at the records and asked, "Are you Vincenzo Stonewright?"

"Yes sir."

"*The* Vincenzo Stonewright of the Stonewright mafia?"

"I don't like that term, your honor. They are my family and I had no control over where I was born."

"But," the judge said, "it would seem that you have a great deal of control over the family's holdings and you used that money to purchase quite a bit of real estate."

Vincenzo shrugged and said, "I was only trying to use my family's fortune to help the desperate people."

"It was blood money," the judge continued. "Money that you and your family gained illegally."

"That's not fair," Vincenzo complained. "It was money that I had wisely held in good Andurian investments. If there had been anything illegal about the money, then surely the empire would have taken it from us before now."

"I'm disgusted by this," the judge growled. "You were profiting from the people's misfortunes."

Vincenzo shrugged and said, "I was helping them and I was expanding my own portfolio. Since when was that illegal?"

"We have always frowned upon washing blood money through supposed legal transactions. These sales are invalid."

"Fine then," Vincenzo said. "That's why I came here to help. Let's cancel the sales and return the money."

"We'll cancel the sales," the judge said, "but you won't be getting your blood money back."

"But you can't do that," Vincenzo replied. "That would make you a thief, and that's illegal. I've spent my life trying to live down my family's legacy. I'm a legitimate business man. I've never been convicted of any crime. These were legitimate transactions. I bought some homes and helped some people whose lives were nearly destroyed by *YOU*. You can't do this. You don't have the authority. If you do this, you'll destroy me."

"If I do this," the judge said, "I'll be destroying your family. I'll be a hero."

"Do you truly believe that everyone in my family is a mobster? The women? The children? The *BABIES*? You'll be taking food from the babies' mouths. I've been a legitimate businessman making money for the family in legal ways, and I'm sure that I'm not the only one, yet you feel that you have the right to strip my entire family of everything I invested when I was only trying to help people?"

Vincenzo was right when he said the judge didn't have the authority, but the judge was an elected official and done properly, this decision could be worth some votes to a higher office. "Mr. Stonewright, do you have council?"

"No, your honor."

"Well I suggest you get some. I'm not a heartless man, and on the off chance that some of what you say is the truth, I'll offer you half of your money back. The remainder will be held in escrow pending an investigation by the organized crime bureau."

Vincenzo wasn't happy. He'd had run-ins with the OCB before, and he didn't trust them, but half the money now with a chance to recover the rest may save his life.

The queen had been sitting quietly in the back of the gallery watching the proceedings. She met Vincenzo in the aisle as he headed towards the courtroom's exit.

Vincenzo hugged her and asked, "What are you doing here?"

"I thought I was going to speak on your behalf, but you did so well that you certainly didn't need me."

Vincenzo pushed the door open and held it for her. "I'm not out of the woods yet. My family will be expecting me to recover all the money, not just half. I think he offered me half as a political move. The whole OCB investigation could just be a smoke screen. I wouldn't be surprised if he has no intention of letting me have the rest."

"What will you do?"

Vincenzo shrugged. "Maybe I can work with the OCB to get at least some of the money back from them. In the meantime, I'll have to try to find some ways to make the rest back."

"That's a lot of money," she said. "How long would it take for you to make that kind of money?"

"Legally?" he asked. "It could take a while. Making fast money is my family's game, if you know what I mean. I might be able to..."

Vincenzo's communicator started whining and whistling. He looked at the screen to make sure it wasn't his mother and said, "Excuse me, but this is one of my business associates."

"Hey Boss," Milton said from the speaker, "I know you told me to keep an eye on the receipts at this place, and they've picked up a little, but not enough. This place ain't never gonna payoff if we don't do something to pick up business. You want that I should go ahead and start making plans for that casino?"

"Not just yet," Vincenzo replied, "The OCB is holding onto half our assets and you know what the books look like. I'm not willing to commit those kinds of funds to building anything just yet."

"All right boss, you want that I should still stay?"

"Yeah. Let's see if business picks up now that the king is patching things up with Vega. If it does, I want you to keep a tally of what kinds of visitors we get."

"Sure thing boss."

The queen wasn't being nosy when she eavesdropped on Vincenzo's call with Milton, but she was interested in seeing that her husband didn't ruin the man. "It sounds like my husband did more than just ruin your real estate deals."

"Yeah," Vincenzo said as he resumed walking out into the atrium. "I still gots a stake in this dude ranch out by Gellian Prime."

"You know, I may be able to help you make it more profitable."

"Thanks, sister, I can tell you're a real sharp dame, but I think we already tried just about everything there short of building that casino, and I'm not risking any money until I gets more of it back from the OCB."

Valentina winced and said, "I don't know if a casino is such a great move for someone trying to distance himself from the stigma of a crime family."

"Tell me about it, but what else can bring in those kinds of smackers?"

"I haven't seen it yet, but I'm assuming you have horses and cowboys and stuff like that."

"Sure we got those. Most of them are fake, of course, but they give it the ambiance."

"What you need is an attraction that can bring in the people, and if you ask me, horses and cowboys should bring in families with kids."

"It should," he said, "but that ain't what's happening. We even thought of building real amusement park rides for the kiddies."

"But," she said, "You still need that one of a kind attraction that will bring people in."

Vincenzo sat down on a park bench that faced a pond with a fountain. Valentina sat next to him and he said, "You see how those flowers over there reflect off the top of the water?"

"Yeah," she said, "It's kind of pretty."

"Well, they got one of those. It reflects the rings of Gellian Prime. That's their big attraction."

"What you need is something that everybody has heard of and already loves, but something that they can only see by going to your ranch."

"Great idea," Vincenzo said, "let me just order one up and have it delivered."

"Okay," she said, "But it won't come free. You'll have to negotiate a contract."

Vincenzo looked at her like she was completely nuts, but something in her eyes told him that she was not only serious, but she already had something in mind to fill the bill. "Alright, sister, I'll bite. What great attraction can I order up that everybody loves and will come pay money to see?"

Valentina jumped up from the bench and struck a pose with her elbows on her hips and her arms extended with her palms up. "Me!"

Francesca followed the king back to his office.

"What?" he asked. "I let your dubious friend out. What more do you want?"

"I am not Valentina. That man was being my sister's friend and we thank you for helping."

"So? Was there something more that you wanted?"

Francesca closed the door. She had a fierce expression on her face that he couldn't read. She stepped slowly towards him and he thought it would be better to step around his desk for the conversation.

She puffed out her chest and sucked in a deep breath, then clasped her hands over her heart and softly sang,

> *"A beguiling play ensnares us now,*
> *My sister, me and you.*
> *How strange I find, my feelings are,*
> *To the man she's married to."*

The king winced at her awkward grammar and replied,

"No stranger than the feelings I
Have nurtured for you two,"

The king grimaced at his own awkward phrase then continued in a monotone voice,

"not you too as in you also but you two as in you both, the two of
you."

Francesca shrugged her shoulders and raised her eyebrows at his even more awkward recovery.

He continued,

"You and she both look the same,
But into different women you grew."

"Really?" she asked. "You grew?" The king just shrugged and she said, "You better let me handle this." Francesca clasped her hands in front of her and sang,

"She says she wants a different life,
I understand not why.
This place has much potential, so,
For her job I apply.

But don't think things can stay the same,
If you take me for your queen.
I set a higher standard than
My sister, as you've seen."

The king's mind swirled in his head. It sounded like she just proposed to him, but he's still married...to her sister no less. She said it like the two of them had arranged it all between them. He meekly nodded his ascent. She was the most assertive woman he had ever known, and he was drawn to her. If there were any legal problems with the arrangement, he had people who could work out the details. It should be easy since they had already agreed to the proposal.

Roy and Harvey entered the elevator and quietly smiled at the other guests.

"So?" Harvey asked. "Did he tell you what he wanted?"

Roy held his finger to his lips and jerked his eyes towards the other guests as he whispered, "Shhh."

The doors opened on the second floor and the other passengers exited, leaving Harvey and Roy alone on the lift. Harvey waited for the doors to close before asking, "Now can you tell me what's going on?"

"Not really," Roy said. "Gene just said to meet him in the Diva's quarters."

"Ahh," Harvey said. "I'm sure glad we didn't spill that to the whole world."

"He said he was getting us in on the ground floor of something really big."

"Oh great, another one of his get rich quick schemes. Since when did Gene become the brains of any outfit?"

The elevator doors swished open and they followed the hall down to the Diva's suite. Harvey knocked, but Roy just turned the knob and let them in. Gene was sitting on a steamer trunk talking to Valentina. "Oh good," he said when Roy entered the room. "You're here. We're going back."

"I'm sorry," Roy said. "We're what?"

"We're going back to Emaude Phlott; to the dude ranch."

"We are?"

"Yes!" Gene nodded enthusiastically. "With the queen!"

Roy glanced over at the queen who was grinning broadly.

"We'll be the queen's personal attendants."

"Technically," Valentina said, "I won't be the queen anymore."

"Yeah you will," Roy said. "Once a queen, always a queen. You may not be the current reigning queen, but you'll still be a queen."

Roy made a funny face and Valentina asked, "What's wrong?"

"Nothing," Roy said. "It just felt strange saying the word 'queen' so many times in a single breath."

Harvey asked, "Hey fellas, what's any of this have to do with me?"

Gene shrugged and said, "I dunno. Why are you here?"

Roy replied, "I just assumed you wanted both of us."

"Nope, not for this part, I just needed my brother."

"Wait a sec," Roy said. "Why would we want to go back to Emaude Phlott?"

"For me," Valentina said. "I have arranged to live and work there so we can get it back on its feet again."

"You're going to work?" Roy asked.

"Don't look so surprised," she replied. "I wasn't always your queen. I used to work for a living. Besides, I'm just there to make appearances and draw in the crowd."

"But why?" Roy asked. "Before we left, we overheard them talking about the mob putting in a casino."

"Yeah," Gene said rubbing his hands together, "It will be a gold mine! I can't wait."

Roy shook his head and said, "It will be a magnet for degenerates and losers."

"That's not fair," Gene objected. "Lots of fine people like to play the games of chance."

"Sure," Roy replied, "but some of them lose their shirts and end up roaming our streets penniless."

"Boys," Valentina interrupted, "We're not building a casino. If things go well enough, we will build amusement rides to draw in the families with kids."

"We?" Harvey asked.

"Awww," Gene said. "I really wanted to play the games."

Roy chuckled. "You can still play the games on the midway."

"We?" Harvey repeated.

"Mr. Stonewright and myself," Valentina replied. "We're going into business together."

Harvey scratched his head and asked, "Are you sure this isn't that Denmark syndrome?"

"Stockholm," Roy corrected him.

"I'm fine," she said. "It was all my idea. I'll stay at the hotel and give the Andurian people a chance to come mingle with their queen."

"Sweet gig," Gene said.

"You don't look convinced," Valentina said.

Harvey shrugged and said, "It's just that Francesca may become queen. What makes you think they'll want to meet you?"

"Really Mr. Kushkin, which of us do you think they would rather meet?"

"She has a point," Gene said.

"I guess," Harvey admitted.

Elizabeth entered the room with Francesca and Gene started jumping up and down on the steamer trunk. "Wait till you hear the best part! Elizabeth! Go ahead and tell them!"

All heads turned to Elizabeth and she said, "On occasion, I'll book the diva to sing there."

"You hear that?" Gene said. "We'll have both of them there! I'm telling you, we're going to be rich!"

Harvey was puzzled. "I'm not sure why having both of them there has you so excited. Besides, the way things are going, do you really think the king is going to let her continue singing?"

"Let her?" Francesca asked. "Nobody *lets* Francesca Vittoria Agostina La Perla sing. They beg her to sing."

"But," Harvey explained, "if things continue going the way they have been, are you sure the king will want you travelling around singing? Wouldn't he tend to keep you at his side?"

Francesca snorted and raised her nose in the air. "Francesca needs no man's permission. I am not being his pet. Besides, I got him the bit part singing in the opera. He'll do whatever I want him to do."

"The king?" Harvey asked. "The emperor is going to perform on stage? Isn't that dangerous?"

"We'll be taking the precautions," Francesca replied. "And he'll be anonymous with someone else's name."

Elizabeth came to Harvey and put her arms around his waist. "Don't be such a glass half empty guy all the time. This will work."

"It won't be that easy," Harvey said. "Do you really think having him perform under an alias will be enough? Moving people around in secrecy can be very difficult."

Elizabeth smiled coyly and said, "That's why the king will need to commission a special office for a flight captain to shuttle him around in secrecy."

"Good luck with that," Harvey said. "There are probably only a handful of people who could guarantee his safety on trips like that."

"So," Elizabeth said. "It will be a very exclusive and highly rewarding job and only the best need apply."

"He's not that easy to work for," Harvey added, "and it could be dangerous too! Who in their right mind would want a job like that?"

Elizabeth just smiled coyly and stared into his eyes.

"Great," he gulped. "You want me to be the royal smuggler."

Chapter 13

Vincenzo shoved the communicator in front of Milton's face and said, "You tell her, she won't believe me."

Milton tried backing away, but he ran into the buckboard and couldn't escape the looming comm unit.

"Tell her," Vincenzo growled.

Milton reluctantly took the device and said, "Mrs. Stonewright. This is Milton. How are you?"

"How am I?" she screamed out of the speaker. "You give me back to my good for nothing two-bit son!"

Milton held the comm unit at arm's length and said, "She wants to talk to you."

Vincenzo walked away saying, "No. You manage the books. You tell her."

His voice squeaked slightly as he said, "Mrs. Stonewright? Hi. This is Milton again. Vinny had to step away."

"Did you call my Vinny 'Vinny'? He's Mr. Stonewright to you!"

"Yes ma'am, but I didn't want to remind you of your husband, Mr. Stonewright, the Don, may he rest in peace."

Her tone softened some as she said, "Well, that was good thinking, but his father was a no account loser just like my Vinny. What do you mean he stepped away? I was talking to him, and I'm his mother."

"I'm sure he would have liked talking to you a bit longer, but we are just so busy here, you wouldn't believe it."

"I don't."

"It's true. We're raking in more dough here than we make in the Starliner Casino."

"Oh? So my Vinny finally built the casino like I told him he should do?"

"No ma'am. No casino. Just tourists. They come in from all over and they're loaded with dough-re-mi."

"No casino?"

"No ma'am, but we were hoping to build an amusement park with rides for the kids. This place is already a gold mine, but I think we could double the take in three years."

"I don't get it," she said. "What's the scam?"

"No scam," he replied. "It's one-hundred-percent legit, and you could say that it has the royal seal of approval."

"And my little Vinny did this thing?"

"Yes ma'am. He may be a genius when it comes to this stuff."

"But what about all that money he lost?"

"Are you still blaming him for that? That money was confiscated because of the many questionable Stonewright enterprises, none of which were his doing. Besides, he's already made all that money back, and he did it legitimately."

She didn't reply.

"You know, Mrs. Stonewright, you should come here for a vacation and see the place for yourself."

"To a horse ranch? I don't think so."

"You could meet the queen. She's dying to meet you, you know. She's always asking your son when she's going to get to meet his mother."

"Why would she ask him that?"

"Because she's a nice lady and she wants to meet his family."

Valentina followed Vincenzo from his office at the resort to the wide lawn between the hotel and the reflecting pond. "Why don't you talk to your mother?"

Vincenzo paused so she could catch him. "She's impossible. She thinks I'm an idiot and can't do anything right, yet she insists that I fix the family fortune."

"But you already recovered the money which was lost."

"Not according to her."

"Can't she look at the accounts?"

Vincenzo sighed. "She could, but I'm so stupid in her eyes that it's not even worth her time to look."

"Maybe she needs a doctor."

"Sure," Vincenzo laughed, "if he marries her. She needs a man in her life so she can pick on him and stop focusing on me."

Valentina stopped walking and asked, "How am I ever going to meet her if the two of you can't find some way to get along?"

Vincenzo stopped and turned. "You don't have time to meet her. We have so many people coming here, I've had to add on more appearances for you to greet them."

"Not more autographs," she complained.

"Yes, more autographs. And don't forget, you need to finish that book about your life in the palace. That will give people something new to have you sign."

Valentina flashed him a half smile and started walking down the path to the reflecting pond. "You mean I have to start that book. I told you, I'm no writer."

"What happened to the ghostwriter I hired for you?"

"Which one?" she asked. "There were three."

"Pick one. If there were three ghostwriters, where's the book?"

Valentina scowled. "They were horrid. Each of them wanted to write a nasty little expose of anything that would embarrass the king."

"So?"

"So?" she asked as she picked up a pebble and flung it at him. "He's not a bad man, and he's going to be my sister's husband. I won't have them write lies about him. Besides, if we publish a book, the lines will get even longer and they're long enough already."

"I know. We need to build the amusement park just to spread out the lines."

"So you need to make nice with your mother so you can get her blessing to use the family money to build the park."

They reached the reflecting pond and Vincenzo gazed out at the rings of Gellian reflecting off the ripples. "You'd think this would be enough of an attraction for everybody."

Valentina put her arm around his waist and said, "But, imagine how long the lines would be if this were the only attraction."

"It's kind of funny," Harvey said, "taking Francesca back to Emaude Phlott. I thought she'd never want to go back there."

"Yeah," Elizabeth agreed. "It wasn't really up to her standards."

"Nothing is ever up to her standards, but that place seemed to irritate her at every turn. What did she call it?"

Elizabeth laughed and said, "She said it was all a cowboy movie and called it Mud Flats."

"Well, there it is."

"Woah," Elizabeth exhaled while looking out the ships cockpit windows, "I don't remember the rings being so beautiful."

"I do," Harvey said, "but it was a different kind of beauty."

"You mean when you slalomed us through the ice to evade the police?"

"I guess that some people just can't appreciate that kind of beauty."

"I'll go tell her we're here."

Elizabeth took the lift to the mid-level where the lounge was located. "Diva? We're almost there."

"Yes," Francesca said, "I am seeing the rings myself. They are being much prettier than I remember."

"You never got to see them from out here, did you? You were unconscious when you were kidnapped."

Francesca shivered and said, "I prefer not to be remembering that ride, but I am really looking forward to seeing my sister again."

Philbis escorted three Vegan dignitaries into the royal conference rooms and showed them to their seats. The king was anxious to get this whole incident behind him and was already seated at the head of the conference table.

The head delegate scanned around the room at those present and said, "I had hoped the queen would also be in attendance, seeing as how she was at the center of this controversy, even if not by her own wishes."

"I understand," the king said, "and I anticipated as much, but the queen is off planet on business that is quite her own. She has agreed, however, to join us via tele-conference." The king nodded to the butler and a large view-screen at the end of the room lit up.

"Can you hear me?" the queen asked even before her image was fully rendered on the screen.

"Yes, my dear," the king responded. "We hear you quite well. Perhaps our guests can introduce themselves."

"Is that Horace?" the queen asked. "Horace certainly needs no introduction."

The lead dignitary stood up and said, "Indeed, your majesty. It is I. This fine gentleman on my right is the secretary of finance, Armani Gumwalt, and on my left, acting as my assistant, is Bernard Kane."

"Little Bernie?" the queen asked. "Your nephew?"

Bernie stood and bowed. "Your majesty honors me with her fine memory."

Valentina nodded her head and said, "You may want to tone down the 'your majesties' since I have abdicated the throne, but we've agreed that I will still hold the title of queen."

Bernie bowed again and said, "As you wish my queen."

Horace nodded to his nephew as a subtle suggestion that he may sit down again. "May I say, for all of Vega, that I hope the queen is well and in a place that brings her the great happiness she so deserves."

"I'm fine," she replied, "in fact, I'm better than fine. You are most welcome to come for a visit. I'm sure you will find it as restful here as I do."

"I would like that," Horace replied. Part of him wanted to visit just to confirm that she wanted to be there and was not marooned on that strange little moon.

"Gentlemen," the king said, "may we turn to the topic at hand?"

"We see no need," Horace replied. "The queen appears quite well, and she is someplace where we can readily audit and confirm her well-being. Vega is satisfied and ready to ratify the temporary truce that has been in place. We see no reason that we cannot resume business as it was before."

"Not so fast," the king replied. "The actions taken by Vega in defense of the queen have exposed a dangerous hole in the empires economy. In order to prevent the collapse of the empire at the hands of our enemies, Anduria has begun the implementation of a dual banking and trading system located in Anduria."

Armani squirmed in his seat. Vega was aware of what was going on. No matter how the king sugar coated it, Vega was losing its monopoly on high finance.

Horace thought Armani would say something, but when he didn't, Horace cleared his throat and said, "Vega, of course, favors any step that strengthens our defenses against financial disaster. If there is anything we can do to assist Anduria, we are at her disposal. Perhaps, in the not too distant future, we can tie our systems together as backups for each other."

The king barely suppressed a smile. He loved to see them squirm. "Anduria is grateful for Vega's offer and rest assured, we will call upon Vega when she is needed."

Valentina knew that her sister was coming. Elizabeth had arranged for Francesca to sing for them at the dinner show. Francesca didn't care that they would be eating. She was here for a different purpose. She stood in the back of the room and watched her sister work. Valentina's shift was almost over and the doors had already been closed to prevent any more tourists until the next show.

Valentina sat on a small throne and greeted the people as they came in; sometimes one at a time; other times she would see couples together or even a whole family at the same time. She kissed the babies and stroked the young girl's hair. She always shared a personal story with every visitor.

Gene stood on her right hand side with a lap tray that he handed to her whenever they asked for autographs. Every signature was accompanied by a personal note. She signed anything they asked her to sign: pictures, books, clothing, and even the little girls' cheeks. Roy had always been concerned that some unruly men would ask her to sign something she would have to refuse, but they never did.

The line of families waiting to see her finally ran down and Francesca approached. "You must be exhausted."

"From this?" Valentina asked. "It's hardly even work, certainly nothing compared to what you do. Speaking of which, aren't you supposed to be singing soon? Let me walk you to the stage."

Francesca hooked her arm into Valentina's and replied, "Only if you can be hearing what I am to say."

They walked arm in arm out of the mini throne room and onto the campus. "I'm listening," Valentina said.

Francesca squeezed Valentina's arm and said, "I am needing to know for sure. This is all so strange, but you won't be hating me if I am seeing your husband?"

"Again?" Valentina asked. "How many times must you ask me this dear sister? He is no longer my husband. I have made a new life. It's okay. He's yours."

"But, this is different. I am needing to have your blessing."

"My blessing? Have you fallen and hit your head?"

"I won't be doing it if you cannot give me your blessing."

"What's with this blessing?" Valentina asked, then in an instant of clarity, she asked, "You mean that he wants to marry you?"

"Stop joking," Francesca insisted. "You know we've already planned the wedding."

"And haven't I already given you my blessing?"

Francesca nodded her head.

"And you are still sure that you wish to do this? He's a charming man, but I didn't find him to be that great in the husband department."

Francesca nodded again and said, "I am not being you."

"Then you have my blessing, again. Where's my calendar? When were you planning to do this?"

Francesca blushed, a rarity for her, and said, "Tomorrow, as if you didn't already know."

"Tomorrow?" Valentina feigned surprise. "That's too soon! How can I get ready in time? I need to get a gift for you! Tomorrow?!? What are you doing here?"

"I want you with me," Francesca said, "and I was afraid you wouldn't come because he was there."

Valentina hugged her sister and said, "Of course I'll be there. I'm already packed. Didn't I already agree to give you away? As long as you're here, we can go back together. Just let me tell everyone that you won't be singing tonight because of a prior engagement. I wouldn't want you to be late for your own wedding."

"No," Francesca said. "Francesca never cancels the show, except when she is being marooned in the cowboy movie, but that's not today. The show must be going on."

"Very well," Valentina said. She walked her sister to the dining hall to the back stage entrance. "You're on in two minutes," she said. "You wait here until you're announced."

Valentina grabbed a microphone and walked out onto the stage. The crowd erupted in applause when they saw her. She bowed and said, "Thank you. Thank you. I love you too, but let me now introduce my very own sister, the number one leading soprano for all the empire, Francesca Vittoria Agostina La Perla. I'm sure you've all heard that tomorrow will be a very special day for her. I'm quite certain that all of you will grow to love her as I do."

Francesca joined her sister on stage and the audience was hushed.

"You may have noticed," Valentina said, "that she is me. Francesca is my twin sister, except, she sings like an angel."

They hugged again and Valentina retreated to the royal table that was always reserved for her. She stood at her table and led the audience in their applause for her sister. Francesca smiled broadly to the audience, then nodded to Victor who started the music and she began to sing.

Harvey stood at the top of the ramp greeting his guests as they boarded his ship.

"Ah," Valentina said, "I see that Mr. Harvey is still in your employ."

Francesca laughed and said, "He is now being the royal smuggler."

Harvey frowned towards Francesca, then took Valentina's hand and kissed it while bowing in the formal manor. "I like to think of myself as the protector of the precious cargo."

Victor added, "I think he really prefers to be called the Czar of Stealth."

Harvey wadded up the manifest he was holding and threw it at Victor. "Ladies, won't you follow me to the observation lounge?"

"So formal," Elizabeth laughed. "I think we know the way by now."

Victor adjusted Harvey's collar and straightened his tie, saying, "It just doesn't matter how big a title they give you, does it? You just don't get any respect around here."

Elizabeth hip-bumped Victor and shoved him out of the way. She finished arranging Harvey's collar and said, "Don't worry. Everyone respects you. They only tease you because they have grown to love you as much as I do."

Harvey wrapped his arms around Elizabeth and said, "My ego could use a little respect right about now."

Elizabeth broke the embrace and said, "If you want some respect, then I suggest you get us to the wedding on time."

Harvey clicked his heels at attention and saluted her saying, "Aye, aye Captain!"

"They should be back by now," the king whined.

The butler leaned back against the king's desk and watched him pace nervously back and forth.

"This is all your fault," the king continued. "You told me to hire that pirate. He's probably holding the whole wedding party hostage."

"He's not holding them hostage," the butler replied. "And, if he were, you'd just pay it."

"I don't make deals with pirates."

"Yes you do, and if you didn't, I'd pay it out of my own pocket. You need this wedding. She's the one."

"Is she?" the king asked. "How can you be sure?"

"Because you're afraid of her."

The king stopped pacing and barked, "The king is not afraid of her. I fear no woman."

The butler laughed and said, "You're almost as afraid of keeping her as you are of losing her. In my experience, any woman whose husband is not afraid of losing her is the most dangerous of all. You're afraid of losing her and that makes her perfect for you."

The king leaned on his desk next to his longtime friend, then jumped back to the center of the room and said, "I can't lounge around here. I need to go see that the hall is in order."

"Relax," the butler said, "I've already seen to all the details. You need to sit down and take it easy. Have a drink even."

The king sat down in his chair behind the desk and drummed his fingers on the blotter. "Where is she? What if there was an accident?"

The butler closed his eyes and shook his head slowly.

Nothing matches the pomp and grandeur of a royal wedding. The cathedral was just outside the palace grounds, but was every bit as ornate as the palace. Four tall white spires marked the corners of the main building, surrounded by smaller structures which in turn were surrounded by a variety of gardens. An ancient graveyard in the back of the cathedral grounds was host to some of the most celebrated members of the king's ancestors, plus a couple more notorious members best forgotten.

The mood within the cathedral was predictably anxious. The queen had addressed the empire on several occasions to quell any feelings of loss or replacement of her position. In truth, since they were twins, the transition may have gone unnoticed if they had kept it quiet, but Valentina had insisted that Francesca deserved the full blown wedding in front of everybody.

The music started and the crowd quieted. Valentina walked Francesca up the aisle, which was a site few were prepared to see, no matter how many times they had been informed about the queen's twin. The king waited at the altar, with Johnny, the butler, at his side.

The sisters weren't unattractive women, but neither were they runway models. Their dark black locks framed their faces in large wavy curls. Valentina's curls splayed out upon her shoulder while Francesca's remained suspended under the white veil.

Francesca shook at her core. Waves of nervousness rattled up into her chest and radiated outward. She wasn't just marrying a man, she was marrying an empire. Valentina squeezed her hand to steady her. They walked slowly and deliberately. Neither of them locked their steps to the music, which they barely heard. Francesca was filled with doubts, and slowed slightly. Valentina knew exactly what her sister was feeling and urged her forward.

At the foot of the altar, Francesca looked hesitantly into her sister's eyes.

"It's okay," Valentina said. "This is what you've dreamed about since we were little girls."

Francesca left her sister to stand next to the king.

Elizabeth stood in the front row and squeezed Harvey's arm.

Francesca's mind was a blur as the ceremony started. It was like she wasn't even there. It didn't need her and proceeded on its own just fine without her. She glanced over at the king who turned now to face her. He took her hands in his and turned her to face him. She vaguely heard someone ask, "Do you Francesca Vittoria Agostina La Perla take this..." Her mind blanked out again. What were they thinking? Did they think she would come this far only to change her mind? What was she thinking? She was already the grand queen of the opera world. She already had billions of loyal subjects who adored her. Why did she need to do this?

All eyes were on Francesca. She stared into the king's eyes. He seemed to expect something. The question! He was waiting for her to answer. Her heart palpitated in her chest as she drew a breath and sang,

> *"Before I say,*
> *I ask of you,*
> *Is this really*
> *What you want to do?"*

The king's heart melted and a great joy shaped his face into a broad smile as he sang in a sweet tenor.

> *"No greater joy,*
> *Could bless my life,*
> *Than for you, my dear,*
> *To be my wife."*

Francesca shared a sly smile with him. Life and wife were obvious, though difficult rhymes, but not bad when so many were watching.

> *"That's good to hear,*
> *I think so too,*
> *I'll say the words,*
> *To you, 'I do.'"*

Guests throughout the church grew quiet. They had heard the stories of the day when Francesca had arrived and the two of them had an operatic argument at dinner. Rumors of them singing in other venues within the palace had also circulated, but nobody expected them to break out in song at their own wedding, and neither had they.

Some guests thought it was a shameful break from tradition. They saw it as making a mockery of the wedding, but most guests saw something else. The king and Francesca had a special connection that they could witness, but few would ever experience.

The king couldn't contain himself and belted out,

> *"My word to you,*
> *I give this day,*
> *With the words, 'I do,'*
> *That I now say."*

Together, they turned to face the congregation and sang,

> *"To those of you who witness this,*
> *We pledge our love within this song,*
> *And form a stable monarchy,*
> *For, from our love can come no wrong."*

They faced each other and kissed while Valentina sang,

> *"The best to you,*
> *is what I wish.*
> *To both of you,*
> *My king and sis."*

Neither of them could hide the shock as they turned to face her.

"Sister!" Francesca exclaimed. "You never told me you could sing!"

Valentina shrugged and said, "You never asked. Don't you remember? We used to sing together, when we were younger, but when I heard them say they were sending us to that opera school in Italy, I stopped."

"Why wouldn't you want to go to school with me?"

Valentina smiled slyly and said, "Billy Paulsen."

Francesca leaned close to her sister and whispered, "But we were only fourteen! You stayed behind to be with him?"

Valentina whispered back, "Billy wasn't so young, but enough about me. This is your wedding. Take us to the reception now. I'm hungry."

"Not so fast," the king said. "All those years. You knew how much I loved the opera, and you never told me you could sing."

"What was I supposed to do? Pretend like I was my sister, the famous opera singer? I am my own person."

Francesca hugged her sister and said, "You were always being a rebel, even before I know about Billy."

The king still shook his head as he took Francesca's arm and led them out of the cathedral to the reception.

"So," Harvey said after putting his ship into auto pilot, "we're going back to that moon, again."

"Yes," the king replied. "We're going to see Valentina's new venture for ourselves."

"And we're going to be singing there," Francesca added.

"Both of you?" Harvey asked. "On stage?"

"Yes," the king replied nervously. "Francesca has talked me into a performance in front of people."

"Not people," Francesca said, "they are diners. We will sing for tourists eating their hot dogs and beans."

"It will be fine," Elizabeth said. "Who knows, you may have a backup career if this king thing doesn't work out."

The king swallowed hard and smiled weakly.

Valentina walked to the center of the stage and the crowd roared. She smiled and bowed over and over, then finally raised her hands to quiet the crowd. "Friends, we have a special treat for you tonight. My sister has come here on her honeymoon, and she has agreed to sing for us tonight. So, with no further ado, please allow me to introduce the most gifted and most famous soprano in this empire and the next, my sister, and your new queen, the great diva, Francesca Vittoria Agostina La Perla."

The crowd jumped to their feet and roared again. Hands were clapped and mugs were banged on the tables. Valentina again raised her hands to silence them. "There's more. Accompanying her tonight will be her new husband, your king and emperor, Marcel Dogian Pernupt!"

The king was a bit hesitant as Francesca led him out onto the stage. She knew what he was feeling and gave him little time to reconsider what he was about to do. As soon as he was in position, she nodded her head to Victor who started the music.

Francesca started the duet. She planned it this way. Once she started singing, he would have no choice but to follow. His instincts kicked in and he sang with gusto.

The audience was stunned. There was no talking among the onlookers. There was none of the clinking of plates and glasses that Francesca hated so much. The audience stared in rapt disbelief that their king would stand on stage and sing for them, then it transformed into a new disbelief that he could sing so well, or for some, that he could sing at all. By the end of the performance, they were simply stunned by the beautiful performance.

Francesca and the king stood before the rapt diners and bowed their heads. The crowd exploded in uproarious approval. The king was a little uncomfortable from the attention. He was more accustomed to being hated and maligned by the people, but Francesca bathed in the adoration. She held her hands in the air and egged the throng of people to cheer louder and louder. She was in her element.

Finally, when she thought it had gone on long enough, she held up her palms to calm the crowd. "Thank you," she said. "I am being happy to bring you this wonderful performance with my new husband. Is he not also a very good singer? How lucky we all are being to have him sing for us. Before we leave the stage, however, I am wanting to say a special thanks to my sister. My sister, who I am still thinking of as our queen, is the most noble person I have ever known. She is being a diva in her own right."

Francesca clapped her hands enthusiastically and led the crowd into clapping theirs as she said, "Please show your appreciation for my sister Valentina, the diva of mud flats!"

The end

Jonni Jordyn was born in Oakland, California in 1957. She started writing at an early age, writing music, poetry, short stories, radio, film, and stage scripts. She didn't start writing novels until later in life, after she retired from playing music, and found herself travelling away from home for extended periods.

She currently lives in Denver, Colorado.

www.ingramcontent.com/pod-product-compliance
Lightning Source LLC
Chambersburg PA
CBHW020743310726
48969CB00002B/402